AN INTERESTING OFFER

"I have a wicked reputation, Miss Hollis. If I lose my earnings for any reason, I'll have to take payment out on your pretty hide."

Randee laughed. "What recourse do I have if you do a lousy job?"

Marsh didn't realize his eyes were glowing as he replied, "Same as mine; take it out on me any way you please."

Randee caught the provocative meaning and saw the look of desire in those enticing blue eyes. His pattern of breathing told her that he was aroused by her and his own suggestive statement. The tension between them stimulated her, and she wondered if her eyes were as telltale as his were. His large, strong hands were lying more than halfway across the table. She wondered if they could be as gentle as they were strong, if they could drive a woman mindless with pleasure. She wanted to slip her hands into his to savor his touch.

Marsh was taken with Randee as well. He pondered how it would feel to have her in his arms, that sunny head lying against his chest or those green eyes fusing with his, his fingers drifting up and down her arms or back, their passions steadily heightening. . . .

PASSIONS WILD AND FREE

JANELLE TAYLOR

ZEBRA BOOKS
KENSINGTON PUBLISHING CORP.

ZEBRA BOOKS

are published by

Kensington Publishing Corp.
475 Park Avenue South
New York, NY 10016

Copyright © 1988 by Janelle Taylor

Seventh printing: January, 1992

Printed in the United States of America

For
Johanna Lindsey, *a friend and a very talented writer whose works have inspired and pleasured me for years.*

And for
Ellen Tanner Marsh, *a lovely lady who writes wonderful and exciting tales.*

Where can Passions race wild and free,
Except o'er lands which
Try our souls,
Challenge our hearts,
And fill our dreams?

Chapter One

"I can't give it up, Brody. The Epson Gang murdered everyone at my uncle's ranch, some they even tortured. Then, they plundered his home and stole his cattle, laughing all the while and joking as if they were happy children playing a harmless game. You saw the ranch before and after their raid. No evil can surpass what those villains did. They should be beaten and tormented before they're hung!" Randee Hollis tossed her drawstring purse on Sheriff Brody Wade's desk and continued, "The Epson Gang destroys everyone and everything they touch. They're terrorizing the countryside in all directions, from Fort Worth to Forts Richardson and Concho and halfway to the New Mexico Territory. To them, nothing is sacred and everyone is a target, even helpless children and dirt-poor squatters and churches of any faith. From what we've heard and read, that band of devils is getting bigger and stronger and crueler each month. They must be stopped, Brody, any way necessary. If the law can't or won't track them down and punish them, then I will. Just as soon as my helper arrives," Randee added.

Brody shook his head and frowned worriedly at the lovely young woman who was standing before him attired in a fetching dark green dress. What flesh was showing was tanned a golden brown, from hours spent beneath an adoring sun. He imagined the concealed portion to be as white and soft as East Texas cotton. Her slender figure barely halted before grazing the five-feet-five-inch mark, but she was an armful of delightful pleasure, a worthy prize for any man to seize.

Although her flaxen hair was covered with a fashionable bonnet today, he knew how it looked when it was hanging down her back. The nearly waist-length mane was almost straight, but very thick and carefree, an enhancement to her natural beauty. Yet, he could not imagine why she had cut the top of her hair to fall into shaggy strands over her forehead, with some of the varying lengths teasing at her dark blond brows. The words *mischievous vixen* came to mind and warmed his body. This afternoon, however, those bangs were neatly tucked into her bonnet and she appeared every inch the lady.

As he mentally searched for a clever and convincing protest to her daring plans, Brody's appreciative gaze continued to wander over Randee's face and figure. Her large green eyes revealed determination to carry out her perilous quest to locate and capture the Epson Gang. Even her dainty chin jutted out with fierce resolve. He wanted to lean forward and nibble on it before tracing the stubbornly set angle of her jawline up to her ear and then over to her lips. He didn't mind the two-inch scar which ran upward from her jaw before her right ear, the result of a childhood fall, from what she had told him. His tongue longed to caress the white line before lavishing attention on her mouth and neck. His body's reaction to the fantasy warned him to drop it.

The lawman tried to sound tough and gentle as he reasoned, "Listen to yourself, Dee. Nobody knows better than you that those villains are more than simple outlaws; they torture, rape, murder, burn, and steal because they enjoy it. They don't know the meaning of conscience, self-control, mercy, or guilt. They don't care who they kill or how much they torture a person. You've seen how they treat women, young and old alike. You can't go after such brutal beasts, with or without help. You'll only get yourself killed."

Randee leaned against the cool bars of the cell and met Brody's brown gaze. "I might not be any match for the Epson Gang, but that won't stop me from trying to destroy them. If I hadn't been locked in the attic during their bloody attack, I wouldn't be alive now. I have to do something, anything, to obtain vengeance and justice. Men who murder and destroy blindly deserve to die."

"I hate it that Mrs. Carson was killed because she didn't hide in the attic with you. I know this situation has you grief-stricken and mad, but you can't go tearing off unprepared. Frankly it's a miracle those bastards didn't burn down the house out of pure meanness. I'd be out of my head if they'd found you that day. Don't you see that you're asking them to come back and try again?"

"I outwitted them once, Brody, and I'll do it again. They'll pay for their crimes; I swear it."

When Randee lowered her head, Brody grasped her chin and lifted it to fuse their gazes. Knowing someone could enter the jail at any moment, he resisted the urge to shake her or to kiss her. He asked, "What can you possibly do without getting yourself killed?"

"With luck, my helper and I can follow them secretly and pick off a few here and there. If their number is reduced, the law might gain enough courage to challenge them. Or we might track them after every attack until we get lucky and discover their hide-out for the

11

authorities. Sooner or later they'll slip up and leave some clues or tracks. Don't worry, I'll think of something safe and sly." She briefly recalled how she had cunningly outsmarted her lecherous stepfather; no doubt his hirelings were still searching for her in New York. The green-eyed blonde realized there was a chance that Payton Slade might see or hear about her newspaper advertisements, but she had to take that risk. Even if he located her, she would never return to her Kansas home and bewitched mother, not while Payton was alive. Randee artfully slipped from between Brody's frame and the confining cell.

Sheriff Brody Wade watched her pace the small office in deep study. He had visited the Carson Ranch many times since the blonde's arrival a few months ago to live with her maternal uncle and his wife. With a little effort, the nineteen-year-old beauty could pass for sixteen. As unconsciously as she breathed, she sent forth an odd blend of lingering innocence and simmering passion, a heady blend which he craved to enjoy. Now, he mistakenly presumed, Miss Randee Hollis was alone, but certainly not vulnerable or scared; he wished she were, so he could ensnare her for his wife. Whatever it took, Brody decided, he must have this intoxicating mixture of vixen and lady. But first, he had to halt her crazy plans before this situation got out of control.

Brody argued in a husky voice, "You're a woman, Dee, a very young and beautiful one. Even with help from somebody, you can't go running after a huge band of cutthroats. And what makes you think a trustworthy soul will answer that reckless advertisement you placed in all the neighboring papers? You'd be alone out there with a total stranger. After he robs you and . . . there's no telling what else, he'll leave you stranded somewhere or make you a tasty meal for some vultures."

When Randee failed to relent or to show fear, the sheriff continued, "What if someone in the Epson Gang sees your tempting offer? It's got to be causing gossip all over this area. As far as I know, you're the only survivor to any of their raids. If you go chasing them or become a threat to them . . ." He grimaced. "Lord help us all, Dee. To be safe, you have to remain here and keep quiet. If they discover they left behind a witness, they'll be swarming over Wadesville looking for you. I'm only one man, Dee. If you lure them here, how can I protect you against so many killers? And how can I defend my town against them? If a hired gunslinger and a large gang of killers aren't perils enough to dissuade you, then consider the danger you're putting others in. And what about marauding Indians and unpredictable weather? It's no work or place for a woman. Please give this up, Dee," he urged.

Even if most of his points were true, Randee knew the lawman was trying to frighten her into giving up this admittedly dangerous challenge because he wanted her to remain here and marry him. He had proposed twice after the horrifying episode, and he had been wooing her for weeks. As no other force was trying to defeat that devilish band, she had to find a way to do so. She owed her uncle, aunt, and friends that much; they had taken her in after she ran away from home, supported her, made her part of their family, returned her joy and spirit, and kept her whereabouts a secret from her wicked stepfather. To watch them being slaughtered like cattle . . .

"I'll confess I'm intimidated by this decision, but I'm not rash or stupid. You know I turned down those first two men because I didn't think I could trust them or

13

believe they could do the job. I promise I won't leave here with just anyone, Brody. But I can't allow those cold-blooded villains to go free after what they've done," she vowed angrily, then gentled her tone to say, "I'll be careful. Besides, I can protect myself—don't forget I'm an excellent shot and rider. And I'm strong and sturdy, so I can handle the rough trails and a hired assistant. Now that the news may be out about a survivor, perhaps it's best for everyone here if I leave quickly. I'm sorry, Brody, but I just couldn't think of any other way to obtain help, or to shock the law into doing something. Maybe my life was spared for a special reason; maybe I'm the only one who can defeat them. That may sound cocky or crazy, but it might be true. No matter, I can't back down, Brody, I can't."

"Dee, you're fooling yourself. No god spared you to become a vigilante who's supposed to go traipsing after vicious bandits. You're getting deeper and deeper into this mess, and I'm frightened for you. What's to stop that gang leader from coming here or sending one of his men to be hired by you, just to lure you into their grasping arms?"

Randee had considered that possibility, but had discarded it with good reason. She hadn't told Brody she couldn't be fooled because she had seen the faces of the bandits who, presuming everyone was dead after their bloody siege, had removed their hoods. That was the secret upon which her survival and success depended, the reason why she personally had to take on this task. She couldn't risk anyone discovering her secret and accidentally disclosing it. With her helper's assistance and protection, she could travel from town to town and point them out for him to destroy. If she shared her knowledge with the authorities, the bandits might go into hiding before they could be reduced and con-

14

quered. Besides, she doubted that pictures of the criminals would imbue law officials with a sudden flow of courage, which they had been sadly lacking since this gang came into power. "I won't allow myself to get trapped by them," she replied confidently.

"Your scheme is full of holes and perils. Those two men you've already turned down might be lurking outside town, waiting to rob you and your hired gun. A five-thousand-dollar reward is too tempting and too large to go unnoticed by bad men. I'm surprised that more than two greedy snakes haven't come around to dupe you. Obviously very few of them read newspapers, or they failed to see your dangerously enticing ad. It isn't going to work, Dee. I can't name a single gunslinger who's that reckless, and you can't go riding off alone."

Randee realized his last sentence contradicted his earlier argument, but she didn't point it out to him. He was worried about her safety, and about not winning her. Brody had been too eagerly pursuing her to notice she didn't want to be ensnared by him, at least not into marriage. Sheriff Wade was a pleasing companion, but he didn't inflame her blood as she knew the right man would. She revealed, "If it doesn't work soon, I'm raising my offer to ten thousand dollars. After all, I am asking him to risk his life by going up against a bloodthirsty band even the law fears and avoids."

Brody shifted and glanced away from her steady gaze. "You understand why I can't go after them, Dee. I'm not a coward, but I know when the odds are against my victory and survival. There's no way I could raise a qualified posse for a shoot-out with nearly thirty expert gunmen. These people are farmers and ranchers and merchants; they can't ride off and leave their homes and families unprotected. I wish I could do this for you, but I'm responsible for protecting this town. A dead brave man isn't good for anything or anybody."

"Brody Wade! Of course I don't think you're a coward. You're only one lawman and you have big responsibilities here. You can't take the time and attention necessary to search for that gang, or risk getting townfolk killed in a one-sided battle. That gang is attacking all over the area; it could take months to track them down carefully." Randee knew that Brody was not the man for what she had in mind, but she didn't want to hurt his feelings or wound his ego. She smiled and encouraged, "I think you're being very wise; it must require enormous self-control to remain where you're needed. You're brave and a good shot, but I need a man who lives by his gun and risks his life daily. I need a man with Ranger blood and spirit, one who thinks nothing about confronting one bandit or twenty, a man who knows how villains think and work. The trouble is that ex-Rangers have settled down and aren't interested in stalking death for a meager five thousand dollars. So, it'll have to be a fearless, intelligent, trustworthy gunslinger."

"There's no such animal, Dee. But even if one existed and answered your summons, what makes you believe you two can succeed?" Randee shrugged, but looked undaunted. "If you've got to do something, why don't you use those dollars to hire a detective agency or a group of ex-Rangers? You don't have to go along and endanger yourself."

"If the Texas Rangers hadn't been disbanded after the war, those villains wouldn't be murdering and plundering today. That was a stupid mistake on the law's part. I'd be willing to bet a stack of money they'll be reinstated as soon as everyone gets tired of criminals

16

eluding justice. And the Army certainly isn't doing anything. We have forts north, east, and south of here, and not a one of them is trying to capture that gang. They act like it's a civilian problem and they're not in Texas to protect us. I realize these outlaws are terrible; but if people don't band together against them, they'll own and control this entire area. As to detectives, we read where several had taken the case, only to give it up after a few weeks or months. Those villains manage to cow nearly everybody." When the man simply stared at her, she reminded him, "You showed me those stories, remember?"

Brody had shown Randee those stories to terrify and discourage her. Instead, they had only made her more determined to fight this battle. "The Epson Gang is large, too big and mean for even a posse to tangle with, much less two people and one of those being a half-grown woman. You've seen and heard what those bandits do. If they catch you two tailing them, they'll take you apart with great pleasure, after they keep you around for a while to entertain them. This isn't a game, Dee; it's a serious and deadly business," he warned.

Randee almost corrected Sheriff Brody Wade for the seemingly hundredth time for calling her by his chosen nickname, especially when he said it with such passionate emotion as he was using again today. Just under six feet tall, Brody was a nice-looking man with brown eyes and hair. For several years he had been the sheriff of Wadesville, a town named after his father. Rumor claimed that "Old Man Wade" had lost his wits during the war between the North and the South while Brody was off fighting for the Confederacy. By the time Brody made it home, his parents were dead and his inheritance was gone.

Brody had offered to buy the Carson ranch or help her find men to run it for her if she chose to keep it, which would be hard because she was such a young woman. Randee had not told Sheriff Wade she couldn't sell Lee Carson's ranch because her mother was undoubtedly the legal heir, and Randee didn't want anyone here learning about Kansas and Dee Carson Hollis Slade. Besides, there was no livestock left to handle. If she hired men to watch over the place and to keep it from falling into disrepair, she could be placing their lives in jeopardy when the bandits returned for another surprise assault. She also hadn't told Brody that she suspected that robbery was not the only reason behind the gang's malevolent actions, if theft was a reason at all. Since everyone and every place was being threatened and destroyed by this hit-and-hide gang, it looked more like an insidious land-grab to her. It seemed that someone wanted all of central West Texas and was using the Epson Gang to clear the land. But who and why? she wondered. Since it was so much land to claim and control, perhaps a group of men were involved. She could not voice her opinion aloud, or she might unsuspectingly alert a clever boss to her knowledge. Then she would be in worse peril than being a sole survivor. If she could uncover the real motive and leader, the paid attacks would cease. A cunning, fearless, talented gunslinger was exactly who she needed for an assistant. She needed a man who knew this territory and . . .

Brody's words cut into her rambling thoughts, "It's too dangerous. You can't go, Dee," he told her matter-of-factly. "If necessary to keep you from such impulsiveness — and protect this town against trouble — I'll lock you up until you clear your wits and forget this nonsense."

Randee's shocked expression was quickly mastered. She grinned and replied, "You can't stop me, Brody; besides, I have an appointment with the dressmaker and I'm late. I'll see you tomorrow." Without allowing him time to respond, she hurriedly departed, forgetting her drawstring bag on his desk.

As she was rushing past the saloon, she gathered up her skirts and gingerly picked a path across the uneven sidewalk boards and around patches of tobacco spittle. Suddenly, the double doors swung open and a playfully scuffling couple bumped into her, causing her to topple off the boardwalk into the dirt street. Instantly the man scooped her up, dusted her off, and rapidly apologized for the accident. At that moment, Randee was flustered, distracted, and annoyed.

Randee slapped at his swiftly moving hands and told him, "Stop it! I can brush myself off. Just look at my dress! It's filthy, and I'm already late for an appointment. If you aren't more careful in the future, you'll injure someone badly." As she straightened her attire, she muttered, "Any decent man would be home working at this time of day, not playing around in . . ." Randee lifted her head, allowing them to view each other for the first time, and halted her scolding.

For a moment, as their gazes locked, both were silent and still. Realizing the victim was the woman that Sheriff Wade was interested in, the nervous saloon girl returned to work to avoid getting into trouble with the smitten lawman. But neither Randee nor the man noticed her hasty retreat.

It was almost one o'clock, and very few people were on the street. Those who were around went on about their business and paid little heed to them. Randee Hollis and the black-clad stranger continued to size up each other as he politely assisted her back to the cov-

19

ered boardwalk and out of the brilliant sun.

He was the first to speak. "I'm sorry, miss. You're right, I was being mighty careless. I just got into town and I've been riding hard and long for days. I guess I'm too tired to think clearly. Are you hurt?"

"I'm fine, thank you," Randee replied, hoping her voice wasn't trembling like her body was. Had she ever seen any man so appealing? she asked herself, then answered negatively. His ebony hair was sleek and shiny, and his attentive eyes were light blue, like a crystal clear stream. He was darkly tanned and splendidly built. His black shirt was unbuttoned to his heart, and she had trouble pulling her gaze from that tanned hair-covered area. She had the wildest urge to snatch off his dark bandanna and wave it beneath her nose, as she was certain it carried the same delightful manly scent which her tingling nose detected on that virile six-foot-two frame. Obviously he had been in town long enough to have a bath and to change clothes, and his pattern of priorities pleased her. His features— brows, nose, lips—were all full and noticeable, but not too large. As if he hadn't shaved today, his face was stubbled with dark hair. It gave him a mysterious and sensual look, which she found most provocative. "I suppose one shouldn't get angry and rude over an accident, but it does present a problem for me. Either I go to my appointment like this, or I make myself late by returning home to change clothes," she mused aloud as she removed her lopsided bonnet to correct its angle and tuck in her long hair.

"You're a little rumpled and dusty, but you still look mighty pretty to me." No, he mentally corrected himself, she was beautiful, despite the visible scar on her cheek and the mussed hair which tumbled over her shoulders. "You can't go around with a dirty face, so the least I can do is clean it off a mite." He removed his bandanna and wiped at the nonexistent smudges, enjoying his little ruse. Judging by her coloring, she spent a great deal of time outdoors, and that conclusion caught his interest. Her skin was as soft as a baby's and she smelled wonderful. He liked the way her green eyes seemed to glow with various emotions and thoughts, a glow which created a gnawing hunger in his loins. Her natural smile and laughter combined with her alluring gaze to increase his warmth and intrigue. As she stood there like an obedient and trusting child, he wondered, was she a lady or a vixen, or a little of both?

When he was finished wiping her face, Randee finger-combed her hair and tried to slow her racing pulse. This man had a very stimulating and disturbing touch, but she shouldn't be allowing a stranger such contact with her body. As she was tying the ribbons to her bonnet, Randee's gaze explored this compelling man further. She observed how he wore his gunbelt secured snugly below his waist and his holsters strapped to well-muscled thighs. She recalled how quickly, fluidly, and purposefully he had moved. He looked as if he were totally relaxed, but she detected constant alertness in his gaze and stance. Every noise or movement briefly captured his probing gaze, yet, he appeared to be only casually glancing at his surroundings. Despite his easy-going façade, his constant guard also had been noticeable in his taut muscles when she had accepted his arm earlier. He was a gunslinger, she decided, but a most unexpected one. Of course, she reasoned, his geniality and warmth and manners could be faked traits which masked a cold and brutal nature. She had seen pictures of handsome gunmen and outlaws, and heard of ones who were pleasant and friendly until provoked. She could not help but wonder how this man would react to a threat or a challenge. What turned a man like this into a hard and tough loner, into a dangerous gun-toting peril?

The ebony-haired man observed how this female was watching him, studying him, and perhaps enticing him. He was baffled, and delighted by her receptive attention. He saw her lift her green gaze and settle it on his whisker-rough face. She looked as if she were trying to penetrate some dark, strong barrier, as if she were trying to see into his head and heart. *Heart?* What a curious word to come to mind! His heart had been dull ever since the first raid thirteen months ago. Besides, a man who lived by his guns shouldn't be thinking about pretty young ladies. Even if she was tempting him, he didn't have time to accept her offer and enjoy her. He had a job to do; he had been sent here to find a man and halt his threat.

Randee pondered offering this man a position as her assistant, or at least discussing a partnership with him. She did not have to ask herself if he could do the job; he exuded prowess. But could he be trusted? Would he be receptive? Manageable? Dare she approach him about her scheme? Would he laugh? Think her crazy or wild? He appeared nice and kind, but first impressions — particularly skillfully controlled ones — could be deceiving and hazardous.

"Do you need me to escort you home, miss?" he asked, seeing that she wore no wedding ring. She appeared strangely hesitant, and he wondered what was whirling around inside that lovely head. "I have some important business to handle with the sheriff."

She mused, a gunslinger needing to see the sheriff? Could it be that he was here about her job? She would know soon. Even so, he had to be questioned, studied, and tested. Randee eyed him up and down, then replied, "No thanks."

The man pulled his hat from its resting place on his back, positioned it, tipped it, and walked away. Randee turned and let her gaze follow him into Brody Wade's office. She smiled, knowing she had an excuse to return to the jail, in case she was caught eavesdropping.

She sneaked to the door just as the stranger was saying, "I'm looking for a man named Randee Hollis. The note in the paper said to ask for him here. I'm interested in the job he's offering." Randee's heart pounded with excitement and pleasure. At last, a real man.

Brody looked the man over and replied brusquely, "There isn't a job, mister. It was all a mistake. I think it's best if you . . ."

Randee stepped into the small office and interrupted Brody. "The mistake is on your part, Sheriff Wade, and the job is still available." She met the stranger's gaze and announced calmly, "I'm Randee Hollis, and the offer is genuine, if you're qualified to fill it."

The man had sensed a presence behind him, but a non-threatening one, so he had ignored it. He knew the girl on the street had just left this room because her fragrance still lingered in the air. "You're Randee Hollis?" he asked with surprise, then saw her smile and nod. "I was expecting a man, not a pretty girl. The paper said it was to help track down the Epson Gang. I'll be glad to do the job, Miss Hollis, but alone."

Randee was vexed by his gaze and tone. Moments ago he hadn't been looking at her like she was a . . . little girl! She thought she had found her man, but obviously she was mistaken. "I'm afraid that isn't possible. I know this task is very dangerous, but it's important to me to carry it out. The job pays five thousand dollars to *help me* locate and destroy that vicious gang,

23

not do it on your own. I have to be there every step of the way or it's no deal."

The man glanced at the sheriff, then back at Randee. "You must be kidding, woman. This isn't something for a female to attempt, not even with the help of a large posse."

Randee scoffed, "If I had wanted to hire a posse, sir, I would have done so. If you know anything about this situation, then you're aware that no force—Army, detectives, marshals, posses, and the like—will take on the Epson Gang. Well, I will! So what difference does it make if your boss is a woman? I was reared on a ranch; I can ride, shoot, rope, and track better than most men, maybe even better than you. Those bandits aren't perfect; they'll make a mistake soon and I'll be on their tails to take advantage of it. I know I can pull off this task, but I doubt you're man enough to assist me."

The man grinned at her provocative challenge. "Do you know how big and clever and mean that gang is? You take off after them and they'll gobble you up like a tasty treat and think nothing of it. If you're so smart, Miss Hollis, you'll go back home before you get hurt."

Randee locked forceful stares with the gunslinger, a curious anger building higher and higher within her. It infuriated her to know this man would have bedded her, but was refusing to take her mission seriously. Flames of fury danced wildly in her narrowed eyes. Her jaw was clenched, and her body was taut. She vowed confidently, "I'm not afraid of the Epson Gang; I'm only afraid of what will happen if they aren't stopped. If you're so scared, why did you answer my summons?"

Randee failed to notice a subtle change in the man's mood, gaze, and stance. His softened tone reasoned, "Anyone with brains should be afraid of that blood-

24

thirsty outfit, 'cause it's walking death. Why are you so keen on killing them yourself?"

"I have my reasons, which I'll explain only to my partner."

The man cleverly taunted, "The sheriff was right; this is a silly mistake. You've wasted my time and energy, woman. I'm not taking any pint-size crusader on a crazy manhunt."

Randee caught the playful gleam in those ice-blue eyes which said, "Convince me." She calmed her voice, and collected her wits and poise. Gluing her gaze to his, she replied, "That suits me fine, sir, because I might not want to hire you. Besides, I haven't tested you. I need a special man for this job, one who's brave, smart, and fearless. I need a man I won't have to worry about betraying me or disappointing me, a man who knows this territory better than the Indians, a man who uses guns better than he wears them, a man who can store his pride and take orders from a woman. I don't need a man who makes fun of me and who doesn't take this matter seriously."

"You're not asking for much, are you?" he teased.

"On the contrary, I'm demanding a great deal for my money. My survival and success will depend on my partner, just as his will depend on me. I have to hire the best, only the best," she emphasized. "You aren't the first man who's wanted this job, and it isn't yours for the asking. I'm not a fool, sir; I don't plan to take off into the wilds with a man I doubt." She retrieved her purse, smiled at Brody, and said, "I left too quickly and forgot this. Then, some careless beast stumbled out of the saloon, knocked me down, and ruined my clothes. Now I'm terribly late for my appointment." She returned her gaze to the gunslinger and said, "If you're interested in the job, meet me in the hotel lobby in an

25

hour so we can discuss it. If you like, you can test me, and of course I'll have to test you."

"What do you mean by 'test' me?"

"I need to see how well you can use a pistol and rifle, how you ride and rope, what you know about this area; see if you understand the criminal mind, if you panic under fire. You know, how you handle yourself and if you're qualified for the job. It's very simple."

The blue-eyed man shook his head and said, "I'm afraid I don't think this job is simple or for real. It sound more like a girlish game to me. What makes you think you can hunt down the Epson Gang?"

Randee parried, "What makes you think *you* can hunt down the Epson Gang? If you didn't want or need help and money, you wouldn't be here. You would be on their trail this very moment, alone like you prefer. I know I'm capable of going on this mission, but you'll have to prove to me that you are." She added, "Unless you're a member of the Epson Gang and you're here to put me six feet under."

The man scowled at her bad joke. "I'm here because I thought Randee Hollis was a man, a rich man looking for adventure, one who needed a guide and protection for his undertaking. I'm not sure I can work for a female with that same idea."

Randee shrugged and said, "Think it over; you have one hour. I plan to leave within two days, whether I hire you or not."

"Dee! You can't do this," Brody protested, "Darn it all, you'll get yourself killed. I swear it, Dee, I'll lock you up before I let you ride out of town alone."

Randee frowned and retorted, "You have no legal grounds to arrest or to hold me, Brody Wade. You know that I have to do this, and you can't stop me. You just told me I can unintentionally lure the Epson Gang here if they learn about my survival. I won't risk bringing them down on you and this town. I'm leaving by Friday and that's that! Good-bye, I'm late." Quickly, Randee left the office once more.

The stranger and the sheriff watched her departure. "Did she mean she's a survivor of an Epson Gang raid?" the stranger asked.

"Yep, and it's filled her head with crazy ideas of catching them. Don't go along with her reckless scheme; it'll get you both killed. And if you try to dupe her or rob her or harm her, I'll chase you down to hell and back. Understand?" Brody demanded coldly.

The man ignored Brody's warning, but caught his meaning. "I haven't heard anything about a witness. Why haven't *wanted* posters been printed up with their descriptions, and rewards set? And what's she doing running around loose? Those bandits will want her badly."

"She didn't see their faces. She was hiding in the attic. Those bastards wiped out everybody on the Carson Ranch and stole everything else. Randee's lucky to be alive, and I plan to keep her that way. You just ride on out of town. She'll get over this foolishness soon."

"Sounds to me like she'd be safer on the trail than hanging around here waiting for the Epson Gang to learn about her."

Brody's eyes darkened as he sighted the intrigued look in the man's eyes. "Leave her be, mister; she's under my personal protection. By the way, what's your name?"

"Durango," the dark-haired man replied as he returned Brody's frosty stare. The two men eyed each other closely and carefully.

"The Durango Kid?" the sheriff probed suspiciously.

The black-clad man leaned against the door. "That's

right, but don't eye me like a vulture, Sheriff; there's no reward poster on me."

"Dee isn't leaving here with no cocky, infamous gunslinger."

"You planning to stop her from hiring me?" the man asked.

Brody's keen gaze slowly covered the man before him. He had met and faced down many outlaws, but he realized this was not a man to challenge, not fairly anyway. Clearly this man was skilled and deadly. Yet, he couldn't back all the way down. Wearing a silver star gave him a little bluffing room that was effective with most men, and he used it quickly. "I'm Dee's friend and guardian, and I won't allow anyone to take advantage of her. I think you should move on before dark. That's what I told Waco Bob, but he didn't listen. If he was a friend of yours, you can visit his grave outside town."

Everyone knew the legend of Waco Bob, a gunslinger reported to have been one of the fastest to ever live. The blue-eyed man smiled and asked, "When you gunned him down, was Bob still weak from where I winged him two months ago? I just couldn't bring myself to kill a real legend, so I only nicked him as a warning."

Brody was annoyed and he didn't answer. "She's mine, Kid, and I won't take kindly to you messing with her. I have lots of friends inside and outside the law. They won't be pleased with you if you rile me. They can make your travels miserable from now on."

"Thanks for the friendly advice, Sheriff. I'll give both offers some thought, yours and hers. Trouble is, hers is a lot more attractive than yours."

"Does that mean your life's only worth a measly five thousand?"

The gunman chuckled and answered, "I don't rightly

know what any man's life is worth, Sheriff, including mine and yours. Do you?"

"Take my advice to heart, Kid, and ignore this offer. You see, I have deputies guarding this office at all times. Check out the top of the bank, the saloon, and the feed store. If you want to be unobliging and make the wrong decision, it'll be your last one."

"And my first one," the gunslinger added with a laugh. "Besides, I haven't challenged your friendly advice, Sheriff. Fact is, I like to stay on the good side of the law. It's much healthier. Frankly, this sounded like a fast and easy way to make lots of money, legal-like. Real shame it's only a grieving woman's mistake. Be seeing you around."

The tall, dark-clad stranger walked toward the hotel, not to pack and leave as he'd led Brody to think, but to await a meeting with Randee Hollis. Without looking, he knew Brody Wade had lied about having concealed deputies. He had work to do, and it didn't include tangling with a hostile sheriff who had flaming loins for that stunning blonde. Hopefully he could carry out his task here and leave without trouble. So, he mused in vexation, *Randee Hollis is a female.* Worse, she was a survivor of the recent raid nearby, and possibly an important witness. Considering her personality, this wild plan wasn't surprising, but she had to be dealt with promptly. Why hadn't he been informed of these dismaying facts? No matter, he had to halt Randee Hollis. . . .

29

Chapter Two

Hands loaded with packages, and over thirty minutes later than she had told the gunslinger to meet her, Randee breathlessly entered the hotel but sighted no one. Mouthing a silent prayer, she glanced into the adjoining dining area, but it was empty. Annoyed with herself for being late, no matter how unavoidably, she breathed deeply to slow her rapid respiration and to calm her agitation. Her face was flushed and damp from her exertion, and her arms were cramped. What she needed was a long, soothing bath; a tall, refreshing drink; and a good, loud scream! He had seemed so perfect for the job, one she was beyond ready to get under way. Even though she had suspected he might not come, she was disappointed. Maybe he had been here at two thirty, she mused optimistically, but had gotten tired of waiting. She approached the clerk at the desk and asked, "Has anyone been here looking for me? I'm late for an appointment."

The clerk was shaking his head as a mellow voice behind her jested, "Are you ever on time for anything, Miss Hollis?"

Randee turned and smiled, more swiftly and eagerly that she wished she had. Her slowing respiration speeded up again, and her cooling body warmed anew. Despite her distraction, she heard the clerk excuse himself to tend to chores in the back room.

With his buttocks propped lazily on the front windowsill, the man was nearly hidden by the open door. She watched him nonchalantly push the door aside with a freshly polished boot. Overlapping his arms on his chest, he stretched out his long legs and crossed them at the ankles. His ebony hair was recently combed, but he hadn't shaved. She had a wild impulse to walk forward seductively, lean intimately against his hard body, and caress that shadowy face before placing thousands of kisses over it. Still attired in the black shirt and pants which made him seem so irresistible and mysterious, he was like a wicked treat luring her into temptation, and perhaps he was. His powerful presence seemed to fill the room and her senses, and she wondered why she hadn't perceived it immediately. Their gazes touched tentatively, then locked tightly. She was besieged by fiery passions which burned wildly and freely within her. She had never experienced emotions and thoughts like these, and she was unsettled by her strong physical attraction to this dark stranger. She asked herself if it was possible to be so moved by a man the first time one saw him, and every time one saw him. *Of course, it is,* her mind shouted, *you can feel his effect all over!* In fact, her attraction to him heightened each time they met. But was it proper, and safe, to react to this extent? Would her hunger continue to mount? She couldn't answer.

Clearly he was fascinated by her too; she read enormous interest in his consuming gaze. Perhaps that was why he had shown up for this appointment, to see her again. That insight thrilled and alarmed her. It was hazardous to be so enchanted by a man, particularly in view of their impending relationship! For weeks they would be alone, solely dependent on each other for survival. But what if he didn't want to work for her?

She realized that only a minute or so had elapsed, even though it seemed more like an hour that she'd been staring at him. She gathered her wits and replied, "Frankly, I didn't think you'd show up after our meeting in Brody's office, but that isn't why I'm so late."

His eagle-eyed gaze noted her appearance and state as he observed her intently. From her behavior and expression, she was delighted and surprised to see him again. He was glad he had her offguard, as he could learn more when a person was flustered. "I would imagine that a pretty woman like you stays busy all the time," he murmured. "But I'm happy you didn't keep me waiting much longer."

She glanced towards the door through which the gaunt hotel man had vanished, and wondered if there was a special reason for such odd behavior. "Why did the clerk mislead me?" Randee queried.

The gunslinger was impressed by her keen wits and self-control. "He didn't know I was waiting for you, and I made him rather nervous."

The man stood and came forward purposefully, his movements well-coordinated. He halted before her and smiled in amusement, his blue eyes coming to life and sending excitement flowing through her.

Randee comprehended how this man could be just as intimidating as he was compelling. She tried not to laugh, because the clerk's timidity wasn't funny, but the gunslinger's expression and tone were. She knew she must play this scene with great care, because he had to take her seriously if there was a chance of hiring him. Too, if they were going to be on the trail together, she had to set the proper pattern for their business arrangement. She couldn't allow herself to be swept away by these wild and crazy emotions, especially by a man who lived with death on his shoulder each day and had done . . . no telling what things during his lifetime.

Yet, there was something about him which told Randee she could trust this man and depend on him. She ordered herself to remain calm and poised and to make a good impression. After all, their first two meetings had been unusual ones. "This has been a rather hectic day. My schedule has been off balance since rising. I apologize for making you wait, but I'm glad you didn't leave." He grinned as if he knew she was nervous but was artfully masking it. "Actually I'm hoping you're qualified for this job and willing to accept my offer, because my patience has run out," she added, but it didn't strip the playful smile from his face.

He mirthfully confided, "The sheriff thought I should leave town, but your offer and demands intrigue me enough to risk irritating him. You could say I'm a very curious man who enjoys a good challenge, and this certainly has enormous possibilities. I'd like to hear all about them, if you have time." He tucked one thumb into his waistband and the other inside his front pocket, allowing his fingers to fan out over his pants. He leaned against the desk and said, "I'm anxious to see if you can persuade me to partner up with a woman, a very young woman."

When he talked, his lips moved in such a way as to draw her attention to them and to cause her to long to kiss him. She liked the way he held his shoulders and angled his jawline, undeniable marks of self-assurance and prowess. It pleased her to see that his hands were clean and his nails were neatly clipped. There was no shiny grease on his face and midnight hair, nor were there grimy marks to say his clothes had gone too long without washing. This, she concluded, was no ordinary man, no common gunslinger, no ill-favored drifter.

Randee promptly noticed many things about him that seemed habitual and natural rather than something done to impress or to fool another person, such

33

as his cleanliness and composure, such as openly admitting to being a certain kind of person who was satisfied with himself and his fate, such as appearing both well-bred and well-trained. So far, he seemed straightforward and candid, and she liked those traits. She had hundreds of questions about him floating inside her head, but doubted he would answer them. Gunslingers were usually loners, and loners usually kept most things to themselves.

Right now, she needed to freshen up, get rid of her cumbersome bundles, and get down to business while she had his curiosity piqued. "If you'll excuse me for only a moment longer, I would like to place these packages in my room before we begin our discussion. My arms are quivering from strain. Do you mind?"

"You're staying here?" he inquired, his surprise honest. "Why?"

"Actually, I'm living here at the present," she responded. "I promise I'll return in five minutes or less and explain everything to you."

The man did not offer to help Randee with her packages because he didn't want to be seen going to her room. "I'll wait in the dining area. It's quiet and private in there. Don't be too long, because curiosity is eating me alive," he teased before leaving her side.

Randee watched him retrieve his hat, enter the dining room, and head for a corner table, which was out of sight from the hotel lobby. She went to her room and piled her packages on the bed, to be sorted later. Removing her bonnet, she quickly washed her face. Randee was glad her complexion was clear and smooth, and she smiled happily in the mirror. Her father had once told her, "There's nothing bad in knowing you're pretty and loving it. Just don't use good looks to tease men, or they'll get too bold and mean on you."

Hastily she brushed her long hair, artfully fluffing

and arranging the fringe across her forehead. She knew that her tawny hair was nearly straight, but it was full and healthy and flattering. She glanced at her soiled dress, but decided not to change and thus make it appear obvious that she wanted to capture the man's attention. She did splash on a nice fragrance, as it was a very warm day and she hadn't bathed since the night before. Ready, she locked her door and left.

Randee approached the table in the secluded corner of the hotel restaurant. The man stood politely, but intentionally did not come around the table to pull out her chair. As she settled herself gracefully, she glanced at what he'd ordered, then at him.

He smiled and said, "I took the liberty of ordering us some coffee and pie. You look like a cream and sugar person," he remarked as he passed the creamer and sugar bowl to her.

Randee returned his pleasant smile and said, "Just sugar, please. You'll like the pie. Mrs. Scott is an excellent cook."

"All she had was dried apples, and I hate apples. But I don't want to hurt her feelings, so I'll manage," he disclosed with a grin before taking a bite. He frowned as he chewed and swallowed the pie.

Randee laughed softly. "Does that mean I'm not to pack any apples for you when we leave on our trip?" she inquired suggestively.

"I'm a trail man, Miss Hollis, so I'll see to picking and packing the supplies. You'll only pay for them and share the cooking." He placed his fork on the small plate and looked at her. "Naturally that depends on whether or not we hit the trail together. You've got some powerful convincing to do. Tell him something; why is your name Hollis if you lived on the Carson Ranch? Are you a widow or an orphan?" As he spoke, he eyed her tumbling blond hair and lively green eyes.

She had features which made a man's fingers want to roam them, and he was looking forward to carrying out that fantasy. He noted that she hadn't changed clothes and wondered if it was because she was too rushed or if she was afraid he might think she was preening for him.

Randee was intrigued by his choice of positions for her. "Neither, Mr. . . . I don't know your name," she commented with a laugh. "I suppose it would be a good idea if we got acquainted first."

"Durango," he replied and watched her closely.

Randee realized he was waiting to see if she recognized his name, which meant she should. She gave it rapid thought and guessed why. "Mr. Durango, or the Durango Kid?" she suggested casually.

"Does it matter?" he asked, leaning back in his chair and flattening his palms on the table.

Randee boldly looked him over and said, "Considering the job I have in mind, I hope it's the Durango Kid. Does that matter to you?"

The man leaned forward, laughed, and reached for his coffee. "You're quick and smart, Miss Hollis. I like that; it can save your life, and maybe mine if we team up."

"I'm glad you approve, Mr. . . . Durango. I'll confess that I'm concerned about you lacking confidence in me. If we partner up, we need to trust and respect each other. This job is difficult and dangerous. Our survival depends on our skills and on how we work together. To answer your question, I was living on the Carson Ranch when the Epson Gang attacked it. Lee Carson was my uncle, my mother's brother. He was killed that day. More accurately, he and everyone else were brutally slaughtered. I survived because my uncle locked me in the attic when the attack began. I remained hidden until the next morning, then walked into town to get help with the burials. It takes a lot of time and strong stomachs to bury so many people. I . . ."

"You don't have to finish, Miss Hollis, I heard all about it when I got into town last night and before I saw you this morning."

Randee fused her misty green eyes to his impenetrable blue ones. "When we bumped each other, you said you had just arrived, had ridden hard and long, and were too tired to think clearly or to walk straight. Which is it, Durango?" she queried his contradiction.

"Like I said, you're quick and alert, Miss Hollis. After our little accident, I didn't see any reason to explain myself to a pretty stranger during a fleeting moment, but I did need an acceptable apology for my bad conduct. Just now, I was trying to stop you from having to cover bloody ground. To be honest, I got in real late last night and rented a room to catch up on my sleep. This morning I took care of some personal chores before I crashed into you. I haven't talked to anyone about the Carson attack, but this doesn't seem the time for you to go into it with me or anyone else. If I take this job, you can tell me everything later, when it isn't so painfully fresh in your mind."

Randee sipped her coffee as she listened to him. He did not appear worried or defensive, or deceitful. She appreciated his concern and kindness and she thanked him before continuing, "It didn't seem safe to remain at the ranch alone, so I've been living here for several weeks. You can decide if being nineteen makes me *a very young woman*. I was raised in Kansas on a cattle ranch, but I left home the end of February. I made it here all alone, Durango, through snow and Indian Territory and the worst of conditions. So, yes, I can handle rough going and rough trails. My father—rest his soul—taught me to be an excellent shot and rider, and a skilled tracker. I have lots of energy and determination, and I'm no quitter or coward. With or without you, I'm going after the Epson Gang and kill them."

"What about bringing them to justice?" he asked, his tone lacking any mockery or enlightening clues.

Randee's eyes flamed with hostility. "Vicious beasts like those can't be brought to justice. It's kill them or let them run loose. I'd rather see them dead—even by my own hand—than let them continue this reign of terror. If you're wondering why I didn't help battle them during the raid, I knew it was useless. We were vastly outnumbered and taken by surprise. Uncle Lee's cowhands were no match for skilled gunmen, and they weren't prepared to do lethal battle at dawn. I still can't believe how fast it all happened. There was no time to defend ourselves. The slaughter was over in less than fifteen minutes. It was like they knew when and where and how to strike. I stayed hidden because I wanted to remain alive to hunt them down and punish them."

He listened attentively, then said, "Hating and talking are easier than gunning down a man, Miss Hollis. Do you honestly believe you can kill a man, face to face, or shoot him in the back?"

Randee had deliberated this point many times before, so she did not have to think twice before replying, "Yes. Don't worry; I won't back down or freeze up when we come face to face with them."

The man studied her for a long moment, and believed her. He grasped her courage and cunning, and realized she wasn't a glory-seeking fool or a brazen female out to shove her way into a man's world. "Do you really think you can defeat that gang, even with my help? Do you honestly believe you can succeed where no man or other force has managed to do so?" Randee nodded, and the man exhaled loudly. "Do you honestly know what's waiting out there for you? They're worse than renegade Indians. They have no

38

souls, no hearts, nothing to hold them back. They'll kill anybody and do anything they please, and enjoy it."

"If you're trying to terrify or discourage me, it won't work. I'm going after them, Durango. I hope you'll come along; I need you. If we follow a good plan and are careful, I know we can destroy them. We just have to figure out how they plan their strikes and carry them out, and foil them. I'm aware of the perils and their savagery, but somebody has to challenge them. I can't let them go free after what they did at my uncle's ranch. God forgive me, but I want to hack them to pieces and send them to hell," she disclosed, balling her fists and clenching her teeth. She met the man's gaze and offered, "I'll pay you ten thousand dollars if you become my partner and we succeed."

He tried to keep his astonishment from showing, but was only half successful. She was serious, but was she a little too desperate? He wondered if there was more to this woman and her mission than she was revealing. He suddenly and disturbingly realized that this blonde had him as off balance as he had her! Yet right now, she looked in perfect control of herself and the situation. No doubt she was as self-sufficient and skilled as she claimed. "How do you know I'm not a member of the Epson Gang, here to find you and kill you? That notice in the paper was reckless. You've exposed yourself."

"I know you aren't one of them," she answered confidently. "If you were, you'd have killed me, robbed me, and moved on by now. And you're too smart to show yourself so openly. You're still sitting here right now because you know I'm serious and you want this job; otherwise, you'd be across the street eating delicious peach cobbler at that new restaurant, instead of gallantly suffering through apple pie. I'll be straight with you, Durango. You're not the first man who's sought

39

this job, but you're the first one I've considered hiring. I don't have to tell you how good you are at what you do, and you know I'm not flattering you by saying you're one of the best — maybe even the best gunman alive. I need a special man, Durango, and we both know you fit that description. I also think you appreciate honesty, and you don't consider my explanation and behavior as being forward and false. Besides, there are some clues about this gang and their so-called random raids which only I know. If you become my partner, Durango, I'll share them with you."

The man leaned forward, propped his elbows on the table, and rested his chin on extended thumbs. His forefingers absently rubbed his upper lip as he stared at her for a while. She didn't look away, and he could tell she meant what she said. This matter had taken a different turn since his arrival: more than likely she possessed valuable evidence, and she was in peril here. That sheriff couldn't protect her or this town if the Epson Gang rode in, for her or for any reason! She was lively and could be lots of fun on the trail, if she didn't slow him down or endanger them. He must not discourage her plans, even though he came here to keep her from perilously intruding on his case. If she had information, he needed it. He had no choice; he had to go along with her until she opened up to him. "What kind of clues, Dee?"

Randee's expression altered noticeably. "Don't call me that."

"Is it Sheriff Wade's private name?" he asked.

"No, it's my mother's name. I've asked Brody not to call me Dee, but he forgets. Don't you start that habit or I'll get very angry," she warned. Nearly every time Brody said "Dee," she thought of how her mother was bewitched and duped by that villainous snake Payton Slade. One day, she would have to solve that nasty

40

problem too. Heavens, how she hated to think of her stepfather getting his greedy hands on Lee Carson's beautiful ranch, like he had done with her father's. Payton had wooed her mother, swept the Widow Hollis off her feet, and taken over everything Randall Hollis had loved and owned. All except for his daughter, and that wasn't from a lack of trying! How blind and foolish her mother was, but maybe all women in love were the same way. As long as possible, she must pretend to be the heir and owner of the ranch so no one would go looking for her Uncle Lee's next of kin. The last thing she needed was Payton Slade in her hair again!

The man watched Randee silently. If she had a mother in Kansas, why had she come here, and alone? What were her anger, fear, and agitation about? he wondered. Like everyone, she had a weak spot, and hers was in Kansas. It was smart and vital to know a person's strengths and weaknesses, and he needed to learn more about this woman's traits and secrets. He should get another U.S. Agent, Willard Mason, to check it out for him. Maybe he could use that information to control her. "Miss Hollis?" he broke into her thoughts.

Her attention returned to him. "You can call me Randee. I was named after my parents, Randall and Dee Hollis. I hate it when people get stuck with nicknames, and it's confusing to go by your mother's name. It's spelled R-a-n-d-e-e, not R-a-n-d-y. I like my name, even if most people think it's a man's."

"It's a perfect name; you look like a Randee," he commented, then suggested, "Let's get on with our business before our privacy is lost. Tell me what you know about the gang and how you plan to locate and capture them. Or how you plan for us to do them in."

Randee realized she had made herself vulnerable to this perceptive man, and she realized how wisely and cunningly he had dropped the touchy subject. It was going to be quite a challenge to work with him without being consumed. Right now she needed to get back on an even keel. "First, tell me about yourself, beginning with your real name. If I'm going to trust you, then you have to trust me."

The man toyed with the last two bites of his apple pie as he considered her demand and insight. This room was quiet and peaceful, and she was captivating company. He warned himself that everything was almost too disarming and pleasant. He was getting too relaxed and comfortable, too open, too drawn to this clever vixen who had perilous schemes on her mind. After a good night's sleep, a hot bath, and delicious food, he felt mellow and soft — like expensive aged cheese. Maybe it was because this was the first time in countless months that he'd felt this way.

Fragrant smells of preparations for the evening meal wafted in from the adjoining kitchen. He wished someone would bring them hot coffee and give him time to think, but the restaurant was actually closed at this hour. Yet, no one would tell the Durango Kid he couldn't sit here and talk. Talk — he was not one for small talk with strangers, especially beautiful female strangers, so this relatively easy encounter surprised him. He warmed to the natural way she returned his pleasant smile and he liked her straightforward manner. Her parents had raised her well. She was confident without being cocky and vain. She was intelligent, brave, and crafty — a worthy companion or opponent for anyone. In all of his thirty-one years, few women had caught his attention so quickly and easily. Still, she was a young woman, and a perilous trail was no place for her. Hopefully he could win her confidence quickly, obtain any facts she had, and leave her somewhere safe while he went after the Epson Gang. For certain, Wadesville was no longer safe for her. She claimed she had been locked in the attic during the attack, but maybe that wasn't true; she knew something crucial. She must, because his gut instinct told him so, and he was rarely mistaken. She wanted revenge, not justice; the same was true of him. He had been after the Epson Gang for thirteen months, ever since they killed his parents and devastated his home, but they had always managed to elude him. If this beautiful golden-haired beauty knew anything that could help him complete his task, he had to get it out of her, any way necessary.

If he had to romance her, then so be it. Some people called him ruthless and cold-blooded, and perhaps he was when it came to dealing with vermin like the Epson band. A firm believer in justice, he had seen the destructive evil of this gang, and he was determined to halt them. Selected, appointed, and authorized by the President, he was accountable only to this country's leader. Furthermore, that gang had stolen three things very precious from him: his parent's lives; a chance to explain his wild life to his heartbroken parents; time to earn their respect, forgiveness, and understanding for what he was doing for this state and country. He had made so many sacrifices to rid Texas and America of countless villains, but because of his mandatory secret life his parents had died believing he had turned out bad. To have confided in his parents might have endangered their lives, and the lives of others in his many cases. He had taken a Presidential oath to silence and loyalty and justice, and he had kept it. Yet, he had always believed the moment would come when his parents would learn the truth about him and be very proud of him; now, that could never be. Knowing the risks and demands, he had accepted this job, but would he do so again? Presently, he couldn't answer that painful question.

He finally responded, "I'm from this area of Texas, but I've been away a long time. My parents are dead, and I have no other family. I'm thirty-one, and I come and go as I please. Considering my reputation, I have good reason to be wary of strangers, even pretty ones. I promise you, the Durango Kid isn't wanted by the law."

Randee believed his claims, but felt he was distorting them in his favor. During his pensive silence, she had read signs of anger, disappointment, bitterness, and soul-deep loneliness in his gaze and expression. Reflected in his blue eyes and revealed in his somber mood, she had grasped an anguish he had endured and a burden he bore. "As far as I know, you've been very careful and smart. Even if you're wanted by the law — unless it's for cold-blooded murder — I'm not interested in any charges against you. Your name?" she prompted.

The man mildly threatened, "If you mention this name to anyone, I'll cut out your tongue, and that's a promise. Marsh Logan."

Randee's alert gaze traveled over the handsome man's face, paying close attention to his eyes, nose, and mouth — places where lies were revealed first. His pupils did not enlarge, his respiration did not alter, and his lips didn't get dry. Satisfied, she smiled and said, "I like it, much better than the Durango Kid. It's a strong name, one you should be proud to carry. Why don't you, Marsh?"

He wondered if she knew he had given her his real name, a risk worth taking to win her trust and assistance. Off and on between cases since last April, he had pursued the murderous band. A month ago, he had been forced to threaten to quit his government job if President Grant refused to let him take on this personal mission. He had won the assignment for a maximum of three months, and one of those months was already

44

gone. He had been checking out each raid site for leads when word came of Randee Hollis' curious advertisement. He had come here simply to prevent "him" from interfering with the case. "We aren't here to discuss me, Randee, just your job offer and plans."

"Can I call you 'Marsh'?" she asked politely. "It's much nicer and less intimidating than Durango."

Not surprisingly, he replied, "I'd rather you didn't until we leave town. Someone might hear you. Not many families are happy or willing to acknowledge a notorious gunslinger as kin; mine was no different. I'd prefer to keep their good name clean and not have the Logan memory stained by my dark reputation. Now, tell me more," he encouraged.

Randee told Marsh what she thought was the gang's motive, but she withheld her knowledge of the gang's identity. She knew he would leave her behind if he didn't need her, considering there were several other fat rewards out on the gang, rewards he might not want to share with a partner. If he viewed her help as unnecessary, he would strike out on his own, and doubtlessly assume she would still pay him for his success! She did tell him, "It's terror strategy to scare everyone out of a certain area; that's the only way you can explain some of the attacks. If we unmask their leader and his plot, the killing and plundering will halt. We'll need to make a map of this area and chart their path. I'm willing to bet we'll see a pattern. When we do, we can beat them to their next target and set a trap for them. We can outwit them, Marsh, I'm positive of it."

"It sounds logical, Randee, but it won't be that simple. Between jobs, I've been pursuing them for thirteen months. Since they're still on the loose, that tells you something. They appear, strike, then vanish. That calls for clever planning and timing. By the time I reach their last target, no clues or tracks are left—if there ever were any."

"There aren't," she remarked immediately. She hastily covered her slip by saying, "After the raid at my uncle's ranch, I looked everywhere—no tracks in any direction. That means they're smart enough to conceal their trail; it also means they aren't worried about taking the time to do so. What does that tell you, Marsh?"

"That they know everybody's schedule in the area. It means, woman, that they spy on their targets, or they have a member who's familiar with the territory and its people. Of course, there are never any witnesses to question. I started this pursuit for the money and the challenge; but after seeing what they leave behind, I want to destroy them. I'm used to fair fights or ones pushed on me, but the Epson Gang cuts down anybody: children, women, old men, whole families. I've always been one step behind them, but no more. With your help and support, I can concentrate totally on catching up or getting ahead. What else you got in mind?"

"They wear dark hoods to protect their identities. I saw that much before I was shoved into the attic. I'm sure they don't stay hidden all the time, so maybe we can discover where they're from or where they hang around. I'm sure I'll recognize some of their voices, their clothes, their mounts, and other things about them. We can visit towns and pick them off a few at a time. We can trim down their number, Marsh, I know we can. Besides, they need a hide-out or at least a meeting point. If we can track them after one of their attacks and find it, we can destroy them." She asked unexpectedly, "Do you know how to use dynamite and can you get your hands on some? From what Uncle Lee told me, it's only been around a few years, but it surely would better our chances with the Epson Gang.

46

He used it one time to clear some rocks to get to an underground stream."

"I can use it, and I know several places we can get some. There's one catch; to keep our plans quiet, we'll have to steal it."

Randee didn't wait before saying, "Fine, whatever's necessary."

He requested, "Let me think a minute and get some points straight in my head." To avoid being distracted by Randee's blond good looks, Marsh lowered his head and focused his blue eyes on the table. He was aware that their departure had to be carefully planned and timed. And this meeting had to end very soon to prevent people, especially that love-besotted sheriff, from linking them together. Secrecy was vital.

Randee observed the man who sat in deep silence before her. His gaze was angled toward the table, but it moved about rapidly as unknown thoughts raced through his sharp mind. She was anxious for him to share those cunning ideas and plans, and she waited eagerly for him to do so. *Marsh Logan,* she mused dreamily. It was a strong, masculine name. It suited him perfectly, just as he suited her perfectly. Here was a man attuned to his prowess and surroundings, a man who had paid dearly for his hazardous and exciting lifestyle. He was a man compelled to take on difficult challenges, provoked to court danger and death, driven to prove he was the best at what he did. Or driven to prove something else . . .

When Marsh lifted his head and gaze, he found Randee watching him intently. As their eyes met and lingered, he realized how much he enjoyed looking at her and being near her. Here was a woman with more than good looks, with far more than sensual appeal, with far more than superficial charm. Undoubtedly she possessed the wits and talents to go on the trail and

47

capture outlaws, but the Epson Gang was different. That gang was large and cruel and deadly. He would use Randee's help only as long as it was safe for her. Then, when the going got rough, he would leave her behind and finish alone.

"We have to hurry, Randee. It's nearly four thirty. I don't want the supper crowd to find us here alone. Besides, we don't need Brody Wade becoming angry and getting into our hair. We have to keep our plans and partnership a secret from everyone, including your good friend the sheriff. We can't afford any accidental slips or interference. You'll need to get to the bank before it closes at five and . . ."

Randee interrupted, "The deal is to pay you three hundred dollars a month for our supplies and expenses, no matter how long it takes. The ten-thousand-dollar payment is already deposited at the bank, but it can't be collected until this matter is settled and I sign the paper to release it. That's the only way I can protect myself from being duped or harmed. Agreed?"

"What about me? Who has the authority to release my money if you're killed during our travels? Once those men are dead and my job's done, what's to keep you from cheating me, Miss Hollis?"

Randee saw the sparkle in his eyes and heard the playful note in his voice, so she realized he was teasing. "I promise we'll figure out some way to protect your investment."

"I have a wicked reputation, Miss Hollis. If I lose my earnings for any reason, I'll have to take payment out of your pretty hide."

Randee laughed. "What recourse do I have if you do a lousy job?"

Marsh didn't realize his eyes were glowing as he replied, "Same as mine; take it out on me any way you please."

Randee caught his provocative meaning and saw the look of desire in those enticing blue eyes. His pattern of breathing told her that he was aroused by her and his own suggestive statement. The tension between them stimulated her, and she wondered if her eyes were as telltale as his were. His large strong hands were lying more than halfway across the table. She wondered if they could be as gentle as they were strong, if they could drive a woman mindless with pleasure. She wanted to slip her hands into his and savor his touch.

Marsh was taken with Randee too. He pondered how it would feel to have her in his arms, that sunny head lying against his chest or those green eyes fusing with his, his fingers drifting up and down her arms or back, their passions steadily heightening . . . . He could imagine lying in the grass with her, near a pond or river, gazing up into a peaceful blue sky or a star-filled night, listening to the sounds of nature and inhaling its scents, laughing, talking, making love . . . .

He shook his head and smiled guiltily, knowing she read the signs of his mounting desire. She didn't smile or frown as she tried not to give herself away. "Back to business," he teased. "Your offer's fine except for one point; I'll need extra money up front to buy you a horse and saddle. Since the Epson Gang always steals the stock and burns the barns, I presume you don't have either one. I'll get them for you in another town to preserve that secrecy I mentioned. After you make your withdrawal, we'll walk past each other on the sidewalk and you can slip the money into my hand. I'll leave today, then you head out by stage on Thursday. Make sure you get enough money to cover a ticket to Dodge City. I'll be waiting for you at one of the relay stations along the way. If we run into trouble passing along the money, I'll come to your room at midnight."

Randee inquired, "Why the sneaky behavior and

separate schedules? Why Dodge City?"

"Because the stage only runs north on Tuesdays and Thursdays. Even if it wasn't too late today, it'd look suspicious for both of us to leave on the same day. It's probably common knowledge that you're a witness and you've been trying to hire a man, or men, to ride down the Epson Gang. If we're put together as a threat, it'll endanger both of us and our mission. It has to appear as if you've given up and left town for a while. People have to think you're on your way by stage to Dodge City to catch the train to visit kin somewhere. We also need everyone to believe I think you're crazy, and I left. Just so Sheriff Wade doesn't get worried or suspicious, tell him you'll come back to him in about a month. Convince him of this tale, Randee, or he'll trail us and intrude." He added, "It might help our cause if we have a few nasty words in public after you pass the money to me. Another thing, store all your clothes except for what you need and can use on the trail. I'll get out of Wadesville by dusk. Tomorrow, I'll find you a good horse and saddle. Then, Thursday I'll pick you up somewhere."

When Randee didn't reply, Marsh finally asked, "Are you afraid I'm trying to weasel you out of four hundred dollars? Afraid I won't meet you along the road? Or have you changed your mind about going?"

"That wasn't what I was thinking about. I was deciding what story to make up to keep Brody off our trail. I'm seeing him for supper, so I'll get it over with tonight. I'll take care of everything else tomorrow. But I'll give you five hundred dollars because I want a good horse and a comfortable saddle. If you've spent as much time on your horse as I've spent on mine, you know what I mean, Mr. Logan."

Marsh chuckled and nodded. "I'll go out the back way so we won't be seen together. After you leave the bank, I'll bump into you, so have the money folded tightly in your hand. From now on, any conversation between us needs to be hostile, understand?"

"Perfectly, Mr. Logan. As for you, stay out of gun-fights and any trouble with the law. I'll see you at one of the depots. Thanks for joining me, Marsh; I'm glad you let me change your mind."

"Did you ever truly doubt you wouldn't win me over?" he jested.

"Honestly?" she queried. He nodded. She grinned and admitted, "Yes, very big doubts. See you around, Durango." She stood, smiled, and left. To give her partner time to get into position, Randee slowly crossed the dirt street and headed toward the bank along the plankway.

Marsh quickly departed by the back door, slipped past several buildings, and entered the rear of a sad-dlery shop. He casually looked around as he watched the bank through the windows. Randee walked slower than he did, so she came into sight shortly. Minutes after she entered the building across the street, three men rode up and dismounted. It was almost five o'clock, closing time for the bank. Marsh watched the way those men checked out their surroundings, and he knew what was about to take place, with Randee inside . . . .

Chapter Three

While the teller was placing her sealed note of instructions in the safe with her ten-thousand-dollar deposit, Randee folded the five hundred dollars for Marsh and stuffed it into her bodice, deciding she could retrieve it and pass it along more quickly that way. The hundred dollars for her stage ticket and expenses until she joined her partner was placed inside her drawstring purse. She was about to leave when two men entered and warned, "This is a holdup. Be quiet and nobody gits hurt." She was pushed roughly into a corner by one of the men while the other one gave orders to the stocky teller.

As the teller followed instructions, the bandit near Randee seized her arm and jerked her toward him. "You stand real close in case somebody comes in and tries to stop us. We got us a pretty hostage, Billy Joe. Maybe we oughta take her with us for a spell."

Randee looked at the man who was holding her. Tobacco juice trickled down the deep crevice beside his mouth. His brows were bushy, and his face was splotched by the sun and bad health. His hair was dirty and uncombed, his breath was foul. She knew his clothes hadn't been washed in weeks; neither had his body. He was a sorry, repulsive sight. Randee glared at him and yanked her arm free of his loose grip.

"I don't think she likes me, Billy Joe," he joked.

"Don't fool with her, Luther. We'll git us plenty of gals later. We ain't got no time to waste. Hurry up, mister, or I'll plug you good."

"What you got in this little purse, girlie?" Luther asked and grabbed it off her wrist. Randee struggled with him for its possession. The annoyed outlaw knocked her sideways to the floor and shouted, "Lay still, girlie, or you won't like what I give you." He fumbled with the drawstring, loosened it, and dumped her things on the floor.

Randee unthinkingly reached for the money, but the man kicked her arm away. She squealed in pain and cradled her arm, rubbing the minor injury. She scolded herself for being so foolish. If rashly provoked, these unstable men could kill her and the teller. It was wiser for her to shut up and be still.

Luther snatched up the bills and grinned, "You're worth more'n I thought, girlie. Looka here, Billy Joe, another hundred dollars."

Merchants were preparing to close for the day, and most customers had left the stores. Families in or around town were busy with evening meals and chores. The street was nearly deserted, an excellent time for a holdup.

Eyeing the man standing guard at the bank door, Marsh was deciding on a course of action when the saddler stammered nervously, "I'm s-s-sorry, sir, b-but it's cl-closing time. Can you come back to-morrow?"

Marsh glanced at the slender man, whose eyes held the same look of timidity as the hotel clerk's. He smiled and ordered, "Go out the back door and be very quiet. Warn the sheriff there's a robbery going on. See that man at the bank door? There are two more inside. I'll

53

try to slow them down while you get Sheriff Wade. First, I need your rifle from beneath the counter," he said, knowing all merchants concealed weapons for protection, even those who were too scared to pull and use a gun.

The man peered across the street, then looked at the black-clad gunman beside him. He appeared too frightened to move.

Marsh teased, "If your money's in that bank, mister, you best fetch the law pronto, or it'll be riding off with those outlaws. I need help, man. Be quick and fetch the sheriff."

Logan's smile and pleasant manner dispelled the man's fears and hesitation. Nodding, he hurried off to do as Marsh ordered.

Marsh quickly checked his guns and the rifle. There would be no time for reloading or cocking hammers. He had to make each of the three shots count. The moment those other two men showed themselves, he had to fire the rifle, toss it aside, and draw and fire his two pistols. He had simultaneously taken on this many men before, but it was different this time for two reasons: First, they could bring Randee out with them to use for cover. If so, he needed to be swifter and more accurate than ever. Second, he was wearing single-action Colts—like the real Durango Kid wore—which had to be hand-cocked after each shot. If only he had on his new Smith & Wesson .44's with rapid-firing trigger control!

Inside the bank, the man behind the teller's cage was nervously shoving money into a canvas sack. Sweat was pouring off his terrified body and saturating his white shirt and black vest. The heat from his face kept fogging his glasses, but he continued to work swiftly.

Randee knew that the Durango Kid was watching the bank. She wondered if he realized what was happening over here. No matter, it was three against one, and she didn't know what he could do about such odds. Her money, she fretted, would soon be walking out the door. Her expense money and Marsh's ten-thousand-dollar payment, she corrected herself. What would he say and do if it was stolen?

Only the five hundred dollars, one month's expenses, was still tucked safely inside her bosom. But there was another consolation, a bigger one: the rest of the Carson money and jewels was hidden on the deserted ranch . . . . She had been smart to deposit only twelve thousand dollars and to bury the rest. She had feared something like this might happen, but had known she would be asked to prove to her partner she could pay him.

"What'cha gimme to return your money, girlie? A big kiss? A roll in the hay?" Luther Crebbs taunted the golden-skinned blonde.

"Put it away, Luther, we gotta git out of here." Billy Joe grabbed the sack from the teller's shaky hand. "Let's go."

Luther crammed the cash into his pants' pocket and threatened, "I'll shoot the first one who moves or shouts."

Randee remained on the floor, pressed up against the wall and huddled over as if in pain and fear. To prevent their using her as a hostage, she pretended she'd been badly injured from being kicked. After all, a hurt woman couldn't ride or would slow them down! Gingerly, she drew her legs up as far as she could, putting the small gun inside her boot within reach.

The instant Luther and Billy Joe joined Homer Crebbs outside, a loud commotion erupted. Shots were exchanged, shouts were heard, horses whinnied and

55

thrashed around, and yelps of pain filled the air. The teller fell to his stomach behind the counter, covered his ears, and trembled with his eyes closed.

Luther — the first to be wounded — stumbled back inside the bank, glanced at Randee and shouted, "Git over here, lady bitch!"

Randee fired her pistol and watched Luther collapse, her shot masked by the gunfire outside as Homer and Billy Joe vainly tried to defend themselves. Other noises reached her ears — the sound of running boots and mingled voices of people who rushed outside to view the incident.

Quickly, Randee concealed the gun. As she did so, she recalled when her uncle had ordered the special leather boots and taught her how to draw and use the concealed pistol. Tears filled her eyes as she thought about Lee and Sara Elizabeth Carson and all of her new friends on the ranch: all gone, savagely murdered by horrible beasts who were worse than these crude bandits.

Suddenly, Sheriff Wade was kneeling beside her and asking if she was injured. Randee looked up at him and said, "I'm fine, Brody. The gunfire just reminded me of the attack at the ranch. Did you get them all?" she questioned, letting him help her to her feet.

Brody knew she would hear the tale of how the Durango Kid gunned down all three men with a single shot each, so he told the truth. Their attention was drawn to Marsh when he entered the bank, slapped the bag on the counter, and said, "Here's the money, Sheriff. I'll be riding out now. This town's too noise and dangerous for me."

The sheriff asked, "What about your rewards, Kid? Billy Joe Greene and the Crebbs brothers have money on their heads."

"It'll take time to be requested and sent here, and I'm

not interested in hanging around Wadesville. When it arrives, bank it for me and I'll collect it later. But guard it a little better than you did this money." Marsh patted the bag, grinned, and turned to leave.

"Wait!" Randee shouted and hurried forward. "Brody told me," she said as she half turned and smiled at the sheriff while unnoticeably pressing the five hundred dollars into Marsh's hand, "how you halted their escape. I want to thank you for saving my money."

As Brody joined them, Randee lowered her head and added, "And I should thank you for making me see how foolish and dangerous it would be to go chasing after that vicious gang."

Marsh inconspicuously slipped the money into his back pocket as he replied, "Like I said, Miss Hollis, if you and some gunslinger go racing after them, the Epson Gang will do worse than eat you two alive. If you can hire a lawful bunch to go after them, I'll be glad to join up for a nice sum. But ride after them alone? I'm not crazy, or looking to die that soon. Even if you stay here, you're in big trouble. Wouldn't surprise me any if that gang comes after you. If I were you, Miss Hollis, I'd hightail it away from these parts."

Marsh had seen her withdraw the money from her bodice as she came forward. The exchange had been made quickly, expertly, and furtively. In fact, his fingers were still in his back pocket, touching the warm, damp bills which had been snuggled between her breasts. He was filled with amazement and humor, and he liked her quick thinking. And her trust. He was supposed to be speaking harshly and condescendingly to her, but somehow couldn't manage it right now.

"That's exactly what I plan to do for a while," she announced casually. "That's why I'm in the bank, getting money for a stage ticket."

Brody asked, "What are you talking about, Dee?"

Randee touched the sheriff's arm and explained, "I was going to tell you at supper. I have to get away from here for a while. I'm going to Dodge City by stage to catch the train there. I plan to visit my father's family in Ohio. Don't worry, I'll be back in four to six weeks. Then, you can help me do something with Uncle Lee's ranch. It's mine now. Don't be angry or difficult, Brody. I need the rest and distraction, and I'm in danger here. I thought I'd pack tomorrow and leave on Thursday's stage."

"So soon?" Brody inquired in dismay. "Are you sure about this?"

Randee was glad that Matt Johnson, Brody's deputy, was keeping everyone outside, which allowed her to carry out her business with Marsh Logan and to be near him for a few more minutes. She wanted to stall the departure of this attractive man, but couldn't think of anything further to say without arousing Brody's suspicions. Knowing she wouldn't see Marsh again for days, she was inexplicably sad and lonely.

Marsh jumped into the conversation at this point. "If you're finished with me, Sheriff, I'll be on my way and let you two talk alone. I'll be heading over to Fort Worth, but I'll contact you about my reward money in a few weeks, Miss Hollis," he said as a polite farewell, then tipped his hat and left.

As if Marsh's departure meant nothing to her, Randee turned to Brody and entreated, "Will you get my money out of the bank robber's pocket? He stole it from my purse after he knocked me down."

The teller locked the retrieved money back in the safe as Brody recovered Randee's money from a dead Luther Crebbs and handed it to her. "I hate to see you go, Dee," he whispered.

"I know, but it's for the best. I wouldn't tell anyone except you, Brody; after talking to that wicked gun-

58

slinger, I'm scared. I never really stopped to think about those bandits coming after me. I was all dreamy-eyed about being the one to capture them, and crazy with grief. Heavens, Brody, what ever made me think and say such stupid things? If I leave now, the town will be safe, you'll be safe, and I'll be safe. Away from here, I can get over this matter. Maybe the law will destroy that gang before I get back and it'll all be over." She looked at the brown-haired man and murmured, "I'm scared, and I'm tired, and I'm miserable, Brody. I need to go away for a few weeks. When I return, you can help me hire some new hands, buy more stock, and move back to the ranch. I loved it there, and I miss it. As terrible as it sounds, this is the best time to visit my kin in Ohio."

Brody couldn't and didn't argue her reasons and plans. "Promise you'll come back as soon as possible?" Randee smiled and nodded. "And you'll still have supper with me tonight?"

"Of course," she replied. "And tomorrow night too, if you wish." As they left the bank, Randee avoided looking at the bandits' corpses and she tried not to dwell on what she had done in self-defense.

At seven o'clock, Brody seated Randee in the new restaurant across the street from the hotel. They dined and talked for two hours.

"You know something strange, Brody? Now that I've made these decisions, I feel so much better. You will watch over the ranch for me, won't you?" she implored in a sultry voice as she smiled into his brown eyes.

Brody didn't care who was watching, his hands closed over Randee's and he squeezed them lightly. "I know you're better. I can see it in those beautiful eyes and in your smile. This trip will be good for you, Dee.

59

With luck, it'll all be over before your return."

"I hope so, Brody. If any mail comes for me, keep it until I get back. I'm planning to leave most of my clothes in storage at the hotel. You'll ask the clerk to guard them carefully, won't you?" Randee knew she was being flirtatious and deceitful, but Brody was eating up the attention and necessary lies. She wished she didn't have to fool him like this, but he would try to stop her or follow her if she didn't carry out this provocative ruse.

"Don't worry about anything, Dee. Would you like more coffee?"

"It's late, Brody, and I have a busy day tomorrow. I should get back to my room. I'll come by your office for a visit when I go out to purchase my stage ticket. Since you don't have any prisoners, we could get Mrs. Scott to prepare us a nice meal to eat at the jail, like an indoor picnic. That way, we can talk and visit privately on our last night together. I mean" — she explained in a whisper and with a blush — "Look around — everyone is watching us and trying to eavesdrop."

Brody knew she was correct, and he was stimulated by her cozy suggestion. "That's a wonderful idea. I'll handle it in the morning."

They walked to Randee's door in silence. She unlocked it and turned to bid the sheriff good night. "I'll see you tomorrow, Brody. Thanks for a lovely dinner. I appreciate your taking care of everything for me while I'm gone. I'll return soon, I promise."

"You know how I feel about you, Dee. I love you and want to marry you. While you're gone, I want you to consider my proposal."

Randee met his adoring gaze and said, "You know you mean a lot to me, Brody. I'll think about it seriously while I'm away."

"If you think hard and fast," the lawman encouraged

hopefully, "you can give me your answer tomorrow night while we're having our picnic at the jail. I'll make sure we aren't disturbed, even if I have to refuse a prisoner lodgings for the night. I'm going to miss you."

Brody glanced around to make certain they were alone, then pulled Randee into his arms and kissed her. To Randee, the kiss was pleasant, but nothing stirring or shocking. She felt Brody quiver and knew she was arousing him. It was nice to know she had such a powerful effect on a man, but she didn't want to tease him unkindly.

She genially freed herself from his embrace. "Someone might see us and gossip. We'll discuss this matter later. Good night, Brody. Until tomorrow," she murmured and kissed his mouth lightly. She entered her room, closed the door, locked it, and went to the bed. She lay down across it and sighed heavily.

She heard Brody walk away before she rose to slip into her nightgown. She had bathed before dinner, so her skin felt comfortable on this cool evening. She put away her clothing, doused the lantern, and eased between the sheets. She was alone in the dark; now she could think about Marsh Logan and their plans . . . .

Randee mentally went over everything that had happened that day. She hated to think about killing Luther Crebbs, but he would have done the same to her. Since she was going after the Epson Gang, she had to be prepared to shoot more men. No, not men, but devilish beasts!

She curled to her side and recalled her first meeting with Marsh. He had been backing out of the saloon while trying to discourage an overly eager workinggirl. The sapphire-clad female had wanted Marsh badly — no doubt for free — and Randee couldn't blame the woman, knowing how terrible some of her customers must be. Despite the woman's fumbling and persistent hands, Marsh's refusal had been delivered kindly and gently . . . .

Randee did not scream as she watched a dark shadow enter her side window and slip toward her bed. Her right hand eased beneath the pillow and she firmly grasped the butt of her gun. She was careful to keep her breathing normal and to lie still, feigning sleep. To prevent a mistake by acting too swiftly, she waited for the man to get closer.

A familiar fragrance teased her nostrils. Apprehension was replaced by anticipation. It was as if thinking of him had summoned him. Yet, she wondered why he was sneaking into her room at midnight. As he reached the foot of the bed and hesitated there, Randee lifted the gun and uncocked it as she said, "I could have shot you, Marsh. I thought you were miles away by now. Is anything wrong?"

Marsh came to her side and asked quietly, "How did you know it was me? It's nearly black in here."

She whispered, "I recognized your smell. That's nice cologne."

"You took quite a risk; I'm not the only man who wears it."

"But it smells different on each man. What if I had screamed?"

"I was planning to sneak up on you and to clasp my hand over your mouth like this," he replied, doing so as he took the gun from her grasp and pinned her body to the bed. "You're quick, smart, and alert, Miss Hollis, but I thought you needed more testing, since my life's going to be in your hands on the trail. If you've got good skills when you think you're safe, then you'll have better ones when you know you're in danger. I'm glad to learn you don't panic and lose your head. Yep, you've got good instincts and skills, Miss Hollis, but you drop your guard too quickly." He laid her gun on the bedside table.

Randee playfully rolled him to his back and promptly placed a knife blade at his throat, one cleverly taken from beneath the other pillow while he was distracted. "Is that a fact, Mr. Logan?" she teased. "What now, my all-too-trusting partner? I could slice your throat before you could move an inch. I wonder if I should cut out your scolding tongue or pardon you. I may not be as good as you, Durango, but I'm not half bad. If you were anyone else, I could have killed you twice by now. Be grateful for my marvelous self-control, and the fact that I need you." She smothered her laughter as she put the knife aside and asked, "Now, what brings you here so late?"

Marsh chuckled softly and admitted, "I'm most impressed." He rolled to his side and propped his head on his folded elbow. He gazed into the darkness toward her, wishing he could pierce its cover. He had enjoyed the brief contact with her and found himself wanting more of it, more of her. "I can see there's no reason to test you further, partner. I came back to make certain you weren't injured this afternoon. I couldn't ask in front of the sheriff, but you were holding your arm when I came in."

"Very perceptive," she murmured, then explained most of what had happened inside the bank. "After what you did today, there's no need to test you further or to doubt that I'll be in good hands."

There was silence for a time as both pondered another meaning to her last sentence. Heavy emotion steadily filled the room as each became more aware of the other and their closeness.

Randee shifted modestly. She suggested, "I think we should talk somewhere else, Marsh. This isn't proper."

"Relax, Miss Hollis. I promise to keep my greedy hands off of you tonight, and I can't see a thing in this darkness."

"You could see well enough to find my bed and disarm me."

"I could see the foot of the bed shining in the moonlight. I planned to follow it up to you. As for the gun, it could only be one place—in your right hand—and I was touching you then. You should try doing things in the dark sometimes; it heightens the senses. There won't always be daylight or a full moon when we're working on the Epson Gang. You should learn how to move about silently and handle tasks in pitch black. Can you saddle a horse and load a gun in the dark?"

"Yes," she replied confidently.

"Sneak up on someone over any kind of terrain?"

Randee sat up, crossed her legs, and held the sheet before her. "I'm not sure, but you can teach me what I don't know. I have worked at night with my father when we were troubled by rustlers, and I was as good as any son could have been; my father said so many times. But I realize foiling thieves isn't the same as creeping up on a large gang of killers. What are you laughing at?"

"You, Miss Hollis. Evidently you don't trust me tonight or you wouldn't be poised to escape. Do you really need to clutch that sheet so tightly? I swear I can't see you over there, and I don't handle a woman who resists me. Relax, I'm nailed to this side of the bed."

"I thought you said you can't see me," she scolded.

"I'm lying on the sheet, so I can feel you pulling on it and hear your fingers gripping it like crazy. If you can't trust me here in town, how do you plan to trust me when we're out there alone?"

"I don't want to make any disturbance here. But out there, if you misbehave, I'll chop off your hand, loudly," she warned.

"If it'll make you feel better, I'll sit in the chair over there. Trouble is, we can't whisper at that distance. Well?" he prompted.

Randee realized she was being foolish because he was making her nervous with his awesome temptation. He wasn't going to harm the person who was hiring him for ten thousand dollars. And he wasn't going to accost her sexually. Maybe she was annoyed because he wasn't coming after her romantically. It was crazy to feel that way, because she didn't want this charming rogue to enchant and dupe her like Payton Slade was doing to her mother back in Kansas. "I'm sorry. You're right. I'm being silly. I'm just unaccustomed to having a . . ."

"A man in your room at night?" Marsh playfully finished for her.

"A stranger in my room," she mildly corrected, just to taunt him.

He promptly changed the subject. "I like the way you protected my wages and pulled off that sneaky exchange. What would you have done if those bandits had made off with my reward money?"

"Since I had already hired you for a specific job and made the required deposit, Mister Logan, it was your money they were stealing. Before the robbery attempt, I left a sealed letter in the bank safe, which guarantees you're to be paid the ten thousand dollars I placed there, *if* you can prove to the sheriff and the bank that you personally defeated the Epson Gang, whether or not I return alive. Naturally I appreciate your rescuing my remaining cash, but the main loss would have been yours. If you care to check, you'll find that your payment is at the bank, waiting to be earned and collected. Whether we have a signed contract or not, it's the only way you can get your hands on that money. It's in our names, Marsh, but the letter authorizes payment to you, so I'm not responsible for its safety. Agreed?"

"So, you do trust me. Well, I'll be damned," he murmured, then chuckled softly. "I appreciate your confidence, Randee; I don't get much of it from people, so I won't let you down, ever. Don't you fret; we'll make a good team, and I won't let anything happen to you." Marsh immediately knew he shouldn't have spoken so intensely, so he hurried on, "I rode out of town and doubled back. Your sweetheart had me followed. Does that mean he doesn't trust you, or me?"

Randee was elated by Marsh's fervent words and tone, even though he hastily brushed over them like a fleeing man hiding his tracks. For certain, Marsh Logan didn't like being vulnerable to anything or to anyone. Did she make him nervous, susceptible, wary? Her pulse quickened and a tingly sensation raced over her exceptionally warm body, making her aware that he had that intimidating effect on her. This man got to her more frequently and easily than was comfortable! To disguise her weakness for him, she reasoned, "Brody's smart. Maybe he wanted to make certain the infamous Durango Kid got out of his territory. Or maybe neither one of us fooled him."

"No way, Miss Hollis. I saw you working him over good in the bank, and in the restaurant tonight. You had him bound tighter than a cow's legs for branding, and he was lapping up your milky words like a starving kitten. I was watching you two from the roof. I thought you never would get back so we could talk. Mighty nice of him to seat you in front of the window across the street; probably trying to show you off or let the other men know about his claim on you." Marsh didn't tell Randee he had sneaked into the room next door so he could overhear her talk with Brody before returning to the roof to slip into her room. "Yesiree, Old Wade was eating up those sugary words you were pouring out.

Are all women this good at fooling reckless men?"

Randee was insulted, so she answered curtly, "I wouldn't know, Mr. Logan. I don't make a practice of duping my good friends, and I didn't enjoy it one bit. The only reason I misled Brody was because you insisted it was vital. So it had better be!"

"You planning to marry that respectable sheriff after you get your revenge?" the words seemed to slip uncontrollably from his lips.

"That's none of your business, and I don't like your spying on me. It's past time for you to leave. I'm tired and it's late."

"Just two more questions and I'll be gone. Where did you get ten thousand dollars? And who shot Luther Crebbs the second time?"

"What do either of those questions have to do with our partnership?" she asked, unnerved by his inquisitiveness.

"Just curious on the first point, and mad about the second one."

"Mad? Why?" she inquired, altering her position to relax the strain on her muscles.

"I don't want a reputation for overkill. That first shot was enough to finish him off in a few minutes. I don't want people thinking I shot a dying man. Who fired that bullet, Miss Hollis? It came from inside the bank and that teller was too scared to move."

"Then you already know it was me without asking. How was I to know he was mortally wounded? He was calling me horrible names and trying to grab me as a hostage. He had already tried to break my arm and knocked me around and threatened to kill me. If you're so damn good with your one-shot kills, why did he have the time and strength to come after me?"

Marsh saw he was antagonizing her over a difficult action, so he explained, "I usually like to give a man

67

time to say his final prayers."

Still miffed, she scoffed, "Do that with the Epson Gang and it'll be us praying for a last time."

"Yes, ma'am, boss lady. Any other orders besides kill 'em quick?" he inquired mischievously to calm her down.

Randee said angrily, "I don't understand you, Marsh Logan! You change every minute or two! How will I ever get to know you so I can trust you implicitly? Be honest and serious, will you?"

"How can I, when I promised to keep my hands off of you? If I'm *honest*, I'd have to admit I've wanted to kiss you ever since I knocked you into the street this afternoon. If I'm *serious*, I'd do exactly that and more, and make you madder than you are right now. Yep, nothing would please me more than to curl up to you and sleep right here tonight. I'm afraid that would complicate a purely business arrangement and dull our wits on the trail. So, it's best if I get moving pronto. I'll see you somewhere along the road Thursday or Friday." Marsh got off the bed and headed for the open window.

Randee's mind echoed his words *this afternoon*. They had only known each other for a few hours, but it seemed more like months. Her thoughts and emotions were running wild and free. The reality of his imminent departure pained and panicked her. She was being so cold and curt with him. What if she provoked him into . . . She hopped off the bed and followed him. "You will meet me, won't you, Marsh?"

The gunslinger turned to make out her face in the pale moonlight, his eyes adjusting quickly. She was looking up at him with those large green eyes which had bewitched Brody Wade earlier. She was moistening those pink lips which had deceived, then kissed, the cocky sheriff. She was interlacing fingers which Brody Wade had held so affectionately at the supper table.

That silken tawny hair fell around her shoulders like a cape of shimmering gold, and he wondered if the sheriff's greedy hands had stroked it. A nightgown, which was the color of his eyes, rested lightly against her assuredly soft flesh, guarding it from his view. Mercy, she was an overwhelming temptation, one he'd been fighting for hours!

He had observed them at supper, being too friendly in public! He had spied on them in the hallway, being too intimate for good taste! He was irrationally peeved over several things: Brody's declaration of love and his proposal, Brody's past and present relationship with Randee, and the romantic picnic scheduled for Wednesday night. When she had said, "Good night, Brody. Until tomorrow," it had been spoken so honey sweet he had gotten sticky just listening!

What, he wondered, was the matter with him? He had never felt or behaved this crazy way before. He was envious of the time which Brody Wade had spent — and would spend — with this enthralling creature, and that was most troubling. Jealousy? Now there was an admission which didn't sit well with him, one which annoyed him just as much as the thought of Randee's marrying the man who had ordered him to get out of town! Marsh chided himself, *Why should I feel and act like I've got a tormenting, unreachable burr in my pants? She's leaving town with me, not Wade. And she's lied to him, but not to me. Besides, she can't be stuck on Wade if she's leaning in my direction!* Then, he mused, there was the curious matter of her withholding crucial evidence from the lawman . . . .

Randee was disturbed by his lengthy silence and intense study of her. She wondered what to do if he reached for her tonight; more so, if he backed out on her and vanished forever. Worriedly, she asked, "You haven't changed your mind about our working together, have you?"

"Nope," he replied as he regained his composure, which wasn't easy, with her staring up into his face. "I just want to make sure Wade isn't trailing you before I show my face. As taken as he is with you, it wouldn't surprise me none if he followed you all the way to Dodge City. So don't get worried if I lay back a day or two. I'll be within sight of the stagecoach at all times, but keep that gun handy. You're good with it and the road can be a dangerous place."

"Where are your boots?" she asked when he, preparing to climb out, placed a sock-clad foot on the windowsill.

"I left them on the roof to prevent any noise. You should lock this window; it's too easy to slip over the edge and get into your room. Be careful, Randee. I won't be around for a while to protect you. If any strangers come to town, hide until they leave. If you're not on the stage, I'll know something's wrong and I'll come back for you."

Randee was soothed by his words and manner. She smiled and said, "Whatever you say, partner." When he glanced over his shoulder at her, she disclosed, "Don't worry about taking orders from a bossy woman, Marsh; I intend for you to make most of the decisions. Out there, we're in your territory, and you probably know what's safest."

In a tone that was half jesting and half serious, Marsh said, "Mercy, woman, you've amazed me again. I've never known a female who was so smart and cooperative. Since women and work don't mix well, I best git before I take another look at you and forget that lifesaving rule."

Randee peered out the window. She watched Marsh agilely shinny up a rope which was tied to the roof structure somewhere. After covering the few feet, he grabbed the edge of the flat-topped building and hoisted himself out of sight. The rope wiggled upwards and vanished. She vainly waited for him to peek over the side and say good-bye.

Randee did as Marsh advised; she closed and locked the back window, as there was one at the front for fresh air to enter. After fluffing the curtains into place, she returned to the bed. As she lay down, she realized that Marsh's manly smell clung to one side of the bed. She boldly rested her face on the pillow there and inhaled deeply, letting the spent air escape slowly. As she did so, she fantasized about Marsh's money being stolen from the bank and his intoxicating threat "to take payment out of your pretty hide."

She rolled onto her back and smiled broadly. "How wicked you are, Randee Hollis," she whispered. "How deliciously wicked."

Marsh had certainly asked a lot of questions and made plenty of remarks about her and Sheriff Brody Wade . . . . And he had returned to town, even though it wasn't necessary. If she had any doubts before about his meeting her along the stagecoach line, they were gone now. Marsh's timing was perfect. Her appointment at the dressmaker's had been to pick up the sturdy trail clothes she had paid the woman to make, mostly from the same material with which Mr. Levi Strauss was making his popular jeans. Her "womanly way" had ended yesterday, so she wouldn't have to worry about it for weeks. Everything was coming together perfectly, with a perfect man.

"Perfect man?" she murmured apprehensively. "Are you too perfect, Marsh Logan? Mama thinks Payton is perfect, but I know better. Am I just as blind and gullible as she is? It's all going so fast, too fast. I have to slow it down. One afternoon, Randee, and you're ready to fall into his arms. What's gotten into you, girl?

71

He's an infamous gunslinger, and we could both be dead before the week's out."

Maybe, Randee decided, that was it: The threat of death and the thrill of danger were drawing her toward . . . the notorious Durango Kid. But was he honestly attracted to her? If so, why? Was she viewed as a "lady" with money and land? A stimulating conquest? Or a profitable one? What a mismatch! A naive innocent attracted to an experienced charmer . . . The love of Sheriff Brody Wade enticing a daring gunman with a talented draw . . . A woman who lived on a ranch becoming entwined with a mysterious drifter who loved to roam aimlessly and endlessly . . . A frontier woman drawn to a man with superior skills and instincts, with restless blood in his veins . . . "Lordy, Marsh Logan, are we really so different after all?"

Chapter Four

Randee Hollis sat in Sheriff Brody Wade's squeaky chair and impatiently waited for his return from the hotel. He had gone to pick up the food which he had ordered from Mrs. Scott for their private dinner. The room was small and cluttered between the cell and the front door, and looked as if it could use a good scrubbing from ceiling to floor. A smelly cigar — which wasn't Brody's — had been mashed recently into a clay bowl on the scarred wooden desk, and its remains continued to send foul odors into the stuffy air. Above the desk, light flickered depressingly from a grimy lantern, the only one lit in the office. She was certain Brody would have arranged a thorough cleaning if he'd been given the time, as these surroundings were hardly conducive to the romance which he so obviously had in mind for tonight.

Randee sighed heavily in the empty office. She wasn't behind the bars, but she felt oddly confined. The urge to jump up and run out plagued her, but it was an impulse to which she knew she couldn't yield. She was tense and weary, and she didn't want to be here. Yet, to avoid suspicions and problems, she knew she had to go through with this evening and had to act natural. *Natural*, she fretted. What was normal behavior for such circumstances? Things were different to-night; she was different! Why ever had she suggested this stupid picnic? She knew why. In her attempts to be kind to Brody before leaving town and to mislead him about her scheme, she had come up with this foolish idea.

Lively music from the saloon reached her ears, but did not lift her dragging spirits. She listened to other sounds from the street: horses' movements and soft whinnies, muffled talk, laughter, quarrels, enticements to cowboys from the working girls, the barking of dogs, and the slamming of doors. Through open windows, she inhaled the scents which accompanied those sounds: food, tobacco, dust, leather, sweat, horseflesh, and more. How she wished she were on the ranch, near a serene pond, beneath a setting sun and rising moon, lying on a blanket with . . . She cautioned herself to get Marsh Logan off her mind so she could deal properly with Brody Wade. She was eager to get this meal under way and over with as quickly as possible.

Today she had packed her garments for the impending trip, and stored her remaining clothes with the hotel clerk. After purchasing her stagecoach ticket to Dodge City, she had tried to visit Brody as promised yesterday, but the lawman had been called to the Sharp's Ranch to settle a land dispute with squatters. She mentally rushed her companion's return, even though her appetite was nonexistent. She wanted to get to sleep so the night could pass swiftly, for tomorrow she would be on her way to meet Marsh Logan and begin their adventure. *Marsh Logan!* There he was again, taking over her thoughts and mood!

Randee heard the thudding of Brody's boots as he hurried across the planked walkway to rejoin her. She returned his broad smile as he entered the office and set the basket down. She watched him close and lock the door, then turn and smile at her again. There was a sparkle in his brown eyes, which reminded her of sunlight dancing on the surface of muddy water. She knew the meaning of that happy sparkle, one which made her feel more guilty about her deception, one which she wasn't in the mood for tonight.

"You sit down, Dee, and let me get everything ready. I'm sorry I wasn't here earlier today and was so late getting back to town. Bill has his ire up about those squatters on his north pasture. If I hadn't gone out there and talked them into moving on, I think he would have shot them all. Seems to me that his temper gets darker every year."

Brody cleared his desk, placed a tablecloth over it, and spread out food and dishes. Lastly, he filled two glasses with wine. Grinning, he said, "I got this from the saloon's secret stock." After lighting several tall white candles and dousing the smoky lantern, he eyed the makeshift table and said, "I think everything's ready."

As he had talked and worked, Randee had wandered around the room instead of taking a seat. The entrapped female had watched the sheriff's actions with mounting dread.

Randee took the chair he pulled out for her, and thanked him. They dined leisurely on slices of tender roast beef, spring vegetables, and hot biscuits with jelly. As Brody feasted happily, Randee forced herself to eat the delicious meal which Mrs. Scott had kindly prepared. They talked about people and events in the area, except for Indian attacks and the Epson Gang, which Brody said would spoil their "lovely evening." When the meal was finished, they sipped wine and spoke of the approaching summer with its many local activities.

Finally, to assuage Brody's worries about her trip,

75

Randee was forced to continue a story about nonexistent relatives. "I haven't seen my kin in years, so I don't know much about them. I got a letter from my aunt and uncle right before I came here. I promised I would visit them this summer, but I really didn't want to go. Now, it seems best. What are you planning to do while I'm away? Attend all of those barbeques, barn dances, and church socials?"

Brody laughed, then nodded with a playful grimace. "It's the sheriff's duty to attend each one and keep the peace. Some men get a little drunk and loud, and sometimes they have to be persuaded to leave early or settle down. Nothing will be any fun with you gone."

Randee mischievously suggested, "I'm sure there are plenty of girls around here who would swoon with pleasure to be your companion for an evening, even if you chose a different one to escort to each function. What better way to fulfill your duty, Sheriff Wade, than by making the local females ecstatically happy? Their parents, too."

"You wouldn't get jealous?" he teased with undisguised hope.

She jested, "Only if you woo them during your kind escort. You don't want to sit alone or stand around on guard all night, and you surely can't dance alone. There's no reason for you not to have fun."

"I'll think about it," was Brody's response. Then he surprised her with a change of topic. "I want to buy a ranch and give up law enforcement by the end of this year. I've saved enough money to make a good down payment and to buy a small herd, if the right place comes along. I was raised on a ranch nearby and I miss that life. After the war, I didn't want to become a cowboy or drover, so I let them talk me into becoming sheriff. Since everything's furnished for me, I've been able to save most of my wages. And I've earned a few

76

rewards from bringing in criminals with prices on their heads. I guess I'm just tired of being shot at every week, and tired of having to chase down killers and rustlers, and tired of breaking up saloon fights and jailing drunks. Mostly I'm tired of being responsible for the lives of so many people that I've known all my life," he admitted freely. "These days, I'm mainly burying friends and looking up heirs to their properties. This job's gotten stale and depressing, Dee. It's time to give it up."

Randee saw how troubled he was, so she stopped joking about his attending any social functions. A few times since her arrival, Brody had mentioned going back to ranching one day, but his announcement tonight was unexpected. And meaningful? she wondered. She nodded in understanding. "It's a terrible job, Brody, but somebody has to do it, and you've done it so well. The folk around here love you and respect you, and appreciate your dedication and skills. Don't feel guilty because you want to give it up and settle down to a peaceful life for a change. You've earned that right."

"I guess it's just hard because so many people depend on me for safety and survival. It gets to be a heavy burden after a while."

"Come election time, let them start depending on someone else. You've risked your life countless times to serve these people. There's nothing wrong in turning the task over to someone else."

Brody's brown eyes brightened and he sent her a grateful smile. "With so many families leaving because of this trouble with the Epson Gang, I should be able to buy something reasonable. I just hate to take advantage of somebody's problem or tragedy. But if I don't buy 'em out, somebody else will or they'll have to leave broke. Anyway, I need to wait for a while. It's too dangerous to begin a new life until that gang is defeated. I wouldn't want them burning down the place faster than I can build it. All I need is a good wife to work at my side."

Randee knew what was coming before Brody continued, but there was no way to stop him.

"I want that woman to be you, Dee. I hope you'll marry me, or at least accept my proposal, when you return from Ohio. You must know you're driving me loco with love for you. I want us to settle down, have a family, build a nice spread. I need you, Dee."

Randee gazed at him for a few minutes. If she told him "no," he might suspect something about her leaving so soon after the Durango Kid's arrival and departure. If she told him "yes," that wouldn't be right or kind. If she told him "maybe," he would wait for her return, while assuming her final answer to be "yes." And she didn't know how long she would be on the trail with Marsh, or if she'd survive her task. But if they won, Marsh vanished from her life, and she returned to live on the ranch — what about her future here? What about a mate and children? What about Brody Wade and his love for her?

"Brody, I . . ." she faltered as his loving gaze locked on her apprehensive green one, mutely pleading with her to respond positively. She forged on bravely, "I'm sorry, Brody, but I can't give you any kind of answer tonight. I don't know what my feelings are, except that I'm very fond of you. I have so much on my mind right now that I can't think clearly and fairly about your proposal. I don't want to take advantage of you by marrying you for the wrong reasons. Presently, I'm scared, I'm alone, I'm vulnerable, I'm . . . I'm too susceptible to your beautiful plans."

She covered his right hand with both of hers and halted his interruption. "Wait, let me finish while I have the courage and words because this is very hard for me. Marriage is a serious undertaking; it's a lifetime commitment. You know all about duties and obligations. It's scary to take on the responsibilities of husband, home, and family. And it isn't right to make a man accountable for a family and property if you don't feel as strongly about them as he does. I don't want to marry you to keep from being alone or because marriage is the proper course of action at a certain age. I want and I need more than a ranch partner, more than a father for my children, more than a spinster saver. I have to make certain I love and want to marry only you. With some distance between us and time on my hands, I can decide what's the best answer for both of us. I promise I'll be back as soon as possible."

Disappointment showed in Brody's expression before he smiled and acquiesced, "You're right, Dee, but it's hard to wait. I'm so afraid you'll meet someone else and forget about me. You're the first woman I've loved, the first one I've asked to marry me. Actually, you're the only one I've wanted to be around me day and night. You made me happy again. I haven't felt that way since before the war. I love you, Dee, and I need you in my life."

Tears glittered in her eyes as she listened to his revealing words. More guilt plagued her until she told herself it wasn't her fault if she didn't share his feelings and desires. She knew she was fascinated by Marsh Logan, but there was no future with a notorious gunslinger. What troubled Randee most was knowing that if the Carsons had been killed accidentally and if Marsh Logan hadn't appeared and if Brody had said these things to her, her answer might have been "yes" tonight.

Soon, she would need someone to help her rebuild the ranch. No, she corrected herself, the ranch didn't belong to her. One day Dee Carson Hollis Slade would learn of her brother's death and that valuable inheritance. Randee asked herself if she could build her life around a ranch she didn't own, the ranch which Payton Slade would claim when he learned about it. If the Carsons failed to write or to answer letters for a long time, her mother would check on the matter. If her mother told her deceitful husband where Randee was . . . Where would she go then? What would she do alone? Who would protect her from her insidious stepfather? Whatever happened, those were her problems, not Brody Wade's. Randee didn't need anyone to take care of her, but she wanted someone special to share her life.

Brody clasped both of her hands between his. "I'm sorry, Dee. I've upset you and spoiled a lovely evening. I won't push you anymore."

"That isn't it, Brody. I'm just touched by your feelings for me. You're such a special man, and I hope my answer can be yes. If it is, I don't want to live on the Carson Ranch; too much happened there."

"It's a marvelous spread, Dee, but I understand. Besides, I want to build my own from scratch. We can choose the spot and plan the house together; then it'll be just what we want. I'll keep an eye on the Carson Ranch until you get back, then you can see about selling it. If you like, I can keep my ears open for a buyer while you're gone."

"I'd appreciate that, Brody," was the answer she had to give.

"I want you to be careful on the stage and train, and to have a good time with your kinfolk. I'm glad you dropped that scheme about hiring the Durango Kid. I was worried. He's sneaky and dangerous, a real bad apple. He walks just a shave inside the law, but one day he'll slip up and get himself hanged. Some of the cold-blooded stories I've heard about him would freeze off your ears to hear them."

Randee almost laughed at the comparison of Marsh Logan to one of the gunman's intense dislikes. She hoped Marsh's colorful reputation was just that, a colorful reputation. To change the subject, Randee said, "It was silly to think I could take off after a band of murderers. I was just filled with anguish and fury, and I was upset because they're getting away with it. Let's don't talk about them tonight. It . . ." Randee was silenced by a loud thudding on the front door. It sounded as if someone was beating on it with a boot.

A man's voice shouted, "Open up in the jail. Marshal Foley Timms here with a prisoner."

Randee glanced at Brody, who was scowling and making no attempt to get up and let the marshal inside. The man kicked the door again, harder and louder, and called out, "You in there, Sheriff?"

Brody apologized to her as he slowly got up to respond. He opened the door and asked curtly, "What do you want, Timms?"

The persistent lawman looked surprised by the terse greeting. He peered around Brody and saw the remains of a private dinner with a lovely woman. "Just passing through and need a prisoner locked up for the night. Looks like I came at a bad time, Sheriff Wade. Sorry to disturb you, but I saw a light and thought you might be reading or napping. I suppose I could tie him to a chair in my hotel room."

Randee saw the opportunity to end this trying evening, so she promptly joined the men at the door. She said, "That isn't necessary, Marshal Timms. It's late and I need to get home." Turning to Brody, she said, "I'll see you in the morning before the stage leaves."

"You don't need to leave yet, Dee. Marshal Timms

81

can keep his prisoner at the hotel with him. It won't be any bother. I've done it several times when jails were full, or towns didn't have one."

"I have a long and hard journey ahead, Brody. I really should get plenty of rest tonight. And I'm sure Marshal Timms sees enough of criminals during the day without having to sleep with them at night. He'll probably be overjoyed to sleep with both eyes closed for a change. The dinner was wonderful. Thank you again. We'll speak in the morning. Good night, Brody. Good night, Marshal Timms."

"I'll walk you to the hotel. It's dark and late," Brody announced. To Foley Timms, he said, "You know where the keys and cell are."

At her door, Brody whispered, "I'm sorry he ruined our evening, Dee. I'll be over about eight thirty to carry your bags to the stage."

"You could hardly let him bring his prisoner to the hotel for the night. If we refused to let a marshal inside the jail, people would wonder what we were doing over there. Then, if we married soon after my return, they'd think there was some wicked reason for doing so."

The grinning sheriff confessed, "I guess the intrusion was good, since you're such a desirable woman and I promised to give you time. This way, I'm forced to behave. Can I have a good-bye kiss?"

They embraced and their lips met. The kiss was more intense than Randee planned or wanted, but she allowed it to run its course. She felt the force of his desire in his taut body and snug embrace. His mouth hungrily claimed hers and she tried to respond.

His hands gently captured her head and he spread rapid kisses over her face before she could caution him to halt. When he did, he gazed deeply into her eyes and vowed hoarsely, "You're my own weakness, Dee, the only thing that can hurt me or harm me. I won't give up my chase until you're my wife. I must have you, I must."

Randee watched the lawman round the corner and disappear down the steps. She felt traitorous to Brody as she dreamily thought, *If only Marsh Logan could feel and say such things* . . .

It was two o'clock in the morning when Randee began to thrash on her bed and to endure a bad dream: She witnessed her father's murder by rustlers who wore the faces of the Epson Gang; she watched Payton Slade woo, wed, and dupe her mother; she saw Dee's husband join the Hollis Ranch to the Slade Ranch and claim it all as his; and she saw how her stepfather's stare got bolder every day.

The dream got worse: Randee found herself trapped inside the barn while her mother was occupied with a bath. She felt Payton's lips and hands on her body. She heard him threaten to kill her mother if she refused him and if she exposed him. She saw her shirt ripped away and Payton bury his face between her breasts. She felt his dirty hand slipping up her thigh. She desperately wanted to scream and resist, but couldn't because Payton had two of his men standing on the front porch, prepared to enter the house and brutalize her mother if she did so.

Randee heard her stepfather say, "It's more fun this way, girl. Keepin' it a secret makes it more excitin'. Even if you told Dee about us, she wouldn't believe you. She would let me strip you an' beat you for speakin' such evil about her beloved husband. I like you bein' real scared an' wantin' to kill me, but obeyin'. It makes me real hard for you. You're my private prisoner, girl. I can do anythin' to you. I'm sendin' yore ma on a trip next week to help out at the Kirbys'.

While she's gone, I'll teach you a few things; you'll probably like 'em. In case you get any crazy ideas, I'm sendin' one of my men with yore ma."

Randee awoke trembling and in a sweat. She was breathing erratically and her mouth was dry. She sat up in the bed and tried to clear away all thoughts of the nightmare, parts of which were real. She fetched herself water to wet her lips and throat, then changed into a dry nightgown. She turned and fluffed her pillow and straightened the sheets.

Randee knew she could never return to Kansas, even if that meant never seeing her mother again. She hated knowing that her mother was fooled by Payton Slade, but ignorance kept Dee happy and alive. Randee recalled how she had left her mother a note which said she was running away to New York to seek adventure. She remembered how she had packed and escaped during her mother's visit to the Kirbys'. She had confided in the Carsons, and finally convinced them that Payton Slade was too powerful to challenge and that her mother wouldn't take Randee's word against her stepfather's. The Carsons had believed her and protected her secrecy. Now they were gone, and Payton Slade would soon be staking his claim on another special ranch. Since she hadn't exposed Payton's wickedness in the note, her stepfather had no reason to harm her mother. But how long would he keep Dee around?

A bold idea entered Randee's troubled mind. Following the destruction of the Epson Gang, why couldn't she hire the Durango Kid to defeat her stepfather? Of course, Payton Slade was not a wanted criminal like the savage gang they would be hunting down legally. Marsh would have to force him into a fight and gun him down! After she explained why she needed Payton killed and if she offered Marsh a great deal of money, surely he would take the additional work.

When the deed was done, she and her mother could force Payton's men off the ranch, or they could move here for a fresh start on the Carson Ranch. Somehow she would convince her mother of Payton's evil, after his death. If Marsh refused the second job, she would plead for Brody's help, even if she had to marry him to get it. "Don't worry, Mother, I'm going to save you from that bastard. If we're both lucky, you'll discover how bad he is before I come after him."

Randee snuggled to her side and closed her eyes. Yes, she mused, they were her problems and she would solve them . . . .

By eight forty-five on Thursday, May 18th, Randee had bathed, dressed, eaten breakfast, and followed Brody to the waiting stage. She listened as the driver explained the rules to the passengers: "Don't drink unless you need to and can share the bottle. Don't smoke with ladies aboard. No cussing or swearing. Don't crowd your neighbor or use him for a pillow. No shooting from the coach unless there's trouble. If we have trouble, be calm until it's settled. Obey these rules and you'll enjoy a good ride. If not, you can be put off anywhere to make your way to the nearest town or station, with no refund."

Randee and Brody exchanged amused grins as the passengers climbed inside the coach. He handed her a limp, paper-wrapped package. "A present to remember me by, ribbons for your hair. Every time you wear one, think of me and what's waiting here for you."

Randee ignored any stares or cause for gossip to hug the man and kiss his cheek. "Thank you, Brody. I'll miss you. Stay safe and well."

As Brody assisted Randee into the coach, the man on the left slid over to give the coveted window area to the sheriff's "sweetheart." The route was posted at the office and on the stagecoach door: Wadesville to Fort Worth to Red River Station on the Texas border, across Indian Territory, and into Kansas to Dodge City. It was alleged to be a dusty, bruising, bone-tiring experience of eleven to twelve days, depending on the weather and any trouble along the way. For the passengers' information and convenience, the schedule was also posted: departure at nine, a ten-minute horse change at a relay station at eleven, a forty-five minute halt for lunch and rest at a home station at one, a ten-minute horse change at another lay station at four, and a halt for the night at six at a home station or town. Since the horses were run fast and hard at eight to nine miles per hour, they were changed every fifteen miles. The driver and guard took their seats, and the momentous journey began at nine o'clock sharp.

Randee waved farewell to Brody and settled back to make herself as comfortable as possible. She was glad to be sitting against the front boot and facing backward, because that was the best bench available. She did not notice the man who began following the stage at the edge of town . . . .

Some of the passengers conversed casually, but avoided the forbidden topics of robberies and Indian attacks. One woman took out her sewing for a while until she realized it was impossible to do such work under such jarring conditions. The same was true of a man who tried to read a book. A youth finally took out a harmonica and began to entertain the passengers with lively music, which helped to pass the time.

Around eleven, the stop at the relay station was brief because the attendant was swift and skilled, carrying out his task in less than five minutes. Passengers were not allowed to leave the coach at relay stops unless it was an emergency.

At twelve-fifty, the stage halted at a home station for

lunch. Randee only picked over the unappealing fare of beans, biscuits, and coffee. Back in the coach, many dozed after the quick meal and exercise. Randee watched the scenery rush by and wondered what lay ahead for her.

They reached Fort Worth on time and the passengers were on their own for the night, after being ordered to be on time for the morning departure. Randee hired a youth to take her bag to the local hotel, where she registered for the night and paid for a bath to be brought to her room. Afterwards, she went to the hotel restaurant for a decent meal, devouring each delectable bite. She doubted Marsh would join her this soon, and she was right. The night passed in fitful sleep and she was up and ready to leave at nine.

Some of the passengers were different today, but things went much the same as the day before. Still, she did not see the man who was stealthily following the coach . . . . Nor did she hear the tales of how the Durango Kid was giving the locals excitement far away in San Antonio . . . . Nor did she hear of the vicious raid on Bill Sharp's ranch near Wadesville . . . .

Today, her tawny hair was becomingly secured by one of the ribbons from Brody Wade. As she fingered it, she pondered the ruggedly handsome lawman and his stirring revelations. Over and over she considered her plans and options, always finding Marsh Logan in the midst of them. He was something to deal with before her task ended!

That night, they halted at a home station. Following another unappetizing meal—served with an edible cake for dessert—they listened to music from a fiddler before the women were sent to one room and the men to a different one. Randee was unaccustomed to bedding down with another person, so she slept little. The other woman was the wife of an Army major, on her way to join her husband, who was stationed at Fort Sill just inside Indian Territory. The woman was painfully shy and talked little, despite Randee's attempts to draw her out for a much needed distraction. At least Indian Territory — one day to become the state of Oklahoma — was heavily dotted with Army posts to protect whites and to keep the Indians on their assigned reservations.

Saturday passed without trouble, and without an appearance by Marsh Logan. The Red River was nearby and it seemed to warn Randee, "Don't cross me or you'll be in deep trouble." As she tossed in the bed with the other young woman, she wondered what she should do if Marsh didn't meet her soon as promised. In the morning, they would leave Texas, placing her closer to Kansas and Payton Slade. By the time she reached Dodge City, if she did, her funds would be too low to catch the stage back to Wadesville. She asked herself if she should halt here and turn back, or continue onward. Once she entered Indian Territory, she had no choice but to pass through it into Kansas . . . .

Randee stood beside the coach with mounting tension and doubts as the stage was ferried across the river boundary. The driver pulled it into a level clearing and ordered the passengers to reload. Randee hesitated a minute, fear gripping her heart. Had she trusted Marsh too quickly and fully? Had he taken her money and . . .

"Miss Hollis," the familiar voice called out as she was slowly mounting the fold-down step.

Randee whirled and smiled, her heart pounding fiercely in relief and pleasure. She noticed Marsh's roguish grin as he told the driver he was picking her up at this point and taking her home. The driver asked if she knew the man and if she agreed to leave the stage with him. Randee smiled at the man and replied, "Yes, sir. It's fine."

Her bag was tossed down and the stage left them standing there. Randee looked at the gunslinger and demanded, "What kept you so long?"

"Getting worried, huh?" he teased. "I couldn't get you sooner, because you were being dogged by Deputy Matthew Johnson. Obviously your loving sheriff asked him to make certain you left Texas alone. He turned back after the ferry started across the river. I suppose old Wade wanted to make sure you didn't hook up with me in Fort Worth. I made the mistake of telling him in the bank that's where I was heading. Must have been that robbery attempt that had my brain dulled. I guess he ordered Johnson to follow you until it was clear we weren't joining up somewhere. Mistrustful sweetheart, isn't he?"

"Maybe he just wanted an extra guard on me for protection," she retorted in annoyance and fatigue. "Brody might not trust you, Durango, but he trusts me totally."

"Is that so?" he taunted helplessly.

Randee glared at him. "Yes, it is so," she replied confidently.

"I see we're tired and fussy today. Why don't we blame it on that bumpy trip and cease this silly quarrel?"

"I wasn't quarreling; you were. Let me get changed and we can get out of here," she suggested to halt the vexing banter.

"Good, 'cause that pretty dress would be hard to ride in. I hope you packed some trail clothes like I ordered."

Randee sent him another icy glare at his last word, but didn't challenge it. She took her bag and disappeared behind the thick underbrush near the river. She quickly changed into a split-tail riding skirt, matching shirt, and boots. She strapped on the holster and gun which her father had given to her before his death in

'68. Ready, she joined Marsh at the horses.

He eyed the dark blue outfit and smiled approvingly. He tossed her a double-sided saddle bag and said, "Put your things in there. A carpetbag doesn't tie well to a saddle."

Randee caught the leather pouches and said, "Thank you." She knelt to stuff her garments inside as Marsh watched her attentively. When she stood, he handed her a hat, commenting that she might not have one and would need it on the sunny trail. Again, she thanked him for his foresight and preparation. She was delighted to find that the hat was a perfect fit.

Before she could check out the horse and saddle he had purchased for her, he handed her a new holster with two guns — Smith & Wesson .44's. "I'll teach you to fire with both hands; it might be handy along the way. These guns don't have to be hand-cocked after each shot, like that Colt you're wearing. I've also put a new Winchester rifle on your saddle."

Randee studied the revolvers and rifle, and was pleased. She lifted the gun and checked its weight. "It's heavier. How's its accuracy?"

"You'll find out when we camp tonight. I don't want that stage or station to hear gunfire. Just watch its kick if you use it before then; it's a powerful weapon. I'm sure you're a good judge of horseflesh and leather, so you'll see I bought you the best of both."

Randee went over the animal thoroughly and skillfully, examining his legs, teeth, eyes, hide, and hooves. Next, she ran her hands over the saddle, outside and underneath. She smiled and nodded her appreciation. "I see you spent the money well, Mr. Logan. Thanks."

"I'm glad you like my selections, Miss Hollis," he replied mirthfully. "They did cost us a mite more than we planned, but they'll prove their worth in the weeks to come. So will those weapons," he added as she traded her prized Colt for the new revolvers.

Randee tied her pouches to her saddle and checked the stirrup length and girth-strap snugness. He told her the chestnut's name was Rojo, Spanish for *red,* unless she preferred to change it. "If she's used to it, there's no need to confuse her," Randee said. She gently stroked the mare's forehead and neck, allowing the animal to accept her touch and smell. She mounted agilely and asked, "Ready to ride, Mr. Logan?"

"Since we can't use the ferry without notice, let's go for a swim, Miss Hollis." With that statement, he headed down the bank to a safe crossing point and guided his sleek black stallion into the water.

Randee removed her boots and held them in her lap to prevent them from filling with water and becoming uncomfortable; plus, she didn't want her concealed pistol to get soaked. She wasn't concerned about her skirt tail getting wet as it would dry quickly in the warm sun and the breeze that would be raised when they resumed riding.

Randee and Marsh forded the river in a short time. Neither one had any trouble with the often dangerous task. Marsh halted long enough for Randee to dry her feet and replace her boots. Accustomed to crossing many rivers during his travels, Marsh had learned how to hold his feet and legs to avoid water-filled boots. But, he realized, Randee's way was simpler and safer — if you weren't being chased.

Conversation was impossible as they rode toward Jacksboro at a swift pace and with Marsh's intense concentration on their surroundings. Randee noted that clearly this was a man who stayed on alert and who constantly gathered numerous perceptions at the same time. They halted briefly around noon, to rest and to water the horses and to eat cold biscuits with baked ham. The sparse fare was washed down with water since Marsh thought it best not to make a campfire for coffee. During that stop, he kept busy and to himself, so Randee did the same.

As they traveled, both had similar thoughts: each other. Both knew that each was being watched and tested by the other. All day, Marsh pushed the lovely blonde hard and fast to test her strength and mettle. Randee surmised his behavior and motive, and proved herself.

Marsh recalled what Randee Hollis had said about hiring a "special man" . . . "only the best." Since it was he who was with her right now — and not the other two applicants she had mentioned — that revealed her high opinion of his prowess. He took the lead to avoid her tempting distraction, as watching her would surely take his mind off of the road.

To the north of them, shortly after Marsh picked up Randee, trouble had struck. A band of renegade Indians, led by the Kiowa Chief Satanta, had attacked the stagecoach which had transported the blonde from Wadesville to the Red River border of Texas. Boldly they had crossed the river and raided the home station where Randee had slept Saturday night. They took horses, goods, and female prisoners; but the white men had been left behind, all dead.

In 1867, the Kiowas and Comanches, fierce tribal enemies, had given up the Texas Panhandle and agreed to settle on reservations in Indian Territory. But the land was barren and promises were broken, so Chief Satanta had rebelled and returned to "the old way."

When the Army major's wife and the stagecoach failed to arrive Sunday afternoon as scheduled, a search would begin immediately. The dreadful evidence would be found by dusk. By Monday morning,

soldiers from Fort Sill would be on the march to recover the captives and to punish the renegade Indians.
And, news of the lethal raids would be sent to the
passengers' and station workers' next of kin in Fort
Worth and Wadesville . . . .

As the miles raced past, Randee studied the irresistible man who rode just ahead of her. No matter how
amiable and charming he was, she always sensed a
protective reserve about him. Yes, she admitted, he
talked to her when it suited him to do so, but he always
revealed very little, especially about himself. One thing
she did know, she was safe with him. If he had been
after the expense money, he wouldn't have joined her at
Red River. If he had been after her for other wicked
reasons, he would have halted and taken advantage of
her by now. Somehow, she had sensed she could trust
him in those areas, even if he kept things from her or
lied to her about himself.

Randee's eyes roamed the sturdy physique on the
saddle before her. Marsh possessed a combination of
visible strengths: physical, mental, and emotional. At
the hotel, he had given her a scant insight to an array
of feelings, but by accident and without his awareness.
It didn't surprise her that he was a wary and private
person, but she hoped he would relax and reveal more
during their journey.

She eyed the strong jawline which was firmly set on
that handsome face. She remembered how light his
blue eyes appeared against a darkly tanned face surrounded by ebony hair and heavy stubble. When he
smiled, it created such an arresting effect, and he
seemed to do it easily and naturally for the "cold-
blooded" gunman Brody had called him. She liked his
intelligence and concern, shown to her by the horse,

saddle, hat, and weapons. This man was a rare combination of traits that potently drew her to him, a man not to be taken lightly or foolishly.

They didn't halt their tiring journey until dark, as Marsh said they needed to get at least halfway to Jacksboro. After tending their horses and setting up camp, they finished off the cold ham-and-biscuits with hot coffee made by Marsh. As both were weary and sleepy, they turned in immediately after eating, with only boots and hats removed. This wasn't the time for conversing about anything, so they didn't. Both were asleep quickly, Randee more deeply than Marsh.

It was shortly after dawn when the gunman awakened Randee and told her it was time to eat and move on. He secretly eyed her for signs of excessive fatigue and fragility, and decided she was doing more than fine on the arduous trail. In fact, she had done better yesterday than most men would have, and without a single complaint or problem or sluggishness. He was most impressed, and surprised, by this beautiful lady who matched his endurance and determination. To keep her from slacking off, or so he mistakenly thought, he did not compliment her on her favorable skills. They ate the beans and biscuits which Marsh had ready almost minutes after she was astir.

Randee furtively observed the handsome man whose ebony hair fell appealingly over his forehead. Shadowy stubble darkened the strong jawline on his bronze face, and his eyes looked very blue and enticing this morning. He hadn't buttoned or tucked in his shirt yet, and that golden chest was most tantalizing. Feeling warm and itchy all over, Randee knew she had to get her mind off the tempting sight of this man. The nineteen-year-old female smiled and stretched after finishing her breakfast. She told him, "You make wonderful coffee, Mr. Logan, and you're an excellent cook."

Marsh realized she was slightly nervous this morning, and he hoped he had guessed the correct reason for her tension: him. As she straightened her garments and brushed her hair, he grinned and teased, "I reckon that means I'm not supposed to be good in those areas because I'm a man. Or because I'm a gunslinger. Fact is, Miss Hollis, I'm on the trail most of the time, so I have to know how to cook good to keep from starving or spending too much time in noisy towns. Let's get packing, woman, or we won't make Jacksboro by nightfall."

At dawn, while Randee and Marsh were beginning their day, the notorious Epson Gang made a bloody raid on a ranch near the Trinity River West Fork, a cattle spread northwest of Jacksboro . . . .

Chapter Five

The pace of their journey was different this morning. Randee and Marsh did not ride as hard and fast as they had yesterday, but their progress was a steady one, and the miles lessened between them and their first destination. At each rest and water stop for the horses, Marsh again kept mostly to himself, and Randee followed suit. She realized that he would have to get accustomed to having another person around all the time. Until the Durango Kid adjusted to his loss of privacy, she concluded it was best to be as unnoticeable as possible.

The blonde longed for a soothing bath and clean clothes, and a soft bed with lots of cuddly pillows. Visions of steaming cornbread, delicious vegetable-and-beef soup, fresh lemonade, and blackberry cobbler filled her mind. She thought of Brody Wade, who was probably yearning for her hasty return and her hand in marriage. Guilt washed over Randee as she gazed at Marsh Logan, and her body flamed instantly with a feverish passion, which Brody had never ignited.

She wondered why this mysterious loner had such a powerful and crazy effect on her, while a dependable, respectable, kindhearted man like Brody felt more like an adopted brother. The two men were so different from each other, and both were so unlike that vile beast, Payton Slade. Randee angrily scolded herself for allowing her stepfather to plague her on this lovely afternoon in late May. She dismissed all three men from mind, and called forth the Epson Gang to study.

When they halted for a longer stop that afternoon, Marsh was in a curious mood. "We'll make camp tonight at a place I know near Jacksboro, the site of the gang's first raid. We'll make our plans and do our maps there." Running his fingers through his black hair, he mussed the windblown locks more than he tamed them. He appeared edgy as he chatted. "During the next few days, I'll teach you some tricks about stealthy tracking and fast movements. I want you as highly trained as possible before we confront those murdering bastards. While we're camped near Jacksboro, you can practice with those new weapons and get that mare used to you." The alert Marsh had noticed her working frequently with the animal since that morning, and he didn't know why he'd added that unnecessary suggestion. It was obvious she knew a lot about horses and earning their loyalty and assistance.

Randee was aware of Marsh's unusual talkativeness and slight tension. She presumed he had had trouble in this area in the past and was placing himself on extra guard, but was trying to conceal it. "Thanks, those are excellent ideas," she remarked. She reasoned that asking him questions right now would only make him retreat further into silence, so she didn't press. She had to be patient until he was ready to open up to her, which he might do after getting to know her better.

"How did your little picnic with the sheriff go?" he inquired.

Randee looked his way, but his gaze was in the other direction. She grinned and queried, "Fine, why do you ask?"

"Just wondering if you kept your head and didn't drop any clues about us," he replied, then drank deeply from his canteen. "Did he act or talk strange? Did he mention me?"

"Naturally he mentioned the notorious Durango Kid; I must say, most unfavorably. But he didn't behave strangely or mistrustfully, even when I made up kin in Ohio and told him all about them. You can relax, Mr. Logan; I remained tight-lipped, like someone else I know."

Marsh half turned and glanced at her. Yep, he concluded, she was smart and quick, and she was witty. He chuckled, causing his eyes to sparkle and a pleasant expression to slip over his face. "Wade told me to steer clear of you, that you belong to him. Is that true?"

"My relationship with Brody doesn't concern you," she responded.

"I suppose not, unless he hears of our little adventure and comes after me with a blood glint in his eye. I don't like showdowns with the law. A furious sweetheart could tangle our plans something fierce. Haven't you learned that jealous men do crazy things?"

She quipped, "Then, make certain we're careful on all accounts. Speaking of arousing suspicion, you were too nice in the bank."

This time, Marsh laughed heartily. "So were you," he retorted playfully. "It sounded smart when I first gave you that order, but I decided it would look strange being hostile to a beautiful lady for no reason."

Randee let his compliment pass as if unnoticed. She watched Marsh stretch and flex his muscular body, and that warm tingle came over her again. Heavens, she fretted, he was such an overwhelming attraction! She focused her attention on Rojo, patting her nose, stroking her neck, feeding her bunches of grass, and speaking to her.

"Another question, Randee," Marsh began, his tone softened like a caress. "You said you left home in February and made it to Wadesville alone. Why did you leave Kansas and why are you afraid to return?"

Before she could master her reflexes, Randee's hand ceased its loving labor. She inhaled sharply and she stiffened. Hastily she commanded herself to relax and to come up with an acceptable answer. Her warring mind refused to aid her, so she snapped, "That's my business! It's none of your affair."

Marsh refuted, "It is my affair if you left trouble back there and it follows you here and involves me."

Randee turned slowly and met his probing gaze. She smiled provocatively and murmured, "Do I look like the kind of person who gets into trouble?"

Marsh's eyes leisurely traveled over her from head to foot. "Yep."

Randee laughed at his amused expression. "Even if I did leave a nasty situation behind, I'm certain my partner can handle any overflow of trouble if it comes our way. But don't worry, nobody's coming to Texas to look for me and to cause you problems. My father's dead."

"Where's your mother?" he asked instantly.

Randee sent him a fake smile. "She's happily married again, and newlyweds don't need a grown woman around their house. Their efforts to gain privacy got to be annoying. Besides, I wanted to live with my kin and enjoy new surroundings, so I came to Texas."

Marsh knew she was lying, but he didn't call her on it. There was no denying that something terrible had happened in Kansas to drive her away from home in the midst of winter. Otherwise, a female of her age would have been given an escort by her parents or kin, or she would have taken the stage. There was a reason why she left quickly and alone. What it was, or who it was, he needed to discover.

Randee knew he hadn't believed her, but she didn't retract her lies or nervously add more to her tale. "What about you, Mr. Logan? Why did you leave home and become a famous gunslinger?"

"For thrills and adventures, Miss Hollis, just like you."

"You men are lucky. You can seek adventure without problems, but females can't. A woman on her own isn't viewed in a good light, and people try to take advantage of her. Yet, you men can go anywhere and do anything you please, and everyone thinks it's fine and even envies your freedom and excitement. When you defend yourself, it's a glorious notch on your reputation. But if a woman shoots a man, it's murder or big trouble. That's stupid and unfair."

"You sorry you're a woman? You trying to become a real man? Is that what this chase is all about?"

"It isn't a joke, Marsh. Try being a woman for a month and you'll see what I mean! We work as hard, if not harder, than men. We labor side by side on farms and ranches, plus take care of homes and children during and after those chores, while the men rest. We doctor the sick, we teach the young, and we hold things together when men go off to war or get killed. But, no, I don't wish I were a man. I just want to be treated fairly and equally when and where I deserve it."

"Is your father to blame for this bad opinion of men?"

Randee's face flushed with anger. "Don't you dare insult my father! He was the best man to ever live. After chores, he always helped around the house because he knew Mother and I were just as tired as he was. He did lots of things men consider woman's work, but he was a strong and brave man and people's jokes didn't bother him. I was referring to the way it is in most homes and situations, where men give themselves, or other men, all the credit for success, as if their wives had nothing to do with it. My father wasn't like that. He did special things to make us happy."

Randee looked out across the greening landscape and envisioned Randall Hollis working out there. "My father never treated me like a son, or wished I were one. He treated me as an equal with the other hands because I earned that right. Just like I'll prove to you I can handle my share of everything that comes our way. I don't care why you agreed to take this job, but my only reason for this mission is to see justice done. I want those bastards dead for what they did at the Carson Ranch. And if it costs me my life, so be it, because it's the only thing in my life right now. Let's get riding, or we won't make Jacksboro by dark."

As she wet her throat after her mild tirade, Randee chided herself for jabbering like a fool. She had to let this bitterness go, this destructive resentment over her father's early death and her mother's marriage to a beast like Payton Slade: one of those men she had been describing! Heavens, she loved her father and missed him terribly. How totally different Payton Slade was from Randall Hollis, and she could not understand what her mother saw in that wicked man. Between the war and her mother's remarriage, Randee's life had been ruined. Then, to come here and to find a new one, only to have it stolen from her . . .

Marsh intruded on her tormenting thoughts, "How's the arm?"

"What?" she replied, unsettled and confused.

Marsh gently grasped her arm and pushed the sleeve up to look at the purplish-yellow area. "Luther Crebbs got you good that day. Did you have it checked to make sure the bone isn't cracked?"

Randee glanced at the healing injury, then up at Marsh. His touch was as gentle as she had imagined it would be. Seemingly genuine concern showed in his eyes, and unnerved her further. "I've taken care of enough breaks to know it's fine, just badly bruised muscle. My arm's still a little sore, but it won't get in the way of our work."

Marsh knew she was fatigued and probably aching from her rough journey, but not once had she slowed him down or asked for special treatment. He also knew that something awful was haunting her, and he understood that feeling only too well. A curious empathy came over him and he wanted to comfort her. "You don't have to behave as strong as a man, Randee. When you need to stop, don't be too proud or embarrassed to say so. I'm used to constant travel; you aren't."

Marsh was standing too close for comfort, and his touch was too disturbing to ignore. Her nose detected a mixture of ruggedly manly smells, which were stimulating. She felt the heat from his virile body, and the heat he was creating within hers. He exuded a tantalizing tenderness that flustered her. She had carried burdens for months and weeks, and she longed to throw herself into his arms to accept the solace he was mutely offering. She dared not behave so weakly and rashly. She had to remain strong and in control, or he would doubt her strength and capabilities. Moreover, his embrace was hazardous to her.

Today he was wearing a tan shirt and snug jeans that vividly displayed his well-built frame. She felt her heart beating strangely, and she inhaled deeply to slow its crazy pace. "I'm doing fine, Marsh. I'm tired and sore, but not enough to make camp this early. I worked and rode every day at the ranch, so I'm in good condition. I'll tell you if I need an extra break. But thanks for being so kind and understanding."

Nimbly mounting her horse, she announced, "I'm ready, partner."

Marsh took off his hat, wiped the sweat from his brow, and replaced it. He tossed two woven sacks of supplies across his saddle, which he had hidden at this rest stop before retrieving Randee. He mounted and said, "Come along, Miss Hollis. We have a ways to go before nightfall."

They traveled until dusk without another stop or word. As the sun was grazing the tree tops near a wide creek, Marsh revealed, "We're almost there. We'll be camping in ten minutes."

"Good. I'm starving and exhausted," she freely admitted.

In a strained voice, Marsh concurred, "Me too."

Randee wondered about his gradual change in tone and aura as they neared this lovely and peaceful spot. She moved her right leg over the horse and dismounted. Bending forward at the waist, she bounced several times to loosen her taut back muscles. Afterwards, she twisted and flexed her limbs to complete unwinding. Her skin was damp and dusty, and her stomach was near to hunger pangs.

As if reading her mind, Marsh informed her, "About a hundred yards downstream, there's a nice water hole for bathing. You look like you need it badly." He grinned and challenged, "That is, if you trust me enough to take advantage of a good thing. While you're refreshing yourself, I'll take cook duty tonight."

"Is this spot safe?" she asked as she fetched her leather pouches. "I mean, is it a secluded one? Any neighbors or squatters nearby?"

"Nobody's supposed to be around for miles, Randee, but I'll keep an extra eye and ear open. I haven't been here in a long time, but it still looked deserted as we rode in." While unsaddling his stallion, Marsh disclosed, "This ranch belonged to people I knew, people killed in that first raid last April. The house and barns were over that way," he told her, pointing to a shady grove not too far from the stream. "It was really something to see.

103

Thirteen months ago, the Epson Gang killed everybody and burned everything to the ground."

Randee observed the man intently. Marsh's bitterness and fury were evident in his voice and stance. "I'm sure your friends would appreciate what you're doing for them, Marsh. We'll catch that murderous band and punish them, then all of their dead can rest easier." She looked around and smiled sadly. "It's such a beautiful place, so tranquil and fertile. Who owns it now? Are we trespassing?"

"There's only one heir and he wouldn't sell for any reason, if the local authorities knew where to locate him. I can't blame him; a homestead isn't something you get rid of just because there's trouble."

Randee eyed the peaceful grove where a home had once stood and a family had lived, unaware of their grim fates. She thought of her father's ranch, her lost home, and a great sadness filled her. "You're right, Marsh, a home isn't something to lose carelessly, or something to have taken from you by force and deceit."

Marsh was intrigued and touched by her melancholy mood. She sighed deeply and shook it off with sheer will power, and he did the same. "You're safe here from all harm, Randee, I promise. And you have my word I'll be a perfect gentleman."

Randee accepted his word and headed off to find the water hole. The light was vanishing quickly and she wanted to see it before dark to make certain no slithery creatures were swimming there. She located it in an area that was screened by bushes and trees. Stripping and entering the water, she barely managed to suppress a shriek of discomfort as the chilly water engulfed her body. She scrubbed quickly with the soap she had brought along and dried off with her worn shirt. Donning a nightgown, she hung her sweaty garments on bushes to dry before packing them. She slipped into the shirt she would wear tomorrow and used it for a robe. Gathering her things, she headed back to camp.

As she neared the fire where Marsh was cooking supper, he glanced up at her before returning his gaze to the task at hand. Suddenly, his head jerked upward and he took another look. Noting her attire, surprise registered on his face and he nearly burned himself.

Randee related, "I can't sleep in confining clothes that I've worn all day, and I'm too tired to be kept awake. Besides, if it's safe for you to visit my hotel room in the middle of the night and safe for me to strip and bathe nearby, then surely it's safe for me to sleep in a nightgown which conceals nearly every inch of me from view. You said there were no neighbors or dangers, so why be uncomfortably modest?"

"You're right, Miss Hollis. I was just taken unprepared for such courage. Sit down and rest a minute. Supper will be ready soon." Marsh watched her place a folded blanket on the ground and take a seat on it, the fiery blaze and cooking meal safely positioned between them. Randee's tawny hair tumbled over her shoulders and shone like polished silk in the firelight, whose loving glow also caressed her golden complexion. As she wearily stared into the colorful flames, their dreamy dance was reflected in her green eyes. Truly, the cotton gown was visually impenetrable, and hardly sexy with that shirt buttoned over it. He knew she was being honest; comfort was her only motive. He was glad she felt so secure around him because it didn't matter what she had on; anything she wore whet his appetite for her.

When they finished eating, he washed the metal dishes in the stream and set them aside for use in the morning. He told Randee, "You sleep here beside the fire. I'll sleep near the water hole, after I bathe. If you get scared or need anything, call out."

"Thanks, but I'll be fine. I camped out plenty of times

105

with my father, so I'm not afraid of the dark or night creatures. See you in the morning." Randee unrolled her sleeping bag and climbed inside. She placed her cherished Colt near her head and closed her eyes. She waited to see if the man would keep his word, and wondered if she wanted him to do so . . . .

Marsh was positive the weapon wasn't there as a warning to him. He noticed which gun she chose to spend the night with and guessed why: Her father must have given it to her and it made her feel safe. He picked up his belongings and headed for the water hole, depositing them nearby. Then, he returned to the fire to retrieve a pan of hot water, told her good night, and left. At his campsite, he used the steamy water and his sharp knife to shave. It was an easy chore to do in the dark and without a mirror, as he had done it this way many times before. He removed his clothes and took a long bath. He needed the cold water to douse the fire in his body, one which Miss Randee Hollis kept igniting at every turn. Noticing her clothes draped on the bushes, he followed her lead and hung his own garments out to dry.

Only a sliver of moon was in the sky tonight, making the area around him dark, much too dark for Randee to see his naked body at this distance. He kicked the sleeping bag and sent it to unrolling rapidly. Climbing inside, he knew that for many reasons he was in for a night of little sleep: He was on the alert for peril, an overwhelmingly tempting woman was sleeping nearby, and his parents had been brutally murdered here. So many old memories and new desires troubled him; so many ghosts haunted him; so much guilt and hunger plagued him. He looked toward the dying glow of the campfire, where Randee was asleep. *Well, Ma, I finally brought a girl home with me, but you aren't here to meet her. Soon, you and Pa will rest peacefully because I'm going to hunt down and kill every one of those bastards.*

106

He lifted his ebony head once more and glanced in Randee's direction. There was no movement in her bedroll, so he assumed the exhausted female was slumbering peacefully. His hands longed to caress her while she was curled enticingly into his embrace. Just knowing she was nearby inflamed his passions. He remembered every inch of her face. Mercy, how he wanted to join her over there!

She was so unlike the women he had known and taken. As with his mother, she had a strength about her, a gentleness, a special quality. She could inspire a man to do anything for her, then help him do it. With her skills and traits, she was a treasure any man would covet. Mercy, he wanted her, but he couldn't allow her to distract him, not until this vital mission was over. No, not even then, he warned himself. She was a lady, and he was a drifter. She was the marrying kind, and he was a loner. She had someone waiting for her, someone who loved her and would do anything for her, someone who could give her a good life. Even if he didn't like Brody Wade and couldn't stand the thought of the sheriff having her, Brody had a lot to offer Randee. It would be wrong of Marsh to take that from her, wrong because she had suffered great pain and loss, and she deserved happiness and stability.

Damn you, woman! Why did you have to come into my miserable life and tempt me so fiercely? I'm responsible for my parents' deaths. If I had been here like any good son, they would be alive. I can't rest until every member of that gang is dead. Afterwards, I'd be on my way to accept another challenging mission. If I was a rancher instead of a hired gun, I could think about you seriously, but I'm not a homebody like your Sheriff Wade and may never become one. Besides, a traitor can't settle on land earned with blood. What could I possibly have to offer a lady like you, Randee Hollis? Nothing . . .

Randee lay very still and quiet, not wanting Marsh to

107

know she was still awake. Just knowing he was bathing and sleeping not far away aroused her to intense desire. She was within a hundred yards of the first man who made her tremble uncontrollably, who made her want to forget everything she knew and was, just to entice and enjoy him!

She was ensnared by Marsh Logan and worried about him. She wondered if as the Durango Kid he ever got tired of his hazardous lifestyle. Surely being on the move and on the alert all the time would eventually cause a once-exciting existence to lose its magic and pull. Did he ever think about settling down? Did he care for ranching or farming? Did he want a home, wife, and children one day? A gunslinger couldn't ply his lethal trade forever. The time came when his eyes and instincts dulled, when his speed and skills lessened — and when someone else took his life, or gave up such a lifestyle. But how did a man simply walk away from a famous reputation? Would other upcoming gunmen allow a colorful and challenging legend to retire peacefully? Would some cocky lawman force him to step over the lawful boundary, just to boast that he had slain the Durango Kid? Death, she fretted, was the only end to such a perilous life. What a terrible waste of such a good man!

Randee listened to the calming songs of frogs, crickets, and night birds. She heard branches with supple leaves tickling each other, and water racing over rocks in the stream. The campfire was down to barely glowing embers, and the partial moon cast very little light. Everything smelled so fresh and clean here. Her soul was enlivened, thanks to Marsh Logan. Could she persuade him to begin a new life, a much different one? Could they become a perfect match and find happiness together? How wonderful it would be to sleep nestled together on the same bedroll, to build a home in this very location, to wake up each morning and do chores together, to create a child and watch it grow, to share laughter and joy and suffering, to be partners in all things . . . .

Marsh Logan was a man strong enough to earn her full respect, her assistance, her total loyalty. She was drawn to him, and she wanted him. She had recognized that truth the moment she had looked up into his attractive face, into those captivating blue eyes. Instantly she had known that here was a unique man, a man she must have.

During the coming weeks, while they were on the trail, she must show him what his life was missing, what he could have if he yielded to her pull. When this dangerous task was over, the Durango Kid must be laid to rest and Marsh Logan must be reborn.

Randee stretched and yawned, coming alert gradually. The sounds of early morning touched her ears, especially the joyful singing of birds. She felt rested and filled with anticipation for the coming day. She propped herself up on her elbows and looked around for Marsh. He was not at his campsite near the water hole, and she heard nothing that might give away his location. She sat up and scanned the area for him, finally spying him on a grassy knoll in the distance. He was kneeling beside two green mounds with wooden crosses: a gravesite.

She slipped behind some bushes and dressed. After finding her brush, she untangled her hair and secured it at her nape with one of Brody's ribbons. The water in the stream was refreshing when she washed her face and hands. She rolled and bound her sleeping bag, and put away her possessions. Since Marsh had not noticed her stirrings and returned, she headed for the gravesite that had him so preoccupied.

He was absorbed in such deep thought that he did not

hear her nearly soundless approach, something unusual for the keenly alert man. Randee read the two markers, and her eyes widened in surprise: "Judith Logan, 1817-1870" and "Marshall Logan, 1814-1870."

Marsh was on his knees, with his buttocks resting against his boot soles. His proud shoulders were slightly slumped and his hands were capping his knees tightly. As she edged to his right side to allow the sun to cast her shadow over his lap, she noticed that his jaw was clenched and his expression was cold. It was so glacial that a chill passed over her body. She jumped and squealed as Marsh caught sight of her from the corner of his eye and whirled toward her. His narrowed gaze caused her to step backward and to say, "I'm sorry if I intruded on your mourning. You didn't tell me they were your kin."

Marsh stood quickly and masked his feelings. "They weren't kin; they were my parents. I need some coffee," he growled, then headed back for camp.

Randee stared at his back as he retreated from the sad spot. His words from yesterday filled her mind. That meant he was the heir of this lovely and tragic spread! If he was an only son, why had he left home? Why had he become a hired gunslinger? Now she realized there was more to his taking her offer than she had known . . . .

As he prepared a fire and made coffee, he answered her unasked questions without looking up. "Before we go on to other matters this morning, we'll clear up this one. What I said in the sheriff's office about why I sought your job wasn't true. It wasn't to earn money from a rich adventurer or to face a new challenge; it was to seek support on the Epson search. I waste time and lose ground when I have to halt to earn expense money. It seems we have a mutual bond and need; that's why we're sitting here. The large reward isn't that important, but I'll take it if I earn it. I also wanted to make sure no reckless glory-seeker fouled up my search, so I hoped to get the money and discourage Randee Hollis from going along. You made that impossible."

At last, he met her gaze. "Nothing is more important to me than my family. Even if they're dead, I owe them, like you owe your kin. Those bastards attacked my home and killed my parents in their first strike last April. I've been trailing them ever since, but they're real clever. I want them dead, Randee, but each one by my own hand. You've got clues and I've got skills, so that makes us a good match. Since I haven't been successful getting to them, maybe I do need your brains and help. I know I can use your support."

"Why did you keep this a secret until today?" she inquired.

"I didn't want anyone else knowing how serious I was about catching this gang. If anyone came around Wadesville after my departure looking for information, I didn't want him to consider me a threat and start watching for me over his shoulder. If I had told you the truth, you could have let something drop accidentally to your sweetheart, to keep him from worrying about you. I needed for Sheriff Wade to believe I only came looking for money and excitement; otherwise, he would have wondered how I could reject your reward and help. When I came to the hotel to meet with you, it was to talk you out of coming along. But after I grasped your talents and motive, plus the danger you were in, I figured it was best to bring you along. You're especially important to me if you can pick out those men from clues you observed."

Randee was disappointed to learn that Marsh had brought her with him only to use her to obtain personal revenge. Yes, she admitted, she was using him too, but she was paying heavily for that privilege, and she hadn't lied about why she was hiring him! No doubt this astute male realized she knew more than she had revealed to him, and was hoping to charm the information from her. She had to keep silent because, when he no longer needed her, he might desert her somewhere and pursue his own vengeful path.

He had endured great pain and would take on any and all obstacles to seek victory. It was good that his commitment matched hers, but could she trust him completely? Only time could provide that answer. Perhaps it was best to let the matter slide for a while as she proved herself to him, and he proved himself to her. She nodded and said, "I understand your reasoning. Actually, I like this motive better than money and adventure; it means you're deadly serious about our task."

Noticing his appearance, she decided to change the subject. "Can I ask you another question?" When he didn't respond either way, she queried, "Why do you always shave at night?" Every time she saw him in the light—that first day in Wadesville, that morning at Red River Station, and now—he had only a night's growth of whiskers. Why would a man have a shadowy face during the daytime and a smooth one at night?

Marsh grinned at her ploy. She was alert and compassionate. "Lots of reasons, my eagle-eyed partner, all having to do with being prepared for anything. If I have to ride out of town or camp real fast, which happens often, I don't have time to shave in the morning. After a hard and dusty day on the trail, it's more relaxing to do it at night, and it keeps prickly whiskers from catching on my bedroll and pinching. It also helps me hone those night skills I told you about. I practice doing it with little or no sound, and without cutting myself. It really sharpens the senses and skills. Makes the old fingers learn to move with an extra light touch, which comes in handy," he teased huskily.

"When are you going to share those skills with me?

You said you would teach me everything you know about survival."

Marsh looked her over boldly and imagined what he would really like to teach her and share with her, and the way she was returning his gaze said she was receptive. "We'll get your training under way after breakfast and our strategy meeting. This mission has to be planned perfectly or we're both dead."

"I believe it's my turn to cook," she reminded him as he pulled out supplies and began making biscuits.

"I'm used to cooking for myself, so it came natural to start the meal. Let's make this a joint venture and we'll be eating sooner. While I finish here, why don't you pour us some coffee and get the meat to frying? I have jars of honey and jam in the supply sack; take your pick."

"Which do you prefer?" she asked as she followed his suggestions.

"Doesn't matter to me. I like them both. Frankly, I only chose things that I like. Maybe I should have checked on your preferences."

She looked through the two sacks and smiled. "From what I can see, Mr. Logan, you did an excellent job with your selections. I think honey's best this morning, because it's the stickiest and we're near lots of water. It does have a sneaky way of getting all over you."

Marsh looked at her and chuckled. He asked, "Do you always reason everything out?"

Randee's hand ceased slicing the meat and she shrugged. "I suppose so," she admitted. She laid the strips neatly in the skillet and placed it over the flame. While she waited for it to begin sizzling, she prepared their coffee. Handing one cup to Marsh, she remarked, "See if that's how you like it."

He sipped it and met her gaze. "Looks as if you know me already. Since you notice everything and recall it, I'll have to be careful with what I say and do. If I make a mistake, you'll never forget it. But of course, talents like those are vital in our work."

After they ate, Marsh began the clean-up chores. Randee laughed and said, "You're marvelous to have around, Mr. Logan. You remind me of my father, kind and brave enough to do what's needed. I like not being expected to do the chores because I'm a woman. You've won my deepest affection and respect."

"Knowing how you feel about your father, Miss Hollis, I take that as the highest compliment you could pay me. On this journey, we're partners, equals. We share everything and anything. Right?"

"I couldn't ask for a more perfect arrangement," she replied.

"Nor could I," Marsh retorted, winking at her.

Marsh eyed her garments. She was dressed in a vest and skirt of material and color that matched the jeans he was wearing — a sturdy, durable, and comfortable outfit for the trail. The skirt was full and it flowed over the tops of her brown boots, a style which made mounting and riding easy and modest. She wore a red shirt beneath the vest, its shade flattering to her golden skin. Her hair, bound today with a red ribbon, reminded him of a field of ripened wheat, and it seemed to call out to him to wander through it with his fingers.

"Do you approve of my taste, Mr. Logan?" she asked merrily.

"I'm beginning to wonder if there's anything about you that isn't flawless. Makes a man nervous to be around such perfection."

Randee shook her head and laughed. "Don't tell me you've made your first mistake, Mr. Logan. I can assure you, I have many flaws."

"Such as?" he prompted, his blue gaze mischievous.

"I think I'll leave it up to you to discover them. That way, if you miss a few, then you'll think I'm not so terrible after all."

"A wise woman, or a cunningly deceitful one — I wonder which," he murmured. A wicked grin eased over his face and he challenged, "Shall we see who outguesses the other first? A sporting game to enliven our spirits and while away the hours when we're not at work."

Randee's defensive reply was, "Speaking of work, shouldn't we get to it? As we play, more people could be dying."

The man in the snug blue shirt and dark jeans walked forward. He looked down into her expressive eyes and jested, "Afraid you'll lose if you accept my challenge, or are you refusing because of Brody Wade?"

Randee stared him in the eye and countered, "I'm refusing because neither of us can afford such a distraction while our lives are in danger. Challenge me again after our victory, and I'll accept."

Marsh teased the backs of his fingers over her flushed cheek, then across her lips. He felt her tremble and read enormous desire for him within her gaze and mood. Yet, she was pulling back from him. Perhaps because it was considered a woman's duty to protect her chastity and to keep a tempting male at arm's length — until he was ready or willing to put a wedding band before carnal pleasures. Even so, he murmured seductively, "Maybe I'll do just that, Miss Hollis."

"And maybe you won't," but I hope you will, locking her gaze to his and astonishing him with her unexpected reply following her retreat.

Chapter Six

Marsh scolded himself for doing just what he vowed he wouldn't do last night, which was to entice Miss Randee Hollis and lead her on a merry chase. Chances were that he wouldn't survive this perilous mission in which he was outnumbered thirty to one. But he had to carry it out for peace of mind. As for Randee, once her novel quests for revenge and adventure were sated one way or another, she'd return home to settle down — and he wasn't ready or willing to change his lifestyle any time soon. He couldn't offer her anything serious or permanent, so he shouldn't raise her hopes with reckless temptations. Nor should he falsely and rashly encourage her to pursue him. The last thing he needed was to have a love-smitten girl hot on his trail. If only she weren't so damned compelling and unique! If only she were older and more experienced in matters of men and sensual pleasures! If only she didn't want and need what he was probably unable to give! If only . . .

To get past the awkward and unsettling moment, he chuckled and playfully winced before agreeing, "You're right, Miss Hollis. Carefree men like me scare off real easy around proper ladies like you who demand all or nothing. Since I don't want my talented hand or my handsome head chopped off for misbehaving with my boss lady, I'll stop playing mischievous games with you."

116

Without appearing shocked or angered, Randee instantly came back with, "And women like me are intimidated by disarming rogues like you who want all for nothing; so that makes us even, Mr. Logan. No silly games, just serious business. Why don't you tell me what you've learned about the Epson Gang while you've been tracking them? I'd also like to know why Texas lawmen aren't doing anything about this grave problem. It's been over a year and numerous raids."

Marsh noticed that she didn't clarify what kind of woman she considered herself, or reveal what she expected from a man. "I'll explain what I know about the law first. Ever since the Texas Rangers were dissolved after the war and the Federal Government refused to allow Southern states to have local authorities, we've depended on the Army and military control for protection and law enforcement. Things weren't too bad for us until Davis became governor two years back. That Republican carpetbagger wanted power and he knew how to get it; he created the State Police. Since they came into control in '70, it's been crazy and dangerous here. They've been accused of official murder, legal theft, and fierce oppression of Confederate families. Those so-called lawmen are full of flaws and they make lots of errors. I doubt they'll be in power much longer, not after President Grant learns what's happening, and he will. Crimes like theirs can't be kept quiet forever."

Marsh knew that Grant was being well-informed through secret reports from him. As he traveled around, U.S. Special Agent Marsh Logan recorded the charges and crimes of the State Police's often ruthless force. As soon as the President untangled some of his seriously pressing problems in Washington and around the country, he would find a way to liberate Texas from the grasps of Governor Davis and his State Police. Until then, Marsh was assigned to handle as many problems as he could, without exposing himself to Davis, the police, the Army, or to any local lawmen. Once his identity as a President's special agent was unmasked, his life and missions would be in jeopardy. Only through secrecy could he carry out good and thorough investigations.

Marsh sipped coffee as his mind wandered for a short time. He was glad when, knowing he wasn't finished, she didn't interrupt. "As for the Army, which is supposed to be protecting the frontier and its settlers, they aren't doing much better these days." He promptly qualified that statement. "That may be too harsh a judgment. They have their hands full with renegade Kiowas and Comanches, especially since Chief Satanta broke from the reservation and is riding free again." His blue eyes danced with amusement as he chuckled and told her, "I bet Phil Sheridan's face is as red as raw meat about now. Not too long ago, he reported that all Indians had been subdued and were living quietly on reservations beyond the Red River. North of us, we have old Custer, who's keeping Indians on the run to reduce them to poverty-stricken, spiritless people who'll sit back and depend on the whites for meager handouts. After that massacre at Washita, he cowed lots of them, but inspired others— like Satanta and Quanah Parker—to bolder deeds. I'm willing to bet my reward that we haven't seen the last of either chief."

"Are those tribes raiding in this area?" she asked worriedly. If so, it could complicate or halt their task.

"Nope, they're mainly working to the north and west of Texas. It's a shame they aren't around to take on the Epson Gang."

"You sound as if you like them and disapprove of their treatment."

"They were great leaders, good warriors who were only protecting their lands and people. I respect them, and I think they got raw deals. What good are reserva-

118

tions on barren lands and broken promises? The whites wanted the buffalo and the Indians' lands. We were stronger, so we took them by force. Then we expected the Indians to calmly accept any peace terms that we offered them. I don't blame them for rebelling. But as far as I know, they won't give us any trouble in this area. We can't expect help from the State Police or the Army, and local lawmen don't have enough men to give chase. We're on our own, Randee. Let's get busy on our map and plans. After that, I'll give you lessons with those new weapons before we ride to Jacksboro and Fort Richardson. We'll see if we can pick up any recent information, then head out to check on raid sites."

Randee waited while he retrieved a map from his saddlebag. He spread it out before them and motioned her closer.

"I've recorded the locations of the raids I know about so far. I've numbered them in order, dated them, and marked the miles between each raid. This way, we can tell how far and fast they move, and see which areas they hit repeatedly. Maybe we'll detect that pattern you mentioned, which could lead us to their hide-out area, or get us one step ahead of them for a change. After talking with you in Wadesville, I realized we think much alike, so that'll make working together easier. You don't have to worry about me getting stubborn or defensive just because you're a woman with superior skills and brains. A good partner is a good partner, be it male or female. I won't try to boss you, so you can relax and speak your mind any time."

"I'm glad to hear that, Marsh. We aren't in a competition; we're a team facing a big and deadly obstacle. We have to respect each other and get along for this partnership to work. I admire you and respect you, and I hope you'll soon feel the same way about me." Randee studied the map and notations. He had done a lot of work, clever work, and she was impressed. She suggested, "What about if you include what time and how the raids occurred? That will let us know when and how they strike. It could provide useful clues."

"You're right again, partner," he sincerely complimented her.

"Do you know anything about Quantrill's Raiders?" she asked.

He glanced at her quizzically. "Yes, why?"

"I'm from Kansas, remember? These raids are similar to those. I was wondering if perhaps some of his ex-members are in this band. They did terrible things in Lawrence and Baxter Springs, just like this gang is doing here. They slaughtered people of all ages and both sexes. They tortured, burned, raped, and stole. They appeared nearly always at dawn or dusk, struck fast and deadly, then vanished. It could be coincidental or just pure evil in similar men."

"You may have something there, Randee, but how could we find out who was in that band and who's still alive? You didn't happen to see any of Quantrill's Raiders at work, did you?"

"No, but I wouldn't be surprised if the rustlers who killed my father had ridden with that vicious beast and are raiding here now."

"Is that why you want to pursue them?"

"No, I only realized the similarities recently and thought I should mention them to you. We must consider every possibility."

Marsh met her gaze and said, "It might be helpful if we can learn more about those raids and men. I'll give it more thought."

She liked the easy way he took her advice and suggestions. Few men would be so receptive, so self-confident as to not feel threatened or annoyed by a woman's knowledge and skills. Few men would allow a woman to be an equal in a relationship, even if Marsh had said otherwise. As her father used to tease, "The doing and the saying of a thing aren't always the same." Randee relaxed even more with him. "What about witnesses, Marsh? Are you certain there aren't any? Maybe they're just too scared to come forward because they know the law can't protect them. I mean, it seems impossible that somebody somewhere hasn't seen something — if only a large band of riders."

"That's a good question to ask during our investigation. We'll list anyone unusual who's around before and after each attack. We might come up with a frequent name or names. You can see by the map that the raids are in this oblong-shaped area." His finger circled the location to which he was referring. "Every raid I know about took place between Fort Worth to one hundred and ten miles westward and a hundred-fifty-mile north-to-south span westward of Fort Worth. Here's my parents' ranch near Jacksboro and the Carson Ranch southwest of Fort Worth. Looks like yours is about halfway between here and Hillsboro. We'll need to check out this entire area and record all new raids. If that gang isn't spreading out, we'll know there's a good reason."

Randee noticed that Marsh said "my parents' ranch," not "my ranch," and "between here and Hillsboro," rather than "between my land and Hillsboro." Recalling his earlier words about a single heir who wouldn't sell out, she wondered why, but didn't ask. As with her, there must be a terrible reason why Marsh had left home and couldn't return, and another grave reason why he kept his motive a secret.

Marsh informed her, "From reports I've gathered, the Epson Gang's size is between twenty-five and thirty strong, a real challenge."

Randee nodded awareness as she said, "But we have Good and Justice on our side. We'll win, Marsh; we must."

"Before this is over, Good and Justice might not be sufficient powers for our survival."

"Even if we only punish a few of them, it'll be worth the risk."

He countered, "Even if they hire more men as soon as we're dead?"

Randee looked distressed at that thought: To die in vain. A reality came to mind. "If those we slay are the ones who killed our loved ones, then, yes, it'll be worth our lives. If they aren't, they've harmed other innocent people and we've claimed justice for them. We can always hope that someone will eventually do the same for us. I'm certain there's a dark reason why somebody wants this large area. All we have to do is discover who and why; then our task is half over."

"Let's get moving, woman. I want you to show me how fast you can mount and ride off, then dismount over there as quickly as possible and take cover behind that tree. Take off," he told her.

"You want this test with or without a saddle?" she inquired.

His brow lifted inquisitively. "You can ride bareback? What happens if that chestnut gallops away after you hop off her back? You haven't been working with her very long."

For an answer, Randee hurried to the reddish-brown mare, leapt on her bare back, and rode swiftly and agilely to the tree. She jumped off the other side and darted behind the designated hiding place. After a moment, she showed herself and called to Rojo. The animal responded instantly, and Randee returned to where Marsh was standing. He was grinning appreciatively.

"Ready for the next test or lesson," she said, careful not to sound cocky. She would be open and honest about her skills, as Marsh needed to know her range of abilities,

122

her weaknesses and strengths. And, she hadn't gotten the impression he would be annoyed by them.

Marsh showed her how to load the revolver and rifle. He watched her follow his instructions rapidly and skillfully, and he smiled again. "Now, let's see how good you are with those weapons."

Randee waited patiently as the man set up targets of various sizes and distances. When he was back at her side, she told him, "First, I need to fire the guns a few times to check their weight, balance, and aim. You have no objections to my familiarizing myself with them, do you?"

Marsh couldn't conceal his look of astonishment. "Certainly not. I'm delighted you know enough to do so."

Randee examined the weapons more closely than she had at Red River. She aimed and fired at the closest target, then eyed her success. She repeated the procedure several times, compensating for each weapon's kick and alignment. She glanced at him and said, "Ready."

The shapely blonde fired three shots at each target, reloading when necessary. "Why don't you check them out before I try it moving?"

Marsh did as she suggested, amazed to find she hadn't missed a single time. He watched her fire while running, kneeling, and lying flat on the ground. After he checked those shots, she mounted Rojo and displayed her matching skills while riding.

Marsh eyed her up and down before asking, "Are you sure you aren't an expert gunslinger whose name I haven't heard yet?"

Randee laughed softly. "My father taught me that nothing is more important than life and being able to defend it. He drilled me every day like I was a soldier. I'm glad he did, because the law isn't usually around to protect you when trouble strikes. I only wish I had been with him that last night. Maybe he would still be alive if I had been there to back him up instead of lying in bed with a cold." Mastering her guilt and pain, she returned her attention to the task at hand. "What about if you blindfold me and I practice loading in the dark?"

"Excellent idea," he concurred. He pulled off his bandanna and walked behind her. Placing it over her lovely eyes, he secured it snugly. "How's that, partner?"

"I can't see a thing." She did the task slowly the first two times, then rapidly speeded up with more practice. She worked until her deft fingers knew the task by heart and could do it under pitch-black conditions.

Marsh observed her closely. His eyes kept returning to her lips as she licked them and chewed on them in deep concentration. Finally, he noted how she relaxed once she could perform the task with expertise and speed. What an amazing, unexpected woman, he mused. Was there nothing she couldn't do, and do well? Mercy, she nearly had him beat in skills! Even so, no twinges of jealousy or irritation nibbled at him, only a curious pride in her ability. Here was a worthy partner, not one to be treated differently because she was a female. Yep, he decided, she's quite a woman. "If you're as good under fire as you are standing here, I have nothing to worry about on the trail." His keen mind corrected, *nearly nothing, only self-control* . . .

Having removed the blindfold as he was talking, Randee returned it to Marsh. "Thanks, partner. You're an expert teacher and you chose excellent weapons. What's next?"

"We'll save your lessons on tracking and stealthy night moves for later. But if you're as skilled at those as you are with riding and shooting, you won't need my help or suggestions. You'll notice we both have dark-skinned horses, which will conceal us better for night work. You've just about gotten Rojo as well trained as Midnight. You're good, Randee, and I'm pleased to be teamed up with you."

"Thank you, Marsh," she told him softly. Nearly always, most men didn't like a woman being as good as or better than them at such skills. Yet, she had to be honest with him to prove she was capable of taking care of herself and any trouble they ran into. Just in case his masculine ego was stinging, she entreated, "Please teach me all you've learned. I know so little about tracking, and nothing about stealth. I don't want my ignorance to get us into trouble. I said I would be your partner in all things, so you'll have to help me keep that promise."

Marsh playfully cuffed her chin and said, "I'm glad you didn't pretend to be a helpless female just to keep from stomping on my toes. I appreciate a talented person who isn't cocky about his or her skills. You have confidence, Randee, and that's as vital to survival as prowess."

"So is knowing one's limits," she remarked.

As she turned to put away her weapons, Marsh inquired, "What are our limits, Randee?"

Without looking back at him, she replied, "Knowing how far and how hard to press, and knowing when to back away. Despite what I said earlier and no matter how badly I want to defeat this gang, I don't want us getting killed. Patience is hard and defeat can be bitter, but a person has to learn when to retreat, or to hold off, until he has the advantage over an enemy or a nasty situation. To enter a battle without at least having equal odds is foolish."

Marsh realized there was more behind her words than she revealed, just as there had rashly been more behind his question. Mercy, this woman had a quick and easy way of getting to him. If he didn't practice patience and retreat, they could both be in deep trouble real soon! He ventured truthfully, "Sometimes there's no getting around death, but I'll protect us as best I can."

She faced him and replied, "I know you will; that's why I chose you as my partner. I would like to make one request. If a moment arises when you can't protect me without endangering your life, please don't take any reckless chances to save me. I need you to finish this mission, or come as close to victory as possible."

"I'll make that promise only if you'll do the same."

Their gazes met in a searching, mutual appraisal. "That sounds fair and reasonable," she answered hazily.

"I want another promise," he added. "Promise you won't go after this gang if I get killed along the way. I don't want you hiring another partner and taking more risks. Promise you'll give it up."

"Would you give it up if I'm slain?" she questioned gravely.

Marsh scowled, and Randee remarked, "Nor can I, Marsh, even if we both know you're irreplaceable as a partner."

The ebony-haired man considered what that gang would do to this woman if they were caught, and he frowned again. *No, Randee,* he thought, *I won't let you get killed or injured. If it gets too bad, I'll have you jailed for your protection before I let them capture and harm you.*

Marsh grinned as he realized that was the same threat Brody Wade had used. Noting Randee's inquisitive look, he chuckled and said, "Well, woman, it looks like we're stuck with each other, so let's make the best of it."

They packed their things, mounted, and rode away from the lovely place. Near Jacksboro, Marsh asked her to conceal herself while he rode into town to ask a few questions.

"Why do I have to wait here? We're partners, remember?"

"I'm known around here. People will notice and remember a beautiful woman riding with the Durango Kid. If we're seen together, word might spread and endanger our secret mission. You did say I could make cautious decisions like this one. I'll be back soon."

"You're right, this time," she conceded. "Be careful, Marsh. Don't let the Durango Kid get talked into a gunfight."

He smiled and nodded, then rode off into town.

Randee dismounted and tied Rojo's reins to a bush. She leaned against a small tree and waited apprehensively for Marsh's return. She couldn't help worrying about his legendary reputation, a challenge to other gunfighters. What if something happened to him? What if he confronted a faster draw? What if he was . . . slain?

"I'll kill you, Marsh Logan, if you get into any danger! You and I have some reckoning to do. I have to learn more about you. I have to have more time with you. Damn you, be extra careful."

Marsh was back in less than an hour. "What's wrong?" she asked anxiously as she saw his dark expression.

"Let's ride, woman. Those bastards attacked nearby yesterday morning. They were right in this area, nearly under my nose! Dammit, I should have been there!"

Randee mounted and said, "Even if you hadn't been retrieving me, you probably wouldn't have been in this area. Calm down and think."

Marsh glanced at her. "I'm not blaming you."

"And you shouldn't blame yourself," she chided softly.

"I know, but they were so close for once!"

They hurriedly rode to the ranch and studied the destruction left in the wake of another merciless attack. Townsfolk had been here to handle numerous burials and soldiers had been summoned to look for clues. Unfortunately, their inexperienced trampling over the area had destroyed any leads that might have existed. The odor of burned wood from a home and several barns still lingered in the air. Wisps of dying smoke could be seen heading skyward here and there. Fresh graves of various sizes were in sight. Savage death and wanton destruction were undeniable.

Randee walked away from the horrid scene, one similar to what had occurred at the Carson Ranch. Tears dampened her eyes and she tried not to cry. She imagined the terror and anguish these people must have faced early Monday morning. When Marsh joined her, she murmured, "How can anyone be so cruel? We have to stop them, Marsh."

Randee was glad the man didn't pull her into his arms for comfort. If he had, she would have burst into tears. Then, he would have thought her too fragile and vulnerable to continue their task.

Marsh wanted to comfort Randee, and to draw comfort from her. It had been weeks after the raid on his home before he had viewed the damage. This was the freshest site he had examined, and it impressed on him how terrible the attacks were. Yet, he couldn't embrace Randee, because it was too dangerous.

"Let's ride to Fort Richardson and see what we can learn there." He headed for his horse. When Randee didn't move, he walked back to her and asked, "Are you all right?"

"Yes and no," she responded honestly. "But don't worry. It only makes me more determined to carry out our mission."

They rode for Fort Richardson, arriving near the post in a short time. "I know," she muttered, "wait here, Randee."

Marsh smiled and said, "Getting smarter by the hour, woman — if that's possible. Hide over there, and try to get some rest."

"How can I relax when you're taking all the risks?"

"You'll get your share of them soon enough, partner. We just need to be extra cautious in this area."

Inside the fort, Marsh met with a soldier whom he had

known for years. The major asked, "What brings you here, old friend?"

Marsh took a seat before the officer's desk. "Just passing through, Jim, and heard about the attack. Any clues this time?"

"Sorry, Marsh, but there weren't any this time either. To tell you the truth, I've been seeking orders allowing us to go after that gang, but permission hasn't come yet and I can't explain why. Really wouldn't matter; I don't know where to look or even where to begin," the officer admitted wryly. "Nobody knew a thing until noon yesterday, when a neighboring rancher went to pick up a breeding bull. It happened at dawn, so they couldn't have put up much of a fight. I rode out there early this morning. Just got back, or I would have missed your visit. A terrible sight, Marsh, worse than at your parents' ranch. Some of the bodies were burned with the house. Lordy, man, they shot down children and women, and butchered some of those folks. That gang comes and goes like ghosts, Marsh. I don't have any idea how to locate or stop them. What are you planning to do with your ranch?"

Marsh knew the man was trying to get off the gory subject, so he let it pass for a time. "I haven't decided yet. It's a good spread, but I'm not a rancher." Marsh knew he would never sell that land, but he didn't want anyone to know that fact, in case someone suspicious came around asking to buy him out. So far, no one had.

The officer asked, "Why don't you come back to work for us, Marsh? We can always use scouts and guides and good soldiers, especially with those Indians acting up again. The Army knows what a good job you did with those Galvanized Yankees during the war, so they'd hire you without a second request."

Marsh recalled his days as the captain of a group of Southern prisoners who had spent their wartime captivity working out west for the Yankees: fighting Indians, protecting settlements and pioneers, building roads and forts, and defending the homes of other soldiers at war. He hadn't been a Yankee, but he hadn't wanted to fight against his country. Since he was a Southerner, the Army deal had suited him perfectly. That was only one of many jobs he had done since leaving home.

As if Marsh was considering his offer, Jim eagerly continued, "The best place to look for work is in Indian Territory, probably at Fort Sill. They've been having big trouble there since those Comanches and Kiowas broke treaty. There was a bad incident Sunday morning just the other side of the Red River. The stage was attacked just a few miles inside the territory. Then, those redskins crossed into Texas and burned the home station. Far as we know, the men were killed and the women were taken captive. Some major from Fort Sill had a wife aboard; he's in a rage. He's got his men on their trail right now, but he can use a good scout and gunman. Most of the passengers and workers were from around Fort Worth and Wadesville. The Army's already sent word to their kin through the sheriff's office."

That news struck Marsh Logan in two ways: relief in knowing Brody Wade would think Randee was gone forever, and sadness in knowing people had died because of differences between the Indians and the whites. At least this way, Brody wouldn't be expecting to see or hear from Randee anytime soon. He decided not to share this news with his partner just yet; otherwise, she might want to contact Brody to relieve his worry.

"I don't want to get back into following orders and schedules again. I like moving around at will." Meeting the officer's gaze, Marsh asserted, "I've been considering the mounting rewards on the Epson Gang and might go after them, if I can round up some other men who can handle a gun and rough going. You heard of any other recent raids?"

"Matter of fact, I have," Jim revealed to his trusted friend. "A ranch near Wadesville on the eighteenth, owned by a man named Bill Sharp. We usually get all the reports, but we can't do anything to halt the raids. I can give you the information I have in my drawer, but you might have competition for those rewards. A U.S. Marshal called Foley Timms was here Sunday before the raid, asking questions like you are. I saw him again early yesterday. He was heading south 'cause somebody saw a large band of riders going that way. Don't know who gave him the information, but he took off after them. He's a fool to go alone. No reward is worth challenging that gang by yourself."

When Marsh finally rejoined Randee, she was pacing nervously. "What kept you so long, Marsh Logan? I've been worried like crazy. I was about to come looking for you. I thought you might need rescuing from their jail. I don't like being left behind to worry."

Marsh grinned. "Would you really break a gunslinger out of jail?"

"I would free my partner if at all possible. Did you learn anything?" she asked, eagerness shining brightly in her eyes.

Marsh concealed the news about the stage and depot attacks, and what Brody must be thinking about now. He told her about the raid on Bill Sharp's ranch, and she was stunned. He went on to relate news of Marshal Timm's possible interference. "He's heading south after them right this minute. If we hurry, we can catch up and pass him."

"If they attacked in Wadesville on the eighteenth and here on the twenty-first, that means they had to ride fast and hard and straight here. Sounds like a preplanned attack to me, not a random one."

"That's my thinking too, Randee. Now, they're head-

131

ing back south because they know people will think they won't return this soon."

"That's exactly what I don't believe, Marsh. That Marshal Foley Timms, he was in Wadesville on the seventeenth. He brought a prisoner to the jail while Brody and I were having our picnic."

"What does your romantic picnic have to do with the marshal and this mission?" he asked, jealousy briefly clouding his wits.

"Not with Brody and the picnic, Marsh! Foley Timms was in Wadesville the night before Bill Sharp's ranch was attacked. Now, he's in Jacksboro the night before this attack. Don't you see? A U.S. Marshal goes anywhere, everywhere, without suspicion. He knows the territory; he can learn about the people. He makes a perfect spy."

Marsh contemplated her speculations and said, "You could have something there, Randee. I've never heard of this marshal before, but he could be new on the job."

"If he's involved, that means the gang headed north or east or west, but not south like he wants everyone to believe. But even if he's not working with them, he wouldn't give away their destination if he's after those rewards or sheer glory. I say we put his name on our list of suspicious people near raids. If he keeps showing up . . ."

"You're a clever vixen, Randee Hollis. I'm glad I took up with you. Anything else, partner?" he said earnestly.

"Not yet," she commented reluctantly. She wanted to reveal the other information in her possession, but it was too soon. She needed more time with Marsh before sharing all with him. "I do have one question. If no one knows who's in that band, why is it called the Epson Gang?" she queried.

"My home was their first attack, but raids near the town of Epson were the first time that wild bunch was given a name for reports and identification. I'm afraid it doesn't hold any clues for us."

"What about members of the gang, Marsh? I saw arms and hands before I was locked in the attic. One man is black, and at least two others are Indians. I would guess Apache from their garments."

"That's a big help, Randee. But we shouldn't reveal those facts to the authorities just yet. If those three men go into hiding, we won't be able to use them to lead us to other gang members."

"I know. That's why I haven't mentioned it before to anyone. They're our only leads, so we can't alert them to their peril. I also remember horses, and mannerisms, and voices. That's why I wanted to get started on this search quickly, because memories dull."

"You also have to be along to identify those men."

"That's right. Only I can recognize those clues. When I hear those voices again, I'll know those men. And I never forget a horse."

Marsh trusted her conclusions and skills. "I'm going to accept your instinct about Timms and the direction of those raiders. Since we don't know where to head, let's follow through with our initial plan from this morning. Southwestward, with stops along the way."

Randee smiled happily. "Thanks, Marsh, that means a lot to me. I'm glad we're learning to trust each other and work together so easily—and to depend on each other."

They rode for hours, checking out any site that came across their path before dark. At each brief stop, Marsh instructed her on how to gather clues and on tracking skills. They were both tired and hungry when they made camp near the ruins of Fort Belknap, a post near the Brazos River, which had been abandoned in 1867. Before the war, it had been one of the largest posts in north Texas. A few of the structures still remained intact, but in disrepair.

133

"We'll spend the night here, Randee. I want to look around in the morning to see if the gang has used this old post for a hide-out or meeting point. But right now, let's find the cookhouse and prepare us a real supper tonight." He headed for the dilapidated building.

Before long, he had a fire going in the stove left behind, and had freshly made biscuits cooking. He pulled a cloth-wrapped package from his saddlebag and grinned. "How does fried chicken sound? All we need to do is warm it. I bought it in town earlier today." He waved it beneath her nose and chuckled when she rolled her eyes dreamily. He set it on the newly scrubbed table. "I was hoping I wouldn't need my canteen, because it's filled with peas flavored with tiny bits of ham. Then, we have these boiled potatoes, if they aren't squashed."

Randee watched him pour the peas into a pot and set them on the rusting stove. She eyed the slightly damaged potatoes and laughed. "You are wonderful, Marsh Logan. How will I ever equal this?"

"I hope you can't. I need to stay ahead in some area. My damn pride demands it," he jested. "Why don't you make coffee, and later you can wash the dishes?"

"Sounds more than fair to me," she replied merrily.

They devoured the entire meal with great delight. Afterwards, Randee cleared the table and did the dishes. Marsh made certain the fire was out, as the buildings were old and would burn rapidly if a spark ignited them.

Marsh informed her, "If we were sneaking around, you'd need to remove anything on your clothing that makes noise, like jewelry or spurs or weapons. You even have to be careful of pants material rubbing together between your thighs, and your garments catching on nails and bushes. And you have to make certain your boots don't scrape on floors or rocks. Even your breathing and scent can give you away. When you're being stealthy, watch sudden or rapid moves from place to

134

place; they're noticed quickly by a lookout, especially an Indian scout."

"What do you do if you have to crawl on your belly over rough terrain?" she inquired to prolong their genial talk.

"Most importantly, make sure you don't squeal if you land on a pointed rock or cactus, or if a creature walks under your nose or over your hand. It's slow going. You have to place your hands carefully, making sure the rocks beneath them won't shift or crunch with your weight on them. Then, you lift your body, shift forward, and lower it; it's like taking a tiny step at a time. If you rush, they'll hear you. Retreating is worse, if you can't get off your belly and have to inch backward. My worst moment was when I inched up to a rock where a rattler was snoozing and I had to remain still for nearly an hour."

"That means you'll have to teach me patience along with those skills. I must admit, it's my worst weakness."

"I'll have to teach you how to endure pain without making a sound, but I haven't come up with that lesson yet. Since you weren't discovered in the Carsons' attic, you might already possess lots of those survival skills. It's late and we have a hard ride tomorrow. Which hotel do you choose, Miss Hollis?" he asked cheerfully.

Randee looked around and selected the sturdiest appearing quarters. "There, Mr. Logan. What about you?"

"I'll take the old arsenal. I love the smell of gunpowder. Call out if you need anything," he told her again tonight.

Randee thought, *The only thing I need tonight is you, Marsh Logan, but I dare not disclose that fact so soon. Heavens, Mother, how would you feel if you knew what I was doing and thinking? Or would you even care about me at all, after your beloved Payton filled your ears with his lies about me? If only I could have found a way to enlighten you, to convince you of his evil, without endangering you and the baby. Somehow I'll find a way to free you. I won't let that bastard outsmart me or defeat me, and I'll never let him hurt me again!*

Marsh was careful not to look at her or to say another word, as things were feeling a little too cozy between them tonight. He promptly went to the crumbling arsenal and bedded down there. Stretched out on his back, with arms folded beneath his head, he gazed at the stars which were visible through the fallen roof. Even if he changed his mind about chasing Randee Hollis, they had known each other only a week, too soon for her to . . . *Forget it, Marsh, a lady wouldn't choose a notorious gunslinger over a respectable sheriff, or life on the trail over a cozy home and family.*

In Wadesville late that night, Brody Wade was talking with Deputy Matthew Johnson. Matthew had just returned from his tracking assignment, but Brody had received his grim message earlier. Brody had been hoping that Randee had left the stage before reaching Red River, but Matthew told him she hadn't.

"Damn it all, Matt! I wish I had stopped her from leaving town on Thursday. Hell, I can't go searching for her in Indian Territory. I wouldn't know where to look or how to find her. With those savages running loose, it's too dangerous and I don't have any authority there. I'll have to depend on the Army to locate her and rescue her for me."

The deputy's eyes widened in shock. "You mean you'll take her back after she's been with them Injuns? Sakes alive, Brody, you know what they do with white women. She'll be too dirty to touch or look at."

Brody scowled. "I don't care what's happened to her. She's mine and I want her back. I love her, Matt. One way or another, she's going to marry me. I just had to make certain that cocky gunslinger didn't try to join her after she left town. I didn't like the way he was eyeing her. I don't know who he is or what he had in mind, but he isn't the Durango Kid. I'm doing some checking on him now, just in case he turns up here again after Dee's return."

More shock filled the man's face. "I'll be goldarn, Brody, you really want her bad. I shoulda knowed it when you made me trail her to the edge of Texas. She's gone now, maybe for good."

"Not Randee Hollis; she's too smart and brave to die easily. She'll be back. Hell, she'll probably escape within a week! You wait and see, Matt; she'll come back to me. She promised."

After a quick breakfast and a search of the abandoned fort, Randee and Marsh continued their journey southward. Wednesday was spent checking out each raid location in their path and making notes on them. They questioned neighbors of past victims, but learned nothing new. The ranches in this area were large and mostly self-contained, with many miles between them. Over and over, they repeated their story of how their homes had been destroyed and they were trying to gather evidence to help the law capture the gang. Everyone wished them luck, but thought them foolishly brave to take on such a task. At each stop, Marsh gave a Fort Worth address to which anyone seeing or hearing anything strange could send the information for him to collect.

Shortly before dusk, they halted and camped beside a river. While she prepared the evening meal, he checked their surroundings to make certain no threat was lurking nearby. He was pleased to find no one around, not even squatters. After supper, Marsh located a safe and private spot for Randee to bathe. She was delighted, especially after not having had a bath last night at the old fort. When she returned to the campfire, Marsh went for a quick swim and bath.

Tonight, they both unrolled their sleeping bags near the fire. Since Marsh said the area was safe, Randee wore her comfortable nightgown. Marsh kept his pants on, but removed his shirt and boots. Both lay on their backs, as if afraid to look at each other.

Marsh's body was tantalized by Randee's proximity. No matter which way he turned or looked, he remained highly cognizant of her allure and their romantic solitude. He couldn't help but wonder how she would react to intimate overtures from him, or if he dared to make any. The longer he lay there in silence, the more his tension mounted. To break it, he commented, "You're doing wonderful, Randee. I'm proud of you. I like the way you never slow us down or complain. You're more than holding up your end of our bargain."

Randee was experiencing that same discomfort of rampant desires. She turned her head in his direction and said, "Thanks, Marsh. I just wish we had learned something today."

"Don't get discouraged. We're mostly on a cold trail right now. One thing I did notice, Marshal Foley Timms's name wasn't recognized. If he visited the area around the times of those attacks, the people who know that fact are dead or gone. If he comes around these parts soon, I hope no one mentions we were asking about him."

She looked skyward again as she asked, "How can we discover who's purchased those deserted spreads? There might be a clue there to a clever land grab."

"While I was in Fort Worth, I asked a friend of mine to check out that angle for me. If he's learned anything by the time we reach Brownwood, he'll have a message waiting for us."

Emotional strain steadily increased in the ensuing

silence as each became more and more ensnared by the other's tempting presence and their secluded camp. Each heard the other's breathing and noticed it wasn't normal respiration. For a time, neither spoke nor moved, but hearts throbbed furiously. They lay there tense and alert, and with mounting desires. It was as if each was waiting for the other to make the first move; yet, both were fearful of the other's reaction.

Randee became so unsettled by Marsh Logan and her feelings that she forced her mind onto another man. She asked rashly, "Do you think Brody has tried to go after me? He was terribly worried."

Marsh was annoyed by the mention of the man who wanted to marry Randee. He mistakenly believed she was breathing heavily because she was daydreaming about . . . his competition, if he wanted to challenge the sheriff's grip on her heart and life. Maybe he should roll over there next to her and show her who the real man was! No, he wasn't one to forcefully or cunningly seduce a woman. And making love to a woman didn't prove to her that you were a real man, or the right man for her. Once he revealed an interest in her, things might get complicated between them. He desired her like crazy, but, no, he couldn't take her unless she wanted him as much as he wanted her. "I doubt it, Randee; it's too soon, unless he lacks all masculine pride," he answered, making sure he kept his voice level and called her the right name to keep her from guessing the turmoil of his emotions. He knew Brody wouldn't ride into Indian Territory to search for her; the lawman was too keen on his own survival. Maybe he should tell her the truth about the Indian attack on the stage. No, not yet . . .

"Does that mean you view worry over a loved one as a weakness? Are you less of a man if you expose your feelings?" she inquired.

"Men are trained to control their feelings, so it's

139

harder for us to reveal them than it is for you women. About the only emotions men are supposed to show are pride and anger, and they can get you into real trouble. I feel sorry for any man who reveals anguish; it's like baring your soul to vultures. I've seen people pick a gentle man to pieces. Either you follow the rules, or you make your own. But if you do, you'd best be able to defend them."

"What I meant, was to reveal your emotions to those involved, like to your family or to special people. My father didn't go around displaying or declaring his love for me and Mother, but he made sure we knew how he felt about us. Most men won't even show their families how they feel about them. Maybe because of pride, like you said. That was my father's reason for playing the masterful man in public."

Marsh jested mirthfully, "I'm glad your father wasn't totally perfect, or he'd be a hard man for you to match in a husband. You sure Brody Wade can fill such large boots?"

"I don't want to mislead you, Marsh. My father was a wonderful man, but he had his faults. All men do. It's just that his many good traits overshadowed the few flaws he had. As for seeking a husband who's like my father, I'm not. I don't want to marry my father's image, but I won't mind if he has similar traits. Too many men view special emotions as weaknesses, and that causes problems for everyone involved. Brody isn't like that. He's a good man, a kind and generous one. He's thoughtful and caring. He's looked out for me since that raid."

"And he loves you and wants to marry you," Marsh added.

To get beyond this vexing point, which she had created, she teased, "Why shouldn't he? Even you said I was wonderful, and you're a hard man to impress or to make such admissions. Surely a strong and uncomplaining woman is worth her weight in gold."

"And Brody made the first strike on your golden treasure."

Randee didn't reply, and her respiration altered noticeably. She remembered Payton Slade calling her his "little golden treasure." Her stepfather had remarked often on her "golden skin" and "golden hair" and her "golden promise." Heavens, how she loathed that vile man! How she longed for every memory of him to vanish! She was glad that the incident with her vile stepfather had not made her bitter and suspicious of all men. But she was more on the alert now than she had been before he entered her life. Randee was fairly confident that no man could fool her as deeply and quickly as Payton had duped her mother, but maybe she was mistaken. A person never knew how he would behave or feel until facing that situation. Sometimes the episode with Payton seemed excruciatingly real; other times, it seemed like a bad dream, something which had never, and could never, happen to her.

"I believe I've touched a sore spot," Marsh remarked unhappily. "What do you say about calling it a night and getting some sleep before we destroy the progress we've made between us?"

"I think that's an excellent suggestion. Good night, Marsh." Randee turned onto her side, away from him, and closed her eyes. Heavens, how she wanted to cry. She blamed her distraught emotions on fatigue, vexation, and a gnawing hunger for the mysterious man nearby. Undemanding sleep was exactly what she needed!

Chapter Seven

Randee was not to enjoy mindless sleep that night. Wicked images and voices prevented peaceful slumber as she witnessed her evil stepfather plaguing her with his insidious advances behind her trusting mother's back. She envisioned Dee Hollis Slade in grave peril if Dee learned of Payton's lecherous behavior. Randee hated the inability to protect and to free her mother. Randall Hollis had taught his daughter to be strong and independent, to be brave and honest, but Payton Slade had stolen those valuable traits.

Caught up in the swirling maelstrom of the past, Randee's slumbering mind waxed between scenes of Dee believing her and scenes of Dee doubting her claims against the man she had married in the fall of '69, and whose child she now carried.

Randee couldn't blame her mother totally for that terrible mistake in judgment. Dee had been distraught by Randall Hollis's unexpected death in '68, as those two had been madly in love and had wed when Dee was sixteen. Life and ranching had been hard on her after Randall's murder, and she had been susceptible to Payton's amorous attentions. Payton had helped Dee Carson Hollis with many problems while he had wooed her wildly. A woman who wanted and needed a strong man at her side, Dee had been swept off her feet by Payton's romantic and persistent siege.

Problems had multiplied following the tragic event. The rustlers who had slain Randall Hollis continued to plague them. Dee felt that the work was too hard and dangerous for a woman with a young daughter. The hands were tense over having a female boss who was too distressed to think straight and who didn't "know how to run a large ranch alone." Suffering from loneliness, anguish, fears, and doubts, Dee had cried herself to sleep nearly every night for weeks.

Many hands and local ranchers started showing hot interest in the attractive Widow Hollis, who had a lot to offer a man in herself and with her ranch. Then, Payton Slade began to call on Dee every few days, offering and supplying help and advice. Things quickly got better, through deceit, Randee came to suspect. Soon, Payton was filling Dee's emotional void and handling nearly everything for her, as if he owned or controlled her and the ranch. He had absorbed Dee as dry earth greedily consumed water and sucked it out of sight forever. Afraid of being alone and of losing the ranch, and in desperate need of love and assistance, Dee had yielded to the man's obsessive desire for her. She had seemed overjoyed to have him take away her decisions and worries. The old Dee Hollis vanished.

Randee had not liked or trusted Payton Slade from their first meeting, but she had been unable to put her finger on why she felt that way. The man was nice-looking and had a good build, but his smile and gaze had always made her nervous. She had tried to convince her mother to wait a while longer before marrying their neighbor, but Dee had been enchanted and duped by the powerful rancher, who had taken over the adjoining ranch only six months before her father's death. In a deed dispute with heirs, Payton, who had powerful political connections, had won possession of the enviable ranch which his uncle had owned for many years. Although Payton had tried his best to become friends with her father, Randall Hollis had remained skeptical of the man and that legal decision. Payton had called on them frequently and had appeared at every social function in the area, always displaying exceptional charm. Even so, Randee knew her father never came to trust or to like the man.

Yet, Randee's dark feelings stemmed from other troubles with her stepfather. The immoral beast had begun his wooing within two months of her father's death in midwinter, a difficult time for anyone to care for a ranch. Dee had been frightened and confused, but instead of turning to Randee, she had leaned on Payton for help and solace. Within weeks, it seemed as if the man was spending as much time on the Hollis Ranch as he did on his own ranch. To protect his future interests, Randee had often thought to herself. By spring, Dee's mourning period had disappeared, much to Randee's dismay, and Dee had turned completely to the cunning devil. All summer the lovers played around like carefree, happy children — except for when they sneaked into bed together like passion-dazed adults. Randee knew her mother would have married Payton during the spring or summer, but the sly bastard had convinced Dee it wouldn't appear right to wed so soon after Randall's demise. He had made Dee wait until late fall, making less than a year of widowhood. Since life was hard on the "frontier," no one had gossiped.

At first, Payton Slade had been too busy with his cunning scheme to turn his wicked attentions on Randee. He had poured his false affection on Dee like a treacherous rain that caused flash floods and great damage. Every time Randee turned around, Payton was all over her mother, like the itch from a fall into a chigger-infested weed patch! During those months before the wedding, Randy had accidentally witnessed and over-heard bouts of lovemaking which had astonished and embarrassed her. With windows open and sex taken anytime and anywhere, Randee had worried over what others might see and think about her mother. But Dee Hollis didn't seem to care about anything except pleasing herself and Payton. Randee could not imagine what Payton was doing to have such an effect on her mother. Had it been true love? Feverish sex? A time of insanity? What tormented and disappointed Randee the most was her mother's almost wanton behavior so soon after losing the man she had loved since the age of sixteen. How, she had wondered, was it possible to give your heart and body to another man so quickly, so passionately, so uninhibitedly?

As the Hollis home was much larger and nicer than Payton's, the man had moved into her father's house, his room, and his bed the day of the wedding. Immediately he had gone to work merging the two ranches to create a powerful and prosperous spread.

In the beginning, Randee had wondered if she merely disliked and mistrusted the man because he was taking over her father's place and possessions, and because her dear mother had changed so drastically since her father's death and since falling under Payton's spell. Dee had been Randall's partner in every area of their lives, but it wasn't the same with Payton Slade. Dee seemed dazed by the man, dependent on him for everything, almost as if she were bewitched! Anything the man said or did was fine! It seemed as if Dee was no longer strong, confident, intelligent, proud, outgoing, or brave. Dee waited upon Payton hand and foot, eagerly and joyfully responding to his every whim and order. She never discussed matters with the man or asked questions or disagreed with him. It was as if Dee would make any sacrifice to keep her second husband, as if her survival was solely in his hands, as if she needed only him to make her happy, as if she actually enjoyed being ordered about day and night!

As the months passed, Randee realized she was not being selfish and unfair and resentful, but it was a long and bitter lesson for her. From the start and to her mother's delight, Payton called Randee his daughter; he kissed her cheek, embraced her, talked to her, and bought her gifts: actions which she overheard him telling Dee were to win the girl's affection and acceptance. Payton was very clever with his pretense, faking wild and passionate love for his new bride while filthy plans roamed his dark mind. The infatuated Dee had been fooled completely, as had Randee for a while. Randee had never imagined her stepfather — or any male family member — capable of being that evil and bold, so for a time she truly had not realized what he was doing and thinking. In hindsight, the green-eyed blonde admitted that she should have comprehended the man's wickedness and her imminent predicament. Not that Randee was too trusting and overly naive; she simply hadn't realized such horrible things could happen to her.

As winter progressed, Payton became more affectionate and genial to her in front of her mother. On a few occasions, he tickled and tussled with Dee before drawing Randee into his crafty game, where hands and kisses swiftly and unnoticeably and *accidentally* touched areas they shouldn't have. Sometimes he playfully chased or spanked the two females, even though Dee and Payton knew Randee didn't like their childish sport. Twice, her mother had scolded her for being a stick-in-the-mud and for not trying to accept her "new father." When Randee had said she was too old for such behavior and didn't enjoy it, Payton had feigned hurt and offense, and Dee had gotten angry with her.

146

Payton had tried to appease and trick Randee by apologizing and backing off for a time. He had even forbidden Dee to scold her for her feelings and "impulsive conduct." He had claimed that in time they would become a close and happy family. Later, he had taken up his merry sport once more. This was the pattern for many episodes that caused Randee to doubt her impressions and suspicions. Since Payton was supposedly madly in love with Dee and was trying to make friends with Randee, why should she imagine he had dirty games in mind?

Some wintry nights, Payton would come into her room to make certain "his little girl" was "covered with warm blankets," at first with Dee and then alone. His short good-night kisses on her cheek moved to quick ones on her mouth, then to longer ones on her lips as he vowed how glad he was to have "the most beautiful wife an' daughter in Kansas." He would lift a giggling Dee and swing her around and around before cuddling and kissing her as if she were the only female who warmed his heart and loins. But when he embraced Randee, he cunningly mashed her growing breasts against his hard chest and often shifted in such a manner as to caress them with his torso: a lewd trick, which Randee didn't grasp for a time because it was done so cleverly and because she was trying to get along with the man to please her mother.

As spring drifted into summer, gradually her mother's husband began to behave more suspiciously to her in private. Sometimes when he came up beside or behind her, his hands wandered to forbidden areas like her breasts or buttocks or thighs; at first, as with his silly games, it was done rapidly and in a way that looked unintentional. Soon, Randee became mistrustful, angry, and resentful. She tried to avoid the man, and prayed the problem would cease. When it didn't, she

147

began to pull away and to glare at him to let him know she had caught on to his ploy. A few times, she bravely hinted at his crude actions—protesting that the way he kissed her and hugged her wasn't proper—and suggested he halt his behavior before her mother misunderstood and got angry with them. Nothing worked, because Payton feigned innocence and ignorance. The vile beast even teased her about her wild and naughty imagination! He claimed there was nothing wrong with him showing her love and attention, since he was her new father, even if he hadn't "birthed her." He told her that Dee would be very angry and upset by such false charges and it would cause bad trouble in their home.

Even as he denied her barely veiled charges, she could still hear him practically admitting them, "Aw, come on, girl. Be nice to yore new pa. We could git along real good if you tried. I know I ain't got much book learnin', but I ain't stupid. You're just stubborn an' vain, girl, like yore ma used to be when Randall was alive. I straightened her out an' I can do the same with you. I'm yore pa now; the law says it's true an' yore ma says it's true, so you best mind me, or else I'll be forced to thrash you. I ain't tried to git in yore bloomers, so you best not tell yore ma such lies. You clean up yore mouth an' head, or I'll have to switch you good behind the barn."

Randee knew that before she took any action she had to discover how tight Payton's grasp was on Dee, as her father had taught her to reason out a problem before acting on it rashly. She had concluded that Payton's actions were not accidental, and certainly not normal. Yet, she realized she had to handle this offensive matter carefully, as it would be her word against her stepfather's. If her mother hadn't been so enthralled with the man, Randee wouldn't have had a dilemma. The situation worsened for Randee when the man made certain he did and said nothing suspicious before his wife and others, denying her any evidence against him. Even so, Randee found a private moment to ask her mother if Payton Slade had the authority to punish her, even if her misdeed was only in the man's mind. Randee had been shocked and dismayed to learn that her mother would indeed allow the man to punish her for any reason which he felt was necessary!

When she protested, Dee had said, "He's your father now, Randee. You must do everything he says. If you anger or disobey him in any way, I'll have to allow him to punish you. He doesn't have any children of his own and he wants to make you his daughter, but you're so mean and rude to him."

When Randee frowned, Dee admonished, "Don't roll those Hollis eyes at me, young lady. I don't like the way you've treated Payton since our marriage, but he's too kind to let me punish you. You've been set against him since we met, and you've made no attempt to get along with him. Don't shake your head *no*, because you most certainly have been ugly to him. He knows you hate him for taking your father's place and it hurts him badly. You should be ashamed of yourself, Randee Hollis. I know your father would be greatly disappointed in you if he witnessed such bad behavior."

Randee became annoyed as Dee almost whined her next words, "Please, Randee, don't cause me any more pain and trouble and grief. Payton won't allow it. He loves me and takes good care of me. I can't lose him too, girl, so I'll do anything to keep him." The woman's eyes narrowed as she warned, "If you say or do anything to destroy my marriage or to make Payton leave, you'll be sorry, Randee."

Randee had stared at her mother in disbelief and anguish. She saw that the blinded woman was serious; her mother would do anything to keep that foul creature! God, how she hated Payton Slade for so drastically

149

changing her mother! How, Randee had wondered, had he done so in just a year and so completely? Suddenly, Randee realized she was entrapped in a terrible situation. The challenge to outwit Payton was a difficult one. She had to discover her limits and work within them. Considering her mother's blind trust and distorted feelings, if she confessed the man's evil to Dee, the woman might not believe her. Or worse, Dee might not care about anything anymore except herself. . . .

Summer and fall passed and their second winter together began. Randee was miserable, too miserable to think clearly. She was worried about her mother's enchantment and sanity. The only reason she hadn't taken action against Payton — despite what he and Dee had said to her — was because he had left her alone for months. She was hoping the problem had disappeared and she wouldn't have to reveal her stepfather's brazen conduct to her mother, who appeared so blissfully happy. Randee knew, if she was compelled to expose the man, Dee's new life would be ripped asunder. Besides being hurt and humiliated, there was no guessing how the woman would react to such a vile discovery. Dee seemed to be living in a lovely dream world, and she seemed to have become só fragile and vulnerable, so immersed in that man. Randee couldn't help but worry that her disclosure might destroy her mother instead of the deceitful marriage. She could never yield to Payton's evil, but she must pretend she had given up her suspicions. She would lie in wait, like a predator, for the right moment to attack. Then, she would strike at him when the odds were in her favor. Yes, she must recall everything her father had taught her, and use it against this crude excuse for a man.

But the day came when Payton started his little games again, under the absurd guise of making peace. Once more, Randee tried to avoid him and discourage him;

and, for a time, Payton was willing to remain only playful and mischievous. To prevent more trouble before she could leave home in the spring—which Randee knew was her only course of action—she attempted to ignore and to repel her stepfather's overtures. By some miracle, she kept him at arm's length until January.

Then, the lascivious incidents gradually increased in frequency and boldness, as if he were calling her bluff. On days that his behavior was particularly bad, she tried to embarrass him by pointing out his misconduct. Once, she even told him she was praying over his sins, but he only chuckled satanically. That night, Dee announced she was pregnant with Payton's first child, and the man seemed ecstatic! He even claimed that God was rewarding him because he had proven he was a good father to his stepdaughter!

After that stunning revelation, Payton played his secret game with skill and persistence. He constantly mentioned Dee's delicate physical condition and highly sensitive emotional state. He hovered over his wife daily, cooing and behaving as if Dee were the new baby or the most special woman in the world. He genially ordered Randee to do most of the chores so Dee could get plenty of rest or get over bouts of morning sickness. He would point out to Randee that her mother wasn't a young or strong woman and that giving birth could be hard, even dangerous for her. He warned Randee not to say or do anything to upset Dee, which could cause her to lose the baby and perhaps take her life. Randee felt the imaginary noose around her neck tighten as her peril increased. Now, she had another life to consider and protect, a responsibility she didn't want.

Payton realized he had Randee in a bind, and he took advantage of her predicament. His favorite ploy was to catch her alone in the stable while she was feeding and rubbing down her horse. Twice she had escaped him before he could touch her, and other times she had persuaded her mother to accompany her so they could chat like they used to long ago, or make plans for the new baby. But when she became too good at eluding him, Payton found ways to thwart her with help from his trusted hirelings. Once more, she was the prey and he was the predator. Her mind swirled madly with questions. How could she challenge him? How could she outwit him? How could she endure this wickedness any longer? She couldn't, as it was getting worse.

Her boiling fury and resentment increased daily until her temper exploded one freezing morning. She hated to hurt her mother by revealing the truth, but she had no choice. The man would not leave her alone! Randee told him exactly what she thought of him. Instead of threatening to expose him to her ailing mother, which she felt would be useless, she rashly claimed she was going to see the law. Surely he could be arrested and punished, or at least put off their ranch! Once his sordid behavior was revealed to the authorities, surely the spell he had over Dee would be broken! Suddenly, she recalled that he had powerful connections to the law and was widely — but undeservingly — respected in this area.

Still, Randee made her bold threats. That was when Payton Slade almost became violent. He had glared at her for daring to scold, refuse, insult, and threaten him. He had terrified her by warning her of her mother's lethal peril if she dared to mention any of this to Dee or to anyone. He had made grim threats of brutality and death, and Randee never doubted he would carry out his claims. As he had ranted and raved at her, she had grasped how mean and evil he was. It was obvious he didn't love his wife or the baby, only the ranch. It was also obvious that he thought he needed Dee and the child for the image he wanted to present, one he didn't want Randee soiling. That relieved Randee because it meant those two would be safe when she left.

Despite the breach between her and her mother, she couldn't bear for Dee and the child to be harmed or slain. With winter's snow and icy cold surrounding them, presently there was no way she could flee her home successfully. She had used up too much time and been too cautious!

Dee couldn't help her; the pregnant woman could only be emotionally and physically hurt if told of this vile situation. The law wouldn't help her because Payton had the authorities fooled. He had vowed to humiliate her if she went to the law, threatening to claim they had been lovers for months behind Dee's back and that Randee was being spiteful because he refused to divorce Dee and marry her! He seemed to know exactly how to make her appear the villainess. Randee had seen him at work on others plenty of times. He had this strange, intimidating ability to disarm and deceive most people, to make them think and act as he desired and without being aware of Payton's control. He swore he would kill Dee and claim it was suicide because of Randee's betrayal, and she knew he was deadly serious. That devil made her realize that even if the law believed her, she couldn't prove her claims, that even her own mother would testify against her and then disown her.

There seemed to be no way out of the sadistic trap. Randee decided she must kill this man to save herself and her mother, but Payton guessed her thoughts. He warned her of the grim consequences, and proved his threat by calling his trusted men to his side and ordering them to rape, torture, and slay Randee and her mother if anything happened to him! The lecherous men had smiled satanically and agreed, revealing the extent of her peril and helplessness. On that bleak and freezing day, fear, dread, and repulsion had consumed her.

Yet, for a time, Payton Slade seemed satisfied with his

secret victory. He did nothing more than sneak a kiss and touch here and there, and to tease Randee about her enslaved position. It was as if the power and control which he held over her was all he wanted from her, as if the excitement would be lost if the dirty secret were revealed. Randee saw Payton and his cohorts watching her every day, so she knew there was no escape possible at this point. She had to endure this bitter situation until Payton's guard slackened and she could slip away. Once she left and the vile game was ended, so would the danger to Dee and the unborn child end. If she kept her mouth shut!

To save her mother's life while she stalled for time to act, Randee tolerated her stepfather's covert attentions. When they were alone, he stroked her hair and flesh and told her how much he enjoyed "their feel in his hands." When she was doing chores, he sneaked up on her to whisper naughty compliments about how beautiful she was becoming and how nicely she was "filling out." If she tried to protest, he would warn her not to talk back to him or disobey. He would come to her room at night to tuck her in and to give her a good night kiss. It was as if the original game of lewd pursuit was still in progress, not as if he had won it weeks ago and had her at his mercy.

Randee came to believe that Payton Slade was mentally ill, that the game was the important thing, not a final victory. So, while she awaited the moment to escape, she played along with him by pretending she was helpless and terrified and would never challenge his power and grasp, which thrilled and sated him. For a time . . .

February of '71 came, and Randee's situation worsened. For greater excitement, the man began to play other games with her: he seemed to be aroused by cleverly handling Randee when his gullible wife was nearby.

One day in the kitchen when she was standing beside the table and cutting up vegetables from the root cellar, Payton entered the cozy room whistling. He sat down very close to her and spread out a cloth and began to clean his pistol. As he chatted cheerfully with his wife, who was making bread on the counter not far away, his hand slipped under Randee's skirt and teased up and down her inner thigh, but never touched her private region. Chills and disgust raced over her body, and hatred burned fiercely within her. When she glared at him and tried to move away, he lifted the loaded gun, pointed it at Dee's back, and grinned evilly. Randee eyed him intensely, and knew he would pull the trigger if she spoke or moved. Her teeth clenched and her eyes narrowed, and Payton smiled victoriously.

After Randee forced herself to stand there, he was content to halt his sport in a minute. Her hand had gripped the knife tightly, shaking as her mind finally persuaded her not to slash the man's throat. If defeating Payton was her only task, he would have been dead that moment.

Another time, Payton spanked her one night before the fire, claiming she had "smart-mouthed" him about a chore. When Dee did not interfere and turned to fetch him a drink, the man caressed the firm buttocks which he had been slapping forcefully only moments before. Randee sneaked a look at her stepfather's face and realized he was stimulated by the pain and humiliation he was inflicting upon her, especially beneath her mother's nose. Instinctively she knew his dark desires and plans were changing rapidly, and her reprieve was running out. Terror gripped her heart. She had to find a way to win!

After that night, Payton began to touch her when Dee was only inches away from them. Randee detested this new sport, but had not decided how to defeat Payton without losing three lives. Some nights she lay awake trying to come up with a plan. She could sneak into her mother's bedroom and slay the man as he slept, but how could she get them away from Payton's cruel men? She couldn't drag a pregnant woman through the snow, nor could Dee endure a long, rough ride on horseback—if her mother didn't go mad at seeing her love shot, and if her mother believed her explanation. . . . She had asked one man—one who had worked for her father and whom she had thought trustworthy—for help, only to have him betray her to Payton. Her stepfather had been furious, then amused by her bold desperation, and had stressed her helplessness. Now, she didn't know whom to trust. For all she knew, Payton could have all of the men on his side! Yes, she could kill him easily, but how to deal with his men and winter?

One morning, Payton shockingly revealed that Dee was going to be away from home for two weeks to help a neighbor, which was a common practice. Randee knew something terrible was at hand. She tried to reason with them about how dangerous it was for a woman in Dee's condition to take a rough trip and to be around sick people. Payton told her that it would be good for his wife to help another woman deliver her baby and then to take care of mother and child, to refresh Dee's memory and skills! Dee, wanting to please her husband, agreed with his plans. Randee knew it was a trick, and dread filled her.

Randee said it would be better if she went to care for the neighbor, but Payton refused, claiming she wasn't experienced and she was needed to do the chores around the house. He revealed that one of his men was driving Dee over in a buggy slowly and carefully, and would remain there with her to make certain she was safe and healthy. Randee caught his meaningful look and realized the man was being sent to serve as a threat. If

Randee didn't cooperate with Payton, Dee would be in peril.

Later that day, Payton entrapped her in the stable to disclose the evil which she had feared. When he told Randee it was time to take full possession of her, she knew what he meant and nearly became physically ill at the thought of his ravishing her. To date, he hadn't made any flesh-to-flesh contact with her private parts; her garments had always been between his hands and those intimate regions. He told her that he would kill Dee and all witnesses at the other ranch if Randee made any suspicious moves against him. She was petrified, but determined to defeat him. She had to take her chances that others would be safe after she was out of Payton's reach. She could not allow that beastly demon to destroy her. Dee was leaving in four days, so Randee knew this was the moment to escape the horror which controlled her life. Surely Payton would not slay his wife when she was carrying his first child, especially if Randee kept his vile secret.

Yet, other horrible speculations had entered her mind since Payton's insidious scheme had been revealed. She had to run away within four days, even though his guard would be heightened at this time. If Payton was allowed the time and opportunity to ravish her, then use her at will, she could become pregnant with that devil's evil seed and never be able to break free of him. Was saving anyone's life worth making that unholy sacrifice? Her stepfather seemed to crave her spirited resistance. Did he enjoy that even more than her mother's submission? If Payton decided he preferred a feisty virgin over meek Dee as his wife, her mother would be in more peril later than she was now. Worse, the insane bastard could try to make both of them his slaves, as Dee would be too afraid and devastated to battle Payton.

Randee made plan after plan, but they all seemed

fallible. She pretended to be totally under Payton's control, which was possible because he didn't come near her as he eagerly anticipated their two weeks alone. At the last moment, he told Randee that he was going along to get Dee settled at the neighbor's house, but he would return by nightfall. He told her there would be several guards left behind to make sure she didn't try to escape, and one would be left with Dee to kill her and their neighbors if Randee disobeyed any of his orders.

Randee could not permit him to continue blackmailing and terrifying her. She made her plan and carried it out. She did not try to dupe Payton's guard or escape while he was gone, as they would be on her trail instantly and all could be lost forever. She packed as many belongings as she knew she could carry on horseback and hid them beneath her bed. She prepared food and supplies and concealed them with her possessions. She took her final look around the ranch her father had created and nurtured, a place which would one day belong to Payton Slade's child because Randee could never return as long as Payton was alive and Dee was under his spell.

Randee was going to miss this place, but it wasn't home anymore. Payton Slade had violated it. She didn't care if the guard was dogging her, because a daily ride shouldn't cause suspicion, and she had to say farewell to this part of her life. Lastly, she wrote her mother a note in which she claimed she was running away to New York to seek adventure and to give Dee, Payton, and the baby privacy. She claimed she couldn't accept Payton in her father's place and she was miserable on the ranch, but she wished them great happiness. She promised to write home after she was settled somewhere, but she knew she wouldn't, because she couldn't risk Payton locating her. She hid the note in her mother's linen closet, where the woman would find it shortly after her return. Everything was done, and she must take her chances.

When Payton returned at twilight, Randee met him at the door in a lovely floral nightgown, with her honey blond hair tumbling over her shoulders. She had scrubbed her body with fragrant soap and dabbed on French perfume. Her green gaze was soft and seductive as she falsely admitted, "I know when I'm defeated, Payton, so I won't fight you anymore. I'm tired of being unhappy and nervous all the time, and scared Mother's going to find out about us. You win; do as you wish."

Payton's eyes traveled over her very slowly, and he grinned. "I knowed you'd see it my way an' obey me. You look real pretty, girl, an' I'm itching to get at you. But we don't need to rush our fun; Dee'll be gone for weeks. It's been a long ride an' I need to get settled."

Randee was delighted to hear that non-unexpected news, and continued her daring ploy. She knew that the man wanted to savor each moment of his game and victory, which gave her time to carry out her devious strategy. "You're such a smart and strong man, so I guess you know what's best for all of us. Since you practically own me, I guess you have the right to do with me as you please. I just had a hard time accepting you and the truth, but I've done lots of thinking today and decided I should be grateful and obedient. You did save our ranch and make Mother come alive again." She enticingly fluttered her eyes as she lied convincingly, "I suppose I was just jealous that Mother was so happy, when I was so miserable. Heavens, she's corralled her second husband before I can rope just one!" She pouted prettily as she fretted aloud, "I don't even have a single beau calling on me. If you didn't tell me how pretty I was getting, I wouldn't even hear it or know it. It's partly your fault I was so jealous and mean, Payton. You are a very handsome man, and I was forced to watch you two having all the fun while I was miserable and alone. And you treated me like a baby most of the time. I'm eighteen, almost nineteen. When am I going to get a chance at love and happiness? That sounds awful and selfish, doesn't it?" she hinted coquettishly.

Observing her submission, Payton beamed with pleasure and satisfaction. "Course it don't, my little Dee. You was scared an' lonely too, just like yore Ma was afore I worked on her good. See how happy she is now? I know how to take care of women, an' I'll take real good care of you. Afore these two weeks are over, I'll have you grinning and humming every day. But we can't tell yore Ma we're good friends, else she'll get mad an' jealous like you was before. She don't want to share me with no other woman, an' I wouldn't want to whip her to make her mind, not with her carryin' a baby."

"Even if Mother learns our little secret, you can keep her from punishing me or getting angry. She'll do anything you say, just like I have to do from now on." As she helped him remove his coat, and hung it on a peg, she said, "I know you're probably cold and hungry and tired, so I prepared a special supper for us. I'm keeping it warm in the stove. I'll serve it when you give the order." She motioned to her attire and said, "I thought you might be eager to get at me tonight, so I thought it best to wear this and be ready to obey."

Some of Payton's interest sagged at her groveling behavior—as Randee had assumed and was delighted to observe. Payton speculated on how he should behave to get the most pleasure from this first night with the fetching blonde. It would be too noisy to beat her, terrify her, and rape her. But he didn't want a soft and pliable pillow beneath him tonight. He had one fawning slave. What he needed now was a hot-blooded vixen. He craved a fiesty challenge, but he didn't want trouble, as he hadn't yet replaced all the Hollis hands with his own hirelings. "We'll eat first, then I'll teach you how to give me pleasure."

160

She licked her lips and pouted sensually as she murmured, "I hope you don't mind that I took a bottle of your best wine from the cabinet for us to share. I don't know about you, Payton, but I need to relax before we . . . turn in for the night. Would it be all right if after supper we lie before a cozy fire, and you can get me a little dizzy before you claim your golden treasure, as you call me. You will be gentle and patient with me, won't you, Payton? I mean, I know I've been mean and rude to you, but you'll forgive me and go easy tonight, won't you? I promise I won't give you any more trouble," she vowed dishonestly, looking and sounding so like her mother.

Payton actually frowned. Randee quickly said, "If you mind, I'll put it back, Payton. Please don't be angry with me. I'll obey. Please, just tell me what you want me to do," she entreated pitifully.

"First thing, don't whine and cower like yore ma. I thought you was a strong an' smart girl, so quit actin' like an old cow who's ready to drop in 'er tracks. You got me all worked up 'cause you was so spirited, like a golden bronc worth a fortune; now, you're actin' like you've lost yore spunk. Git it back, girl, 'cause I loved it. If you don't, I'll have to provoke you into findin' it agin," he teased as he pinched her right nipple. He chuckled when she squealed and unthinkingly smacked away his hand. "That's more like it, so keep it up. Pour yourself some wine, girl, but give me whiskey. After supper, I want you to put on some old clothes, so I can rip 'em off of you. That's real excitin' for a man. If you want me to, I'll give you the first lesson by the fire, but I want you to tussle with me. You know, girl, give me a little fight, like you don't really want me to hump you. A woman who just lays there or yields happily ain't no fun, no challenge."

Randee understood perfectly. She put on an innocent expression as she replied, "If that's how you like it, Payton, of course I'll pretend to battle you. I think there are some old clothes in that chest in the spare room. If not, I'll find something for us to use. We'll hurry with supper so we can get started with . . . my lessons."

As she poured him a drink and herself some wine, Payton chuckled and teased, "I think you're excited about tonight, ain't you?"

Randee's back was to the man, so he couldn't see the hatred and cunning deceit in her eyes. Her voice was velvety soft as she whispered sultrily, "Does that mean I'm wicked, Payton? I've watched the way you carry on with Mother, and I've heard you two . . . playing in the house and barn and bed at night; it seems so . . . so exciting." She used his favorite word and saw anticipation flush his face as she turned toward him. "I'll be nineteen in April, so I'm a grown woman, a woman who doesn't know anything about men. Don't you think it's time I learn about such things? And who better to teach me than you, my handsome and virile stepfather?"

Payton's mood began to change as he conceitedly assumed she was not cowed but actually tempted by ravenous desire for him. The surge of a new kind of power and ecstasy charged through him as he convinced himself he had bewitched and conquered an old enemy. This girl who had once hated, resisted, and avoided him was now eager to bed him! Her gullible mother had become such a slave to him that Randee craved to learn how and why the woman was so enchanted by him! No, the girl wasn't a coward; she was a brazen vixen! He laughed heartily. "Why, you sly little trickster," he jested. He gulped down his drink before accusing devilishly, "You've been wantin' me an' this all along. I got you real hot by spyin' on me an' Dee, just like I planned. You didn't know I was gettin' you ready to be cooked one night, did you?"

"Payton Slade, that was mean and cruel," she scolded playfully. She swiftly adapted her strategy to his changing moods. "I couldn't help but get all stirred up, and it made me real irritable. There you were, heating me up and coming after me, when I was too scared to let you have your way. My father would have killed us if he'd been around to catch us carrying on behind Mother's back. And I was afraid one of your men might tell somebody by accident; you know men get loose tongues when they get drunk."

She forcefully quelled her repulsion and bravely snuggled against his chest. As her fingers toyed with his shirt, she murmured sweetly, "I don't want to hurt Mother, but I can't help craving you, Payton. I know this is wrong, and we can get into terrible trouble if I got pregnant, but I don't care anymore. It's been too hard rejecting you and trying to be good. I thought if I made you mad at me you would quit tempting and tormenting me with these crazy feelings. But every time you touched me, I got all weak and hot inside. I've really tried to keep away from you, because you're Mother's husband, but I can't keep lying about my feelings for you. Besides, I have to obey you, don't I? So I'm not to blame for being bad. We've got two weeks alone. Isn't that . . . exciting?" she finished and laughed provocatively.

Someone knocked on the kitchen door, and Randee unthinkingly headed to answer it. Payton halted her by pointing to her scanty attire. She blushed at her oversight and stepped behind the door, amusing her stepfather. She winked and grinned as she hid there, convinced that she had her insidious stepfather right where she wanted him.

The foreman asked if there were any further orders for the night. Payton smiled and said, "Take care of everythin' for the next few days. I'll be real busy here at home." Randee kissed and erotically licked her stepfather's fingers, which were curled around the open door. Payton added, "Make sure I ain't disturbed for any reason. I'll

163

talk to you when I take a rest in about three days. For no reason, understand?"

The foreman grasped the evidence of a successful seduction in progress: the hard bulge in Payton's pants, the telltale flush on the man's face, the smell of Randee's perfume on his shirt and in the air; the rancher's heavy breathing, the muffled sound of movement behind the door, the victorious grin on his boss's lips, and the fiery glaze in Payton's eyes. He acknowledged his orders and grinned knowingly. "Nobody will come near this house until you give the word, boss."

After closing and locking the door, Payton looked at Randee and chuckled. His hands covered her breasts and fondled them, and Randee smiled disarmingly. "We'll eat later, girl. You got my stick hotter than a brandin' iron that's been in a campfire all day. You go find them old clothes while I have me another drink or two."

Randee was thrilled to get her victory under way. It would have been difficult to swallow a single bite. She briefly tolerated Payton's touch, as she didn't want him catching on to her lies. She kept herself from tensing and paling when he asked a hazardous question.

"You sure you want me this bad, girl? This ain't no game just to get me on your side 'cause you're scared, is it?"

Randee boldly trailed her fingers over his protruding groin as she whispered seductively, "I'm probably hungrier than you are, Payton. You've had plenty of loving from Mother, but I've never had any. I want you to teach me all you know, and we'll practice those lessons day and night until Mother's return. then you can figure out a place we can meet safely. Where do you want me after I'm dressed?"

"I'm burnin' up. Let's get on with it right now," he said, lust shining brightly and feverishly in his eyes. He reached for her garment.

She captured his hands and warned, "Wait, Payton; this is Mother's favorite gown. She'll miss it if I burn it afterwards, and I'll have to if it gets torn. Let me change first. I want you to . . . to rip my clothes off like you promised. Please. You're always so gentle and playful with Mother. I want it to be different for us, lots of fun and real exciting. You be the lusty rogue and I'll be the reluctant virgin. We can play all kinds of games before Mother's return. We'll take turns making them up. Of course, I'll learn more as we go along, so don't get disappointed with me too soon."

Lecherous laughter filled the room and the man eyed her greedily. "I knowed you'd like the same stuff I love. Go on, but hurry, girl."

Randee kissed him lightly on the mouth and hurried away, thanking him and humming happily. She peered around the dark corner of the hallway and watched the man hastily down two more drinks of strong whiskey. Things were going better than she had planned or dreamed. She had assumed she would only have hours tonight to get away, but her lustful stepfather had given her "about three days" before either of them would be missed. In that length of time, she could travel far away from this awful existence. She slipped to her room and quickly donned an old dress, then returned to find Payton sprawled on the floor on a blanket in front of a colorful fire.

"I'll get the wine and join you in a moment," she told him, needing a weapon that wouldn't arouse his suspicion. Thankfully, he didn't argue with her or halt her, but downed another whiskey.

She sat down beside his prone body, sipping the rosy liquid as she did so. "Is wine supposed to relax you or stimulate you?" she asked.

Payton took another drink, too enticingly provoked to

be aware of his recklessness and peril. "It does both, girl. Finish it quick 'cause I'm more than ready for you," he told her as he stripped off his shirt and started to work on removing the pants.

Randee was glad he hadn't undressed while she was gone, as this was placing him in a nearly helpless position. As he bent forward to yank his pants off his legs, Randee smashed the wine bottle over his head. When he collapsed unconscious to the blanketed floor, she smiled vengefully and pummeled his chest to relieve her tension and fury. Lying there almost naked and powerless, his pale body didn't look intimidating anymore. Randee's hatred and desire for revenge seemed to ooze from her every pore, and she struggled to control herself.

She stood and looked down at him, delighted to have that beast helpless at her feet. She could not stop herself from kicking him in the ribs several times; she wanted him to suffer as she had suffered. Heavens, how she wanted to slay him with her bare hands! But she couldn't. If anything happened to Payton Slade, her mother would face his men's wrath after Randee's escape. She couldn't even leave this evidence behind for her mother to suspect attempted rape; that, too, would endanger Dee's life and the baby's. She had no choice but to protect Payton's guilt, and that infuriated her. At least she could punish him slightly! And one day she might find a way to return and destroy him!

Randee quickly re-dressed the despicable man and roughly rolled him to the cellar door. She gave his limp body a kick and sent it tumbling down the stairs, uncontrollably enjoying every thud it made against the wooden steps and hard dirt floor. She silently prayed that his body would have countless bruises and scratches when he awakened. She went down into the dim area, which she had prepared earlier. The lantern was aglow and everything was as she had left it. She bound the man

166

securely to one of the support beams, then gagged him.

Randee glared at him and refused to bind his wound, which was still bleeding. She checked it and knew it wasn't a fatal injury, only a painful one. She smiled as she envisioned the headache and predicament to which Payton Slade would awaken in a few hours. She wished she could linger to witness it, but she dared not waste precious time — just as she dared not leave him naked to freeze or to catch a deadly cold. The lantern would burn until sometime tomorrow, then he would be in the dark, a nighttime inkiness that matched the blackness of his mind! He would be cold, but it wouldn't kill him or harm him in three days. Nor would going without food and water for that long. If it was that long. She had missed one point. When smoke failed to come from the chimney for a while, his men would come to check on him. She would leave the cellar door open to make sure they located the vile bastard, but only to protect her mother!

Randee cleaned up the broken glass and straightened the house, in case any dangerous clue had been overlooked. She placed the food on the table to keep it from burning and sending out an alarm. After making certain that all doors and windows were locked and curtained, she piled her possessions on the kitchen floor. She changed into warm and sturdy trail clothes, and strapped on her Colt. Quickly she looked around to make sure she hadn't forgotten or missed something.

Randee entered the cellar to check on Payton Slade, to get her last view of him and his predicament. He was still unconscious. She stared at him, her anger and hatred surfacing again. She had the urge to tear out his hair, to scream at him, to cut him into tiny pieces, to pulverize his wicked head with her gun butt, to slap his face over and over. She despised these feelings of violence which this man had created within her, made worse by the fact she could not seek justice for his vile deeds and thwarted intentions. She had to let him go free, unpunished, unmasked. She had to let him go on duping her mother and others. If only she dared to challenge his men and risk their obedience to a dead man. But she must not, as they would probably obey Payton, because they were just like him and would enjoy such dark deeds. A bitter mixture of anguish and helplessness consumed her. She realized that if she didn't get away from him quickly, she might kill him anyway! "I'm not your little golden honey bee; I have a terrible sting which you'll feel one day. Just wait and see! This isn't over between us!"

At midnight, she stoked fires in every hearth, hoping that one of them would burn just a little longer than the others and allow her more time to escape. Considering Payton's orders to his foreman, she had no idea how much time she would have before the search was on for her. With snow and ice on the ground, it would be slow traveling until she got further south. Too, she had to take the time to conceal her trail and time to be wary of perils along her journey to freedom.

Suddenly, the true episode began to fuse with a nightmare about the way it might have taken place months ago: Somehow Payton got free before she could leave the house, and captured her. She saw herself bound to her mother's bed, and the man was laughing wildly as he ripped off her clothes. She saw his grinning cohorts standing nearby, eagerly awaiting their turn with her as punishment for her treachery. She watched Payton strip off his garments and fall atop her. . . .

Randee thrashed and whimpered until Marsh went to her side and tried to awaken her. When he succeeded, she flung herself into his arms and trembled violently. Marsh comforted her with his strong embrace and gentle words, his lips finding hers along the path to solace.

Randee responded feverishly as she clung to him. Their mouths feasted greedily and they savored their snug contact. Caresses and soft words were exchanged, and more urgent kisses. Moans of desire were heard in the peaceful area, and passion's flames burned brighter.

Suddenly, Randee began to struggle with Marsh, as she was not completely awakened from her slumber and, in her confusion, the handsome Texan had become her evil stepfather who was lying atop her and preparing to ravish her brutally. She clawed at him and screamed, "Get off me, you filthy bastard! I hate you! Touch me again and I'll kill you. I swear it, threat or none! I won't let you do this to me!"

Marsh realized what was taking place and he withdrew from her, despite the height of his rampant desire, which cooled quickly as the beautiful blonde became a fierce wildcat. They struggled for a time before he pinned her to the ground. "Randee! Wake up! It's only a bad dream!" he shouted at her as he shook her arms.

At last, the nightmare loosened its vicious grip and released her. She sat up quickly and breathlessly. She looked around, rapidly regaining her senses. She met Marsh's probing gaze, but did not smile or blush. Finally she said, "I'm sorry if I disturbed your sleep and alarmed you. I haven't had a night . . . bad dream in a long time. Next time, leave me alone and I won't get violent with you." With Payton Slade so fresh on her mind, Randee could not allow herself to turn to Marsh or to any man just to escape the nightmarish evil of her stepfather. If, or when, she yielded to Marsh Logan, it had to be for the right reason, the only reason: loving desire.

When Randee lay down and curled onto her side away from him, Marsh eyed her with intrigue. She had called his name and briefly surrendered herself to him, until some dark shadow had terrified her. He considered her words—earlier and tonight—and wondered at their meanings, as she had not been speaking to him or battling him. This ravishing vixen had a frightening secret, one that had chased her from Kansas and had driven her from his arms tonight.

From her wild rantings, someone had tried to take advantage of her, someone she hated and wanted to slay. Twice she had mentioned "a nasty situation." Had she been forced to defend her honor by killing a man? Had she perhaps been married to some cruel man whom she had fled? Had her home been stolen from her through deceit or force? After her father's death, had she been left homeless and helpless? Had her mother been compelled to marry some awful man to escape the few options open to widows and orphans: a schoolmarm, a seamstress, a second marriage, a cook, a prostitute? Had this female faced such choices? Or perhaps her mother and stepfather hadn't wanted her around after their marriage. If, as she had once claimed, revenge was the only thing in her life at this point, where did that leave Brody Wade? Was the sheriff nothing more than the lesser of many evils? How could Marsh help her, or have her, without dealing with her troubled past? Unintentionally, he spoke aloud, "Randee, don't you think you should tell me about this problem which haunts you?"

Chapter Eight

Randee arose the next morning and made coffee before Marsh began stirring. She had no way of knowing that he had been awake a long time, but had remained still and silent to allow her more sleep after her restless night. Without putting on his shirt and boots, Marsh vanished into the trees and bushes to her right. Randee sipped the dark liquid as she watched his departure. He had glanced at her, then left camp without speaking. Perhaps he was still annoyed with her about last night, and he had every right to feel that way. She had been hateful and rude to him when he was only being kind and . . . passionate. She had refused to answer his question and explain her crazy behavior. Overwrought and muddle-headed at the time, she had told him, "We're both loners, Durango, so let's keep our noses out of each other's private affairs. I appreciate your concern, but I don't need a manly shoulder to cry on or a strong arm to protect me. I can take care of myself; if not, then it's time I learn how. This is a business arrangement, nothing more. Unless you want to begin mutual revelations by telling me all about the mysterious Marsh Logan alias the Durango Kid. But frankly, I don't think strangers should trade secrets."

Randee sighed heavily and berated herself for her silly conduct. They had been getting along so well; now, she had probably ruined their budding friendship. Ranting like a wild woman was no way to open up a quiet man! She had nearly had him convinced that she made a perfect partner; then, she had behaved like a spoiled child or shrewish female! Her turbulent mind flashed back to last night. Stars above, how that man could kiss! She got all hot and tingly just recalling their amorous bout, one cut too short because of Payton's memory and intrusion. She had left Kansas and that beast behind, but he still journeyed within her. Since she could not forget him or deal with him at this time, she had to come to terms with his lingering spirit. He had almost ruined her life in Kansas; she could not allow him to do the same here in Texas.

Dee's baby was due in mid-August, and today was May twenty-fifth. She knew her mother was safe and well, because the Carsons had received two recent letters from Dee: one shortly after Randee's arrival, which the Carsons had answered without betraying Randee's presence, and one just before the Carsons' deaths — which, fortunately for Randee, had been answered immediately. Hopefully, since Payton hadn't appeared at the ranch, he and her mother believed she was elsewhere. For a while, no correspondence would be expected or missed. That should give her time to seek justice for the Carsons and to find another place to begin the new life she wanted.

Randee was relieved that her assumption about her mother's safety had been correct, and that her reluctant silence had paid off. It distressed her to know that her mother was lying every night next to a husband who was so evil and deceitful. Yet, self-sacrifice could extend only so far, even for loved ones.

Randee fretted over what Marsh was thinking and feeling today after her contradictory actions last night. She had reached out to him, then angrily rejected him. He had responded ardently, but for what reason? Because she was Randee? Or because she was an available woman who was tempting him? If they became lovers, how would she feel

172

when she watched him ride out of her life after this task was ended? Was a brief blaze of passion with him worth what it would cost her later?

Randee squirmed nervously. She knew she would feel better if she washed the dirt and oil from her hair, so she grabbed a strip of drying cloth and headed to the river with her soap and clean clothing. Since it was daylight and cool at this early hour, she kept on her gown as she waded into the narrow river. It was chilly, but she adjusted gradually to the water temperature. She ducked and wet her long flaxen hair, then lathered it. She washed it twice and bathed before climbing onto the grassy bank, refreshed and calmed.

Marsh saw her from their camp and observed her. He knew she hadn't been after his life history last night; she had simply wanted him to back off from his curiosity and painful questions. He hadn't spoken upon arising this morning, to give her time to clear her sleep-fogged mind and to break the silent strain herself. For certain, some ghost was riding her back and she didn't know how to get it off. There had to be clues in his words to her last night, because she had reacted strangely to them and they had triggered a nightmare. Whatever was haunting her caused her to resist his touch, perhaps any man's touch. Yet, she had responded passionately to him. Yes, to him. She had murmured his name several times, not Brody Wade's or another man's. That fact pleased and warmed him, more than he found comfortable, because it meant he was as drawn to her as she was to him. How long could he master his emotions, when she was experiencing the same ones?

The realization that some foe had, or had had, a grip on this woman annoyed him. If it was possible, maybe she would let him help her get free of that trouble after they completed their mission. But unless he won her trust, she would never expose her problem to him, and it could also intrude on their task if left unresolved. That thought warned him not to allow this breach between them to continue. Perhaps he should take the first step toward peace in case she was too proud or afraid to do so. He headed for where Randee was standing, a wet gown clinging most provocatively to her shapely body. She was bent forward drying her hair when Marsh joined her to ask playfully, "What are you doing, woman? You bathed last night."

Randee wrapped the cloth around her hair and straightened. She smiled and replied, "I couldn't wash my hair last night because I don't like to go to bed with it wet on such a chilly night. I figured it could dry while we're riding today. Am I messing up our schedule?"

"Nope," he answered just as pleasantly. "I'll get breakfast ready while you dress."

Randee glanced down and noticed how the soaked garment was stuck to her flesh, outlining it perfectly and immodestly. She blushed, a reaction that was unusual for her. She hastily picked at the material to loosen its grip. When Marsh chuckled, she looked up at him.

"Sorry, Miss Hollis, but you look most appealing in that garb. I'll get back to camp before I forget we're practically strangers."

Randee watched him turn and leave, grinning broadly. She couldn't help but smile. He could be such a gentleman, and such an enticing rogue. This was a man of many traits and, so far, she liked them all. She surmised why he had approached her and was delighted by his generous overture. They had been alone for days and under most stimulating circumstances; yet, he had not pressed his advantage. She liked his self-control, and she liked him, very much.

She slipped into the bushes to dry off and dress. Removing as much water as possible from her hair, she let it hang free to dry. Then she gathered her belongings and joined Marsh at the fire. After tossing her wet gown over a low-hanging branch, she sat down opposite him. He handed her a cup of coffee and smiled again as his gaze lazily traveled over her from head to foot. He was still shirtless and barefoot, and he looked so at ease with her. His uncombed ebony hair was mussed sexily, with wisps of it teasing over his forehead. Her tension and troubles faded from mind and body. She felt good. She felt alive. And she realized it was this man's effect on her.

Heavens, his eyes looked so blue and compelling against his dark skin. They were expressive eyes, which often talked louder and more often than he did. Her gaze followed the furry black hair that covered his chest, narrowed over his ribs, then widened again around his navel. He was lean and muscular, and his body was well-toned. Her appreciative gaze returned to his handsome face. As he absently stroked his jawline while he cooked their meal, she suddenly realized he hadn't shaved the night before.

"Do you want me to fetch you some water to heat for shaving?" she offered politely.

His gaze came up to meet hers. He grinned as he rubbed his whisker-rough jawline. "I'll skip it until we camp tonight, but thanks."

Randee grasped a handful of her hair and squeezed it tightly, holding it for a moment before repeating the action on another area. Marsh's brow lifted inquisitively, and she laughed, "It keeps my hair from being so straight," she explained without his asking.

He watched the areas wave and curl beneath her artful touch. She took sections along the edges and rolled them over and over, and her tawny locks hardly moved when she released them. Using her fingers, she fluffed her shorter bangs and made them feather across her forehead. As he handed her a plate of food, he jested, "I've never seen anything like this before. You women use all kinds of beauty tricks to ensnare us men. Mighty interesting, partner."

Randee laughed before retorting, "I can see you've never had a sister or a sweetheart, Durango, or you'd know that bunch-curling is quick and easy."

"Especially on the trail," he added mirthfully. As he ate his meal, his amused gaze remained on her. She looked so lovely and calm this morning. No trace of her troublesome night lingered in her mood or appearance. He hoped it was his companionship, as hers had a wonderful effect on him. He had never found being around another person so easy and enjoyable, and he wasn't ready for this feeling to leave any time soon. His mother would have liked Randee, and he was sorry those two could never meet.

Twenty minutes later they broke camp and packed up their possessions. Marsh walked around her before she could mount the chestnut mare, eyeing and touching her hair. "I have to see if this worked," he informed her as she twisted to follow his movements.

He halted on her right and studied the two-inch scar before her ear. He estimated it to be around four or five years old. It was wider than a knife wound, but hadn't cut deeply enough to cause permanent damage to her facial muscles. Nor was it an ugly or repulsive scar.

Aware of his intense scrutiny, she related the story of how she had gotten the scar, "Since you're too nice or afraid to ask, Marsh, I'll volunteer the information. In happened in '67 while I was making and setting traps for ground squirrels that were pestering us. My father didn't like to kill anything if it wasn't necessary, so we trapped them and took them miles away before releasing them to find new homes. I was concentrating so hard on my task that I didn't realize trouble was approaching; at least I thought it was trouble," she remarked with a laugh. "I heard something strange and looked up to see this huge furry beast running toward me. I'd only seen pictures of wolves and knew they were dangerous creatures. When he leaped at me, I panicked and fell backward, and the hatchet in my hand caught me here," she said, running her finger over the white line.

When she didn't continue, he asked anxiously, "What happened then? Did he attack you or did you slay him?"

She lowered her voice to a serious tone. "He jumped on me and attacked me . . . with a thousand licks," she finished amidst merry laughter. "He belonged to a new neighbor and had been raised from a cub. He was only a playful wild pet. Of course, he almost got shot when my father heard the first scream and came running to help. He saw me tumbling around with a big wolf and blood flying everywhere. It's amazing how much a little place like this can bleed."

"You were mighty lucky, Randee; wolves can rip flesh to pieces."

"I'm afraid Bo was in more peril than I was. He ran free once too often and was shot by mistake. It was sad to lose him. Sometimes he went hunting with a group of us and he saved me from danger several times. He always knew where the snakes and pitfalls were located. Someday I'd like to get a good dog like Bo was."

"When you settle down, you can," he remarked.

She looked into the distance and murmured, "I hope so, if I'm ever allowed to remain in one pla . . ." She halted and said, "You ready?"

"Let's ride, partner," he agreed as he mounted his black stallion named Midnight. As they galloped over rolling hills, Marsh speculated over her slip. If "nobody's coming to look for me" as she'd told him, why was she on the run? Why was she teamed up with a famous gunslinger in pursuit of a savage band of outlaws? It was hardly the way to go unnoticed for very long. Where had she gotten the ten thousand dollars? She had skills which few men, much less a woman, possessed. Could she be a criminal, or from a family of criminals? Was she truly Randee Hollis? Truly the Carsons' niece? How had she become the only survivor of an Epson raid? There were many curious things about this beautiful vixen, things he wanted and needed to know. It sounded as if someone was pursuing her and tormenting her. That was bad. He wanted to probe her meaning, but let it pass for now.

At the Red River stage depot, the Epson Gang was eyeing the unmistakable remains of an Indian attack. Since the station was already destroyed and no signs of rebuilding were in progress, their job in this area was over, at least for the present. They rested for a while, then left for the next target, passing over an attack which would have provided Marsh and Randee with a valuable clue to their motive . . . .

Randee and Marsh made good progress that day as the raid sites were further apart in this sparsely populated area where large ranches dominated the open range. At each stop, Marsh instructed her on how to gather clues. She was amazed by the man's knowledge and skills. He explained how to detect the age of a campfire from the condition of the coals, and how to date someone's passing, by broken grass or scratches on rocks. He showed her how to read tracks from their depth, clarity, and style. She listened closely and intently.

"Most blacksmiths have their own marks, if you know what to look for. That clue can tell you where the rider had his horse reshod, and it helps you stay on the right man's trail when tracks overlap on roads. If you know an area, Randee, you can judge when a track was made by the moisture in the depression, or the lack of it. If there's been a sandstorm lately, but the track doesn't have any dirt inside, then you know your rider passed by after the storm. The same is true with rain and snow. When you have blades of grass trampled, you can check the breaks on them for moisture. If you get really good at it, you can tell a horse's size and its rider's weight from the depth of the impression. It all comes with time and experience."

Around two o'clock, they heard gunshots in the distance. Randee watched Marsh halt to listen and to speculate. She remained quiet and alert while he made the decision to ride that way.

"Let's take it slow and easy, partner," he cautioned her.

"I'm glad you aren't suggesting I remain behind again. How else can I learn anything and gain experience if I don't get involved?"

He glanced at her and grinned as he admitted, "I want to, boss lady, but I know it's useless. Besides, I might have need of your skills. From those sounds, more than a few guns are at work. Close your eyes and listen a moment. You'll see what I mean." Marsh observed her, knowing he had to discover just how good she was, even by thrusting her into danger. Watching her, somehow he just couldn't believe she was wicked or guileful. Whatever trouble she left behind in Kansas couldn't have been her fault.

Randee obeyed. She smiled as she opened her eyes and said, "You're right; each gun has a different voice. I've never noticed that before. I can learn so much from you, Marsh Logan; you're a genius."

"Not really, partner. I just like to stay alive and healthy. And I'll keep you that way, too." Her adoring smile and genuine compliment warmed him from head to toe, and he wanted to yank her into his arms for a hug and a kiss. Mercy, what a time to be distracted!

They rode toward the sounds, which grew louder as they neared the trouble. Marsh halted her again for a moment to study the situation. "No chances, Randee Hollis. Understand?" he ordered, then galloped off ahead of her to challenge the five bandits who were trying to stop and rob the stage from Fort Worth to El Paso.

Randee and Marsh came up behind the bandits before they realized they were under attack. Marsh used the butt

179

of his rifle to knock one masked man from his saddle. Because he hadn't fired an alerting shot, it allowed them more time to get closer to the other bandits. Randee followed his lead by skillfully lassoing another man and dragging him from his horse. By that time, the people on the stage realized that help had arrived, not more bandits.

Marsh wounded two men and Randee disabled the fifth man. The stage halted, and the driver hopped down to help his rescuers with the prisoners. He shook Marsh's hand and slapped him on the back.

"We're awfully glad to see you, mister. I thought we were goners for sure. They winged the guard before we caught wind of 'em."

Marsh and the driver bound the men securely while Randee was retrieving the two men who had fallen a ways back. As their horses had run off, she made them walk toward the waiting stage while she held a gun on them. Slightly injured, neither bandit challenged her skills and loaded gun. The few passengers aboard stepped from the coach and thanked Marsh. As the driver took care of the guard's wound, Marsh chatted with a small boy who was very frightened.

He hunkered down before the boy and smiled, his blue eyes and white teeth enhancing his awesome appearance. He was dressed in black today and his face bore a two days' growth of dark whiskers; yet, he exuded gentleness. "It's over now, son, so you can relax. We have those bandits all tied up and ready for jail." Marsh saw the lad sniffle and wipe at his tears. He knew the boy was embarrassed by his weakness. Marsh stood and pulled a silver coin from his pocket, then squatted again. He held out the gift and said, "Take this lucky coin and keep it with you all the time. When trouble strikes, hold it tightly in your hand and say, 'I won't be scared until I know I have good reason.' It's worked for me for years. My papa gave it to me when I was your age and it taught me real courage. You keep it and practice with it. I bet the next time I see you, you'll be braver than I am."

The boy accepted the coin, stared at it, and clutched it tightly. He looked up at Marsh, who had stood, and smiled. "Thanks, mister. I won't ever cry again, not with my lucky coin to protect me."

Randee watched the child's mother gaze into Marsh's eyes with a look which revealed more than gratitude. Twinges of jealousy and annoyance nipped at her as Marsh returned the smile and genially chatted with the overly friendly female. When the woman rested her hand on Marsh's arm and asked if he would please escort them to the next relay station, Randee felt as if cat's claws were going to spring out of her fingertips to protect her property from that hungry creature. That humorous thought caused Randee to smile and to relax. She had no claim on Marsh Logan, so he could behave any way he desired with the woman, whether she was a widow or somebody's wife.

Marsh called Randee over to him and remarked to everyone, "This is my partner, a real lady who knows how to handle any kind of trouble. She deserves more credit than I do. If she hadn't been with me today, I couldn't have handled all those bandits."

"I saw how you lassoed that varmint, miss. Never seen better riding and roping in my life," the driver praised her.

The woman looked Randee over, and gave the impression that she considered the blonde to be anything but a lady. She smiled falsely, but did not add her thanks to the others' gratitude. Randee glanced at the woman as if she were trivial, but smiled at the little boy.

Marsh suppressed his amusement with the two women. He told the driver, "I'll help you tie them tightly to the roof, Sam, but we can't ride that far out of our way. I'm afraid we're running very late as it is. The relay station is less than ten miles away. I think you can make it that far without more trouble."

The guard agreed, "We'll be fine, Sam. This arm's better now."

The woman earnestly implored Marsh to escort them, making subtle overtures right in front of everyone. Marsh smiled at the boy, tousled his sandy hair, and said, "Sorry ma'am, but we're on a tight schedule. The station isn't much further down the road. If there's more trouble, this fine lad will protect you. Isn't that right, son?"

The boy grinned broadly at Marsh's confidence in him, and nodded his head vigorously. His small chin was raised proudly and his little chest was stuck out bravely. But the attractive woman frowned when she did not get her way, and Randee saw how unpleasant it looked to show one's peevishness in public. Randee exchanged smiles with the little boy as Marsh secured the prisoners to the stage roof. She was aware of the woman's envious stare as the men worked above them. To help out, Randee gathered three horses and tied their reins to the back of the stage, placing her out of the woman's sight. Marsh helped the passengers into the coach and waved to them as it pulled away.

Marsh suggested, "Let's round up those other two horses and unfetter them before we get under way again. I don't want them running loose with bridles and saddles. They didn't look too well-kept. Maybe they'll join up with a wild herd and enjoy their freedom."

Randee concurred with his compassion. After the task was done, she mischievously eyed him up and down, then burst into laughter. "I wonder what those people would have said if they'd known that their champion was the notorious Durango Kid. I hope it doesn't disappoint you that not everyone recognizes such a famous man." She and Marsh grinned at each other. "Every time I turn around, you amaze me again. You were very good with that little boy. What an unexpected and surprising man you are, Marsh Logan. You can be as hard as a rock or as soft as cotton. I wonder, are you for real? Or is this only a clever act to keep me off balance?"

"Actually it's a cunning trick to win you over to my side," he teased, licking his lips seductively.

"Then you're wasting time and energy, Marsh, because I've been on your side since you knocked me down in Wadesville."

The black-clad man chuckled. "The same is true of you, Miss Hollis, one amazement after another. You were good back there, very good." He had been more than pleased with her riding, shooting, wits, courage, and assistance. "I don't have any more worries about you."

"I wish I could say the same," she replied, looking sad.

"What do you mean?" he inquired confusion.

She disclosed pointedly, "We both know you would like nothing better than to leave me behind as soon as you don't need me anymore."

Marsh edged his horse closer to hers and met her challenging gaze. His hand went behind her head and pulled it forward. Before kissing her passionately, he devoured her with his ravenous gaze and said, "Then make certain I need you all the time."

After he released her, he instantly galloped away. The shaky female stared at his back as her fingers stroked her tingling lips. She inhaled deeply to slow her racing heart, then took off after him.

Around five, they halted to rest and water the horses at a spot where a seep was located near a pile of large rocks. Randee strolled around while Marsh leaned against a heavy boulder and watched her. She felt his gaze locked on her, but pretended not to notice it or him. After a time, she turned and said, "You must travel a lot to know this state so well. Do you ever get tired of moving around all the time?"

"I haven't yet," he replied, dreading this line of talk.

She tried another question to draw him out, "Do you ever get tired of being provoked into gunfights? Tired of killing men who only want to prove they're faster and better than the Durango Kid?"

Taking his eyes from her for the first time since they halted, Marsh removed his hat and tossed it on a nearby rock. He rubbed his sleeved arm over his forehead to remove the sweat that was beading there. He hated to deceive her, but he was only pretending to be the noted gunslinger. Like it or not, for now, he had to continue that ruse in case she was captured and questioned by anyone. He met her direct gaze and answered as honestly as possible, for himself, and the real Durango Kid, "I've never killed any man who didn't deserve to die more than I did. A man in my position can't turn his back on a challenge and walk away without being called a coward or getting shot in the back. Neither one appeals to me, Miss Hollis. Believe it or not, I don't go looking for gunfights, but I don't run from them either. I earned this stupid reputation by defending myself, not by searching for trouble and excitement. I guess trouble has a sneaky way of finding me and shoving me into a corner." He looked at her and hinted, "Surely you realize that most colorful legends are half fiction."

Randee detected the hesitation in Marsh's gaze, voice, and reply. She felt that he was responding in the manner which he presumed she expected, and she found that intriguing. "Fiction or not, it can get you killed one day. How long can a gunslinger of your status hope to win every challenge? Tell me, Marsh, when the senses and skills dull, what happens to men like you?"

He stared her in the eye and answered too casually, "We usually wind up as a notch on somebody else's gun."

"Knowing that doesn't bother you?" she probed worriedly.

"It hasn't yet," he replied, trying to sound nonchalant.

"Does the constant threat of death make your life more exciting?"

Marsh chuckled in an attempt to relax her. "It certainly

184

gets the blood to rushing and the body to moving. Yes, Randee, I guess it does," he admitted. "Doesn't danger have the same effect on you?"

"Danger, yes, but terror and death, no," she told him.

"But aren't they one and the same?" he reasoned. "People face death every day, in every challenge, in every peril, in every breath. Think about those stage passengers. They could have been killed if we hadn't of happened along at the right moment. You could have caught a deadly cold today from a chill, by washing your hair. At any time you could get thrown or trampled by your horse. We could bump into the Epson Gang any day and provoke them into killing us. You could have been shot in that bank holdup. Or killed . . . during a stage robbery on your way to Red River. There could be a rattler ready to strike you from beneath that rock. Death surrounds us every moment, woman. That's why I live from one minute to the next."

"Are you ever afraid of anything?" she asked.

"I try not to be. And if I am, I try not to show it," he admitted.

Randee murmured reflectively, "I would be terrified if I could be gunned down at any moment. Why aren't you?"

Marsh shrugged. "Terror keeps one on alert, Miss Hollis, and being alert keeps one alive. You don't think it's exciting to face stimulating challenges each day?"

"I don't find terror or continuous fear exciting or stimulating, especially when there's nothing you can do to conquer it and it feeds on you every day and night like a ravenous vulture. If fear is only a temporary condition, you have hope and you know it'll be over soon. But if there's no end or relief in sight, that's terror. Surely an outlaw experiences terror each day. He's always running scared of the law. He can't ever let his guard down and relax fully. The terror of capture and hanging is with him every moment. Is that exciting? I think not, Marsh. Surely it's much the same with a famous gunslinger. Any day you could get pushed over that skinny mark which separates the law and crime; then you'd be running for your life instead of drifting by choice. Would your life still be exciting and stimulating?"

"Like I said, Randee, I live for today. At least that's true for now. This is me, woman. I'm not ready or willing to change, so I'll have to take my risks. Just like you, I have problems to solve."

Randee couldn't ask him to explain, not after telling him to keep his nose out of her private affairs. "Sometimes the only way to fight a problem is to retreat. Don't you ever back away from a battle or opponent? Have you never felt that the other man was stronger and that you had lived your last day?"

"I guess I've always felt it was better to die than to feel helpless. Nothing sticks in a man's craw worse than being a coward. And nothing is more unforgivable than forcing a man to look like one."

"Sometimes there's no way around being or feeling helpless, but that doesn't make you a coward. Maybe you don't think much about your survival and future because you have only yourself to consider."

"That's why I stay alone, so I won't have any worries to slow me down or control my actions. I don't want to be responsible for another person's life. Considering the fact that my parents are dead because their son was off living his own life, should tell you I'm not good at protecting anyone but myself."

"That sounds awfully pessimistic to me, Marsh."

He politely refuted, "I'm only being realistic, Miss Hollis. A pessimist is always gloomy, and thinking the worst of everything and everybody. I'm not like that, am I?"

She reluctantly told him, "I must admit, you appear totally satisfied with yourself and your hazardous lifestyle."

"Do I hear a bit of resentment in your tone?" he teased.

"It's more like envy, Mr. Logan. Or should I say, Durango?"

"I guess it's according to which man and life you envy."

Randee sighed heavily, then asked, "Aren't you both the same?"

"Every person has many sides, Randee, including you. If you had a choice, which man would you prefer as your partner? Be honest."

Without hesitating, she disclosed, "Marsh Logan."

He looked surprised. "Why?" he asked, highly intrigued.

"Because he'll stay alive longer than the Durango Kid, and I need my partner around for a long time."

Marsh studied her for a while and felt her pull on him. He could tell that she was as tense as he was, but she never broke their interlocked gaze. He smiled almost sadly and revealed, "Would you be shocked if I told you I wish I were only Marsh Logan again? That isn't possible, Randee, and never will be. Too much has happened since I left home."

Randee nodded and replied, "I know what you mean, Marsh." She stretched and yawned as if very tired. "We should get moving, or we won't make that wonderful campsite you mentioned earlier. Oh, yes," she added, "None of those bandits were gang members."

"Are you certain?" he asked, dropping the other subject as she had.

"I'm more than positive they weren't at the Carson Ranch. I thought of something else this afternoon. Do you think those squatters on Bill Sharp's ranch were gang members in disguise? That would be a perfect way to hang around until everyone arrived for the attack."

"I'm lost." He confessed ignorance of her meaning.

"The day before I left Wadesville, Brody was called to the Sharp's Ranch to handle trouble with squatters. That next morning, the Epson Gang attacked there. Could it be coincidental?"

"Probably, but it wouldn't hurt to start checking for a pattern there. I'll mark it on our list of clues. Randee," he started hesitantly, "I want you to know you have nothing to fear from the Durango Kid."

"I know, Marsh, thanks. Will you promise me one thing?"

He laughed. "Another promise?" he jested, winking at her.

Undaunted, she pressed, "Promise me you'll remain Marsh Logan as much as possible on this journey."

"If you knew what he was like, you might not ask that."

"Do it anyway," she entreated.

"For a long time I tried to be anybody except Marsh Logan; now you seem to like him better than who I am today. That worries me."

"It shouldn't, because you're more Marsh Logan than you realize. Your father would be very proud of you and what you're doing."

"Would he, Randee?" Marsh asked a little sarcastically. If he had been home where he belonged, his parents would be alive today! And he would have been home if his father hadn't driven him away! Marsh could still recall the anguish, rebelliousness, disappointment, and resentment which had filled him years ago. Thank God, he had learned the truth two years past about his father's treachery in '56, even though the old man had died believing his son still hated and disrespected him, died believing Marsh was "a bad apple." Maybe that was why he hated apples and could hardly get them down, because they symbolized what his parents died believing about him.

As if knowing what the man was thinking and agonizing over, Randee said, "You're wrong, Marsh. You would be dead, too, if you'd been home that day. Don't let the past rip you apart and force you into death's eager embrace. You're too good to die, and it isn't too late to change your life. You aren't the heartless and selfish person you claim to be, Marsh Logan, so stop trying to convince me you are. If you're afraid that by being yourself you'll provoke me into chasing after you, I promise you have nothing to worry about where I'm concerned." She mounted up and rode off before he could argue or agree.

They traveled until darkness had almost encompassed them. Marsh showed her where to camp, then unloaded their possessions and rode off to check out the security of the area. Randee prepared the fire and started their evening meal. When Marsh returned, he tended his black stallion, then went for a soothing swim in the river nearby.

After joining her, he inhaled deeply and said, "That smells good."

"Only because you didn't have to cook it," she teased. "I might as well confess that I'm not very good in the kitchen, if you haven't noticed already. My mother preferred to do the cooking, so I have little training in that area. Be patient and a good teacher, and I promise to learn more. Did you see anything suspicious out there?"

"No one around for miles, partner, so you can have your coveted bath. I swear, not one peek," he teased huskily. Mercy, how she made him more nervous every hour they spent together. He was afraid of getting her injured and slain. He was afraid of resisting her, but more afraid of yielding to her pull. She wasn't a woman merely to enjoy physically; she was a woman who became a vital part of you, like eating and breathing. If he allowed her to get to him, then what would happen to both of them when they parted? It would be selfish to only live for today where she was concerned. Not knowing her past, he feared saying or doing the wrong thing. If her trouble was over another man, that could determine if and how she responded to him. If he pressed and she wasn't ready . . .

Randee interrupted his line of thought, "If I didn't trust you, Marsh Logan, I wouldn't be here tonight."

He jested mirthfully, "Do you think that's wise, Miss Hollis? You are the most tempting creature I've met to date. The only reasons I've kept my self-control are thoughts of losing my hand and that reward. I didn't scare you this afternoon with my impulsive conduct, did I?"

"You, impulsive?" she taunted with a skeptical grin.

"Not in the past, but I find it happening frequently around you."

"Is that good or bad?" she questioned, her heart pounding.

"Considering the danger we're facing every day, probably bad."

"Frankly, Mr. Logan, I think you're right."

"I was afraid you'd agree with my stupidity."

They both laughed. She passed him his plate and said, "If it's too bad, maybe you'll cook every day from now on."

"No way, woman. If you're messing up on purpose to avoid your share of the chores, you'll be sorry."

"Isn't that what you men usually do to get out of them?"

"Mercy, what kind of monster have I linked up with?" he teased.

"Challenge me, Durango, and you'll find out."

"Will I like what I unearth, my golden treasure?"

Randee's smile faded, as did her joyous mood. "Will you please not use that phrase again? Nothing golden, all right?"

"It's easier to fight a battle when you understand it, Randee. Since you can't tell me about it yet, just tell me when I make a wrong step. Agreed?" As she nodded, Marsh saw unshed tears glistening in her green eyes as she mutely thanked him for his kindness. He smiled and said, "Somewhere along the trail you've had a rough time, Randee. I'm sorry I wasn't there to help you."

"So am I," she confessed honestly, hoarsely. "Maybe you will be next time, because I don't think my past is dead yet. Please, no jokes or compliments about golden treasures and promises, or golden hair and skin." She licked her dry lips and revealed slowly, "Just so you can be prepared in case that Kansas trouble does locate me here, I'll tell you all about it soon. I didn't exactly lie to you about being pursued, because I honestly don't believe I can be traced here — not after the false trail I left behind. Just so you won't worry, I'm not running from the law and I didn't steal that ten thousand dollars. My uncle hid it in the attic with me before the raid. Since it was his money, I thought it should pay for bringing his killers to justice. Please don't ask any questions, because that's all I can tell you tonight." She set her plate aside and excused herself to take a bath.

Marsh retrieved the whiskey from his saddlebag and took a deep drink from the bottle. He realized this was either going to be a very long and painful night, or a very short and blissful one. . . .

Chapter Nine

It was neither kind of night for Marsh. He was more fatigued than he realized, and the whiskey had relaxed him more than he had intended, causing him to fall into a deep sleep before Randee returned to camp.

Noticing the slumbering man, Randee moved quietly to avoid disturbing him. She knew he had to be very tired after their long journey and his continual guard, which required light sleep. He looked so peaceful — and vulnerable — lying there. She was glad he could relax so fully for a change, as it had to be extremely demanding to remain on full alert around the clock. Since no one was in the area and it was late, they shouldn't be in any peril tonight, a fact of which he must be aware. She was careful not to make any noise as she put away her belongings and climbed into her sleeping roll.

Randee decided that she made Marsh just as nervous as he made her, and that experience probably was new and difficult for him. He was not a man who wanted to be vulnerable to anything or anyone, as his survival could depend on being hardhearted and clear-headed. Carefree loners like him often believed that strong emotions — those which were distracting, demanding, and consuming — usually made a man feel defensive and anxious, made him reluctant to surrender any part of himself to another person for fear of losing some special edge which he possessed over others. Perhaps he was also concerned about what he had witnessed between her and Sheriff Wade. Perhaps he worried that she might, or could, fool him as easily and insensitively as she had deceived Brody. Somehow she needed to let him discover that she viewed the two men differently, that she would not dupe him romantically or in any other way. Soon, she would reveal everything about herself and this task, and he would realize she could be trusted implicitly. He would realize he could be himself around her, that he could tell her anything, that he could depend on her fully, that he could finally lean on someone for understanding and comfort and help. Yes, she decided wishfully, she had to prove that she could be all things to him: friend, partner, companion, confidante, and . . . yes, his lover.

The more she was around Marsh Logan, the more she wanted to get to know him better and the more she liked him. No, her mind refuted, the more they were together, the more she came to love and desire him. Perhaps that was what made Marsh different from the other men she had met and known: She liked him and she loved him. It was possible to feel either emotion without the other; but when both were felt for the same person, it was rare and wonderful. Perhaps that was the secret to real love, lasting love, powerful love: truly liking and respecting the person you loved. And, despite his lifestyle and reputation, she respected him and admired him, as he had enjoyed his stimulating existence without going afoul of the law.

Hopefully Marsh would come to feel the same way about her before this mission ended one way or another. If she had him pinpointed correctly, he was the perfect man for her, and she couldn't imagine being so wrong about him after all the time they had spent together. All she had to do was convince him she was perfect for him and persuade him to give up his deadly lifestyle. If only he would let down his guard so she could sneak past that loner-fence which surrounded him. As she drifted off to sleep, she was envisioning them together on his land, building a wonderful life as newlyweds. . . .

At dawn the next morning, the Epson Gang made another vicious raid above Fort Worth.

As they traveled that day, Marsh kept thinking about what Randee had hinted at the night before. As much as he wanted to have her explanation, he dreaded it, because he assumed she would want him to open up to her after she did so with him. As long as he could keep quiet, he wouldn't have to lie to her again, verbally that is. For some strange reason, he found being deceitful with this woman as vexing as it had been with his parents. Maybe it was because she was as special to him as they were, and that probably explained why he was becoming more apprehensive around her. Since she was getting to him, he warned himself to watch his step with her. At least one thing was clear to him now; her problem was personal, not criminal. He was surprised at how deeply he had slept last night, and was more amazed that her stirrings hadn't aroused him. Either he had been awfully tired or she was becoming good at stealth.

They halted at midday to eat and rest. Marsh pointed to tracks nearby and asked, "What can you tell me about them?"

Randee studied them for a moment, then replied, "Two riders passed this way during or right after a heavy rain. I can tell that because of the number of hoof prints, and the ground had to be mushy when they were made, because they're deep and unclear. The dirt around them has dried and hardened enough to crumble into the tracks, and the grass isn't newly damaged. I would guess about a month."

Marsh grinned in pleasure. "I would guess the same thing. What else have you learned?"

"I guessed two riders because the prints are about the same depth. I don't think a supply horse would weigh that much. They were heading northwest, possibly to Santa Fe."

"Excellent, partner. Looks as if I'll have to keep you around."

Randee smiled and thanked him. She withdrew a ribbon from her stuffed saddlebag and secured her hair behind her nape. The day was getting warmer and she wanted to stay as cool as possible. As Brody had intended, the blue ribbon reminded her of him. Yet, she hastily dismissed him from mind, to deal with him much later.

They rode until late afternoon and halted again. Marsh suggested a longer rest break for the horses this time, because the day was hot and humid, a condition which tired the animals more quickly than usual. His shirt and hat were sweaty, so he removed them and hung them over his saddle horn to dry. Unrolling his sleeping bag, he stretched out on it.

Randee tossed a blanket on the ground and took a seat. She noticed the way the sun seemingly caressed his bronzed flesh and caused his ebony hair to shine. She watched beads of sweat glisten on the furry mat on that hard chest, and her eyes roamed over his flat stomach and powerful shoulders. She wanted to press her lips to every spot that shone in the sun's glare. She imagined how hot and smooth each area was and how sensuous it would be to carry out her thought. There was very little breeze to ruffle his hair, but it was mussed from his hat and damp with perspiration. Her gaze drifted over his

195

strong features and darkened jawline. He was so entrancing she could have stared at him for hours without ceasing. His eyes were closed; yet, he was frowning slightly as if the brilliant sun was penetrating his lids. She wondered what he was thinking and feeling at this very moment. Who, she pondered, was Marsh Logan and what haunted him from his past? She yearned to know anything and everything about him.

Her green eyes wandered past his slim hips and long legs, which were crossed at the ankles. His faded jeans fit him snugly, but not indecently. She eyed the metal buttons and brazenly wondered how it would feel to unfasten each one and to slip off his . . . Randee squirmed on her seat and glanced away from the tempting sight which had her mind and body traveling rapidly in a dangerous direction.

Marsh lifted his shoulders, propped himself up on his left elbow, and shaded his eyes with his right forearm. "Is something wrong?" he asked.

Randee's gaze returned to him. The sun was slightly to his left, causing provocative shadows to dance over his masculine frame and to darken his face. She saw how the muscles rippled over his abdomen from his position, and how those in his left arm bulged from the pressure of his weight on it. Both fists were lightly balled, and moisture gleamed on his tanned arms and face. His azure eyes were squinted as much from curiosity as from the bright sunlight. She should have known he would sense her bold scrutiny! She inhaled deeply and exhaled, its sound ragged in the silence which surrounded them. "The humidity is terrible today," she remarked to stall for recovery time. "It makes you feel as if you have a rock on your chest. I'm almost drenched."

Marsh looked her over snailishly. Perspiration was glistening on her face, and her cheeks were flushed. Despite wearing the hat he had purchased for her, Randee's nose was very pink today. He was mildly surprised that someone so tanned could sunburn so easily. He wondered what shade the rest of her body was, and knew he would learn that secret one day. It was inevitable; his gut instinct told him so, just as it told him what was disturbing Randee this afternoon.

With her hair pulled back and secured loosely, the soft and enchanting angle of her jawline was most noticeable. He wanted to trail his quivering fingers over her satiny flesh and becoming features, and he must do so soon or go crazy with longing. His gaze roamed the damp fringe of tawny hair across her forehead. He had the urge to blow on it, to make her bangs dance and to cool her face. The color of her eyes reminded him of new grass and leaves in the spring, and he was aroused by the way they were resting on him. Her lips were made for kissing endlessly and he craved to taste them again, even if it did inspire his head to spin more wildly than drinking a full canteen of Indian mescal. That one kiss had been much too brief, and he hadn't held her in his arms. Mercy, she was a breathtaking creature, the only one whom he'd ever had trouble resisting. He wanted to pull her down beside him and make rapturous love to her beneath the blazing sun. Yep, this woman made his unleashed passions race wild and free like an unbroken stallion. He cautioned himself to clear his head of such wanton thoughts, or his tight jeans would reveal his urgent desire!

Marsh finally spoke, "We'll make camp in another abandoned fort tonight. There's a lake nearby, so you can take a nice, long swim if nobody's around. I can use one myself," he remarked, mopping sweat from his brow and above his upper lip. "If we're lucky, it'll rain soon and cool things off a bit."

She sighed dreamily and stretched to loosen stiff muscles. "Both rain and a swim would be wonderful. I can hardly wait. This humidity is oppressive. I feel as if my hair and clothes are sticking to me like old syrup."

He chuckled as she stood up and strolled around. "Makes you kind of restless and miserable, huh?"

She glanced down at him and remarked, "You must be uncomfortable too, or you wouldn't have your shirt and hat off."

"I'm so used to being alone that I do things without thinking. I'm afraid I have little or no modesty, Miss Hollis, but I hope you don't mind me making myself comfortable for a spell," he teased.

"Why should I? You never complain or object when I get comfy around camp. Just don't let that hot sun cook you to misery."

"If it did, would you take pity on me and doctor me?"

Merry laughter came forth from Randee as her expressive eyes glowed with mischief. In a playfully sultry tone, she responded, "I would be delighted to have you at my mercy, Mr. Logan. Why, these little ole hands are itching to get at you, to see what you're made of. I doubt men like you even know the meaning of pain. And even if it found you, you'd suffer in silence, wouldn't you?"

"I'm afraid you overestimate my strength and courage, Miss Hollis, but thanks for the confidence in me. Frankly, I hope I never have to prove to you what I'm made of; you might be disappointed."

"In view of your immense reputation, Durango, I find that malarky impossible to swallow. Have you ever been wounded?"

"A nick here and there, but nothing serious. What about you?"

"Not yet, and I hope that's one experience I never have. What will we do when we catch up with that gang?" she inquired.

"Try to trim it down a few at a time without arousing their suspicions. We'll pick up dynamite in Brownwood next week."

"Do you think it's safe to let people see us together?"

"Won't matter much. News is probably out about us already."

"I was referring to the Durango Kid showing his handsome face in a town where he could get challenged and slowed down."

"Contrary to popular opinion, woman, I'm not recognized everywhere. Fact is, I doubt anyone there will know who I am." He skirted her question with an honest response.

She argued softly, "You're the one who underestimates yourself, Marsh. I've only been in Texas for three months and I know who the Durango Kid is: a handsome, blue-eyed, black-haired rogue who rides a black stallion and dresses in black and who's matchless with guns and prowess. Surely the locals are even more familiar than I am with a colorful legend like you. Actually I'm surprised we've gotten this far without trouble. I would think countless men are dogging you this very minute, hungry to consume you and increase their weight."

"Then, don't you think it's a mite foolish of you to be tagging along with such a dangerous man?" he speculated mirthfully.

She shook her head. "I can't imagine any place safer than being with you. I said, plenty of men are probably after you, but I doubt all of them put together could defeat you. You see, Durango, I've heard most of the tales about you, so I know I'm not in peril being with you."

"Are you sure about that, Randee?" he inquired huskily.

"Why shouldn't I be?" she cleverly parried. "From what I've heard and read, nobody can be trusted to keep his word more than the Durango Kid. And few men dare challenge him anymore. Is it boring to have people too scared to compete with you, to give you that rush of excitement when danger and death are sitting on your shoulder?"

"There's nothing boring about peace and safety," he replied too quickly, leaving himself open to Randee's next remark.

"Then you don't mind not killing and fighting all the time, and you're willing to start fresh after this job. Good."

"Why is that good?" he asked, his curiosity piqued.

"Because I don't like to think of Marsh Logan entangled in such a deathly web. If you don't enjoy the existence of a notorious gunslinger, then you don't mind giving it up for survival, which is what I want for you, Marsh. Whether you realize it or not, or even admit it, you're a good man, a very special one, and I wouldn't want to see you slain in some senseless gun battle over who's the fastest draw. This isn't a simple game or competition; the rules are harsh and defeat means death or maiming." She urged him gravely, "Back away, Marsh, before you get in too deeply. Please, after this is over, go home and rebuild your ranch. You won't be sorry. If you need money to start life anew, I'll try to arrange a private loan between us, and you do have that ten thousand dollars coming to you for this job. Don't waste it living as Durango. Let Marsh Logan use it for his survival and happiness."

Marsh's heart was beating swiftly at her show of concern and generosity. He had to think and speak like the real Durango Kid. Now he grasped why the Kid lived and felt as he did, because there wasn't a Randee Hollis in his life! How could any man not respond to this unique female? In many ways, she was part woman, part child. She was wise, yet a trusting innocent. She was inexperienced, yet a potent seductress. She was a daring

200

vixen, yet a gentle angel. She was reserved, yet open and direct. How could any man not be tempted to make compromises, changes, where she was concerned? If he were the real Durango, she was offering him a tempting path of escape from a perilous existence! And for a reason that touched him deeply. "I'm a gunfighter, a drifter, a gambler, a scout, and a rogue. I'm not a rancher or a farmer, Randee. I come and go when and where I please. What about being bored into old age?" he had to counter.

Undaunted, she reasoned, "If you get the ranch going again and hire a good foreman, then you can still come and go as you please. But you'll have a home, Marsh, a safe place to rest, a place to relax your guard when you need to. And everybody needs to on occasion."

Speaking for himself this time, Marsh asked pointedly, "What happens when my old enemies come to call at my ranch? A man in my position earns plenty of foes, men with long memories, men who'll stop at nothing for revenge. You think I want to see my home burned and my family killed twice? A little peace isn't worth it, Randee."

Believing Marsh to be the real Durango Kid—a famed gunslinger who had managed to remain just inside the law—sadly, Randee could see his point about being unable to settle down peacefully and safely. He had taken a path which was once stimulating to his male ego, a path which now prevented him from enjoying the life of a normal man. Since a legend remained a challenge as long as he lived, the Durango Kid would be compelled to watch his backside forever, and that reality pained her deeply. It meant he would never endanger those he loved. . . .

Randee knew it wasn't wise or kind to pressure this man about seeking a life which he believed was out of reach. When—not if—the time came when Marsh wanted a new life, he would take any risk to obtain it. All he needed was something, or someone, to make those risks worth taking. She had observed his expressions and mood; he wasn't a lost cause, even if he thought he was. She couldn't tell him he was wrong about being unable to change, because maybe he wasn't. No one could know more about the life of a gunslinger than the man who was one. If she persuaded him to retire and others made it impossible, she could get him killed. "For now, I agree with you, Marsh; it's too dangerous for you to drop the strength of the Durango Kid. But rest assured that I'll guard your back for as long as we're together."

Marsh felt that he could truly depend on this woman; he could trust her, lean on her, listen to her, and even follow her. Yet, it wasn't smart to reveal such things to her any time soon. "I know, Randee, and I'm grateful. You're the only partner I've had, so that should tell you how much confidence I have in you."

The green-eyed blonde smiled and said, "It feels good to trust another person so much, doesn't it? We are friends, aren't we, Marsh?"

"Yes, Randee, we are, and we'll always be good friends."

"I'm glad, because you're the only one I have right now."

Wisely, Marsh bit his tongue before reminding her about Brody Wade. He knew she was being sincere, and he liked that motive. He smiled and said, "It's time to move on, partner. Get saddled up."

"Yes sir, Mr. Logan, right away," she responded laughingly.

Randee was awed by the lively appeal of the land. Countless varieties of wildflowers crowded meadows or grew in every spot they could take root: Indian paint-

202

brush, goldenrod, groundsel, milfoil, green milkweed, bluebonnets, verbena, and many more. The contrast of colors and shapes was breathtaking. In many areas, the floral covering was so thick it looked as if someone had spread exquisite blankets over the ground. Prairie grass was abundant in this area, as were deer and antelope, which were feeding on it. Her eyes were dry from staring all around her. The hot sun was lowering itself toward the horizon, but there were enough trees to provoke shade, especially with their new growths of verdant leaves. The landscape had a wild beauty to it, mostly free of man's damaging intrusion. She understood why everyone — Indian and white — who saw this land craved it.

As they neared the fort ruins, she spotted prickly pear cactus, evening primrose, and Spanish daggers surrounding the ghostly site. Marsh told her that Fort Phantom Hill had not survived the harsh duty and numerous desertions which were inspired by monotony and loneliness. After enduring many hardships and perils following its construction in 1851 to protect this area from marauding Indians, the post was closed four years later. Shortly after the Army pulled out, the fort burned, except for rocky foundations, tall chimneys, and three stone structures: the guardhouse, powder magazine, and commissary. Marsh also told her there were several lakes in the area, including one large one south of the post, along with the Brazos River.

Randee glanced around, imagining the number and kinds of creatures which must be inhabiting those abandoned buildings. For certain, she would be more than satisfied to sleep outside tonight! She looked in each direction and saw nothing to indicate anyone was around within miles. They seemed so far from civilization, almost as if they were alone in the world. The sun was nearly set, casting golden shadows about them. A pleasant breeze stirred the leaves, grasses, and flowers, and cooled her warm body. The fragrant blending of floral scents brought a smile to her lips. She was tired, but not exhausted. A curious feeling of tranquility washed over her gently, causing her to forget their reason for coming to this area. She felt so safe and happy with Marsh, so totally at ease, so responsive to him.

"Looks as if nobody's been here for months," Marsh concluded aloud. "This is another place we can mark off our list of possible hide-outs and meeting points. We'll head for Brownwood tomorrow. If there's only four or five stops along the way, we'll reach town sometime Tuesday. We'll take a nice rest in a comfortable hotel, and pick up new supplies and dynamite there."

Randee added quickly, "And have our washing done. Else, these clothes will soon be dirty beyond redemption."

"I can tell you're a woman used to daily baths and fresh clothes," he teased as they unsaddled their horses, allowing the chestnut mare and black stallion to graze and drink nearby. "We'll have time to get our washing done and enjoy a little extra rest. Just make sure you don't get spoiled before we hit the trail again."

She responded merrily, "Don't worry about me, partner. The blood of a newborn adventuress is flowing through me, thanks to you. I like being a drifter for a change; it's nice to see so many things and places. It's so peaceful and beautiful way out here."

Marsh gathered scrubwood for their campfire while Randee took out the supplies for their evening meal. They had gotten used to working together on the chores, so few questions were asked as they carried them out this evening. Soon, they were sitting on either side of a colorful blaze and eating their meal. When they finished, they worked together to wash the dishes and to put away their supplies.

Marsh shaved the dark stubble from his face as Randee watched. When he finished, she remarked, "You don't use a mirror, but you never cut yourself. That amazes me. You must have a real steady hand."

He tossed the black-dotted water aside and rinsed out the metal bowl. "In my job, it pays to have one, Miss Hollis, but it comes from practice. You want more wood on the fire?" he asked as he gathered his belongings, obviously planning not to sleep nearby.

Randee looked at the dying blaze and replied, "No thanks. I don't think it'll be chilly tonight. If so, I'll snuggle in my bedroll."

"I'm going to bunk down on the other side of that wall," he told her, pointing to the half-finished stone corral behind the last remaining structure. "Why don't I close my eyes and you try to sneak up on me? I'll call out when I'm ready, and when I first hear you."

"Practice my nocturnal skills? Sounds like fun."

"This is work, woman, and it might save our necks one night."

Marsh walked behind the four-foot-high wall and spread out his sleeping roll, whistling as he worked. He removed his gunbelt, hat, and boots, and laid them aside. Unbuttoning his shirt nearly to his waist, he stretched out on his makeshift bed and grinned roguishly. He called out, "Ready any time you are."

Randee draped her agile body over the stone corral and asked, "Is this stealthy enough for you, partner?"

Marsh stood and playfully chided, "You cheated; I wasn't ready."

"Hopefully those bandits won't be ready either," she jested.

"Any time tonight that you want to try it again, do so. The more practice you get, the better for both of us."

"See you in the morning, or before," Randee hinted merrily. She returned to her campsite and put out the fire, as she didn't want him to see her coming the next time. She called out, "Stay put, Logan. I'm going to bathe and change." She smiled when she heard him promise not to move an inch. After gathering her saddlebags, she walked to the water to freshen up and to change into her nightgown.

When she was back in her place, she informed him, "All done."

"Good night, Randee," the mellow words came from the darkness.

"Good night, Marsh," she murmured almost too softly to be heard.

Randee wondered how long she should wait before trying to sneak up on him again. Would he be expecting another attempt so soon? Would he lie awake for an hour or two, anticipating her defeat? Would she . . . She heard a noise behind her, grabbed her pistol, and whirled to check out her peril.

Marsh was squatting nearby, grinning broadly as he waved the stick which he had just broken to catch her attention. "That was fast, woman, but too late to defend yourself," he teased.

"I wasn't expecting you to test me tonight. I thought I was the one doing the training," she said, explaining her lapse.

Marsh came nearer as he informed her, "This is part of your training, being on guard for a surprise attack."

"You're right," she admitted, "And I failed this time."

"Don't get discouraged, partner; it takes time and practice."

"What happens if we don't have enough time and practice?" she asked worriedly. "I don't want to get us killed, Marsh."

"You won't, Randee. Take my word for it."

Randee replaced her pistol and sighed heavily. Floral scents filled the night air and stars twinkled overhead.

206

She did not flinch when Marsh reached over and removed the ribbon from her hair. It felt good when he spread the tawny mane around her shoulders.

Marsh eyed the ravishing creature, and desire consumed him. He wanted her badly, but he didn't know if he should make a move on her. To tempt them like this was crazy, perhaps unfair to her.

Randee knew this was the man she had been looking and waiting for, the man with whom she wanted to share herself. She sensed his desire and hesitation. His quivering hand stroked her cheek and he gazed longingly, undecidedly, into her eyes. His touch was so gentle for a strong man, and his mood spoke so loudly for a quiet one. She yearned to yield to this force which was stronger than she was. It was foolish to fight their attraction, and it wasn't wicked to surrender. She could never win a battle of resistance, so wasn't it wiser to give in to such a powerful passion? She hesitated no longer. She knew this was who and what she wanted, needed, if only for a while.

Randee eased to her knees before him. Her hands grasped his face and drew it to hers, boldly and bravely sealing their lips. Marsh's arms encircled her trembling body and pressed it tightly against his hard one. His mouth seared hers, revealing the extent of his matching desire. His lips traveled her face, pressing kisses to every inch. His respiration was ragged, as was hers. Their mouths fused again, swiftly, urgently, hungrily. As his hands wandered up into her thick hair, her head drifted backward to allow his lips to roam her neck. Her hands slipped down his chest, beneath his arms, and around his back.

Almost breathlessly, Marsh separated them and warned, "I'm a man without a home and a future, Randee. I'm a loner and a drifter. I don't want to mislead you. I can't make you any promises tonight just to entice you into surrendering, much as I want you like crazy."

Randee's gaze met his. He could cleanse her of her dirty past. His touch could erase that of Payton Slade. Her willing surrender could remove the guilt and shame of her helplessness with her stepfather's lewd demands. Yet, that wasn't why she wanted and needed him. She loved him and desired him above all other men. She told him hoarsely, "Here and now are all that matter. No promises, Marsh, from you or from me. We need and desire each other, so that's all that counts tonight, nothing more."

Marsh knew that Randee wasn't playing hard or easy to get. She was just being honest with herself and with him. He liked that. She knew what she wanted — him — and she wasn't afraid to follow her desires. She wanted to do things, enjoy life, and do so with him. "What about Brody Wade?" he had to ask.

"I don't love him, Marsh, or want to marry him. We're just friends. I know he loves me and I hate to break his heart, but I have no choice. I feel bad about leading him on before I left town, but you said it was necessary and I believed you. I'll tell him the truth when I see him again. If I'm lucky, he won't want me after he learns I've been spending weeks alone with the Durango Kid."

"You sure you want to discourage him? He's a respected man, one who'll settle down and make you a good husband and home."

Randee knew what he was doing, being kind and defensive and protective, so she wasn't angry with him. This thing was meant to be between them, and she must open his eyes to it. "Brody's a good man, Marsh, but he isn't for me, and I know you don't believe he is. I have a ranch and the money to rebuild it. I'm strong, smart, and brave. I don't need a husband to take care of me. After I get things going at home, I can leave my foreman in charge and sneak off every so often with you to enjoy adventures. That way, I can have both lives: respectable lady rancher and carefree vixen. I'll pay you well for guiding me around and for letting me join you for a little fun and excitement. I swear, Marsh, I won't be a clinging vine. I'll return home whenever you say so. Don't you see?" she tempted, not caring if she were being forward, "It's a great deal for you — money, fun, and the company of a sensuous woman whenever the mood strikes you. That is, after you train me to be a partner in all ways."

"That isn't fair to you, woman. I would gain far more than you."

"Not really, Marsh. With you, I can be myself, and I need that every so often. I know we can't become a couple, and that isn't what I'm suggesting. But what's wrong with sharing good times together? I'll tell you what; don't answer yet. Get to know me and you'll see that you can trust me to keep my word. No demands, no promises, no commitments, no complaints, and no chasing after you. Just two close friends who need and want each other on occasion."

"Your offer isn't tempting, Randee; it's outright irresistible, just like you are," he murmured huskily, then kissed her tenderly.

Slowly, Marsh and Randee sank to her sleeping roll, embracing, kissing, and caressing. Passions wild and free took control of them and carried them over sensous territory which hadn't been explored before tonight. Soon, they were undressed and lying flesh to flesh beneath a full moon and blinking stars.

Marsh was very gentle with her, although his leisurely pace was hard to control. He craved her desperately, but held a tight rein on his desire to make her his completely. His deft fingers trailed enticingly over her soft skin, aware of its intense heat from burning desire. His lips did the same, lighting here and there like a busy butterfly who wanted to taste every floral spot within his reach. He kissed the hollows of her throat and felt her pulse racing madly beneath his tongue. His lips roamed to her left breast and his warm tongue circled its brown center before his mouth gently conquered the taut peak. He felt Randee arch toward him and inhale deeply as he stimulated the protruding bud. Not once did she try to halt his actions or protest them; she was fully committed to this exploration of pleasure with him.

Randee was caught up in a wonderful spiral, which was lifting her skyward with blissful sensations, lifting her to race ecstatically among the stars and moon. Her senses were alive with need, alive with rapture, alive with torment, alive with Marsh Logan. Her hands wandered over the smooth, hard muscles of his back. She felt them ripple seductively with his experienced movements. She loved the feel of them beneath her hands. She loved the contact of their flesh, flesh which was clinging together, flesh which was aflame with passion.

Marsh's talented fingers teased over her pelt-soft skin, exciting each area that he stroked. He was enthralled by the way she was responding to him, and his body intensified its sensuous siege on hers. He caressed her tenderly, urgently, skillfully. He wanted to tantalize her for hours, giving her pleasure while pressing her to greater need. His loins pleaded for relief, as he had not taken a woman in quite a while. His mind had been on other matters and he hadn't seen one lately who tempted him to steal time from his busy and solitary schedule.

Marsh's fingers explored her shapely figure, slowly making their way downward to a region where none had entered before. The fuzzy forest that guarded her virginal domain was incredibly soft and was shaded a little darker than her long blond mane. Ever so gently and carefully, he roamed the newly discovered territory. It was not an invasion or intrusion, as she shifted to welcome his arrival. Her brave invitation intoxicated him more potently than any whiskey he had tasted. His senses were spinning with a greater hunger for her, one he had to feed soon or pass out from starvation for her.

Randee's eyes were closed as her wits swirled about dizzily in a whirlwind of yearning. Marsh Logan was what a man should be, although he was different from all others. She craved to have him in her life forever. He made her feel so alive, so whole again, so strong and brave, as if anything were possible. He was kind, good, tender, unique; he just needed something, someone, to give him direction, to give his life new meaning. She wanted that someone to be her.

When he thrust within her, there was only a brief instant of discomfort. She felt him hesitate a few minutes as she adjusted to his presence and to the vanquishing of her virginal barrier. Her innocent mind did not know that he was also remaining still as he fought for control over his quivering manhood. He inhaled deeply several times, his warm respiration at her ear causing her to hug him more tightly and to spread kisses over his face to let him know she was all right. She heard him moan and felt his embrace tighten. Joy raced through her. It didn't take an experienced woman to know that this man was reeling from pleasure and desire, and an urgent need to continue their climb to the Mount of Rapture.

As Marsh began to move within her, Randee caught his pattern and pace and matched them. Both were stimulated beyond caution or restraint. They labored together lovingly until sheer bliss seemed to burst around them like a shower of stars falling from the heavens above. They kissed and caressed as they rode out the beautiful storm of passion. Gradually they relaxed into each other's arms and closed their eyes to savor every moment of this special experience. Marsh was lying on his back and Randee was nestled against his

211

side, with her arms resting over his chest. He had drawn her blanket over their naked bodies, and one hand was covering hers while the other was wrapped around her bare shoulders. It was not a time for talking, only one for introspection and acceptance of what had just occurred between them.

Soon, the sated blonde was sleeping peacefully. Marsh stared at the full moon overhead, his wits entangled in a quandary. Now that he had taken Randee Hollis, didn't he owe her something, even though she had vowed no demands and promises? Had he provoked this seduction just to force himself to make a decision about her? To explore his feelings? To test them? To test hers? Now that she belonged to him, what was he going to do about her? With her? He didn't know.

Commitment was a scary thing, even to a brave and fearless man as he was reputed to be. He hardly knew this woman, but he was powerfully drawn to her. Was it more than physical desire? It certainly seemed that way! Was she the one woman whom he couldn't forget or live without? Didn't his being unable to resist her answer that intimidating question for him? Was she the one whom he wanted as his wife and as the mother of his children, if he ever decided to settle down? From what he had observed, she was perfect for both. Was she the one with whom he wanted to spend the rest of his life? In good or bad times, he would be responsible for his family and home. Did he want a permanent place to live? One woman? Children? Duties? Did he want to ranch or farm all day and spend every night with her? With another woman? With any woman?

Marsh knew that his troubled past colored his view and answers. His father had taken up with another woman, betraying his mother, the wife whom he had sworn to love and to cherish above all other females. How much of Marshall Logan's blood ran within his son? Would he also become bored, do the same, and break Randee's heart? He had left home at seventeen — hurt, disappointed, resentful, bitter, and rebellious. Those self-destructive feelings and his father's wicked secret had plagued him for years, had hardened his emotions, driving him from place to place and from reckless deed to deed in search of peace of mind.

As he had done countless times before, Marsh wondered, should he have told his mother about his father's selfish deceit? No, it would have destroyed her. Should he have remained at home to battle his father, to punish the fallen man, to protect his mother from another slip? Would his parents still be alive if he had? Who could say what a person's destiny was, or if he had any real control over it?

He had visited home only three times since leaving there: twice to see his mother, and once to see both of his parents. That last visit in '69 had been a tough one, as his father had pleaded for his understanding and forgiveness, had begged him to return home and to give up his perilous life. His father had related the details and motive for his one moment of weakness, of insanity, of betrayal. Marshall Logan had told him of how he had been tricked by nature, tricked into self-punishment for being a failure and a coward, tricked into proving he was still a man. His father had revealed how scared he was after nearly losing his entire herd and all his crops the year when Marsh was sixteen. His father had spoken of how weak, vulnerable, helpless, and terrified he had felt. He had spoken of how a father and husband had enormous responsibilities and was expected to be strong each moment of his life, even when he needed a shoulder to lean on, perhaps even to cry on. Yet, he had confessed to being too proud and stubborn to allow his wife and son to offer that urgently needed solace.

As the dreadful story had unfolded, Marsh had understood his father's feelings and actions, a terrible mistake in judgment during a time of depression and weakness — which the younger Marsh never knew existed, or could exist in his cherished father. Their neighbor's wife had hated her husband and had used his father as a means to punish her verbally and physically abusive husband. While helping their neighbor with chores to earn money to save his own land, the elder Marshall had succumbed to the woman's brazen overtures — and to the irrational need to hurt his hateful neighbor for making him grovel to keep from losing all he owned and loved. Fortunately, the man had never learned of his wife's deceit, else Marshall Logan would have been slain!

For a year after discovering that dark secret and needing to inflict as much pain as he himself was experiencing, Marsh had fought with his father over anything and everything. Their battles had had a terrible effect on his dear mother. Since birth, Marsh had been his father's shadow; he had loved and respected the man, had viewed the man as perfect. The haunting incident had destroyed that bond, those feelings. As a strapping teenager, he had been unable to understand and forgive his father's Achilles' heel. Yet, he had kept quiet about the episode. Unable to break his mother's heart with the truth and unable to remain around his father, he had left home the following summer. Over the years, and especially during this last one, doubts had eaten viciously at him. Despite his father's confession, Marsh had been unable during that last visit to expose himself to his parents; now, they would never know the truth about their "wayward son," their "bad apple to the core." Marsh could still hear his father asking, "How can I ever forgive myself for destroying my only son? I hate hearing those awful things about you, because I know I'm responsible for them. Don't keep challenging death, son, or it'll grab you for sure one day."

He had left home to complete a dangerous mission, planning to return and explain himself afterwards. The Epson Gang raid had denied him that chance forever. Presently, he was involved in the most perilous mission of his life, and he couldn't allow this radiant creature to remain at his side for very long, or she would wind up slaughtered like his parents. The longer they were together, the harder it would be to send her home, and the more she would resist his order.

Could he risk hurting Randee in any way? Risk hurting himself again? Like him, Randee had experienced many hard times. Did he have the right to give her more, even unintentionally? If he couldn't commit to her because of his emotions or mission, he would cause her terrible pain. No matter what she said, sleeping together would lead her to believe he was making unspoken promises of a future together. If only he could be totally honest and open with her! But he couldn't, because it could get her killed. He needed to wheedle that information from her and send her home as quickly as possible, before any contact with that violent band. Marsh admitted that he wanted her badly, but he would rather give her up than get her injured or slain.

He glanced down at the honey-colored head on his shoulder and felt the warm body nestled against his. He shouldn't have taken possession of her until his dilemma was settled; yet, he wanted her again this very moment. The best thing for both of them was for him to return to his own bedroll and forget this happened.

His troubled mind taunted, *Forget?* There was no way he could forget it, only ignore it. Gingerly he eased from her side and walked to the river to bathe. Afterwards, he stretched out on his bedroll and closed his weary eyes, unable to sleep for a long time.

Chapter Ten

Randee yawned and stretched, then smiled happily as she recalled the previous evening's dreamy episode. She felt wonderful this morning and wished her lover was still at her side. Holding the thin blanket against her bare chest, she propped herself up on her elbow and looked around for Marsh. She spied him riding in the opposite direction, a lengthy ways from camp. She concluded that he was giving her privacy this morning, to bathe and dress, and she was touched by his consideration.

Randee glanced down at her bare body. Strange, but she did not feel disconcerted or embarrassed. She closed her eyes and envisioned their passionate bout upon her bedroll. Last night had been rapturous in his arms. He had been so gentle, so skilled, so utterly satisfying. How blissful it would have been to awaken in his embrace, to make love to him again this morning, to be a part of him forever. Maybe, she mused with a grin, Marsh was the one who was feeling shy and disquieted. After all, she had boldly seduced him, and he might not know what to expect from her today after her brazen conduct last night.

She looked at his dusty retreat and wondered how

long he would stay out of camp. If he had remained here with her, they could have talked and shared their special . . . Twinges of alarm nibbled at her. Maybe he was too uneasy about their intimacy, too anxious about how she would view it and how she would behave from this point onward. If a man didn't know what to do and say during an awkward situation, he usually tried to avoid it, like Marsh was doing this very moment. If he felt the same way she did, he would be lying next to her; they would be talking merrily and making love, savoring the bond which they had created last night, whether he admitted to one or not.

Randee gathered her possessions and went to the river to bathe and dress. The water was chilly, but she didn't mind. She needed the nippy temperature to refresh her, to awaken her wits, to stimulate her sluggish body. Later, as she brushed her hair, she worried about the reason for Marsh's absence. Maybe that blue-eyed rogue was afraid she would go back on her word not to make demands on him. Maybe he didn't know what he wanted from her at this time, or even realize that he did want something from her! From what she had heard and read, men were skittish and defensive creatures, so she must not make him more nervous than he already was. As best she could, she should act just like she had before last night's event. . . .

Which was exactly what Marsh Logan did when he returned to camp thirty minutes later, to a nice breakfast prepared by Randee. Without eyeing her too revealingly, he flashed her a genial smile and said, "Thanks, boss lady. We should eat and get on the trail pronto."

Randee noticed that he didn't mention last night or his dawn ride. Nor did he act any differently to her than before her surrender to him, as if nothing uncommon had taken place between them. She took his lead and behaved in a like manner. She passed him a cup of coffee and a plate of food as she jested, "I cooked, so you have to clean up. It's a lovely morning, isn't it? Not as humid today."

Marsh took a deep breath of fresh air and smiled, aware she was letting him off the hook, at least for a while. "Yep, it's a nice day for traveling." After a few bites, he said, "Your cooking has improved, Miss Hollis. This is very good."

She laughed, then replied, "One can hardly mess up biscuits, salt pork, and gravy."

Marsh chuckled and refuted, "Yes, one can; I've seen it done many times. Doughy biscuits, watery coffee, burned bacon, and gluey gravy . . ." He wrinkled his nose and forehead before adding, "Blah."

"I guess you're right," she conceded. "Of course, I owe my new skills to a very patient and talented teacher. Thanks for the lessons."

Remembering what she had said last night about training her to be his "partner in all ways," Marsh felt his body grow warm and tense. He wanted to ask her if she was all right this morning, but dared not open the delicate subject. He hoped he hadn't hurt her last night; she hadn't acted as if he had at the time. She had been so passionate with him, so giving, so responsive, so eager and greedy. His breath caught in his throat just recalling that delightful episode.

Marsh eyed her furtively when he thought she wasn't paying attention. She looked fine; no, she looked radiant, beautiful, tempting. Mercy, how he craved to seize her and make wild love to her again! She was being so kind today, so true to her word, so undemanding. Lordy, but he hoped it wasn't a clever feminine trick to disarm him. He hoped she would continue to give him time and patience to sort out his feelings, because he was more unsettled now than he had been last night or before his tension-releasing ride. Although she had promised not to be a "clinging vine," he had feared to find one awaiting him at breakfast. Now that he'd spent a short time with her, truthfully, he could deal with a weepy woman better than this composed and cordial one!

Randee was cognizant of Marsh's keen study and obvious confusion—perceptions which she gathered from his voice, movements, respiration, and expressions. She was increasing his apprehension by behaving calmly and friendly, by acting as if last night didn't exist! She decided to continue along this same path, as he didn't really want to get into anything personal today. Perhaps his manly ego just couldn't understand how she could ignore him after a night of ecstasy in his arms! No doubt he was wondering the usual things: did he harm her? Did he give her pleasure? Was she embarrassed to face him? Did she want him again? Would she start chasing him and driving him loco? At least that was what she *assumed* were the usual things.

She started to drop a few hints to relax him, but changed her mind. *Let him stew a while,* she decided. *It'll be good for such a confident man to be uncertain for a change, to wonder and worry about obtaining a victory. Let him learn how to communicate if he wants answers. He has to open that door between us before I can step inside. If he doesn't want me to, then don't humiliate either of us by . . .*

Marsh nudged Randee's shoulder and asked, "You awake?"

The blonde hadn't realized how long she'd been entrapped by deep thought. Marsh had cleared the remains of their early meal and put out the campfire. He was packing up their supplies and trying not to stare at her. Randee stretched and smiled. "Need any help, partner?"

219

"All done here. You ready to ride?" he asked.

Randee nodded, then went to saddle Rojo. She climbed upon the chestnut's back and kneed the mare into a lively gallop. Marsh swiftly caught up with her and rode just ahead of her — on purpose, she decided, to place him, instead of her, in the line of vision.

Marsh wondered what thoughts and feelings had had her so ensnared back in camp, and which ones were racing through her this very moment. Maybe she wanted, or needed, to pretend last night never happened. Maybe it had been an impulsive act, or one to satisfy her feminine curiosity. Or worse, an unpleasant and painful experience. Maybe she was relieved that he was also ignoring it and she was showing her gratitude by being so nice. *Damn*, he silently cursed, *not knowing is torment*.

They traveled over terrain which was a blend of rolling hills and flat grassland, Mainly northward, dark mesas loomed in the distance, poised for all time beneath a very pale blue sky today. Every so often they encountered dry spots with sandy beds and countless prickly cacti. On some high hills it seemed as if one could see into forever, and one grasped the immense size of this territory. In many areas, there were numerous trees and bushes; in others, fertile valleys were covered with lush grasses and multicolored wildflowers. There was plenty of water around, making this section excellent ranch land.

At their first rest stop, Marsh strolled around away from where she was limbering up her taut body, muscles that were tense but not because of their steady journey. It amused her to watch him trying to act natural while trying to avoid her, and perhaps also avoid some kind of confrontation which he didn't know how to deal with just yet. If only she knew more about men and how their minds worked, she could figure out a way to settle down this anxious rogue!

She leaned against a tree and closed her eyes. She wondered why life and love had to be so difficult at times. Her original reason for being with Marsh was receding like a water line during a drought. All she wanted now was to be with him; yet, she had to pretend it was only revenge that was driving her onward, or he might send her home for a lack of concentration and dedication! If he was nervous now, he would be worse if he discovered he had become the center of her life!

Randee opened her eyes to find Marsh staring at her oddly, worriedly. She sent him an amiable smile as she joined him at the horses. She hastily massaged his wrinkled forehead and teased, "Quit frowning, partner, I'm not collapsing from fatigue yet. I was only daydreaming about building my ranch after our mission is over. I think I'll have more stables this time; I like raising horses better than cattle."

He handed her the chestnut's reins. "That's a great idea 'cause you're very good with them. Rojo obeys you without a second thought."

She mounted the mare and looked over at Marsh, who was sitting astride his sleek stallion. "Too bad my hired help doesn't do the same," she playfull taunted, then raced off laughing gaily.

Marsh observed her from the rear, noticing how well she sat her saddle and how ravishing she looked today in a dark blue riding skirt and white shirt. Her tawny locks fanned out behind her and whipped about in the wind she was creating with her pace. He had the urge to race up beside her, yank her from her saddle, and crush her in his arms as his mouth devoured hers. His forehead still tingled where she had touched him, and her silvery laughter still sounded in his ears. What a sneaky little vixen she was, tempting him again today while trying not to frighten him off! If he wasn't wrong, she wanted him, and wanted him badly. Yet, she was being careful not to intimidate him, and he deeply appreciated that kindness. It must be hard on her, not knowing what were the right things to do and say. But he couldn't tell her, because he didn't know either!

They had halted near a cluster of trees for the midday meal and rest when they heard noises from movement of some type. Both looked toward the dark spots on the horizon. "Is it a herd of animals or a band of Indians?" she asked as Marsh lifted his field glasses.

He gazed through the optical device and replied, "Neither."

Randee's only thought was about losing Marsh during a battle. Her heart lurched heavily as she murmured, "The Epson Gang?"

Marsh lowered the glasses and looked over at her pale face. She was breathing erratically and trembling. "Settle down, Randee; it's only a group of wagons heading westward, probably for California. They can't see us over here, and we don't need to make contact."

She realized how he was observing her and how she must appear—like a petrified female, a weakling, and a coward. She closed her eyes and inhaled deeply to steady her respiration and heart rate. Finally she looked at him and said, "I'm sorry, Marsh. For a moment, all I could think about was losing the people I love. There's so much they don't know, so much I haven't told them. For an instant, I didn't think there would be time to do so. When we get to Brownwood, I need to write my mother. She's expecting a baby in August and she's probably worried sick about me. I've been selfish not to let her know where I am, that I'm safe and well. I won't panic again; I promise."

Marsh sensed that Randee was referring more to him than to her mother or anyone else. He almost challenged her words, wanting and needing to hear her speak the truth. *Truth,* his mind echoed; the truth was that they were safe this time, but what about the next one? What if it had been the Epson Gang and they had been sighted?

Randee shook his arm lightly and vowed, "Honestly, Marsh, I won't panic again. Surely I'm allowed one slip."

Knowing he was the reason for her error, he couldn't fault her about it. Besides, if peril had been nearby, they probably would have gone unnoticed or escaped. No damage had been done, so she didn't need to suffer unduly. "I didn't see a slip in your courage and skills, Randee, only in your attention. If we had been attacked you would have done just fine because your instinct for survival would have taken control of you. You were only distracted by personal problems for an instant, but that's exactly why you shouldn't allow your emotions to ensnare you on a dangerous trail. I'm not angry or disappointed. In fact, it was probably an excellent lesson in alertness, for both of us."

Randee grasped the unspoken warning in his message: if they had been absorbed in each other, they could have fallen prey to their worst enemies. This matter was a deadly serious one, something she had allowed herself to forget. She had to stay on guard, or she could get them killed. More so, she had to stop distracting Marsh Logan with her brazen flirtations. This man had dual sides, and both parts depended upon his wits to survive. Her amorous behavior was dulling those wits, so she had to quell it. "You're right, Durango. I let my guard down and that was stupid. I won't allow my private affairs to interfere with our mission again."

"We're both guilty, Randee. My mind was elsewhere too. From now on, partner, it's strictly . . ." Marsh halted and stared past her. After placing his finger to his lips to indicate silence, he pointed beyond her to where a herd of pronghorns was grazing peacefully.

Randee watched them for a while, stealing some of their tranquility. She had wanted to tell Marsh about her past today, but it wasn't the right time, not with them battling their strong attraction to each other. She didn't want to influence his thoughts and feelings by revealing what a hard time she had endured, so she would wait.

Marsh was glad he hadn't finished his discouraging statement, because he doubted that things could remain strictly business between them. No matter how hard she was trying to conceal it, he knew that Randee was distressed by his apparent rejection. Clearly she was trying to abide by his rules and desires, and she was baffled by his conflicting signals to her. He stood and flexed, telling Randee it was time to leave.

The landscape remained much the same: lush rolling hills, valuable grazing land, brilliant wildflowers, plenty of water, and lots of trees and bushes. The trees, mostly oaks and mesquites, had a northward bend because of this area's weather. With short trunks and bushy limbs, many trees looked like giant green balls hanging close to the ground. It was so verdant and lovely along this route to Brownwood.

At dusk, they tended their horses and camped near the head of what would one day be called Pecan Bayou. With little conversation between them, they prepared their meal, ate it, then cleaned up together. To avoid being noticed by anyone in the area, Marsh doused the fire and denied himself a shave. The water nearby was shallow, dirty, and snaky, so Marsh asked her to wait until the next night to take a bath. Having studied their surroundings, Randee promptly agreed. Uncertain of this area's inhabitants, Marsh also insisted on no campfire and on their sleeping close in case of danger. Again, Randee concurred. It required some effort, but both eventually slept fitfully. The following morning, their pattern was much the same: cook, eat, clean up, and leave.

During their first stop, she thought Marsh was napping. It amazed her how fast he could drop off to sleep, to awaken instantly if something caught his always alert ear. She wondered what embittering experiences and disappointments that man had faced during his lifetime, what incidents had made him such a loner. Sometimes she sensed a soul-deep loneliness about him; yet, he always seemed in control of himself and his emotions. His roguish smile or playful grin belied what he had endured since leaving home. Again, she wondered what had driven him away. He must have loved his parents deeply to agonize over their deaths, to risk his life to destroy their killers.

Marsh "Durango Kid" Logan was such a contradiction to her. He was a legendary gunslinger; yet, he was the most caring and gentle man she had known. He seemed arrogant at times but it was nothing more than extreme self-confidence. Often, he seemed totally elusive and unobtainable, yet he had yielded to her once and she knew he wanted to do so again. He was serious, but he had a wonderful sense of humor. He was strong, but he was also vulnerable. He was fearless, yet he was afraid of committing to her, to anything except a deadly challenge. He was self-reliant yet he seemed to need her, need her in many ways. Randee saw those facts and insights reflected in his blue eyes and heard them in his tone when he didn't realize his guard was too low. It was hard for Marsh to trust, hard for him to share himself, hard for him to depend on anyone but himself, hard for him to show a weakness of any kind. Yet, she loved him and wanted him.

During their midday meal break, she wondered which was more distracting: being ill-fated lovers or fighting their mutual attraction. It was their late afternoon rest stop that ensnared them. . . .

The day was exceptionally hot and muggy. Randee felt as if her garments were glued to her moist flesh. Her hair was damp and her bangs were stuck to her flushed face. She struggled to remove her riding gloves, but they were resistive because her hands were hot and sweaty. She tossed her hat aside and knelt by the water's edge to splash her face with tepid liquid. She unfastened the top few buttons of her shirt and removed her bandanna. Soaking it in the shallow stream, she rubbed the cooling cloth over her neck and upper chest. She was miserable, but mostly it was because of this emotional stand-off.

She glanced over at Marsh, who was lying on his back under a shade tree. Heavens, how she wanted to go and pounce on him! The Epson Gang and their cruelties seemed unreal today. All she was aware of was Marsh Logan and her love and desire for him. Randee actually felt as if she couldn't breathe, as if she would perish if she couldn't have him or at least put an end to this stress. She trembled and wanted to cry, and she hated feeling so weak and helpless.

She called out to the reclining man, "Stay where you are, Marsh, because I'm going for a swim. I can't stand this heat and sweat any longer."

Marsh was on his feet and at her side in an instant. "Wait a minute, woman! I haven't checked out this area. What if somebody's nearby? Can't you wait until

226

we camp for the night?"

She locked her gaze to his and made her decision to end this torment. She replied, "No, I can't. I'm so tense I could scream. Be kind and stand guard for me," she entreated.

He suggested, "Why don't I teach you to shoot left-handed? That should take your mind off . . . the heat."

Randee looked him in the eye and revealed, "If you stand anywhere near me, Marsh Logan, my tension and heat will be worse! You best get away from me before I do something we'll both regret," she warned. When he looked as if he were afraid to open his mouth, she forged on bravely, "I can't stand this strain any longer. We can't go on pretending nothing happened between us back there, even if nothing happens between us again. As long as we ignore the problem, we'll be tense and guarded. I just want us to be ourselves, to be relaxed with each other again. Surely this is the worst way to handle a touchy matter. I know it's hard for you to trust another person, to lean on somebody, to share any part of yourself. It doesn't mean you have a weakness, just because you occasionally need someone else. Can't we just enjoy each other while we're together?"

Marsh's sky-blue gaze fused with her earthy-green one. He admitted hoarsely, "I have to agree with you, Randee. If we don't stop avoiding the truth and ignoring each other, this is only going to get harder for us. The trouble is, I don't know what to say and do in a situation like this, because I have no experience with one. It makes me nervous knowing how you feel, but it makes me just as nervous not knowing. I'm afraid of hurting you, because I'm afraid you'll expect too much from me if we get close, and I don't like being scared of anything. I just feel so damn guilty about taking advantage of . . ."

Randee's fingers pressed against his lips and prevented the rest of his sentence from coming forth. She reasoned desperately, "Don't you realize that I'm the one taking advantage of you, Marsh? I'm the one who started this both times because I want you, and I'll take you on any terms. I'm not being reckless or impulsive. That was the most wonderful experience I've had. Knowing what I do, how can I back away now? We're adults; we're free to act on our desires. There's no reason why we can't sleep together if that's what we both want. Please believe me and relax. Don't you see, this restraint is more demanding and dangerous than simply enjoying each other?"

Marsh locked his gaze to hers and deliberated her enticing words. She was very smart and honest for such a young woman, and he wanted to be convinced that he wasn't misusing her. "You're right, Randee, this strain has to end; it's driving me wild," he confessed. "But are you sure you've thought this situation over carefully? Are you positive you understand I'm offering you nothing in return?"

Randee clasped his whiskered jaw between her hands and looked up into his worried eyes. "I've had almost two days to ponder this matter, and this is what I want. I accept your feelings, Marsh, and I won't put any strain on you to change them."

As if a secret signal had passed between them, they melted into each other's arms, and their lips meshed feverishly. They kissed, embraced, caressed, and excited each other. Having fought these desires since Friday night, they were consumed by fiery passion, by a burning need for each other. Despite the damp clinginess of their garments, they were rid of them quickly and were sinking into the lush grass near the water's edge. Their mouths and hands worked eagerly and ardently, as if no force could halt their union.

Little stimulation was required to bring them to boiling level, as they had been simmering for each other. Quickly, the flames beneath them increased, and they bubbled with entrapped energy. Hotter and hotter their bodies burned, and steamier their spirits became. Soon, Marsh was within her, and she rejoiced at their reunion. Rapidly they scaled passion's peak and wavered on its blissful precipice, eager to tumble over its edge, yet reluctant to end this wonderful madness. The top to their kettle of passion blew off and sent their steam of desire racing skyward in happy release. Ever so gradually their wits returned and their bodies cooled.

Marsh gazed down into Randee's lovely face and smiled. "Do you realize that you're the only person to ever steal my wits and control?"

Randee laughed and teased, "Why not, Durango, I paid for their use. You're costing me ten thousand dollars, so you'll have to earn your money one way or another. Is this such a bad requirement?"

"Since you are the boss lady, I have to do as you say."

"Good," she murmured, kissing him provocatively. "No more restraint, Marsh, let's just be ourselves. Give me whatever part of yourself that you can share; I'll expect nothing more."

As he nibbled on her ear, he teased, "That's mighty generous of you, ma'am, because I'm a greedy cuss."

"And I'm a greedy vixen," she replied with a laugh.

"Since it's getting late, we'd better camp here for the night. You start supper while I take a look around," he suggested happily.

Randee watched him get up, rinse off in the nearby stream, and dress. She admired his lean, hard frame. He was so utterly enchanting, she couldn't be blamed for her weakness for him. She liked the new glow in his eyes and the sunny smile on his lips. His expression was one of possessiveness, and that delighted her.

Marsh glanced at her and said, "Up and dress, woman. I'm not about to leave you lying around like that to tempt any passerby to steal what's mine. In case you don't know it, I'm a selfish critter."

Randee grinned at him and obeyed, bathing and dressing quickly. As he mounted and left, she sighed dreamily. She liked this brave change in Marsh, one she shouldn't point out to him.

While Marsh scouted the area, Randee prepared their meal. They ate upon his return, gazing at each other across the campfire and smiling frequently. For the present, both were totally content. They made love again and slept peacefully on bedrolls, side by side.

The following morning, Randee awakened to find Marsh resting on his side, propped up on one elbow, and watching her with a grin on his face. She smiled and asked merrily, "What are you looking at?"

He bent over and kissed her nose before replying, "You, woman. You constantly intrigue me. I've never met any female with more passion and fire than you have."

"I hope that's a compliment, Mr. Logan, because you taught me all I know, so far."

"I best remain your only teacher, woman, or . . ."

"Or what, partner?" she asked, suppressing her laughter.

"I'll tan your hide," he informed her with a chuckle.

"Then, make sure you hold class often, so I won't have to go looking for lessons and pleasures elsewhere."

"Is this often enough?" he inquired huskily as he rolled her onto her back and moved atop her, sealing their lips. . . .

Following a late start that day because of a lusty bout

of lovemaking, they rode at a swifter pace, with few stops, in order to make camp that night at a lake not far from Brownwood.

As they ate supper, Marsh told her, "I didn't want to get into town after dark, so we'll ride in tomorrow and check things over."

"Don't forget, you promised we could have our washing done and sleep in a real bed."

"So I did," he replied, and caressed her cheek. "To prevent gossip and trouble, we'll need to take separate rooms at the hotel."

"Separate rooms?" she echoed in disappointment.

"Don't fret, my hot-blooded vixen, I'll sneak into your room after dark. Frankly, I'm getting used to sleeping with you and I like it."

"So do I," she readily admitted, delighted that he could.

"But tonight, we'd best stick to our own bedrolls. We're close to town and somebody could drop by."

They had made love twice yesterday and once this morning, so it wouldn't be so difficult to refrain tonight. "Does that mean no swim and bath?" she asked.

"Let's not take any chances tonight. I wouldn't want to call attention to us by having to kill some lusty intruder who couldn't resist you. I'll get you one at the hotel tomorrow."

"I suppose we should turn in. We have a busy day ahead."

Marsh embraced her and kissed her, then tucked her in for the night. "Sleep well, Randee, I'll be nearby."

How she longed to say, "I love you," but it was unwise. "Good night, Marsh," she murmured, her tone and gaze filled with the emotion that she didn't give voice to.

At dawn on Tuesday, there was another brutal raid on a ranch just below Fort Richardson, the first one since the attack on Friday above Fort Worth.

They reached Brownwood before noon and headed for the hotel. Marsh said, "I'll get you registered and carry our things to our rooms. Then I'll take the horses to the stable."

"What's our story, if anyone asks?" she inquired cautiously.

"I'll register as Marsh Logan and you'll be my cousin Randee Logan. We're heading for Austin to make a cattle deal. Hopefully we won't attract too much attention."

"Maybe you'll go unnoticed because Durango doesn't normally travel with a companion, particularly a woman."

Marsh looked as if he was about to say something, but changed his mind. "Is there a problem?" she asked.

Marsh hated lying to her, especially now, but he couldn't reveal himself to her. "If I get into any trouble here, get out of town fast and meet me back at the lake."

"You will be careful, won't you?"

"I promise to behave myself," he teased to relax her.

The town was quiet on a Tuesday morning. Yet, those who were around noticed the arrival of the beautiful woman and the gunslinger. Marsh's profession was readily noted from the way in which he wore his guns and carried himself. They halted before the hotel and dismounted, then collected their belongings and entered the clean structure.

After signing up for two rooms, Marsh carried their possessions upstairs and left them there. He had paid for Randee to have a bath and food brought to her room, and for a local laundress to come over to pick up their dirty clothes for washing and ironing.

He tied his garments in a bundle and left them with Randee. "I'll see to the horses. Then I'll get a bath and a shave, maybe get this hair trimmed if I like the looks of their barber. It makes me nervous for anyone but me to get near this neck with a sharp blade. I'll join you for supper at six. Get some rest and do whatever chores you women usually do while men are out."

"Yes, sir, Cousin Marsh. You want me to meet you downstairs?"

"At six sharp, woman, and don't be late this time," he jested.

After the laundress departed with a promise to return their clothes the next morning, Randee eagerly devoured the delicious meal which she was served. Later, a large tub was brought to her room and filled with warm water. Randee locked her door, stripped, and stepped into the inviting tub. She used the fragrant soap, which her uncle had purchased for her, and scrubbed with delight. When her hair and body were clean, she dried them and wrapped a bath sheet around herself while she worked with her hair, plaiting it for waves and fullness. Anticipating a lively night in Marsh's arms, Randee stretched out on her bed and took a nap.

After leaving their horses at the livery stable, Marsh had his shave, haircut, and bath. Then, he dressed in clean clothes: a powder-blue shirt and dark pants. The ebony-haired man picked up a telegram, then returned to his room to read it. He was not surprised to learn that a large company was indeed purchasing many of the ranches which had been terrorized by the Epson Gang. Located in Fort Worth, the Mid-Texas Land Company was run by a lawyer named George Light, but the "owners" and their plans were confidential.

233

Marsh's contact — Willard Mason — said he would keep working on their identities, but was unsure of how to obtain them from the tight-lipped lawyer.

Marsh wrote a letter to his contact in Fort Worth, as he didn't want such news put into a telegram, which could be intercepted more easily than a sealed letter. He requested that a U.S. Marshal Foley Timms be checked out, and also asked that any available information on Quantrill's Raiders be gathered and held for him. He said he would arrive in Fort Worth in seven to ten days. He also requested that a map be drawn up showing the locations of the land company's purchases.

Marsh walked to the stage office and paid for the letter to be delivered to Fort Worth. When he heard talk about the destruction of the Red River Station, he decided this was a good time to share that news with Randee, leading her to believe he had just learned about it. He no longer felt . . . threatened by Brody Wade's hold over her, and revealing this information now could prevent trouble between them later. He hoped Randee would keep her word about no pressure on him until he could work out some details in his life, if he survived this mission.

Marsh sat at the table, drinking coffee and wondering what was keeping Randee. Surely he had given her plenty of time for her chores. He had told her to meet him at six sharp, and it was nearing six thirty. Crazy thoughts raced through his worried mind. Had she decided to end their partnership and drop him? Was she still upstairs? Was she afraid to be seen with the "Durango Kid"? Had this whole situation been a clever trap set for him by those devious State Police, who didn't want anybody exposing them? No, there was no way anyone could know his real identity. Yet, Randee

Hollis was a highly skilled expert for a Kansas farm girl, and that daring notice in the newspaper . . .

"Don't beat me, Cousin Marsh, but I fell asleep. That bed was so comfortable, I couldn't resist trying it out," Randee quickly explained her tardy arrival. "I'm sorry."

Marsh looked at the exquisite creature before him. She was the perfect image of innocence and beauty. She was wearing the dress she'd had on when he'd retrieved her from the stage. It was a little rumpled, but she looked breathtaking. Randee leaned forward to whisper, "If you don't stop staring at me like that, Mr. Logan, someone will suspect a shameful secret about us. They'll probably tar and feather two cousins who bed down together."

Marsh chuckled, rose, and seated her politely. He bent over to whisper in return, "Then, don't look good enough to eat when a man's starving. I was getting worried about you."

As he reclaimed his seat next to hers, she smiled and teased softly, "Good, 'cause that means you missed me. Tell me all the news."

"Later, when we have privacy." When she smiled eagerly, he playfully warned, "Behave yourself, woman, because we're attracting too many stares. Or I should say, you are."

"Let's not be ornery because we didn't get a nap, too," she teased.

"That isn't the reason for this nasty mood. I warned you long ago, men do crazy things when they get jealous."

As she shook her napkin and placed it in her lap, she replied softly, "Then, don't get jealous. After all, you have no reason to."

"Are you sure about that? It seems there's a respect-able sheriff waiting for your return with hopes of marrying you."

Randee glanced at him oddly and her smile faded. "Are you trying to ruin my supper even before it's served? Forget about Brody."

"Sorry, Randee, that was naughty of me. I'll explain later."

Randee leaned toward him and said almost inaudibly, "Listen to me, Marsh Logan; you don't have anything to worry about where other men are concerned. I'm yours for the taking, any time and any place, and for as long as you want me. Is that clear?"

Marsh smiled and said, "As clear as new glass, Cousin Randee."

Their food was ordered and brought to their table by a middle-aged woman in a drab cotton dress. Eating silenced them for a while, and both savored the tasty fare, including a berry pie.

After their highly pleasing meal, Marsh suggested they take a leisurely walk to appear like normal guests. Randee accepted his arm, and they strolled down one side of the street and up the other. She felt the taut alertness in the man beside her, although he appeared perfectly relaxed to everyone they encountered. She noticed how the men eyed his strapped-down holsters and seemed to cringe in fear, and how the women eyed his handsome face and flushed with undisguised desire. The neat, clean-shaven rogue tipped his hat, smiled, and spoke to everyone they met during their walk.

When no one was around, she asked, "What are you up to?"

Marsh glanced at her and asked innocently, "What do you mean?"

"Don't pretend with me, Marsh Logan; I know you too well."

He chuckled heartily and said, "Checking over the layout for my business tonight. You remember, pick up a little dynamite?"

"What time and where do we strike?" she asked.

"Not we, me," he corrected her. "I can get in and out quicker and safer alone. I'll come to your room after it's done."

Randee knew it was useless to argue his valid point, so she nodded acceptance of it. It was nearly dark by the time they reached the hotel and went to their separate rooms.

It seemed like hours passed as the nervous blonde awaited her lover's arrival. She wished she had asked him what time he was going to pull off his theft, so she wouldn't worry unnecessarily. The moon was just leaving its full stage, so it was still bright outside. As she anxiously paced her room, Randee hoped he was dressed in his black outfit so he couldn't be sighted easily during his . . . crime. She wondered what she would do if anything happened to Marsh, as she had been the one to suggest using dynamite to compensate for their being outnumbered.

She brushed her long hair again and fluffed it around her shoulders. She was wearing her last clean gown, but she wished it were prettier. Perhaps she could buy a lovely one before leaving town tomorrow. "Don't be silly, girl," she said to herself, "that would surely give you two away."

Randee scolded herself for fretting constantly, as Marsh Logan was the Durango Kid, a man with matchless skills and prowess, a man who couldn't get caught during a simple robbery in a small town! She dabbed on more of the enticing cologne from her bag, and sprinkled some on the bed covers and pillows. Noting the late hour, she wisely doused the lanterns and forced herself to sit down, as her pacing might be heard below. Soon, she heard several gunshots and stiffened. She trembled and her breathing grew erratic.

Quickly, she cautioned herself to calm down, or Marsh would arrive to see her panicky again.

An hour went by, and no Marsh. Randee peered outside, but could see nothing because her room was on the side of the hotel and a view of the front street was impossible. She dared not pace and make the floor squeak, but her nerves were shattered by fear. She prayed for Marsh's survival. Maybe he had been forced to make a run for it. He had told her to meet him at the lake if trouble arose.

What if she couldn't? What if they came and arrested her because she had entered town with him? She would never betray him to the law, even if they beat her or threatened to hang her! Would Marsh try to rescue her? What if they were both captured? They had promised not to endanger each other, but would either of them keep that hasty vow?

More time passed, and Randee knew that Marsh should have returned by now. It was almost two o'clock in the morning. She couldn't get those gunshots out of her mind. What if he was injured badly or . . . ?

"I love you, Marsh Logan. Don't you go and die on me." She sat on the tiny sofa with her arms wrapped around her updrawn knees and with her chin propped on them. She closed her eyes and prayed, *Please, Marsh, come back to me safe and sound.*

Chapter Eleven

Randee jumped when a hand nudged her and a voice whispered, "You can stop worrying, partner. I'm home without a single scratch."

Randee lifted her head and stared into the darkness, desperately needing to see for herself that he was all right. She laughed softly to conceal her quavering voice and murmured, "How do you do that? I didn't hear a thing."

Marsh sat down beside her and drew her into his arms. He noticed her trembling; yet, he teased, "Probably because you were dozing, when I thought you'd be pacing the room with worry."

Randee cuddled against him. "I was, until I realized how much noise I was making on this creaky floor. If anyone's below me, they would think it odd, don't you imagine? Are you sure you're all right? I heard gunshots hours ago. And yes, I panicked."

Marsh stroked her silky hair as he explained, "I'm fine, honestly. I was just delayed by a few helpers who decided to rob that merchant on the same night I had chosen. I barely sneaked away before they awoke the guard outside. It seems he's been robbed lots lately and was prepared for trouble tonight. I got in and out fine, but those other fellas didn't fare so well. That shooting rousted the sheriff and deputy, so I had to hide until they ceased their search. It would have been difficult to explain what a stranger was doing on the street after midnight, and following a robbery. I've got the dynamite concealed outside of town. We'll pick it up as we're leaving. I even left him money to pay for it, but I imagine those bumbling fools took it."

"Why would you do that?" she asked, mystified.

He playfully tugged on a lock of tawny hair as he replied, "I'm a gunslinger, woman, not a thief. I was merely making a late-night purchase, one I didn't want to explain to that merchant."

"Thanks, Marsh," she whispered, snuggling closer to him.

Marsh didn't have to ask why. He knew. "I'm sure you're exhausted. Do you know what time it is?"

"Past time for my loyal and talented employee to fulfill his duty to me," she merrily quipped. "I had a nap, remember? If you're too . . ."

Marsh silenced her with a ravenous kiss and tight squeeze. He lifted her in his arms and carried her to the bed. He stood her beside it and removed her nightgown before laying her down. Quickly, he removed his ebony garments and joined her.

They laughed softly as the bedsprings squeaked and the floor creaked. "Sounds like we'll have to be real careful tonight."

"Don't tell me you're missing the wide open spaces and all that privacy?" he teased, kissing her ear and tickling her ribs.

While suppressing her giggles, she jerked to and fro as she tried to capture his mischievous hands. "Stop that, Marsh, or we'll have our neighbor below complaining."

"About squeaking bedsprings? You could be having

a restless night," he murmured, then sensuously assailed her ear and throat.

"If he's over sixteen, he'll recognize a certain pattern."

"Randee Hollis, what a wicked mind you have," he roguishly accused, then caressed her from neck to thigh.

"It's all your fault, Marsh Logan; you're a bad influence on an innocent lass."

"Am I now?" he queried, tickling her again.

"Yes, you are, and I love every minute of it, except this one."

Marsh ceased his sport and began to press kisses over her satiny skin. "How about this one?" he asked, his mouth and hands roaming her body freely and wildly.

Randee thrashed upon the bed, driven mindless by his lips and fingers. Suddenly she didn't care how much noise the bed and floor made. She allowed Marsh to do anything he pleased, because everything he did pleased her. She felt totally uninhibited, utterly responsive, and blissfully receptive to this man whom she loved and desired passionately.

Every time Marsh made love to Randee, he enjoyed it more, even though each experience seemed the ultimate in lovemaking. In the past, taking a woman just once had satisfied his desire for that female. But with Randee Hollis, he couldn't seem to have her enough, or have enough of her. It was as if she gave him matchless pleasure and total satisfaction; yet, each union only increased his desire for her, like some magical potion that whet his appetite for a treat he could never devour completely, for which he could never sate his hunger.

Randee's senses spun dizzily as Marsh lovingly labored on her body, stimulating her in ways he hadn't used before. . . . Every time they fused their passions, she couldn't imagine anything feeling better than the past union of bodies and spirits; yet, each time was more wonderful than the last. How could she absorb more pleasure without bursting with joy and rapture? What Marsh was doing now with his hands and lips was causing colorful stars to dance happily before her closed eyes. She loved this man deeply, in and out of bed, and she could not imagine her life without him.

Marsh was starving for her, but her responses were entreating him onward to explore bolder ground with her before feasting greedily at her banquet table. She smelled like wildflowers. She was as soft as costly silk. She tasted like honey, all over. She was driving him mad with the urge to take her wildly and freely. She was a wanton innocent, who stirred his blood more fiercely than any challenge had.

He entered her masterfully, and she locked him within the demanding embrace of her legs. With tantalizing slowness, to avoid that noisy, telltale pattern she had teased about earlier, he entered and withdrew from her beckoning paradise over and over again. She was right; he shouldn't be jealous of other men, of Brody Wade. She could never respond to another man as she was responding to him, never. Surely this experience had to be as unique, as powerful, as overwhelming, as enchanting for her, as it was for him.

Suddenly his manhood erupted in a frenzy and he feared that his loss of concentration and self-control had denied her a similar release. He didn't have to worry, because she was clinging to him as ecstasy consumed her from head to foot. Grasping her level of victory, he surged forward and conquered any lingering restraint. On and on they rode passion's crest together, as if this blissful moment would never end. But, soon, the golden aftermath engulfed them and brought them tenderly back to reality, like a gentle bird returning them from paradise.

Marsh kept kissing her until she was breathless, as if he were drinking life-giving liquid from her lips. She wondered if he realized what his behavior was revealing to her. Obviously not, or he might cease it. She cuddled into his arms and sighed tranquilly.

As they rested in each other's embrace following their blissful exertions, Marsh entreated, "Don't write to your mother just yet. She'll get more worried and come looking for you, or send someone to do it for her. We can't afford any intrusion at this point. Agreed?"

Randee's heart thumped madly as she read between the lines of his sentences: he wanted and needed more time alone with her to study his feelings. "Don't worry, Marsh, I can't write to my mother. If I do, my stepfather will come looking for me, and he's the last person I ever want to see again. I have to tell you why I left home, but please don't judge me too harshly," she implored, then slowly related what had taken place in Kansas.

She continued in a ragged voice, "I despise him, and one day I'm going to kill him. If you're not tired of me when this task is over, I'd like to hire you to help me rescue my mother from that beast. I'll pay you whatever I can. I still have money left over from the Carsons."

When Marsh remained silent and rigid, Randee worried that her story had filled him with disgust for her weakness. "Maybe I'm to blame. If I hadn't been such a coward for so long, he wouldn't have gotten such a grip on . . ."

Marsh rolled atop her and cut off her remaining words with a pervasive kiss. "Don't you ever blame yourself again, woman. If you'd tried to battle a bastard like that, you and your mother would be dead. If we live through this mess here, I'll get him for you, him and his men."

Randee hugged him tightly, and tears of relief slipped from her eyes. Marsh wiped them away gently and kissed each misty eye. "The Carsons lied about my whereabouts to protect me. They took me in and treated me like their own child. I owe them, Marsh; that's why I have to avenge their murders. It was a difficult journey to Texas alone, but I made it just fine. I used every trick my father had taught me about concealing my trail. If Payton had suspected where I was, he would have come after me before now. The trouble is, once Payton learns about the Carsons' deaths, he'll try to take over their ranch, or sell it. I can't let him do that; I have to stop him. The good part is, as long as everyone in Wadesville thinks I'm the heir, they won't go looking for another one. That gives me time to . . . I don't know what."

"Then, we have an unexpected problem," he hinted.

"What do you mean?" she asked.

Marsh told her about the stage attack by Indians. Thank goodness, he could say truthfully, "They were talking about it when I was in the stage office to mail a letter to my friend in Fort Worth. I'm sure Brody Wade knows you're missing by now."

"You don't think he believes I'm dead, do you?"

"I hope not, and I doubt it. Since the women were captured and the Army's after them, he's probably waiting around for your rescue. He knows you're strong and brave. When we get near Wadesville in a few days, I'll go into town to collect those rewards and see what I can learn. I don't want you showing your face unless it's necessary."

Randee hoped his highest motive was to keep her away from Brody out of jealousy. To find out, she teased, "Is that why you were so nasty at supper, afraid

244

I'd insist on relieving Brody's worries by riding head-long for Wadesville?"

"The thought entered my mind," he admitted after a chuckle.

"Don't worry, partner, I'll follow your orders."

"Thanks, woman. We'll take our chances that Brody won't go looking for any Carson kinfolk for a while." Marsh didn't hesitate before adding, "In case that Payton bastard and his men come looking for you, stick real close to me. I won't let them steal you or harm you."

Randee was thrilled to hear that news, that he had another reason for keeping her around a long time and that he was so protective and possessive. Marsh knew she had no place to go except the ranch, and Payton could locate her there. She was glad she had revealed her past to him tonight. "I'm glad you understand what I told you and why I was keeping it a secret. I was so ashamed."

"You have no reason to feel guilty or embarrassed, woman. You were caught in a trap, and you freed yourself as soon as it was safe for everybody concerned. I like the way you reason things out and use self-control. Frankly, I'm glad that bastard drove you to Texas so we could meet. Where would I be without my talented partner?"

Randee's heart was touched by how easily he related his feelings. Surely it meant he was opening up to her, softening his heart, trusting her. Surely they both realized how special they were to each other, even without commitments between them.

After his confession, Marsh's keen mind warned him of his slip. He couldn't let them get too close just yet, not with this hazardous mission still looming over their heads like a ravenous vulture who was waiting for them to die. Yet, it was becoming too easy to be totally relaxed around her. He had to keep his head clear! It was good to have this insight into Randee Hollis. She was strong because of all she had endured and because of what her father had ingrained in her. She could stand as tall and straight as any man, and he was proud of her. Somehow, he had to slay that bastard for daring to touch and terrify this special creature who was stealing his heart and wits!

But right now, he had to slow down this runaway relationship. He murmured in her ear, "I was born a rambling rogue with dust in my veins, so I'll need a good challenge after this one's over. I'll go to Kansas with you later, and rid your home of that sorry piece of manhood. I'm sure your mother will be overjoyed to get you back home again, especially with a new baby to tend. She'll need help with the chores, and you know a lot about ranching. You two won't have any trouble after he's dead. Of course, you two might prefer to take over the Carson Ranch; it is one of the best spreads in Texas."

In her mind, Randee heard Marsh close the carelessly opened door between them as he panicked after his revelation. It wasn't unexpected, but at least he was opening it a crack here and there, and that gave her hope that it would remain open one day. "I'll pay you well for your time and trouble, Marsh, and I'll be grateful for the help. But I want you to find a safe way to get rid of him; I don't want you getting into any trouble because of me. Maybe you can use your earnings to start up your ranch again one day."

Marsh chuckled. "Me, become a rancher or a farmer? I left that life behind long ago, Randee. I was born to wander, woman. At heart, I'm a restless man, a carefree adventurer."

She tickled his stomach as she replied with a lightheartedness that she didn't feel, "I know, Durango, but

246

times change. You'll get old and tired eventually and need a safe place to rest."

He jested unwisely, "If I live long enough."

Randee smacked his chest with her fist and ordered gruffly, "Don't ever say that again, Marsh Logan! You're too smart and fast to get killed before you get out of this dangerous existence you love." Here was a man who thought he had everything he wanted and needed: youth, good looks, prowess, freedom, money, jobs of his choice and timing, a legendary reputation, and valuable land. Why should he want to complicate such a carefree and satisfying existence by taking on a wife, or a full-time lover? How could she prove to him that he needed one more thing to complete his life and happiness?

Marsh changed the topic by revealing, "I did get some news today. There's a rich group in Fort Worth buying up most of those spreads, the Mid-Texas Company. My friend couldn't find out who owns it or what they want with so much land, but he's still working on it. A lawyer named George Light referred to the owners as "them," so there must be more than one behind those curious purchases. That letter I sent out today asked my contact to see what he can learn about Foley Timms and Quantrill's Raiders. Hopefully he'll have some facts for us when we reach Fort Worth next week."

"If we can unmask an illegal land grab, maybe we can stop these killings without having to challenge that gang face to face."

"They still have to be killed or captured, Randee. Stopping their raids is only part of my mission. They have to pay for their crimes."

"You sound more like a marshal than a hired gun-slinger," she jested. "But you're right; they have to be punished, all of them."

"You know you can quit any time you want out,

247

Randee, and I'll finish this task for us. I don't want you getting hurt or slain."

"That's very considerate of you, Mr. Logan, but I'm along for the entire ride. You might need someone to protect your backside."

"Right now, I'm more concerned with my frontside," he said huskily, then began making love to her for the second time that night.

Marsh was gone when Randee awoke. She sponged off, using the water bowl and pitcher in her room, then dressed. Shortly, the laundress arrived to deliver their clean clothes. Randee placed Marsh's things on her bed and packed her own garments. She knocked on Marsh's door, but there was no answer. Hungry, she went downstairs to see if he was waiting there for her. He wasn't, so she sat down to eat alone. He had probably eaten earlier and was out gathering information.

Just as she finished her meal, she noticed people gathering along the wooden sidewalk outside the restaurant windows. She paid for the food and headed for the hotel door to check on the excitement. Her heart nearly stopped in panic. Two men were standing in the dirt street, preparing for a duel, and one was Marsh Logan. . . .

Randee moved back inside to the window, as she didn't want to distract her love with her fear and presence. She glued her wide eyes to the awesome scene before her. She felt nauseous with alarm, and she was trembling. Her entire body felt cold and numb, like death. She watched Marsh closely, noting the signs of a skilled gunfighter: his agile walk, his controlled stance, his confident expression, his keen alertness, and the way he wore his guns strapped to muscled thighs. His hat was resting on his back, allowing everyone to see his ice-blue eyes, which revealed a steely calm. Marsh exuded prowess. No hint of fear showed itself in his carriage or looks. He was dressed in that snug and sexy black garb, and his jawline was dark with stubble. His body was loose, as if he didn't have a care or worry. He was intimidating, a sight to strike terror in the heart of the bravest man. She wondered why any man would recklessly challenge him and invite certain death.

Randee glanced at Marsh's challenger, and knew this battle could have only one ending. Even at a distance, she read fear and uncertainty in the young man's body movements and expression. That man was nervous, and stupid to challenge the Durango Kid. She saw him finger his gun butt, as he was wearing only one pistol, whereas Marsh had two. He was wearing a hat that was slanted downward to block out the sun, which he was facing, another mistake on his part.

The tension mounted as each of the two opponents seemingly waited for the other to make the first move. The witnesses were still and quiet. An eerie silence surrounded the entire scene, perhaps because death hung heavy in the still air.

Marsh called out in a steady voice, "It doesn't have to be this way, boy. You can step off the street as easily as you stepped onto it. This day is too pretty for dying, and you don't stand a chance of beating me to the draw. Go home, boy; I don't want to kill you."

Suddenly, Randee's heart lurched as another man stepped into the street and took his place at the challenger's side. She wanted to race upstairs and fetch her guns to help Marsh, but there was no time. All she could do was observe the deadly drama being played out in Brownwood. Her respiration came in short, shallow gasps. Her mouth was dry, and she could hardly swallow. Her heart was thudding so forcefully that she wondered why it didn't explode within her chest.

"Come on, Durango, you can take both of us, can't you?" the second man taunted to unsettle the fearless man in black.

Randee glared at the two killers whom she recognized from the raid at the Carson Ranch. Randee stared at Marsh and wondered why he needed her along to identify the gang if he could do so . . . .

The confrontation came to an end. Guns were drawn and shots were fired, and the two men opposite Marsh lay dead on one end of the dusty street. Marsh casually holstered his weapons, put on his hat, and walked toward the hotel. The crowd rushed into the street and surrounded the challengers, laughing and chatting excitedly.

Randee turned and fled to her room, locking the door behind her for some reason. She sat on the edge of the sofa and stared at the floor. She had never seen a man move as swiftly and nimbly as Marsh had. Those two men had about as much of a chance at victory as an icicle beneath a blazing sun! She had heard how skilled he was, but now she had witnessed it, and was still amazed.

Reality settled in on her. The man she loved and was traveling with was a . . . No, her mind argued, refusing to even think the terrible word. Yet, she could still see him in her mind's eye: poised confidently and nonchalantly as he waited to slay two men who never stood a chance against his superior skills. Would it be this way in every town they entered? How many men had he slain? How many more gunfights before Marsh was the one lying dead in the street, with insensitive people crowding around him to view his famous body? Could she hang around until that grim day?

She jumped up to pace the floor, unable to think along those heart-wrenching lines. Did it matter that he had tried to dissuade them from attacking? Did it matter that they wouldn't allow Mar . . . the Durango Kid to leave without battling them? Did it matter that they were killers with the Epson Gang? Yes, it mattered greatly.

There was a knock on her door and she knew it was Marsh. She turned and looked at the barrier between them, realizing it wasn't the only one, and sadness filled her. She walked to the door and opened it. Without looking at him, she turned and went to the bed to gather his clean clothes. "The laundress returned these. You'll need to pack them."

Marsh watched her, then asked, "You saw what happened?"

"Yes, I was downstairs eating. Are you all right?" she inquired, wanting to rush into his arms and cover him with kisses.

"As fine as anyone can be after being forced to shoot two men," he replied, his tone sounding oddly strained.

Randee looked at him and asked, "Who were they? Why did they want to battle you?"

"Just two fools looking to increase their reputations."

"Killing the Durango Kid would certainly accomplish that goal. It wasn't a fair fight, two against one."

"I knew which one would draw first. That first kid was real scared, so I knew he'd move slow. That second man was cocky, so it had to be him. If I hadn't of taken them down today, they would have trailed us for another shot at me. I didn't want to endanger you."

When she didn't speak, he tried to break the tension by adding, "A trick you maybe can use one day is knowing when a man's ready to draw on you. His fingers will twitch and they'll graze his gun butt nervously. Once he loosens his fingers, he's ready to pull his pistol. If you think you're faster and he's stalling, wiggle your own fingers and he'll panic and draw. An-

251

other thing to know, Randee, if a man's wearing two guns, he'll draw the one on the hand he favors. You can tell which one by noticing on which side he fastens his belt. See," he pointed out. "I'm left-handed, so I run my belt through my pants' loops in this direction. Don't go by a man's holsters, because they're usually made alike."

"That's very clever and astute," she remarked, impressed.

Randee walked to the window and gazed outside. If it was only a coincidence that those two men were gang members, she needed to know and not let unfair suspicions breed within her. Besides, it was time to tell Marsh she could identify the raiders, as he would see the ranch attic soon and guess her tightly guarded secret. By revealing it now, she would prove her trust in him. Too, those men whom he had been challenged to slay might have been after her . . . .

"Something's troubling you, woman. Spit it out," he coaxed.

Randee faced him and asked, "Did you know those two men?"

"Most men reveal their names after a gunfight. If they win it, they stand around in the saloon, drinking and boasting."

"Then, your answer is no," she pressed.

"That's correct. What's your point," he asked, baffled.

Randee divulged softly, "They were members of the Epson Gang. Maybe they were sent after me and you were in their way."

Marsh walked over to her and stared down into her face. "You're trying to tell me something important, aren't you?"

"My uncle's ranch had small open spaces in the attic, just beneath the overhanging roof, for releasing heat in

252

the summer. The coverings had just been removed because winter was over. By walking across the beams from one side to another, I could see everything that happened all around the house. After the killings, the gang members removed their hoods to search the house and finish their grim work. I saw their faces," she confessed.

Marsh had suspected this news, but it still stunned him to hear it revealed. "Do you realize how much danger you're in, woman?" he asked. When Randee nodded, he said, "I'm glad I got you out of Wadesville, but I doubt those men were searching for you. There was another raid below Fort Richardson yesterday, so they couldn't have gotten here this quickly. Maybe they were advance scouts or riding on their own now. I'm glad you finally told me the truth, Randee. This means I'll have to guard you more closely."

"I'm sure you suspected I knew more than I was telling. That's why you agreed to bring me along, wasn't it?"

"You're right," he admitted, then grinned. "I should have known you were too smart to fool."

"You are, too, but I was afraid you'd leave me behind if you no longer needed me for clues."

Marsh made another admission, "I would have, if things got too dangerous for you. But now it appears as if you're safest with me, considering you've got that gang and your stepfather looking for you."

"There's something else, Marsh. The entrance to the attic is hidden behind a chest in one of the bedrooms, so those villains didn't find it or me. If they spy on their victims beforehand like we suspect, then they knew about my existence. Obviously they must have thought I was away that morning. I heard them searching the house, and I saw the mess they made after I left the attic."

When she halted for breath, he assumed she was finished, and ventured, "Like you said, when they couldn't find you, they probably figured you were gone somewhere. They wouldn't have known you were around that day if you hadn't placed that notice in the papers. That was rash, woman, but it can't be changed now."

"That isn't my point, Marsh. Remember all the raid sites we've visited?" He looked puzzled until she added, "Everything was destroyed. Yet, they didn't burn the Carsons' house. Isn't that a bit strange?"

Marsh thought hard for a minute. "There has to be a clue there, woman. If they didn't know you were hiding inside, then it couldn't have been to spare you. But who would want that house?"

"I don't know. Uncle Lee built it, and he's been the only owner of that land besides the Indians. But it must have been left standing for a reason. I just can't think of one."

"I'll put it on our list of curious clues. See there, I need to keep you around just for using your brains."

"Among other things," she jested seductively.

"Mercy, woman, I am a bad influence on you. I may have to wash your mouth out with soap before this week's over."

They laughed and embraced.

"Are you in any trouble about that shooting?"

Marsh shook his dark head. "Things like that happen in every town all the time. There's no law against self-defense."

"If those bandits hear about you gunning down two of their men, they'll be after both of us. We should get moving fast, partner."

After having slept late and being slowed down by the gunfight and long talk, it was early afternoon before they left town. They gathered their possessions and walked to the livery stable. They mounted Midnight and Rojo and left Brownwood behind.

They had planned to check out Camp Colorado, a post evacuated in '65, but Marsh told her it was unnecessary. He'd learned the day before that there were numerous farmers in the area, and no one had had any trouble with Epson Gang raids. In a way, that was good, because it meant that section was out of the attack area. So far, all raids had remained inside that oblong territory which Marsh had mentioned—a clue they both found intriguing, but not yet enlightening.

They retrieved the dynamite from where Marsh had concealed it the night before, and continued their steady journey northeastward. With stops here and there to check old raid sites and to rest, Marsh and Randee made it to a nice camping spot before dark, twenty-five miles beyond Brownwood.

Thursday was much the same, and they camped near the Leon River shortly before dusk. After Marsh checked out the surrounding area, they took a swim and made love by the river's edge. Afterwards, they lay snuggled together on overlapping bedrolls and talked.

He told her about many of the odd jobs he had done since leaving home at seventeen: frontier guide, freight-wagon driver, cowhand, scout for wagon trains, and trail boss. Several positions surprised her when he added to the list: small-town deputy, guard for gold shipments and payrolls, and shotgunner for a stage line. He didn't mention his work with Galvanized Yankees during the war, which had led to his selection as a government agent for President Grant. Nor did he tell her that many of those jobs had been covers for secret

255

missions.

"I can't imagine the Durango Kid earning a living by working for the law or by holding down a steady job. You must have been countless places and seen all kinds of things."

"Yep, I reckon I have, Miss Hollis. Maybe I'll tell you all about them one day, if you're real good and patient."

"Both are near impossible for a headstrong vixen like me, but I'll try my best," she vowed amidst intentionally skeptical laughter. "You've done an awfully lot of things in less than fifteen years. Can you tell me why you left home?" she asked hesitantly.

Marsh released his hold on her and flattened his back against the ground. He folded his arms and tucked his hands beneath his head. Sighing deeply, he stared at the stars above him.

Assuming it was a touchy matter, she quickly said, "If you prefer not to talk about it, I'll understand. I'm too nosy at times."

Marsh slowly and painfully related most of what had happened between him and his father. "I just couldn't look him in the face anymore. We were fighting all the time, and tearing my mother apart. I figured the best thing to do was leave home before things got worse. By the time I learned the truth and understood his side, it was too late. I was already set in my ways, and all I could bring them was trouble. Now that they're gone, I have no home and parents to return to, if I ever got that yearning. I'm used to being on my own. It might be selfish, but I like it that way."

Randee did not take offense at his last few sentences, as she had known his feelings from the beginning, and now she understood them even more. Just because they differed from hers, that didn't make either one of them right or wrong. She had to stop hoping and believing he would change for her; she had to accept him for the way he was — which had to be wonderful since she had fallen in love with him. To this man, home represented anguish, disappointment, betrayal, weakness, entrapment, and resentment. As with her, he had felt as if he could never return. He had made a life for himself elsewhere, nowhere, and it suited his current emotional needs. "It's a shame you and your father couldn't have worked out your differences before you were forced to leave home, but I understand your reasons and feelings. If you hadn't left home and learned the skills you possess today, you wouldn't be alive to use them for justice. And without them, Marsh, you couldn't have saved your home and parents. Don't you realize that? Please, stop challenging death to prove you're stronger and smarter than it is. Fate chooses the moment for us to be born and to die. All we can do is fill the time between them with as much happiness as we can find. It isn't a fatal flaw to grasp as much of life as you can hold."

He turned his head to look at her. She had sat up while speaking and was stroking his bare chest as if to comfort him. Moonlight sifted through her tawny hair, bathing it and her body in a silvery glow. If she realized she was nude and uncovered to the waist, it didn't show on her lovely face. Her breasts were firm and supple, and her skin invited his touch. She looked like an angel sitting there, one come to save him from himself. How could he not want her, take her?

"Come here, Randee," he entreated huskily. "I need you."

The request was a simple one, a stimulating one, a revealing one. Randee went into his arms and sealed their lips. They made love passionately, as if battling unseen ghosts and cleansing their souls of them.

As she watched him sleep afterwards, she recalled

how he had said *need*, not want. She smiled happily and joined him in slumber.

Friday evening, they reached the town of Granbury, which was beautifully situated on a tranquil lake. In 1854, Thomas Lambert had united his settlement with another one called Stockton and made it into a thriving little town. In '59, a man named Jacob de Cordova had accumulated land scrip—certificates indicating the right of the holder to receive payment later in cash— for more than a million acres. Billing himself as the "Publicity Agent for an Empire," he had lectured throughout the East to promote interest in Texas.

Marsh and Randee had dressed as simply as possible and registered as a couple, hoping to go unnoticed in this town so close to Wadesville.

As they prepared to go downstairs to eat supper, Marsh said, "I felt naked coming into town wearing that Colt of yours just to keep from attracting attention to us. We shouldn't have come here tonight."

"How else will we gather information if we stay out in the wilds?" she teased to calm his unusual tension. "You couldn't leave me alone out there while you rode in alone. I may be a nuisance, Logan, but you'll have to endure me for as long as we're partners."

Randee was gazing out the window as Marsh retorted, "You're anything but a nuisance, woman. You're more like—"

"Marsh, come here quick," she told him. When he joined her, she pointed to three men standing outside the saloon talking. "There's three more of them. What'll we do? You can't take on three men."

"Not fairly," he replied, a cold edge to his voice as he eyed the half-Indian, the gaunt Mexican, and the burly black man.

258

"Either the gang's nearby, or those men are resting between raids."

"For certain we can't ask questions with them in town. I'll fetch you some supper to eat up here, then I'll take a look around."

"What if you're recognized?" she asked worriedly.

"I should have said sneak around, woman. I won't take any unnecessary risks, so stop fretting. This has to be done, Randee. And, no, you can't tag along. Stay put so I can concentrate."

"Damn you, Marsh Logan, if you get hurt out there alone . . ."

Marsh silenced her with a heady kiss. When their lips parted, she warned, "That trick won't work every time, Mr. Logan."

"I know, but it's fun trying it," he jested mirthfully.

"You are a vexing devil," she accused.

He kissed her again before replying, "And you are a beautiful angel. Relax, woman, haven't you heard I'm indestructible?"

"No one is, not even the Durango Kid. Please be careful."

Marsh brought her meal back within fifteen minutes, changed into his ebony garments and left the room.

It was too dark and Marsh was too skilled to be visually followed outside. Randee picked over her food to pass the time. She had waited for Marsh Logan all of her life; now she was waiting to see if he was lost to her forever . . . .

Chapter Twelve

This time, Marsh returned shortly after midnight, frowning and weary. He looked at her and said, "I got them all, but I didn't learn anything from those bastards. They were as close-mouthed as I would have been. I just didn't expect them to be so stubborn and brave. That worries me, woman." He stretched out on the double bed without undressing and rested his arm over his eyes.

Randee watched him from her side of the bed, and decided to keep silent until he was ready to explain what happened tonight. He needed to get things straight in his head and rest a while. Maybe killing wasn't as easy for him as she had imagined it would be for a gunslinger. Or maybe he was just depressed over this frustrating matter. He was accustomed to getting what he wanted, until tonight, until this gang. Clearly he wasn't used to defeat of any kind, and it felt bad to him.

Finally he sat up and half turned to her. He was glad she had given him time to relax and think before asking any questions; most women would have been jabbering away the moment he returned. When she smiled encouragingly, he reached out and caressed her cheek. She cocked her head sideways and nuzzled his hand with her eyes closed, looking serene and radiant.

He liked the way she gave him space and comfort when he needed them, and he needed both tonight. He felt better just having her nearby, better than if he'd had a shot of aged whiskey. Yep, it was good having somebody special to share good and bad times with, somebody to talk to, somebody to lean on for a change, somebody who understood him and his crazy moods.

He revealed wearily, "I hid their bodies, so we should be able to leave in the morning without any problem. I wish we could ride out now, but we can't risk grabbing someone's notice. Once they're missed, along with those other two, somebody's gonna get awfully curious about their deaths. 'Course, we knew this was going to happen sometime. I just hate drawing them in on us and endangering you. Are you sure you won't go somewhere and hide until this matter is over?"

"Please don't ask me to leave you alone to face this peril. I'll be fine, honestly. If you leave me somewhere, you'll only worry about them locating me and that'll destroy your concentration. We're better off sticking together. Did you stop to think that maybe they were more afraid of their boss's wrath than afraid of you and death?"

"That must be true, because they died in silence. It's just that men like those are usually cowards when they don't have their cohorts surrounding them. They played innocents up to the end."

"I'm glad you got them, Marsh, because they weren't innocents. That Indian was the one who killed my uncle. He slit Uncle Lee's throat, then dropped his body to the ground and viciously kicked it over and over. And that Mexican raped and beat the housekeeper before slaying her. I wanted to look away from such horrors, but I watched so I could remember each one of them and despise them enough to kill them when the time came."

261

He drew her tawny head against his chest and stroked her hair. "I'm sorry you had to witness such savagery, but they'll pay, every one of them. I swear it."

"If those raiders are working nearby, what are they doing with all those stolen cattle and goods? They'd need a large place to corral them and store everything. Plus room to alter their brands before selling them. How can that much activity and stock go unnoticed?"

"Somebody big and important is protecting them. Maybe those infernal State Police are in on this mess. Whoever it is, their boss knows enough about this territory to hide them good. Darn it all, we can't stop every large cattle drive and check brands and ownership, so we're right back where we started, with nothing but questions and more questions. Dammit, Randee, we need a lucky break in this case!"

She noticed his last word, but assumed it was a holdover from his deputy days. She heard his heart thudding swiftly as she hinted, "Maybe you can pick up some current news in Wadesville tomorrow."

"If those bastards are spreading out in local towns to rest a while, I wouldn't know a stranger in town if I bumped into one. But I don't want you going there, with them in this area. By now, they could know about your threat and be waiting around for your return."

Randee realized how worried he was over her safety, and it warmed her. "I'm not arguing with your order, Mr. Logan, so calm down. Why don't we get some sleep and talk about this in the morning?"

"Sleep isn't what I need, woman; you are."

Randee leaned away to look up into his smoldering gaze. "I was hoping your needs matched mine tonight." She unbuttoned his shirt and removed it, then pulled off his boots. Marsh stood beside the bed and eased out of his pants. He watched Randee lift her gown over her head and toss it to the floor before he doused the lantern and joined her. He pulled her into his arms, and simply held her for a long time.

Mercy, she had become a special part of him! Maybe that was why he had failed tonight, a lack of attention and the urge to get back at her side quickly, an intoxicating arrangement that could end at any time. Maybe he hadn't used enough time and pain to withdraw information from those bastards. But he couldn't leave her behind; she was in too much peril, and he needed her every day . . . .

"Woman, you're driving me crazy," he murmured in her ear as she spread fiery kisses over his neck and chest, aware of how easy things were between them, including total intimacy. Being together like this seemed as natural as breathing.

Randee rolled him to his back and straddled him, sensuously gathering his erect manhood within her receptive body. Randee felt that same closeness, that same powerful, but gentle, bond. It was as if they had always been a part of each other and always would be. As she made unrestrained love to him, she whispered almost breathlessly, "You affect me the same way, Marsh Logan. If we have to die together, what better way than this?"

Thoughts of nothing, including perils or doubts or hopes, intruded on their blissful world in that small hotel room. No inhibitions, modesty, or worries came between them as they captured a pleasure and closeness that few couples found even after years of lovemaking and marriage. Their hearts were united as tightly and rapturously as their bodies were, and their passions ran wild and free, never to be leashed again . . . .

Saturday afternoon, Randee remained hidden in a thick grove of trees while Marsh rode into Wadesville to see Sheriff Brody Wade. Marsh wouldn't allow her to visit the ranch, speculating that someone might see her there. He told her he was afraid those raiders might check it out to see if she, or anyone else, had returned there.

Randee knew Marsh was right, because the house had been spared for some unknown reason. If that boss wanted it, surely he would have it guarded to make certain it remained abandoned. As she sat there alone, she tried to come up with uses for the targeted area of attacks. It was a large territory, so whoever wanted it so badly had to have plenty of money and a special reason. Who was rich enough to purchase so much land? she wondered. Who was powerful enough to control it after his gang was dismissed? What purpose could it serve? As Marsh had said, endless questions without answers, yet.

Marsh leaned against the door jamb in Brody Wade's office as he waited for the sheriff to get his money and the release paper to sign. He watched Brody intently, as the man kept glancing at him oddly, and he recalled how Brody had had him and Randee followed.

Brody noticed that the man wasn't wearing all black today. Instead, he was dressed in a medium-blue shirt, dark-brown leather vest, and faded jeans. Still, he looked intimidating and self-assured. "I was beginning to think you weren't coming back for this reward money; it's been over two weeks. I suppose a man like you who earns blood money with his gun doesn't need a measly two hundred dollars. Sign this," Brody ordered, shoving the paper at Marsh.

Marsh picked up the money and stuffed it in his pocket without even glancing at it. "A man can always use money, Sheriff, for good whiskey and a pleasing woman here and there."

"Speaking of women, that fair-haired girl you met here last time was kidnapped by Indians at the Red River crossing. You interested in earning a reward from me to go looking for her?" Brody asked, eyeing the other man closely for his reaction.

"That's a shame, Sheriff Wade, she was a real looker. By now, she's probably the personal slave of one of those red bucks. You sure you want her back? Most white men wouldn't."

"I ain't most white men," Brody snapped coldly. "You interested or not? I'll pay you a thousand dollars plus expenses."

"That's a healthy bundle for a small town sheriff. You sure she's still worth it?" Marsh asked, propping his boot on the chair before Brody's desk and laying his arm across his raised thigh.

"Randee Hollis is worth far more, but it's all I have in savings. I was going to use it for a down payment on a ranch. But what good is a ranch without a wife? Not that it's any of your business, but we're supposed to be married when she returns. You're a drifter, a gunslinger. Why not spend your time doing something good for a change? She's a special woman, and I don't want her living as no squaw."

Marsh suspected that Brody was feeling him out for information, baiting him for answers. He didn't bite rashly. "Trouble is, Sheriff, I already have a higher paying job awaiting me in Austin. A rich rancher is having problems with some rustlers and I've agreed to get rid of them for him. He's offering five thousand. Can you better that offer?"

Brody glared at the cocky man and sneered, "You know I can't. Dammit, man, you met her! She's sweet, and innocent, and gentle. She doesn't deserve a fate like that. She has money; I know she'll up the reward if

265

you locate her and rescue her."

"Best I recall, you warned me to stay away from her. You sure you would trust me on the trail with her? I wouldn't if I were you. Why don't you go after her? She's your . . . *friend*, wasn't it?"

Rage colored Brody's cheeks a bright red. His brown eyes blazed with fiery hatred and contempt. His muscles were taut and his fists were balled tightly on the desk. His request for help had been to probe for information, but it was actually a good idea to hire this rogue to do a job he couldn't do himself. He tried to compose himself as he scoffed, "I don't know anything about Indians or Indian Territory. It would take a skilled gunman like you to find her and rescue her."

"Thanks for the compliment, Sheriff, but I can't afford to lose that job in Austin. It'll keep me in pocket money for a long time. Besides, that little gal appeared mighty feisty to me. I wouldn't be surprised if she tricks those redskins into bringing her home before dark."

"You're a cold and cocky son of a bitch! You don't care about anybody except yourself. One day somebody's going to kill you."

Marsh retorted flippantly, "Plenty have tried, and plenty more will, but I don't die easily. I can't risk a sure five thousand on the hope I can find her alive and she'll honor your offer with her money. Once she's free, you two might decide to double-cross me and keep the money; that would be a fatal mistake for all of us."

Infuriated, Brody nearly shouted, "Sign that release and get out of my office! In fact, get out of my town!"

As Marsh lifted the writing quill, Brody warned icily, "And sign your real name, which ain't the Durango Kid. I've seen him."

Marsh chuckled, further irritating the man. "Durango is my cousin. We look alike, so people are always

266

confusing us. He doesn't mind if I use his name once in a while to make people either take notice or steer clear of me. If you don't believe me, ask him the next time you see him, which shouldn't be too long from now. I hear he's riding up this way soon." Marsh signed the paper and tossed it to Brody.

The scowling man lifted it, read it, and frowned again.

"Be seeing you around, Sheriff Wade," Marsh said. He left to buy supplies, aware of the frigid gaze boring into his retreating back. Yep, he decided, that sheriff could be trouble if he wasn't careful.

Brody eyed the paper skeptically, then looked puzzled. Where had he heard or read that name before? he wondered. *Storm Hayden, is it? We'll just see why that name sounds vaguely familiar* . . . .

Brody called his deputy into the office and ordered, "Matt, follow that snake and see what hole he slithers into. And don't lose him this time. I don't trust him, and I'm gonna find out why."

Marsh knew Deputy Matthew Johnson was observing him as he visited the mercantile store and gun shop. He chatted genially with both shopkeepers, learning of two raids near the center of that oblong area which was marked on the map in his saddlebag. He must have guessed right; those bastards were fanned out to avoid grabbing anyone's attention while they awaited orders for their next raid. He wished he could ask if a Marshal Foley Timms was, or had been, in this area, this town, but Brody Wade might check with these townfolk to see what questions he asked. And such questions would appear too suspicious.

Marsh grinned as the incompetent deputy tried to dog him when he left town. He took the road southward to indicate a ride to Austin as he had claimed. He was amused at Brody's challenge of his identity and hadn't minded signing a name which he had used long ago during one of his missions. There was no way Sheriff Brody Wade could investigate "Storm Hayden," because the man didn't exist, and all information about that false identity had been ordered destroyed years ago. For certain, he didn't want Brody discovering he was Marsh Logan, at least no time soon. After a few miles, Marsh tricked the careless deputy and doubled back to join up with Randee.

When he reached the place he had left her, she wasn't there. Her saddle and possessions were piled beneath the tree, but Randee and Rojo were nowhere in sight. A fear such as he had never experienced before charged through his body like a bolt of lightning. Nervous sweat beaded on his forehead and above his upper lip. His heart thundered erratically, altering his respiration to a rapid pace. He searched the area and noticed a line scratched on the ground, an arrow pointing westward. Obviously she had left of her own free will, and left him a message of some sort. He dropped their supplies and his saddlebags near hers, mounted Midnight, and followed her trail.

It was one of the longest rides Marsh had ever taken. When he finally sighted her, joy and relief flooded him. He forcibly mastered his visible panic, a new emotion for him. Now he understood that same reaction in the beauty before him, and he would never fault her with it again. He sneaked up to where she was hiding in a gully, which was densely edged with trees and bushes.

The green-eyed blonde smiled and motioned him close enough to whisper into his ear, "Three more raiders, Marsh, camped over there. Two of them rode past the place I was waiting for you, so I followed them here. They joined that third man. I was very careful. I used the skills you taught me about removing anything that could make noise. I didn't take any risks, and I was about to come fetch you for help."

Marsh peered between the heavily leaved limbs and saw three men lying around a campfire, drinking and talking. It didn't appear as if they were expecting any other gang members to join them. He whispered, "I'm riding into their camp to see if they'll drop any clues. I'll pretend I'm looking for a job." As Randee started to protest, he told her, "Take your rifle and train it on that man in the tan shirt. If there's trouble, you get him and I'll take out the other two. Watch him close, woman. Don't let him finger that pistol too long before shooting him. I don't want any bullet holes marring this handsome body, and you don't either," he teased as she composed herself. "Ready?"

She looked him in the eye and said, "Ready. Be careful."

Marsh smiled, kissed her lightly, then sneaked back to his black stallion. The surge of energy from an imminent challenge filled him. He was proud of Randee; she had done everything right this time. Between the two of them, she wasn't in any peril, so he relaxed. He called out, "You there in camp, rider coming in."

Having used the standard announcement before approaching another man's camp, Marsh slowly guided his horse in that direction. The men roused themselves instantly, all three coming to their feet and staring at Marsh. Randee aimed her new rifle at the center of one man's back, the one in the tan shirt, the bearded one whom she recalled vividly from the Carson Ranch attack. She did not allow her attention to stray for a single moment, as her love's life depended on it.

Marsh casually reined in a few feet from the three men. "Got any coffee to spare, or a sip of good whiskey? I've been riding since dawn and I've got a thirst which would shame a desert. I can pay fifty cents for a share of your supper, but that's about all I got until I find some work around here." Making sure to move unthreateningly slow, he dropped Midnight's reins to the ground and jested amiably, "Hell, these ranchers want to work the hide off of you for a few dollars a month. Got to be an easier way to make your pockets jingle."

"Rest your butt on that log, stranger, and help yourself," said the man in faded Army clothes. "Where you from?"

Marsh dished up some beans and poured himself some coffee, then took a seat on the suggested log. "Down San Antonio way most recently. Had to leave real quick for shooting a deputy in the leg. 'Course, he deserved it. Got real mad when I spent my last two dollars on his favorite saloon gal. But a man's gotta have his releases. Shame though, 'cause she weren't worth dying for. Some new gal in Digger's Saloon, who didn't know much about pleasing a man." Marsh chuckled wickedly, then sipped the hot coffee and shoved beans into his mouth to stall for time to study the men. He noticed that they remained standing, a bad sign because they were displaying ready-to-attack stances. He set his coffee cup on the ground and held the metal plate between his hands, as it would be easy to toss it aside to draw his guns. Knowing Randee had the tan-shirted man in her sights, he concentrated on assessing the other two villains. "Damn, that's good. My belly's been chewing on my backbone for hours. You fellas know anything about work in these parts? I need money real fast to keep from starving."

"Ain't much work in this area, stranger. Too many ranchers been run out by that Epson Gang," another man informed him.

Marsh knew the three men were openly studying him as hard as he was furtively studying them. "Seems like the only paying job around here is with them," he teased, filling his mouth again.

"If you don't mind the law running up your backside, I guess it is."

"Can't say I do, but it's happened a few times," Marsh hinted.

"I figured that, by the way you wear your guns," the first man remarked, resting his right hand on his pistol butt.

"You can relax, friend; I ain't wanted in this area."

"You wanted someplace else?" the third man finally spoke up.

"Maybe. Does it matter?" Marsh asked, staring the man down.

"Not to us, but it might to the local law if you hang around these parts very long," the first man told him.

"Too dull around here. All I need is some money in these pockets and I'll be riding out. You boys live around here or just passing through?"

"Just passing through like you, mister."

"Need an extra hand at anything?" Marsh asked pointedly.

"Nope," the first man replied quickly. The leader of this resting party nodded to his two friends, then suggested, "Why don't you pass those guns over before we talk any more? I got a strange feeling in my gut about you. If I like your answers, I'll give 'em back."

Marsh's gaze shifted from one man to the next. "The Durango Kid don't hand his guns over to nobody. If you want 'em real bad, you'll have to risk taking them. But don't call me out unless you're ready to die on this beautiful day. I ain't looking for a fight, boys, but I'll be obliged to give you one if you make any moves I don't like."

The three men stared at Marsh, then exchanged rapid looks. "We've heard about you, Kid. Why didn't you just give us your name up front? What you doing in this area?"

When they didn't relax their stances, Marsh knew he hadn't won them over. He told himself to be ready for trouble to strike any minute. "Like I said, boys, looking to earn a dollar or two while I rest up a spell. Then, I'm heading down San Antonio way for some unfinished business. Got any objections?" Marsh's ice-blue gaze was cold and confident, and he saw how tensed and excited the raiders had become.

"You got a price on your head?" the third man asked oddly.

"Not that I know of. But if I did, it'd take more than three cowpokes to take me down and collect it."

"You sure you're that good?" the first man asked skeptically.

"You wanna try me and find out?" Marsh challenged.

It happened quickly. All three villains grabbed for their weapons. Marsh dropped two of them dead, and Randee shot the third man. He looked her way and signaled her over to the campfire. He checked the bodies to find none of the three breathing.

When Randee reached his side, he grinned and hugged her. "See, woman, I told you that you wouldn't panic. Thanks."

"You took a big risk, Marsh Logan; I could have reacted too slowly. I'm not used to showdowns like you are. What did they say?"

Marsh repeated the conversation, then added, "I knew they wouldn't spill their guts either, so there was no reason to wing one to question, then have to finish him off later. We need to get moving quickly in case somebody heard those shots and comes to investigate. I want to check their pockets and saddlebags and release those horses."

While Randee unsaddled the animals and freed

them, Marsh went through the men's clothing and possessions, finding nothing useful except money.

Not having been given time to think about killing a man, Randee defensively ignored her necessary action. "We'll have to bury them," she remarked absently.

"We don't have time or a shovel to use. They're cold-blooded killers, woman, so they don't deserve a decent burial. We'll leave them to rot in the open, just like they left their victims."

Randee inquired softly, "Don't you think that's being cold and hard, Marsh? We're not like them."

Marsh looked at her. "We'll shove 'em into that gully. We have to get moving pronto. I heard about two new raids nearby in the last few days. That means those bastards headed straight here from the Fort Richardson area. We've got eight of them, but there are plenty more around. There's another problem; Sheriff Wade still doesn't trust me. He had that deputy of his follow me again after I left town. I lost him before I doubled back to meet you. He could be searching for us right this minute, just to make certain you aren't traveling with me."

"What did he say about me?" she asked.

Without mentioning Storm Hayden, Marsh repeated the curious conversation and teased, "He still has a fever for you, woman. A real shame, since you belong to me now. If he finds us together, it'll stick in his craw and he'll become a pest. You know I can't afford any trouble with the law, especially a lawman who's sweet on my partner."

Randee didn't want to discuss Brody Wade with her lover, so she asked, "Did you hear anything about that Marshal Timms?"

"Nope, and I couldn't risk asking about him, not the way Sheriff Wade was having me watched and dogged. Let's check out those new raid sites before we head for

Fort Worth."

They rode for hours toward the center of the target area, with Marsh on constant alert for any sign of danger around them. When they camped that night, they ate cold food, which Marsh had purchased that morning in town. He didn't want a campfire, which could draw the attention of anyone nearby.

"This business is getting hard and dirty, woman. Now that you've had a foul taste of it, are you sure you want to continue with me? I can take you to Fort Worth and have my friend there guard you until it's over."

"My mind's made up, Marsh; I'm sticking with you. Maybe these killings will work in our favor. If those gang members think their boss is having them weeded out because their task is almost done, we might gain an advantage over them if they get nervous and mistrustful."

"I thought about that angle too. But it might only make them more cautious. If they get to watching their backsides, it'll be hard to sneak up on them. But if we're lucky, we can get more of them out of the way while they're separated, before they learn about their friends' fates."

Marsh didn't shave that night and he didn't allow them to make love or sleep together so he could remain on full alert. Every time Randee awoke and glanced his way, he was awake, on guard.

On Sunday morning and late Sunday afternoon, they checked out the two attack sites. One was totally abandoned and destroyed, but squatters nearby answered some questions for them. A Marshal Foley Timms had been in the area before and after the raid, asking questions and looking for witnesses. As with all other times, nobody saw or heard a thing, or so they claimed.

At the second site, fresh mounds of dirt loomed before their vision, and the smell of burned wood still lingered around the wanton destruction. Marsh examined the area for tracks and clues, and cursed to himself when he found neither. They rode to the next ranch, to find the owners packing to leave. When questioned, the couple fearfully told Marsh and Randee that they were pulling out to start fresh in a safer place. Considering the farmer had several children and a pregnant wife, it was a wise, but difficult decision.

This time, however, Marsh was given a clue. The shaky man said, "I was hunting early that morning and saw that gang leaving the area. They were heading northwesterly. Must have been twenty-five or thirty of them. They had bushes tied to the tails of Joe's cattle and they were moving real slow. I couldn't see too good, but I'd swear there was something covering their horses' hooves, like cloth sacks. I got to get my family out of here before they hit us. There ain't hardly a ranch or farm around which ain't been attacked once or twice. I ain't waiting around until they find my place and kill us all in our sleep."

"Do you recall a U.S. marshal coming by to see you lately?"

"Sure do," the man answered Marsh's query. "His name was Foley Timms, a real big man. Said he'd been on their trail for nearly a year. I didn't tell him nothing 'cause I didn't want to get involved. I was afraid he'd make us hang around and answer more questions."

Marsh smiled genially. "Don't you worry. I won't tell him anything you've told me. Which way did he light out?"

"Toward Granbury," he said.

Marsh knew the man didn't have time to sell his land and was probably near broke this time of year. He pulled out the two hundred dollars reward money and pressed it into the farmer's hand. "I appreciate your help, sir. You take good care of your family."

The man stared at the money, then looked up at Marsh, his eyes misty. "This is real kind of you, son. We can sure use it."

"With luck, maybe I can use the information you gave me to stop those . . . that gang. Before you sell out here, check back in a few months to see if they've been stopped. You got a real nice place and I would hate to see you lose it. Why don't you try working and camping just the other side of Fort Worth for a while? They're not doing any raiding over that way. If we can help the law defeat that gang, you can return home before harvest time."

The man smiled and shook Marsh's hand gratefully, accepting the wise advice. They talked a few more minutes before the man told them, "You two be careful, 'cause that gang is bad, real bad."

"We will. Good luck to you."

Marsh and Randee mounted, waved, and rode northwestward. They halted at the spot where the farmer had told Marsh he'd been concealed. Marsh looked over the area closely.

Randee asked, "Wouldn't dragging brush cover any trail made by slow movement?"

"Most of it, and the weather would finish the task. That Indian riding with them is real smart; he knows all about concealing tracks. Obviously he's tailing them and removing all signs of their passing. No trampled grass, no broken limbs, no rocks turned over . . ."

"What now?" she asked, hunkering down beside him.

"If they kept going this way, they'd be heading into territory which we've already searched pretty good. Somehow, I doubt they're hiding around Fort Richardson. It's my guess they were only skirting other ranches to keep out of sight. You can bet they know where every spread is located."

"What about Marshal Timms? You think he's their scout? Or boss? You think he's heading to Granbury to see what happened to those other men?"

"Whoa, woman, not so fast," he teased. "I have my suspicions about this Timms, but we'll know more about him after we reach Fort Worth. Who knows? Maybe he's a real lawman and he has contacts sending him news of strangers in towns. Coming around after a raid doesn't intrigue me, but doing it before so many certainly does."

On Monday, they followed a similar pattern, and camped a half-day's ride from Fort Worth.

On Tuesday, they rode a few hours eastward before making camp. While Randee prepared a quick meal, Marsh scouted the area. After eating, he shaved quickly and doused the small fire. Again they slept separately and Marsh remained on tense alert during the night.

They entered the large town of Fort Worth and dismounted before a hotel. Again, Marsh rented two rooms and registered them as cousins. He left Randee to eat, bathe, and rest while he went to see his friend and to gather any available news.

Randee turned their dirty garments over to the laundress who came for them. After eating, she took a long bath and washed her hair. While she awaited Marsh's return, she did their mending, the task reminding her of home and her mother.

She halted and stared ahead blankly. How was her mother? What was Payton doing? Was he still searching for her, or had he given her up as lost property? Would her mother and the child be all right until she and Marsh could rescue them? Which problem was the most important to her: defeating this murderous gang or helping her mother? She couldn't defeat Payton alone, and Marsh wouldn't head for Kansas until this grim task was over, so the choice wasn't hers.

If she tried to go home and thwart that evil beast, she would only manage to place herself and her mother in new peril. She had to forget about Payton Slade until . . . The door opened and Marsh entered.

She was sitting cross-legged on the bed, with their sewing. He came forward and sat down on its edge. Her homey task seemed to make him nervous, so she set it aside and asked, "Any news?"

"You don't have to do that, Randee. The laundress can take care of it for me," he replied, ignoring her question.

"I hope you don't mind, Marsh, but I needed something to occupy my mind and hands. This is one thing mother taught me to do well. If you object, I can leave it for . . ."

He interrupted to drop the subject. "If it uses up some of that abundant energy, fine. I just didn't want you doing more than your share of the chores, partner. Is that what you were thinking about when I came in, your mother?"

"I can't help but worry about her. She was so foolish to marry that deceitful devil. He's lied to her and used her, and she's blind to his flaws and the truth. She's living with a man she doesn't even know. You won't forget your promise to help us after this job is over, will you?"

"You have my word on it, woman. Would it make you feel better if you wrote her a letter to let her know you're safe and well?"

"It's too risky, Marsh. I don't want to remind Payton I'm alive somewhere. We don't need his intrusion when we're facing such peril. I have to believe she'll be fine until we can rescue her." Randee sighed heavily. "What if she doesn't take my word against his? What if she hates me for having him killed? Even if he's worthless, she loves him."

Marsh realized she needed this small and comforting talk, so he didn't halt it. "Whatever happens in Kansas, you'll have to accept it. The most important thing is saving her life, not pleasing her."

Randee told him what her mother used to be like with her father, and how she was with her stepfather. "He's draining the life from her, Marsh, and it torments me. If only she could come to her senses and forget him, maybe she could become Dee Hollis again."

"Change is hard, Randee, sometimes impossible for one reason or another. You have to realize that she might not want to know the truth about Slade. Or she might know it already and is simply ignoring it because she doesn't want to lose even a bad life. It's hard to start over with a new life. It's worse for women when there's no man . . . no father or husband to care for them. Saloons are filled with widows and orphans. You said your mother wasn't the kind of woman who wanted to be on her own. What happens after Slade's dead, if she won't let you go home or refuses to live on the Carson Ranch with you?"

"I don't know, Marsh. I've never thought about the points you just made. One thing for certain, if she marries again, surely he can't be as wicked as Payton Slade. I want him out of her life, at any cost."

Marsh replied, "I know, and I don't blame you."

"Let's talk about something else. What did you learn today?"

"I got a map of the purchases by that land company. They've gotten hold of most of those spreads. But as far as my friend can learn, it's all been very legal. He says

279

that company is planning a big promotion back east like Jacob de Cordova pulled off. You remember, the man from Granbury who did the same thing years ago. They're planning settlements and smaller spreads to get this area more populated. If they build towns, they'll make a fortune with stores and such. But he still can't get hold of any names."

Her eyes brightened with a bold idea. "If they make an offer on the Carson Ranch, maybe I can learn who's behind it."

"Not yet, woman. I want you kept out of this as long as possible."

"You're too protective of me, Marsh Logan."

"If you get them sniffing after you and they are involved, our mission could fail before we get close enough to stop them."

"What about if I try to get a job with that company or that lawyer? I might can learn something on the inside," she ventured.

"It's too dangerous. From what I can learn, there's no such lawman as Marshal Timms. He saw you in Wadesville. If he dropped by either office, he'd notice you in a second and get too curious."

"Doesn't that mean he's involved? Isn't this that lucky break?"

"Not if he's new on the job or if he's working under a false name."

"Then, we're still nowhere," she murmured dejectedly. "If this whole job is dangerous, why not take a few risks to get ahead?"

"Not yet, woman," he stated firmly. "I know what I'm doing. We have to stay patient and be cautious or we'll ruin everything."

"Is it because of me, Marsh? Am I causing you to hold back?"

Marsh's gaze locked with hers and he smiled. He

asserted, "You're keeping me from acting rashly just to get vengeance. What you're doing to me is keeping me alive and careful."

"The moment that isn't true, please tell me," she urged.

He caressed her cheek as he promised, "Don't worry, I will. We might have more help, or interference, to deal with. Seems as if the State Police and Army have been ordered to get moving on this case. That could explain why there haven't been any raids since last Friday and why those villains are separated and laying low for a while. I want us to rest here tomorrow, then head back toward Fort Richardson on Thursday. If they're spread out in camps, maybe we can locate some and get rid of them a few at a time like we planned."

"That sounds good to me," she concurred.

"Before we leave town, I want you to meet my friend. If there's any trouble, you come to him and he'll protect you."

Randee caught the meaning between his words. She didn't want anything to ever happen to him. From now on, she wouldn't flinch at doing anything to get this matter over with so Marsh would be safe.

"It's suppertime. You hungry?" he asked, lifting her hand and playfully nipping at her fingers.

"Not for that kind of food," she responded meaningfully.

He chuckled and teased, "What do you do, woman, read my mind?" He pulled her into his arms as she grinned happily . . . .

Chapter Thirteen

Randee sat at the oblong table in Willard Mason's home eating, listening, and talking with the two men. Now she understood how the forty-year-old man gathered so much information for Marsh; Willard worked for the local newspaper, of which he was part owner. That also explained how Marsh had learned of her bold advertisement. The older man had expressive hazel eyes, and a nice build for a man who worked sitting down most of the time. His salt-and-pepper hair made him appear distinguished, and he smiled frequently. She liked this friend of Marsh's and felt that he was an honorable man.

Randee was wearing the only dress she had with her on this momentous journey, washed and ironed by the hotel laundress just in time for this unexpected occasion. Her flaxen hair was shiny and full after its thorough washing, and she smelled wonderful after her fragrant bath. She knew she looked lovely tonight, and she was glad because she wanted to make a good impression on both men.

She and Marsh had slept late that morning; or rather, they had stayed in bed making love and resting. Later, they had strolled around for exercise and diversion. He had purchased a gift for her, a coin-shaped silver necklace with Spanish words which she couldn't read. He had told her it said, "Friends now and forever," but his sly grin had made her doubt him. When he said he needed to make ammunition purchases, she had pretended to look around in a dress and hat shop. The moment he left her there, she had hurried next door to ask the man what the words meant. The merchant had smiled cordially and translated them: "You are in my heart forever." Knowing Marsh could speak Spanish, she had thrilled to his secret message. If actually he had unintentionally or guilefully sent her one . . .

Randee's attention returned to the two men seated with her. She listened to them discuss this tragedy which was attacking her beloved Texas. She noticed the easy rapport between them, and she liked this cordial side of Marsh Logan. He seemed so at ease with this man and in this homey setting, so unlike what she had imagined as the character and personality of a renowned gunman. She could not help but wonder, was Marsh—the Durango Kid—as matchless and relentless as he was reputed to be? He seemed like anything but an "often ruthless" gunslinger. Those notorious stories about him couldn't be true; he was too gentle, too kind, too caring, too sensitive! Even when he slew evil men, he didn't seem to enjoy it, and surely she would perceive such malevolence in him. A cold-blooded killer had to possess satanic tendencies in order to continue such a grim lifestyle. Why did she doubt that Marsh was living the life he truly loved and wanted? What was the truth behind this man she loved? Was he so accustomed to being strong and self-reliant before others that he battled showing any emotion or taking any action that might be misconstrued as a weakness? Was this intrepid male afraid to bare his soul to anyone, except to her on occasion?

She wanted to know so many things about Marsh, especially in matters that concerned her. She had to be patient, or risk scaring him off. He had been hurt at a crucial, impressionable time in a youth's life. She knew some of the things which drove him onward, which haunted him, which made him as he was. But to see him like this, and like he had been yesterday and last Sunday, gave her hope and confidence about reaching and winning him.

Willard was saying, "I honestly don't know if that company's involved in something evil. They could be just taking advantage of a terrible situation. Smart businessmen do that, Marsh. That gang can't terrorize this area forever. Think what their investment will earn them one day. All they have to do is buy up the land cheap, hold it until the trouble is halted, and then sell it for a hefty profit. When I interviewed George Light several times, he said he was the one who informed that group about the valuable possibilities for future development of this area. He's responsible for locating sellers and handling the deals. He says those men don't want to reveal themselves until they're ready to begin their progress, which is after this trouble is settled."

"You think it's legitimate or a cover?" Marsh inquired.

Willard shrugged his shoulders and replied, "It's too soon to tell. I don't have enough facts to make a conclusion one way or another."

Randee asked, "What about this Marshal Foley Timms? Don't you think it's odd that he's always around when trouble strikes?"

"Texas lawmen are strange animals, Miss Hollis. Some have crazy ways of working on cases." He laughed as if he'd told a joke. "Are you forgetting that you met him while he was delivering a prisoner?"

"That's what he claimed," she replied skeptically. "For all I know, it could have been a ruse to take a look around Wadesville without arousing suspicion. There was a raid nearby the next day."

"Did you recognize the prisoner?" Willard asked.

Randee glanced at Marsh quizzically. He told her that the man knew she could identify the raiders, and would keep their confidence. Randee looked dismayed at discovering that Marsh had revealed her valuable and perilous secret to another person, even to a close or old friend of his. To her, this newspaperman was a stranger, a man who published other people's secrets. For all she knew, Willard could be the clever boss of that murderous gang!

Randee was annoyed that Marsh hadn't discussed this vital matter with her before sharing her information with anyone. Marsh was hired by her, not Willard Mason. She was the one paying the expenses and offering the reward. She was the one who deserved Marsh's first loyalty. Marsh was the only one in whom she had confided, and she had not meant for her secret to go any further than her lover's ears.

Both men realized how vexed Randee was at this news, but it was Willard Mason who coaxed amiably, "Don't fret, Miss Hollis, Marsh knows I can be trusted. I would die before exposing either one of you; I swear it. In exchange for helping you two get to the bottom of this trouble, he's giving me the full story afterwards. It's a matter of deep friendship and good fortune between us."

Randee eyed Marsh again before her probing gaze settled on the entreating face of the older man. Since it was too late to change anything, she had to accept Marsh's faith in Willard. Besides, she did have a good feeling about the hazel-eyed man, and her father had always told her to trust her gut instincts. Doing so was the reason she was sitting here tonight with Marsh Logan. Going back to his friend's previous query, she answered honestly, "I really didn't notice Marshal Timms's prisoner that night. At the time, I had other things on my mind. I was leaving town the next morning to join up with Marsh, and I was trying to keep my friends there in the dark about my plans."

Randee was glad that Marsh didn't tease her in front of this man about her past romance with Sheriff Brody

Wade, or mention that she had been in Brody's office for a cozy and private picnic. Suddenly she wondered what all Marsh had confided in his friend. Did Willard Mason know *everything* about Marsh, about her, about their journey together? She felt her cheeks grow warm as she realized that this man might know all about her past and about their current intimate relationship.

Marsh noticed the change in Randee's mood and he wondered what was causing it, what she was thinking. He hadn't told her much about his friend, and nothing about Willard's being his secret contact for government work. Both men were covertly employed by President Grant, facts which must be kept a secret from everyone, including Randee. Maybe she was just miffed because she hadn't been consulted before he exposed their information and plans to his "old friend."

To get past the awkward moment, Willard reminded her, "Marsh told you to come to me if there's trouble on the trail and you two get separated, or he's injured. Please, don't try to take on these ruffians on your own, Miss Hollis. They would take you apart while smiling."

Randee knew this man had sent his wife and children to visit kinfolk to avoid danger if he was discovered helping Marsh unmask those villains. They were all in peril, but it was something which had to be done. She asked, "How long have you two known each other?"

Willard and Marsh glanced at each other and chuckled. "Years," the newspaperman replied. "I met Marsh when he was a guard for the Carver Freight Line. I did a story on him after he singlehandedly foiled a robbery attempt by six men. If anybody can take care of you, Miss Hollis, it's Marsh Logan."

"I'm sure of that, Mr. Mason, that's why we're partners."

The man smiled, then got up to serve dessert. Randee looked at Marsh, who was grinning broadly. He shrugged and quipped, "What can I say, woman, the man admires me to a flaw?"

"Nothing," she replied, "since I do, too."

"That's dangerous, woman, since I'm a no-good rogue."

"Are you, Marsh?" she retorted, then went to help Willard.

It was dusk when they headed back to the hotel. A man stumbled out of the saloon and crashed into them, just as Marsh had done at their first meeting. Randee stared at the man, her face paling and her body going rigid. The man didn't apologize; he simply sneered at them and headed down the plankway, weaving drunkenly. Randee was breathing heavily as she turned to glare at him.

"What's wrong?" Marsh asked worriedly. "Is he one of them?"

"He was one of the rustlers my father was trying to catch just before he was killed. I shot him in the arm, but he got away. I'll never forget his face. I'm going after him. I'm going to kill him this time," she vowed angrily. "He's the reason my father's dead. If it weren't for him, I wouldn't be in this mess. I hate him."

"You get back to the hotel. I'll go after him and get him. You're too upset to think straight, and that's deadly."

"It's my problem, and I'll handle it," she argued. "You're always taking the risks and leaving me behind. We're partners, Marsh."

He grabbed her upper arms and shook her right there in public. "Do you remember when I said you kept my head clear and kept me alive because I was too personally involved in this case? That's what I'm doing for you now, woman, repaying you. Go to your room and wait for me. Dammit, Randee, that's an order. I can't let you get arrested here. Get moving before he's out of sight."

Randee frowned at him, but followed his command. She paced the floor until he returned. She asked unremorsefully, "Did you get him?"

His steady blue gaze met her fiery green one. "I persuaded him to talk first. Seems you're more than right about Payton Slade. He hired those rustlers to harass your father and to . . . kill him. He's been trying to join up with the Epson Gang, but he couldn't locate them. He won't ever harm anyone else again."

Randee sank to the bed, feeling numb with anguish. At last she knew the truth, but it didn't relieve her, because her problem in Kansas still existed. Now she knew how deadly her stepfather was, and she despised him all the more for his evil and greed. Not only had he taken her father's life, Payton had stolen Randall's land and wife! "I'm going to kill him, Marsh; I swear it, and I don't care what Mother says or does afterwards. She can believe me or not, but he's paying for my father's death."

"When we get to Kansas, we'll figure out how to defeat him. Since we have no evidence against him, we'll have to walk carefully, or we'll be in worse danger from the law than he is from us."

"I don't need evidence to kill him! I suspected he was behind that trouble we were having, but I didn't want to accept the whole truth. How could I have been so blind and stupid? Such a coward? I should have killed him the first time he looked at me sideways! I didn't use my instincts, Marsh, and he got away with murder and theft. He's duped my mother and driven me from my home."

"You were young and innocent, Randee. You were hurting from your father's death and trying to hold on to your ranch. Don't blame yourself. If anyone knows how rash a youngster can act, it's me. Back then, we didn't know enough and weren't strong enough to handle problems like those. I promise he'll pay for your father's death."

Randee started to weep, the past few years of torment overwhelming her. "I should have been with Father that night. I . . ."

Marsh drew her into his embrace and held her tightly. "You would be dead, too, Randee, just like I would be if I'd been home. We have to accept the fact we aren't to blame for those deaths. We had to get away from home to learn about life, to become adults." He spread kisses over her face and pulled her down to the bed. He comforted her with his tender embrace until she went to sleep, as it was not a time for making love, only one for offering solace.

Marsh gazed down at the sleeping figure beside him. His heart went out to her. Never had he wanted to protect and love anyone more than Randee Hollis. If he didn't feel his duty to avenge his parents and to halt this siege on innocent Texans, he would . . . He would what? he asked himself. Lordy, he fretted, was he ready and willing to settle down? Could he commit to one woman, to this woman? He was used to traveling around, thinking only of himself and his work. Could he take on the responsibility of another person, of what it all entailed? He had made so many enemies, foes who didn't even know his name. What if he unmasked himself and they learned his real identity? Would they harm his love to get at him, to punish him?

His love, his mind echoed. Was Randee Hollis his true love? He looked over at her, sleeping peacefully in his arms, fully clothed. If it wasn't only physical desire for her, then what else could it be except love? *Lordy, woman, look what you've done to me . . . .*

As they were dressing to leave the Fort Worth hotel on June eighth, Randee remarked, "I wish you'd told me about your tight bond with Willard Mason so I wouldn't have been caught by surprise last night. Are you sure you can trust him so completely? How much does he know about our relationship?"

Instantly Marsh comprehended what had troubled her last night at the table. He responded, "I don't know what he suspects about us, but I didn't reveal anything about our personal attachment. Even if he guessed the truth about us, he wouldn't say anything about it. Are you sorry we . . . we've become so tight?" Is that what she had meant by the "mess" she was in, her carefree affair with him? "Do you want to call a halt to it? Go back to strictly business? I'll understand."

Randee asked herself if she were ashamed of her behavior with the man she loved. Did she regret her sensuous actions? Would she change them, now or in the past? She explained carefully, but honestly, "In most people's eyes, it isn't proper for two unattached people to sleep together, but I'm not sorry we're so close, Marsh. We both know how hard it is to find and share an equal partnership like ours. We can't merely discard it because of life's rules. We're carefree adventurers, and adventurers get their stimulation and victories from breaking those stiff rules. We're friends, confidantes, and lovers, as well as partners and companions. We've made no promises to each other, because neither of us knows how long we'll want each other."

She stroked his bronzed cheek as she told him, "For now, we desire each other and need each other as lovers. But one day, we might only be good friends, or even partners again. This attraction between us is very strong, Marsh, so we have to use it up while we're together. It's like . . ." She halted briefly, laughed, and continued, "It's like an itch which has to be scratched frequently or we'll go crazy. Once it's soothed, we'll both move on to new territories. Even if we can share only this time or short times in the future together, isn't that better than allowing this hunger to chew away at us because we're afraid it'll become more than a ravenous appetite one day? Whatever happens between us, Marsh, now or later, a bond will always stretch between us because we've shared a special time in our lives, a special part of ourselves. But I would prefer we keep our relationship a secret to avoid gossip and problems later when we go our separate ways."

Marsh appreciated the way she never acted helpless or clinging to seize his attention or sympathy. She held her own ground, or she asked for help when necessary. She was strong, smart, and brave. He was pleased by her words and attitude. She was living up to her end of their bargain and that relaxed him. He smiled and nodded.

She told him, "We have to be careful about this trail of bodies we're leaving behind. We have only my word they're criminals. As far as the law can see, men are being killed and they don't know why or by whom. If we're caught, we have no proof. And I doubt the law would take the word of a naughty vixen and the Durango Kid."

"That means we'd better not get caught. All we can do is keep moving and looking for more of them to destroy. Let's get busy checking out the center of this suspicious circle," he suggested, referring to the oblong targeted area of attacks.

They left town and rode slowly but steadily so as to not tire the horses in case they met trouble and had to make a run for their lives. This area was dense with trees, offering plenty of concealed campsites for those dispersed outlaws; so today, they had to be even more cautious with their travel and search than they had in the past.

For their early afternoon rest, they stopped beneath a cluster of trees whose overhanging branches were so low, the tall man was forced to sit on the ground while he ate his meal. Their horses were grazing contentedly nearby, and the day was very warm.

Randee had eaten quickly, then stood to exercise before taking to her saddle again. She grasped a small trunk and leaned backward, flexing her neck and shoulders and waist. Her hat was lying on the ground and her long hair was blowing gently in the same breeze that stirred the leaves around them. It seemed so peaceful here, so private. When they were alone like this, danger always seemed unreal, or far away. She closed her eyes and sighed dreamily as she recalled Marsh's gentleness last night when she had needed it so much.

As Marsh asked if she were restless today, she turned her head in his direction, causing wisps of tawny hair to blow across her face. She smiled and shook her head as she lifted one hand to brush away the tickling strands. She threw her head back and shook the carefree mane behind her to make it behave. But the mischievous wind swirled through it again and whipped it around her golden face and green eyes. She laughed, then sought a ribbon to secure it behind her head. Before doing so, she teased the silky length of ribbon through her fingers and pondered its purchaser, Brody Wade.

Randee frowned slightly. It wasn't fair or right to keep that man waiting for her when she had no intention of accepting his proposal. He had to be worried deeply about her safety and survival. Soon, she needed to let him down easily and kindly, and Marsh shouldn't object.

Marsh watched the array of emotions flicker across her lovely face, and he knew something important was running through her keen mind. He wondered what would happen to this vital woman if he was slain during this mission. Was he being selfish and cruel to her by allowing her to dream of a future with him? She wasn't the kind of woman who should be a man's mistress, not even his. She was the marrying kind, the motherly kind, the home kind. Was he spoiling her for accepting another man, another life, if he was taken from her? Where would she go? What would she do? He mused on the information which he hadn't shared with her about her father's death. He had given Willard Mason the names of the other rustlers which that bastard in Fort Worth had divulged to him, Payton Slade's hirelings. He had asked his friend to check them out for him. He wanted to know if those men were still employed by Randee's stepfather at his ranch in Kansas. He had also secured Willard's promise to take care of Randee in the event of his death . . . .

They rode about one-third of the way between Fort Worth and Fort Richardson before halting to camp for the night. While Randee started their evening meal, Marsh scouted every direction from the old barn to make certain no threat was in the area.

After he returned while it was still light, they ate, doused the campfire, and concealed their horses in the barn. As dusk began to settle around the secluded barn, they climbed into the loft to sleep. Marsh opened the loft door slightly so he could watch and listen for any sign of danger, and he placed their weapons nearby to be prepared. Aged straw filled the area and crackled when they walked on it. Marsh unrolled their sleeping mats and told her to get some rest.

Any day could be their last one, and Randee yearned to spend this one in Marsh's arms. When he turned to look at her, she was gazing at him with a look that said, I want you and need you.

Marsh felt his heart speed up and his loins inflame. He glanced outside and weighed their chances of discovery and peril. It was doubtful that any traveler wouldn't be camped by this hour. He walked over to her and looked down into her entreating eyes. He didn't speak as he unfastened the buttons on her calf-length denim dress. When her belt halted him, he removed it, then continued with the few remaining buttons below her waist.

Marsh eased the garment off her shoulders and it slipped to the dusty floor. Randee stepped out of it and shoved it aside with her foot. With trembling but deft fingers, Marsh loosened the ribbon ties on her chemise and pulled it over her head, tossing it atop her dress. He undid the knot in her bandanna and cast it aside. Kneeling, he removed her boots, then stood to complete his bold task by releasing her bloomers and drawing them off her shapely legs. His igneous blue gaze roamed her naked flesh and branded it anew as his own.

Quickly he discarded his clothes and boots and pressed their naked bodies together. He shuddered with overpowering desire for her, and was amazed that she had this potent effect on him every time they made love. His fingers drifted up and down her sleek back as he passionately assailed her mouth with hungry kisses. He felt her fingers bury themselves in his ebony hair as she pulled his mouth more tightly against hers. Slowly he guided her down to their sleeping roll.

Moonlight entered the loft door and bathed them in a seductive glow. As his mouth moved down the silky column of her throat, it encountered the silver necklace and he pressed his lips to it before trailing them downward to her breasts. The words on that shiny circle were true; she would be a part of him forever, no matter their fates.

Marsh tantalized and stimulated her until she was quivering with urgent need. She knew he felt the same way, and she unleashed all her passion upon him. Holding nothing back, they kissed and caressed until ecstasy's flames engulfed them and seared this blissful moment into their minds forever. They made love wildly and freely until their craving for each other could not be restrained a moment longer, and they feasted on love's treats until their enormous appetites for each other were sated, for a time.

Late Friday afternoon, Marsh noticed fresh tracks

near a creek, and they gingerly followed them. He told her, "Until those gang members link up again and find some of their friends missing, we have the advantage of surprise. They think they're smarter than everybody else, so they won't be expecting anyone on their trail."

She reasoned, "What about the State Police and Army? Didn't you say they were on the case now? And there could be others around like us, or Marshal Timms, if he isn't one of them."

"I'll believe we have help when I see it, not before. Hear me well, woman; if I say get moving, you ride like the devil's pursuing you and don't look back. I mean it, Randee. If I go down with a wound, don't you dare stop and try to help me."

"If you think I'll leave you lying there to . . ."

He grasped her face between his hands and kissed her roughly. His eyes bored into hers as he warned, "I'll finish myself off before I give you reason to come back for me. If I'm wounded, I'll hold them back while you get away." Randee was shaking her head and trying to protest, but Marsh was holding his hand over her mouth to prevent it. "Don't worry about me. I've gotten out of worse predicaments, with more than one wound to slow me down. Dammit, woman, they'll rape you over and over, all of them, then slice you into little pieces. It's time you realize you can't buy them off, or reason with them, or defeat them alone. Swear you'll leave, or you're going no further."

Randee wanted to fling herself into his arms and reveal her love before they rode toward this evil lair of human wolves. She couldn't, because she didn't want him distracted by personal matters. When she relaxed, Marsh released his grip on her mouth and arm. His demand was a difficult one to honor. She knew he wouldn't leave her behind if she were wounded. And he had to be exaggerating his past escapes, because he had told her once before

295

that he'd never been seriously wounded in the past. Yet, she didn't want him worried about her, and she knew he would recognize any deceit in her. She inhaled deeply and vowed, "I'll follow your orders, partner, all of them."

Marsh eyed her closely and knew she was telling the truth. He smiled and revealed, "I'm not a fool, woman. I'm not seeking death or glory today, so I won't take any crazy risks with our lives. This is the clearest my head's been since I started this task over a year ago. We check out this camp, then decide what to do about it. Agreed?"

Randee could not resist hugging him and thanking him. She twirled her hair into a ball and stuffed it under her hat. She checked her weapons and signaled she was ready to go.

Marsh leaned forward and kissed the scar near her right ear. He teased to lessen her anxiety, "Make sure you don't add another war stripe today, 'cause I like this pretty face as is. I'm letting you continue with me because I trust your word and skills," he said, without adding, *because there are only three sets of tracks and between us we can take on that many villains*.

When they neared the area where smoke was visible above a distant clearing, Marsh and Randee left their horses and prepared themselves to attack. After making certain they were wearing nothing that would make a noise, they covered the remaining half-mile on foot. They stealthily crept to within fifty yards of the enemy camp and studied it.

Marsh frowned as he noticed there were many obstacles to their easy success. First, there were five, not three, outlaws in the clearing. Second, their horses were tethered to a rope that was stretched between two trees, cleverly within reach for a quick escape. Third, the way the camp was situated, they couldn't sneak any closer in daylight without taking a big risk of being sighted in an area that had very few trees for cover. Fourth, from where he and Randee were hiding, there were tree trunks in just the right places to hinder accurate firing, especially since three of the men were lying down, making bad targets. The other two were playing cards and drinking whiskey.

The worst problem were the three civilians present. One, who looked to be a local farmer or rancher, was bound securely to the tree which was nearest to the campfire. He was, perhaps, a hostage or an unfortunate passerby. The other two visitors were females, probably saloon girls from Jacksboro, Marsh concluded, noticing the face paint and attire of the one who was still clothed. She was draped wantonly over one of the card players and obviously was trying to distract him from the game. The other female was lying naked between two men on a blanket, laughing and sharing herself with both. The last man was reclining on his side, watching the lusty sport and urging them to get finished with the girl so he could use her.

The woman sat up and lewdly teased, "Hold yore stallion in yore britches a while longer and I'll give 'im a ride he won't n'er forget. There's plenty of me to go around. You boys got all night and half of tomorrow to get yore fill of me and Skizzy there." She returned to her task as the other female got up to pleasure the complaining man.

Marsh glanced at Randee, whose eyes were bravely fastened to the campsite and whose cheeks were a bright pink. He nudged her, and motioned for them to retreat to their horses.

On the return trip, Randee fretted over somebody sneaking up on her and Marsh one day during an intimate episode. She wondered how those two females could do such wicked things. She understood how a destitute female could work in a saloon, could pleasure customers one at a time in private rooms. But to carry on like that in the open with several men watching or participating simultaneously . . . Didn't those women realize what monstrous devils they were giving themselves to? Didn't they care? The thing which disturbed Randee the most was the women didn't appear scared, coerced, or reluctant.

Marsh told her, "It's too chancy to get close enough to attack that camp with other people there. Even if we waited until after dark, there are too many of them to capture or control. If we go in now with guns blazing or sneak in tonight, when hell breaks loose, it could be a disaster." Marsh went on to expose his cunning plan, "Let's ride to Fort Richardson and see a friend of mine there. He can get his troop here before dawn and take care of this mess for us. That way, we won't be involved when news leaks out. Our presence will be kept secret so we can avoid notice for as long as possible. The most important thing is defeating them, whether it's by our hand or not."

Randee realized he was taking a different position today by allowing someone else to slay those gang members. Maybe she had him thinking about something else besides himself, besides only his problems and his goals. Maybe she had given him a reason to care, to live, to change. She smiled and concurred, "That's very clever, partner. We certainly don't want innocent people getting killed, and we don't want any of those beasts escaping to warn the others about us."

Since it was Friday night and half the soldiers were given the evening off, while the others were given Saturday evening off, it was easy for Marsh and Randee to get near the fort unnoticed.

As they dismounted, she laughed and said, "I know the routine by now, partner. Just hurry back."

Marsh grinned and headed toward the gate on foot. He was glad to find Jim alone in his quarters, reading and relaxing. He explained what he had found and how his friend could take the glory for killing or capturing five Epson Gang members at dawn.

Jim asked, "How do you know they're gang members?"

Marsh had to lie slightly. "I've been tracking them for days, since the scene of their last attack. I couldn't take them on alone because there are too many of them. They've broken up into small groups to lay low for a while. I've been tailing five of them. When they settled down for a long rest nearby, I figured it was the perfect time to get help. It's them, Jim; I saw their faces."

The officer seemed to relax at hearing there were five men and not thirty or more. "If you're right, all I can do is arrest them and you'll have to testify against them. It'll be your word against theirs, if you live till the trial. If it were left up to me, I'd gun them down myself. But I'll have other soldiers behind me, so I have to act under orders."

Marsh hadn't considered this intrusive angle, and he was furious with himself. He had assumed his friend would be delighted to defeat even a part of that vicious gang. By trying to save lives — his, Randee's, that captive's, and those two prostitutes — he had overlooked the unbending rules and orders of Army life. "Damnation, man! They're killers. If we put them in jail, their friends will only break them out. And if I step forward as the only witness, that'll stop any future pursuit, because they'll know about me."

"I'm sorry, Marsh, but I can't just ride into their camp shooting."

An idea came to mind and Marsh asked, "Why not? They have three prisoners. There's one old man tied to a tree, and two saloon girls being used. I couldn't risk getting them killed during an attack; otherwise, I'd be gunning them down right now. If you can rescue them, perhaps they'll testify for you so I can stay out of sight."

The officer smiled broadly. "That's all I needed to know, old friend. I've seen what those sons of bitches do. I'll be happy to get rid of a few. I'll make sure to take my best shots and to warn them those outlaws are very dangerous. I'll tell everybody that a local brought me the news about their camp and hostages. I'll get them for you."

"Thanks, Jim. I'll head out after the others." They shook hands and Marsh left Jim to roust his men for a dawn raid.

Upon Marsh's return and revelation, Randee remarked, "A dawn raid by the law — how clever and appropriate. What now, partner?"

They camped in a safe place where they could see the troop returning to the fort so they would know the climax of that raid before continuing their journey. By seven, the soldiers were riding past their hiding place with five bodies and three survivors.

Randee was glad to see that the two women were frightened now. Maybe they knew other members of the gang and would expose them to that grinning officer. Most of all, she was relieved to see that the old man was still alive and uninjured, and only one of the soldiers had a slight wound. Slowly but surely, she and Marsh were winning this war, and winning it without innocent casualties. Thirteen raiders were dead, but how many more existed? At least seventeen, plus their scouts and spies and their boss — and possibly new members to replace those slain.

She absently fingered the silver charm around her neck as she gave thanks for this new victory, for their survival, and for her love.

Marsh said, "Well, that's done, and we're still alive and safe. Let's make a wide circle along another route back to Fort Worth. This picking off a few at a time is easy and smart. Let's pluck some more villains, partner."

300

*   *   *

They rode all day, finding nothing suspicious or dangerous. It was nearly dark when they happened onto an old hunting shack, which was near to collapse. They camped nearby, where lush grass for the horses grew abundantly beside a large stream which was excellent for splashing and bathing. They cooked a light meal, ate, and cleaned up their dishes.

When Marsh became amorous beneath the half-moon and stars, Randee was apprehensive. She worried about someone watching them from the bushes as they had spied on those saloon girls and outlaws. She couldn't relax and surrender uninhibitedly. She explained her problem to Marsh, who didn't laugh or persist or argue, or try to cajole her as if she were a silly woman or small child.

"What about the shack?" she hinted shamelessly.

Marsh glanced at it and shook his head. "It could come tumbling down on us, woman. Why don't we just snuggle up and get some sleep? We'll be in a cozy hotel bed in a couple of days."

Randee met his gaze and echoed, "A couple of days? I don't know what you do to me, Marsh Logan, but I want you all the time, and days sound like forever. I'm being foolish, aren't I?"

Marsh smiled and nestled her closer to him. "Nope. If you can't relax, then you can't enjoy me, and I insist that you enjoy me every time I enjoy you. Listen to me, Randee. I don't blame you for wanting privacy; so do I. Let's wait until we have it. Nothing makes you hungrier for food than when you can't eat for a while — makes it taste better when you finally can savor it."

Randee smiled at him and embraced him. "You're a wonder."

"So are you, Miss Hollis," he teased with a heady kiss.

When their lips parted, she confessed hoarsely, "I'm

301

glad you rode to Wadesville that day and became my partner."

Marsh pressed her honey-blond head against his chest and held her possessively. "Yep, so am I," he admitted.

Marsh and Randee didn't know it yet, but the easy parts were over . . . .

Chapter Fourteen

By noon the following day, it was particularly hot and humid. It was so muggy that their perspiration refused to evaporate and it dampened their garments and flesh. Breathing seemed difficult, and a feeling of misery chewed on them. Marsh taught her how to cool off by riding beneath a vast cloud, which cut off the blazing sun.

As they paused in the natural shade, Randee commented, "That's a good trick, Mr. Logan. I can tell you're used to being out in the open most of the time. You know a lot about nature."

"Why, thank you, Miss Hollis. I appreciate you appreciating me," he teased merrily in an exaggerated Southern drawl.

As the day progressed, so did the imminent threat of a violent storm within the next few hours. The massive white clouds and blue sky vanished. The firmament darkened steadily until it looked like a deep, slate-blue backdrop which was sewn tightly to the rich green landscape on the horizon. The contrast of intense blue and green was breathtaking as Randee looked across the flat land before her line of vision. It was as if, as far as she could see, the earth was a verdant blanket which

303

suddenly became a dark-sapphire barrier that loomed overhead to all points of the compass. The wind gusted ominously, causing the grasses to wave wildly to and fro and refreshing Randee and Marsh.

The heat lessened quickly as breezes grew stronger and cooler. Randee's hair whipped about until she halted to twirl it and tuck it beneath her hat. In the distance, thunder rumbled like boulders being rolled across heaven's floor. On the horizon, brilliant streaks of lightning flashed rapidly across the sky, warning of the violent drama which nature was about to stage in this area. The rumbling grew louder and nearer. The sky became a pearly gray, hinting at how much water was entrapped above them. It was strange, but a burst of energy and excitement filled Randee as the weather changed. She felt so alive, so much a part of nature, so close to it, so affected by its wild beauty.

Marsh reined his horse and dismounted. He quickly withdrew the map from his saddlebag, unfolded it, and scanned it. "We have to find shelter fast, woman. We're in for a long and violent storm. If no one's around, we can take shelter here," he told her, pointing to one of the ranches that was marked as abandoned and sold on his map.

Earsplitting thunderclaps sounded almost overhead, and Randee thought she felt their vibrations within her chest. Lightning danced wildly just beyond them, its jagged lines traveling swiftly from heaven to earth as if they were luminous skeletons attacking the land. "That's fine with me," she agreed, glancing at their intimidating surroundings. It looked as if the sky was nearly bursting with water. She knew the storm's fury would be unleashed soon, and she wanted to be inside.

They galloped toward their new destination, actually heading further away from Fort Worth. The wind was blowing forcefully, and the thunder growled like an angry bear who'd been awakened rashly from his hibernation. The horses were getting nervous as the startling thunderbolts zinged and boomed around them. Marsh and Randee knew they had to hurry to make the ranch before the tempest assailed them.

The house and barns weren't burned because the family had sold out, packed up, and left the perilous area. They rode to the barn, dismounted, and unsaddled their horses. After securing both gates, they quickly tossed hay to the animals. Using two well buckets, Randee drew water while Marsh carried it to the trough and filled it. With food, water, and shelter, the horses would be fine for days.

The wind grabbed and shook tree branches as if trying to viciously rip the limbs from their trunks and, failing to achieve that destructive aim, snatched at their green leaves and sent them scurrying across the dirt yard. Flowers, which had been brought from back East somewhere, were being yanked about rudely; their petals were torn off and sent flying to join the severed leaves.

Marsh and Randee carried their possessions into the house. Much of the furniture had been left behind during the family's hasty departure. They checked the root cellar and found that plenty of food had also been left, probably because there was too much to carry away in an already overloaded wagon. Randee was surprised to discover old clothes inside the house, left behind in the family's hurry to leave this lovely place. Recalling that she had seen a smokehouse and a garden, she asked Marsh to see if any meats had been left while she rushed to pull fresh vegetables for a stew.

Peals of thunder roared like dynamite charges going off in rapid sequence. Lightning flickered like glowing fingers splitting the heavens so that brilliant light could burst through the cracks which they made. The intensity of the storm increased. Suddenly a torrential rain began, drenching Randee and Marsh before they could return to the house.

They laughed as they rushed inside and dropped their burdens on the kitchen floor. He remarked humorously, "I surely hope this stew will be worth getting soaked for, woman."

"It will," she vowed with a merry laugh.

The deluge of water poured down, sounding like meat sizzling in a frying pan. Randee closed the door and turned to the dripping man. Irrepressible giggles came forth and she said, "I haven't played in the rain in years. After the heat and humidity we've been enduring, it feels wonderful." She wiped streams of water from her face.

"We'd better get dried off before we catch cold, woman."

Randee chose the main bedroom for her task. After drying off, she pulled on a comfortable nightgown, then spread her wet garments on a rickety chair. She rubbed the excess moisture from her hair and braided it. When she returned to the other room, Marsh had slipped out of his wet clothes and had donned only a dry pair of pants. She watched him finger-comb his ebony hair before she headed into the kitchen to begin the stew, which would take hours to cook.

Marsh joined her there to build a fire in the large stove. Randee cut up the meat and vegetables and placed them in a pot to simmer. She knew Marsh was eyeing how she was dressed, and she didn't mind.

He walked into the adjoining room, removed supplies from his saddlebag, spread out a blanket on the floor, and sat down to clean his weapons. While their evening meal was cooking, Randee opened the front door and watched the weather.

The thunder was almost deafening. Like rattling tin,

it crashed and echoed across the heavens. The rain poured down so rapidly and heavily that the ground was saturated in minutes, making visibility practically zero. Winds gusted around the house, slanting the large drops of water and sending any loose object airborne.

Randee watched the children's swing as it was tossed about in the strong currents. "Isn't it a shame they had to leave such a lovely place because of those villains?"

Marsh glanced up from his chore and nodded. The homey setting and mood were nice, but scary. He asked unthinkingly, "If you can't destroy Payton Slade or return home or get possession of the Carson Ranch, what then, Randee? If I'm killed during this mission, where will you go? What will you do?"

Randee leaned against the door jamb and looked at the man on the floor nearby. "I don't like talk about failures, Marsh."

Now that the subject had been broached, Marsh had to know the answers to his troubling questions, so he persisted, "You need an alternate plan, woman, in case the worst happens."

Randee sighed heavily and replied, "The Carsons had plenty of money hidden, so I'll be fine. If we fail, which we won't, I'll find some place to settle down and begin a new life. I can buy a store, or a hotel, or a restaurant, and earn a nice living."

"Are you sure I'm not spoiling things for you later?"

"What do you mean?" she inquired, observing him closely.

"I just worry about you getting too accustomed to my being around all the time. What happens when I'm not?"

Suddenly Randee felt depressed by his words and mood. "I've kept my end of our bargain, Marsh, so why do you keep fretting over it? If this thing between us is meant to be more than a temporary affair, it'll happen whether we try to halt it or encourage it. If not, we've shared some special times together. We both felt this strong attraction at our first meeting when you crashed into me. Whatever it is between us, I don't know, but we have to allow it to take its course. It's like a fire. When we met, it began smoldering, then burst into flames to burn brightly and fiercely. We have no choice but to wait and see if those flames dwindle and go out, or if they remain glowing embers to be rekindled from time to time when our bodies need its warmth. Whether it burns for one week, one month, one year, or more—even if nothing comes of it—we have to use it while it's there."

She jumped as several thunderbolts shook the area around the house. "I'm not ready to settle down either. For one thing, we have important work to do, here and in Kansas. Secondly, I watched my mother lose the man she loved, and it nearly destroyed her. I'm not ready to give Fate the chance to do that to me. I'm young and there's lots I want to see and do. I'm not trying to hog-tie you, so relax."

Before Marsh could reason or argue, Randee had the impulse to race outside into the pouring rain and use that swing to get rid of her abundant energy. She did just that, to Marsh's amazement.

Marsh tossed aside the things in his hands and bounded after her, shouting, "Where are you going, woman?"

Randee hopped on the swing and started it moving, swaying back and forth rapidly. The thunder roared around her and the rain pelted down on her, soaking her instantly. She threw her head back and allowed the refreshing water to race over her face and body.

Marsh grabbed the ropes and tried to halt the swing, slipping to his knees in the mud. "What are you doing?" he asked worriedly.

"Enjoying life," she shouted back over the loud rain, wind, and thunder. She laughed gaily at his frantic expression.

He halted her movements and urged, "Come inside, woman, you're getting drenched. You'll take a death of a cold." He noticed how the gown clung to her wet flesh and seemingly vanished in its saturated condition. As she looked down at him, her bangs glued themselves to her forehead and the water ran swiftly off each strand. He watched it bead and drop from her stubbornly set lips and chin. What an unpredictable and tempting creature she was!

The swing lurched forward in a forceful blast of wind, sending Marsh to his butt in the mire. He yanked Randee from the wooden seat, pulled her across his lap and sealed their mouths. He closed his eyes to prevent water from pelting into them. The violence of the weather assailed them, driving them into a heated frenzy for each other. His hands locked around her buttocks, holding her tightly against his groin.

Randee's legs straddled Marsh's thighs and her toes dug down into the mud as she closed any remaining space between their straining bodies. Her hands wandered over Marsh's rain-slicked body and roved through his ebony hair. She thirsted urgently for this man who was intoxicating her with his bold behavior.

Their lips feverishly meshed over and over, creating a white-hot heat within them. He unbuttoned her gown and slipped it off her shoulders to allow his hands to roam her naked flesh. His mouth trailed down her throat, tasting the sweet rainwater and savoring her urgent need for him. His mouth teased over the wet flesh and drifted into the inviting canyon between her breasts. She arched backward to permit his hungry exploration of the taut peaks. She ached for him and encouraged him to continue his loving assault on her body and wits.

Marsh's hands gripped the nightgown and wiggled it upwards, bunching the saturated material around her hips. She was wearing nothing beneath her thin garment, and his fingers tantalized the bare skin of her thighs and buttocks. He hunched his back to reach her breasts and stimulate them with his fiery tongue. Suddenly they fell backwards into the mud, but didn't release each other. They playfully rolled in the mushy bed as they caressed and kissed passionately, wildly, freely, urgently.

Finally they parted only long enough for Marsh to struggle from his clinging wet pants and for Randee to yank off the confining gown. They made no attempt to end or delay this heady madness by dashing into the house to make love there. It was one of those rare moments when emotions and inhibitions were unleashed and allowed to race where they would. The violent weather was no deterrent. It was, in fact, an erotic stimulant, the potent instigator of this carefree union.

Marsh moved atop her quickly and sealed their mouths, blocking the pounding rain from her face. Their tongues mated in a sensuous dance as he drove within her time and time again. The explosive thunder vibrated the ground beneath them and urged them onward with their task.

Randee felt water dripping from Marsh's hair onto her face and she closed her eyes to protect them from the stinging drops. Joy and ravenous desire charged through her as powerfully as the lightning charged across the ever darkening sky. In her ears, her pulse throbbed and her heart roared as loudly as the thunder which surrounded them. Neither modesty nor hesitation entered her mind as she thrashed upon the miry ground beneath her lover. She desperately needed this unrestrained fusion of their bodies and spirits, and she clung to him as she rode out the maddening storm within her. She didn't care if she was getting filthy, as the mud could easily be removed later from her hair and body. All that mattered at this moment was having Marsh Logan in this wild and wonderful manner. As she stroked his back, the mud spread over it, then over his muscled shoulders and arms as her fingers drifted down them.

Marsh captured Randee's face between his hands and kissed her greedily. He felt the torrential rain beating almost painfully against his naked body, but he didn't care. In fact, it seemed to drive him onward in his uncontrollable quest to make this carefree vixen a part of himself. The heat of their bodies increased, and it was surprising that steam didn't rise from the entwined lovers as the chilly rain continued to deluge them. They labored until rapture was ready to burst within them and carry them beyond the reality of the storm's fury.

Thunder boomed and lightning flashed, but they couldn't halt their search for sheer bliss beneath the swaying tree. When ecstasy was obtained, they clung together and savored every drop of their lusty bout in the sensual mud. Dirt-filled drops splattered their joined bodies as they lay there recovering from the staggering experience. At last, both were aware of the pelting rain which bit into their tender flesh.

The blue-eyed man propped his elbows on either side of her muddy hair and gazed down at her, shielding her face from the downpour of water. "You're crazy, woman, but I'm damn glad you are."

Trying to breathe normally, she grinned and remarked, "That was wonderful, wasn't it?"

"Yep, it was," he agreed, smiling broadly, tenderly.

They kissed again, leisurely and more calmly. They laughed and hugged, and the heavy rain could be ignored no longer.

"We're filthy, Mr. Logan," she teased, rubbing her hands over his dirt-blackened frame.

He rolled aside, stood, and pulled her to her feet. With the aid of the pouring rain, he washed the mud from her shapely body, then repeated the action on his. He grinned and said, "All clean now."

Marsh picked up their dirty garments and took her hand to walk back to the house. He dropped their clothes on the porch and turned to find her holding up her unbraided hair to a forceful stream of water that was pouring over the edge of the roof. He stepped forward and helped her rinse the dirt from her tawny head. When all traces of mud were removed, he squeezed out the excess water, then pulled her into his arms. Water ran off their bodies and puddled at their feet while slick flesh rubbed against slick flesh. Neither minded that they were standing outside naked, as no one was in the area.

They stood there a long time, embracing and kissing tenderly. They felt relaxed, despite the increased intensity of the storm. When a bolt of lightning struck the large tree and splintered off a large limb which crashed loudly to the muddy ground, they both jumped and looked that way. The swing was broken, and the place where they had made passionate love was concealed. Fusing their gazes again, they laughed merrily at their narrow escape.

"Let's get you dried off and warmed up, woman."

"I just got cooled off," she jested, leaning forward to nibble at his neck. She snuggled against his hard body and sighed peacefully. How she wished this were their home and they would never have to leave it because of any peril or other reason.

Marsh wrapped his arms around her and rested his cheek atop her head. A strange mixture of calm and excitement filled him. He wondered if it would always be this way between them, stimulating, spontaneous, satisfying, heart-stoppingly fantastic, and tender.

The wind began driving rain upon the porch and they moved closer to the door. The air was cooling rapidly, and both shuddered. They laughed as they realized they were still soaked and naked, standing there *au naturel* as if it were the most common behavior in the world.

He grasped her face between his hands, lifted her head, and looked down into her green eyes. Shaking his head roguishly, he murmured, "You steal my wits and self-control at every turn, woman. What am I going to do with you, Miss Hollis?"

"Enjoy me for as long as you can put up with this headstrong vixen," she quipped, drawing his head down to seal their lips.

When their mouths parted, they entered the house hand in hand and closed the door. Randee went into the kitchen to stir the stew and stoke the stove. Marsh dried off and wrapped a thin blanket around his hips, tying it at his waist. He returned to the porch and draped their dirty garments over the railing to allow the forceful rain to wash them.

Randee headed for the bedroom to dry off and don another gown. Marsh followed her and did the task himself. As he worked slowly and gently, he realized why he had been moody earlier. These strong emotions were unfamiliar, were downright intimidating, but he didn't know why. Yet, he didn't want to analyze them today, or he'd be compelled to accept them and deal with them. Deciding what to do about Randee Hollis was one of the toughest decisions of his life. He could be killed any day, any time. If he gave up his present lifestyle, would he miss it? Would he be content to share this woman's life? Had he pressed his luck too many times? Could he keep challenging mortal danger without paying a lethal price? Could he start living and relaxing, stop being on constant guard every day? If he resigned, would he be crazy in a week, a month, a year? What would his existence be like if he didn't travel all the time, if he never got shot at again, if he never engaged in another fight or duel, if he stayed out of the rain and cold, if he wasn't alone, if he did "normal" things for a change? He had come to think this was the only way to live. But was it? Once in while, shouldn't he listen to his heart and not his head?

Randee mischievously fluffed his damp hair and scolded, "Stop thinking about unsolvable problems or you'll create ugly frown lines on this handsome forehead. We're warm and safe tonight, and we have a hot meal simmering in the kitchen. For a change, Mr. Logan, relax and enjoy life, and your seductive servant," she added merrily. As she caressed his strong jawline, she coaxed, "We're good friends and partners, Marsh, so let's not complicate a perfect situation with fears and doubts. Surely there's nothing wrong with being a little wild and crazy every so often. Can't you see, we don't need any demands or promises to harass us? Isn't that enough to appease you for a while?"

Marsh's hands cupped her shoulders gently and he smiled into her entreating eyes. "Do you know how to play poker?" he asked.

"Do I what?" she asked in confusion.

"Do you know how to play poker, the card game?" he clarified.

"No, but you can teach me if you like."

"I have a pack of cards in my saddlebag. It'll be fun to play for a few hours while that storm rages outside.

After we eat, we'll build a cozy fire, spread out our sleeping rolls before it, and play cards till bedtime. I might even share a nip of my best whiskey with you. You did say partners are supposed to share everything, didn't you?"

Grinning, she replied, "I did, didn't I? Well, partner, how about doing your share of the kitchen work? Supper should be ready soon, so we best get some biscuits to baking, and yours are better than mine. I'll set the table and make the coffee."

"I don't recall seeing a table," he teased, following her.

"You're right. How about if you build that fire and spread out those sleeping rolls after you make the biscuits? Then we can picnic before that cozy fire."

At the word *picnic,* their gazes fused and they exchanged grins. As they worked at the kitchen counter, Randee remarked, "He built her a nice home. I wonder if they'd come back after this mess is over."

Marsh responded, "If anybody knews where they went, we could have the authorities notify them about coming back home. Course, they could be settled some place else by now."

"It's terrible to lose your home, to have to walk — no, run — away from all this work and beauty. It makes me sad and angry."

"One day, this area will be filled with settlers. Then, no gang will be strong enough to push everyone aside for some evil reason."

Reflecting on this vile injustice, Randee vowed, "We'll unmask those bastards! We'll cut 'em down in their tracks and they won't ever harm anyone again."

"Mercy, woman, you're talking just like me. From now on, I best watch my language around an impressionable young lady like you."

She laughingly informed him, "You've already

spoiled me, Durango, so it's too late to change your bad conduct and speech now."

"It's never too late to cha . . ." Marsh fell silent as he whirled and pretended to see why the door had been flung open with a crash. He knew the wind had done it, but it had saved him from making a slip.

He glanced at Randee and chuckled before going over to close and bolt it. "While you finish here, I'll check the other door and windows. We don't want any unexpected guests tonight." He left the room to tend his chores.

Randee watched his hasty retreat with a sly grin. Nobody would be out in this violent storm. They were alone in a cozy and secluded setting, a homey one, which made that carefree rogue nervous. She suppressed her laughter and continued her task.

They ate before a warm fire, then cleared the area for their game. Marsh explained the rules as he dealt the cards. They played several hands, with Marsh winning all of them.

"No fair," she jested, "You're an expert at this. Be kind and let me win for a change. Didn't I tell you I'm a bad loser?"

"If there's one thing I know about you, woman, it's that you want to be treated equally. That means winning on your own, and without cheating or being duped."

She grinned and replied, "You've got me there, partner."

"There and everywhere," he responded huskily.

Randee's eyes slipped over his manly frame, still attired in only a thin blanket. He had shaved while she was finishing their supper, and his handsome face was thoroughly arresting. Heavens, how she loved and desired this irresistible male!

"Your turn," Marsh hinted, running his tongue over

316

his lips.

The room was glowing provocatively from the colorful fire. The storm was still howling and raging outside, with rain beating loudly on the roof. Randee reached forward and took the cards from his hand and cast them aside along with hers. She pressed him onto his back and whispered seductively, "I have the winning hand this time, Mr. Logan, so I'll collect my prize right now." Her fingers loosened the knot at his waist and she boldly pushed the covering aside. Removing her gown, she reclined beside him and reached for him.

As she drove him wild with pleasure, he teased, "If this is your prize, you greedy vixen, then I'll let you win every time."

"What a good sport you are, Marsh Logan. Now, lie still; you're distracting me from my lessons," she replied, then returned to work on him sensuously. . . .

The storm did not subside until late the next morning. When the rain halted and the sun came out, Marsh roused himself from Randee's side and went outdoors to look around and to flex his stiff body. Sleeping on a hard floor was much different from the soft earth, he decided, as he rubbed his aching back and neck.

Randee joined him, stretching and yawning lazily. She inhaled deeply and smiled at her enchanting lover as he drew water from the well for their morning coffee. What a blissful night she had spent in his arms, and she craved many more like that one. She watched Marsh as he labored effortlessly. He was wearing jeans and boots, with his shirt rolled and draped around his neck, wrinkling it beyond any form of neatness. He possessed a hard, firm, smooth physique. He was so strong; yet so gentle. Clearly he went shirtless often, because his torso was bronzed like his arms and face. The sun obviously adored him, for it seemingly caressed his face and body each time they were exposed to its loving glow. She felt her body warm as her gaze followed the hairy pattern on his chest and stomach. He was such a skilled lover, such a tender and giving one. How she would love to spend the rest of her life with this special man. . . .

Together they prepared their morning meal, and ate it while making their plans for the next few days. Then, they reluctantly packed to leave the serene homestead. They had made love nearly all night before the entrancing blaze, then dropped off to sleep just before dawn to claim six hours of slumber. It was nearly two o'clock when they saddled their horses and rode away from the towering tree with its broken swing. They rode until dusk, then made camp. Tonight, Marsh was back on alert, and they slept separately.

On Tuesday, the Epson Gang made a daring and bloody raid on a ranch near Jacksboro, one within a few miles of where their friends had been slain and where Fort Richardson stood. . . .

Randee and Marsh scouted the area gingerly as they made their way back toward Fort Worth. It was a beautiful day. Everything was lush and green following the much needed rain. The sky was a clear blue overhead. The air smelled clean and fresh. Wildflowers grew in abundance and brightly colored the landscape.

Around five, they came upon evidence of a large herd of cattle moving northward. Cautiously they followed the tracks until dusk, then sneaked up to the nocturnal grazing area.

Marsh recognized the brand of a huge ranch in southern Texas. Using his field glasses, Randee eyed the drovers and trail boss. She looked at Marsh and shook her head, sighting none of the raiders amongst that group. He motioned for them to move out before they were spotted and fired on as would-be rustlers.

They traveled a safe distance from the cattle drive and made camp. He told her, "If nothing comes up, we'll make Fort Worth by tomorrow night. We'll check with Willard to see if he has any more clues about that land company and Marshal Timms. Then, it's time to get bolder."

"What do you mean?" she questioned eagerly, worriedly.

"It's time we do something to flush those raiders into the open."

"Like what, Marsh?"

"I'll explain when we get together with Willard."

When they reached Fort Worth, it was after dark. They rode to Willard Mason's house, but the newspaperman wasn't home. They headed for his office, but it was empty too. Marsh scowled.

They returned to the man's home and waited for two hours. Marsh knew they were both tired and hungry. Finally he said, "If he was out for the evening, he'd be back by now. He's one of those early to bed and early to rise people. I don't like this, Randee. Somebody could have gotten annoyed by Willard's inquisitive nature. If anyone's on to us, the hotel would be dangerous. I want you to stay with a friend of mine tonight while I do some snooping around."

"Who? Where?" she asked. "Why can't I stay with

319

you?"

"Women aren't allowed in saloons, and that's where I'll pick up any information available tonight. Please, trust me and bear with me."

"Darn it, left behind again," she grumbled jestingly. Seriously, she concurred, "I'll obey you once more, if you promise to be careful."

"I have to be, or my partner will kill me," he jested.

When they reached their destination, she eyed him oddly and reminded, "I thought you said women weren't allowed in saloons."

"A good friend of mine owns this one. It's the nicest in Texas or anywhere else. Hopefully this is the last place anyone would think to look for you. Just remember to behave yourself after I leave."

"Very amusing," she scoffed, punching him in the side.

Randee waited just inside the back door while Marsh went to locate and speak with his *good friend*. Through slightly parted curtains, she viewed the lush interior of the fancy saloon with its numerous lanterns and elaborately carved furniture. She saw men playing a variety of games. She saw pretty girls in lovely dresses serving them liquor and laughing with them. It wasn't what she had expected, especially after the sight she had witnessed near Fort Richardson recently. She eyed the opulent establishment and realized there must be a lot of money to made with prostitution, gambling, and whiskey. She listened to the music, a combination of piano and a lovely female voice. Soon, she decided that Marsh's friend owned and ran a nice . . . house of masculine pleasures. She couldn't wait to meet this friend of Marsh's, as a man didn't usually grin like that when referring to a male!

At last, Marsh returned to where she was waiting in the shadows. Behind him was a ravishing female with flame-colored hair, fiery sapphire eyes, and skin as white and as soft as cotton. She looked to be in her mid-thirties, but Randee wasn't certain. The woman was dressed in a sexy dark-blue gown with black lace trim, but she wore very little face paint. Twinges of jealousy stabbed at Randee as she wondered what their past and present relationship was. She had known there had been other women in his life because he was a very virile and handsome man, but she had not expected to meet any of them! Doing so made her remember that carefree side of Marsh Logan, and her tenuous hold on him. Yet, she smiled genially as Marsh introduced them.

The beautiful woman shook Randee's hand firmly and smiled. Miss Sloan Peters told her, "If you're wondering where I got a manly first name like Sloan, I was named after my mother's family. But you can call me Pete; most everybody does, especially my friends."

Randee caught her hint and smiled. "Thank you, Pete. It's a pleasure to meet a close friend of Mr. Logan's."

Sloan Peters playfully shook Marsh's arm as she teased the man, "I'm glad Marsh rescued you from those kidnappers and is escorting you back home safely, but this extra good deed surprises me. Marsh is a born drifter, who usually minds his own business. Surely your parents must be wealthy and he's expecting a fat reward."

Aware that Randee didn't know what story he'd told the woman, Marsh quickly injected, "I didn't have any choice but to save her after I practically rode over their camp in the dark. They didn't want any witnesses, so they tried to gun me down. Afterwards, I couldn't just leave a pretty girl like this in the wilds, especially after she promised me her parents would pay hefty for her rescue and return." He chuckled before saying to Randee, "Begging your pardon, miss, but no offense intended. Miss Hollis is a real lady, Pete, so you treat her that way while I'm out tonight. She's been through a rough time, and doesn't need anyone poking her with embarrassing questions. Just tell the girls she's the daughter of an old friend, who's passing through town and wanted a short visit with you. Like I said, two of those varmints got away and they won't be kind at all if they locate me again. Just hide her for the night so she can get some rest, and I'll pick her up by noon tomorrow."

The flaming redhead replied, "Don't you worry, Marsh, she'll be just fine here. She can bunk with Flossie, one of my best girls. It'll do Flossie good to have company. She's been sad lately. You don't mind sharing a room with another woman, do you, Miss Hollis?"

The blonde smiled and shook her head, and used the good manners which her mother had taught her. "Please, call me Randee, and of course I don't mind sharing Miss Flossie's room, if it's all right with her. I don't want to inconvenience anyone, but I'm grateful for your kindness and help. Mr. Logan said he could depend on you."

The surprised woman glanced at Marsh and mischievously rolled her sapphire eyes. "He did, did he? My goodness how we've changed, my handsome loner. Whatever's happened to you since our last visit?"

"Don't you go teasing me unmercifully, Pete. I'm too exhausted to defend myself. One good deed doesn't change a man like me."

"But it's a start, isn't it, Randee?" the woman coaxed merrily.

The blonde gazed at Marsh as if evaluating him in looks and conduct. "I wouldn't know about Mr. Logan's past character, but he's been absolutely wonderful to me," she remarked, sounding like a young girl who was smitten by her handsome champion, as she should be.

Marsh realized that Randee was having fun with this game. He teased, "You're prejudiced, Miss Hollis, because I saved your hide. Don't you fret anymore; I'll have you home safe and sound real soon."

"I can hardly wait, Mr. Logan. Trail life is very hard and demanding. I cannot imagine why you love it so dearly, or why you think badly of yourself. You've been so kind and polite, and you've taught me so many things. I shall never forget you and this experience."

Sloan Peters was astonished by the passionate undercurrents she perceived passing between Marsh Logan and this radiant creature. Their desire for each other was as evident to her as the sexy shadow on Marsh's strong jawline. Sloan was amused, warmed, and pleased to find the man's heart softening toward a female, especially toward one as nice as Randee Hollis. She had known Marsh for years, and she liked him more than most men. This blonde was perfect for Marsh, but did he realize that fact? If she pointed it out to him, he would become defensive and would strengthen his resistance, so she smiled happily and kept silent.

Marsh said, "That's awfully sweet of you, Miss Hollis, but I couldn't live any other way. Trail dust is in my blood."

The older woman told him, "Go on about your business, Marsh. I'll take good care of Miss Hollis for you. She'll be safe here."

For hours, Randee sat cross-legged on the double bed in Flossie's room, listening to the girl talk eagerly. The flame-haired owner of this plush establishment had given the brown-haired girl the night off and had sent a bottle of champagne to the room for them to enjoy. Randee had never drunk the bubbly spirits before, but liked the taste. Nor had she sat in her nightgown on a stranger's bed, savoring girl-talk with another female of her own age who was a professional lover. Her curiosity got the best of her, and she asked Flossie numerous questions.

The attractive brunette had downed most of the champagne to lighten her sagging spirits. Slightly inebriated and thoroughly relaxed, she laughed and teased, "Before you leave in the morning, you'll know as much about men as I do. Lawsy, they love their women well-trained and loose-thighed, and ignorant of the word *no*. But I get tired of no choice in the matter and person. Half the time I don't get the ones I like, and the other half I get the ones I don't like." She fell backward on the bed giggling. "Lawsy, Randee, but I wish some handsome rogue like your Storm Hayden would come along and rescue me."

Randee concluded that Flossie didn't know Marsh's real name. Assuming everyone knew Marsh's other identity, she used it, "His name is Durango, Flossie. Surely you've heard of the Durango Kid. I don't have a lasso on him; I doubt any woman ever will."

Flossie pushed herself to a sitting position and laughed wildly. "He's joshing you, girl. I've spent many a night in bed with the Durango Kid, and that isn't him. Don't you know who you're traveling with? He calls himself Marsh Logan, but his real name is Storm Hayden, a real tough critter who shoots straight and fast and asks questions later. How'd a lady like you get tangled up with an outlaw like that?"

Randee gently corrected the girl, "You're mistaken, Flossie; he really is the Durango Kid. I've been traveling with him for weeks, so I know I'm right about him."

Flossie eyed her sympathetically. "I hate it that he's got you fooled, Randee, 'ticularly since your blood's hot for him. Like I said, I've had the Kid inside me several times, and I've seen him in showdowns in that street outside. He's one of Pete's best friends and customers, so I know the Durango Kid by sight and feel. Your man ain't him; I swear it. I saw one of your sweetie's old posters in Pete's desk; I guess she saved it as a souvenir. It said *Storm Hayden,* said he was wanted *Dead or Alive.* He had a real big reward on his head. Best I recall, the poster was from Kansas or Nebraska."

Chapter Fifteen

Randee stared at the mildly intoxicated female with brown hair and eyes. How, she asked herself, could Marsh not be the Durango Kid? She thought hard for a minute, and realized no one had confirmed who Marsh had claimed to be; no one had called him by that legendary name. She had accepted his word about his dual identities, but why would he lie to her? How could her love be an outlaw, a wanted man, a criminal with a price on his head? How could he dupe her so easily and for so long? Even if he had deceived her in the beginning, why continue the deception after knowing he could trust her, after they had become so close? Yet, Flossie had no reason to make up such a wild story, and there had not been time and opportunity for either Marsh or Pete to have instigated a cruel ruse like this. She needed more information before Flossie passed out for the night.

She shook the brunette's arm and asked, "Are you sure that 'wanted' poster was for Marsh Logan? Maybe it's only someone who looks like him. Please, Flossie, think hard," she pleaded.

Flossie responded confidently, "I don't have to think again; I know it was him, because I heard them joking about the reward poster one night. And, I've seen her tickle him and call him Storm. But don't let on to him or Pete I told you the truth. I ain't got no business being in her office and desk nosing around. Pete would be furious; she'd fire me. Promise me you won't tell them what I did."

"I won't say a word to either of them, Flossie. But I need more facts. What did the poster say about Marsh, I mean Storm?"

While trying to clear her wits, Flossie answered, "Something about murder and robbery. I remember it was a big reward, thousands of dollars. I looked at it a long time because I was shocked to learn such terrible things about a man I knew. A real good artist drew it. He looked so handsome and scary in that picture. And I know it said *Dead or Alive*, because that worried me. I was always scared some lawman would shoot up this place trying to capture him while he was here with Pete. Since he changed his name and he ain't from Texas, I guess few people in these parts know him as Storm Hayden. Pete's crazy about him, and so are you, Randee, so I guess he's not all bad. I surely wouldn't turn him in for no reward, big or little." Flossie sighed deeply before telling why. "Because he ain't no man to betray. Lawsy, Randee, I've seen him make more than one man back down just by glaring at him with those icy blue eyes. Lawsy, girl, he can put the fear of God and death in you with just one stare. A man like that can be as heartless as he can be hot-blooded. You never know which mood you'll find him in, and the wrong one can cost you plenty."

"Can you remember which state or territory he's from? It's real important to me," Randee probed, hoping it wasn't . . .

Flossie saw how upset the girl was, so she complied, "It seems like I read *Kansas* on the poster. But I remember hearing them joke about what he did in Nebraska, so I could be wrong. Who knows? Maybe he's wanted in both places, or lots of places. Or maybe he ain't wanted anywhere anymore. It could be that he's served his time in prison and is free now. I can't imagine Pete befriending a criminal."

Randee shook her head and refuted, "He's too young to have served a prison term for murder and robbery. Why would he tell me he's the Durango Kid? Why not stick to using Marsh Logan?"

Flossie admitted, "He favors the Kid a lot, so I can see how some folks might get fooled, by mistake or on purpose. Maybe he lied to you because he was trying to impress you, Randee, or maybe he was scared you wouldn't like him if you knew he was an outlaw. Pete told me you're real special to him and to take good care of you. Lawsy, what have I done?" she murmured fearfully. "I shouldn't have opened my mouth. Darn that champagne for clouding my brain!"

"Please don't be upset. I'm glad you told me about Storm. He's been tricking me for weeks. I believed everything he told me. It isn't right for a man to trick a woman and use her badly. Damn him!"

That statement hit Flossie forcefully. "That's right, girl; men shouldn't use us badly, but they do if we let 'em. Sometimes they say crazy things when they want a woman to do certain things," Flossie murmured, staring into blank space with a sad look in her eyes.

"What's wrong, Flossie?" the blonde asked gently. "Why were you snooping through Pete's desk? Were you looking for money to run away?"

"Steal from Pete?" the prostitute scoffed incredulously. "Never! Pete pays us girls good and gives us a home and protection. It's not like it is in most saloons. I love Pete, and I would never harm her. I was looking for information about her daughter. I didn't even know she had one until a customer of mine . . ." She hesitated and looked afraid. "You can't reveal this to anybody. Swear it, Randee."

Randee realized that the girl needed to talk desperately, talk to someone who would be gone soon with her secrets, someone who would understand and honor her confidence. "I swear, Flossie."

The nervous female glanced toward the door and lowered her voice before she revealed, "I have this customer I don't like. Like?" she echoed, then laughed coldly. "I hate him. Pete doesn't allow the men to harm us, but I can't tell her about this bad man. He threatened to kill me, Pete, the other girls, and Pete's daughter. He's big and mean, and he has lots of friends just like him. He would do it, Randee, honestly he would. That's why you have to keep your mouth shut about him. I was going through Pete's desk to see if I could find any pictures of her child, maybe with the father. If this man knows her secret, then maybe he's the father. I didn't find anything. If I had, then I could have told Pete about him and his threats. His name's Carl Bush. he has hair redder than Pete's, and cold black eyes. He injured his right leg in the war, so he walks with a limp. When it's paining him, he's meaner than a cornered badger. He comes in every so often and I have to let him use me like he wishes and keep my mouth shut or we're all dead. This is my home, Randee; I can't leave Pete's place. What am I going to do?" she wailed.

Randee was horrified by that news and description. *Carl Bush.* Her mind echoed the name of the leader of the Epson Gang. She dared not tell this saloon girl who she was pleasuring, else she would expose her own secret. If that villain came to visit again soon, Flossie might confess his peril to him in order to save herself and those she loved. She shouldn't do or say anything until she talked with Marsh . . .

Marsh. Was her deceitful lover really Marsh Logan? Recalling his behavior at the Logans' graves, she decided he must be the real son of Marshall and Judith Logan. But was he also this notorious Storm Hayden? Several facts struck home within Randee. If he wasn't the Durango Kid, then all the stories about that famous gunslinger weren't about her love! Everything she thought was true about him wasn't! Yet, he was an expert with guns and prowess. Had he pretended to be the Kid just to get her job? For the money, or another reason? Did he go around claiming to be Durango just to avoid perils and challenges which could unmask his real second identity? Who was Storm Hayden? Was *he* the life Marsh Logan was fleeing, trying to forget, the deadly threat hanging over his head every day, the reckless mistake of his youthful rebellion, the reason why he couldn't start over anywhere for fear of being located and captured?

Randee looked at the weeping girl on the bed near her. She put her arms around the brunette and entreated, "Don't cry, Flossie, men like that get themselves killed every day. Just don't do anything to upset him when he comes to visit. If he gets real mean, you can always kill him in self-defense. Since Pete wouldn't want such bad word spread about her nice place, she'd probably find somebody to get rid of the body secretly. That way, everyone will be safe here."

"You mean, kill him?" the girl asked, wide-eyed and pale.

"Isn't that better than allowing him to hurt you and those you love?" Randee reasoned.

The female shook her dark head vigorously. "I couldn't harm anyone, Randee, not even Carl Bush. I'm such a coward."

"If you were a coward, Flossie, you wouldn't have snooped in Pete's office! You've braver than you think.

330

I tell you what, I'll try to get Marsh—I mean Storm—to gun him down in a duel. Will that help?"

"Would he do that for us?" the pretty prostitute asked hopefully.

"He'll have no choice. If he helps us, we'll keep his secret. Doesn't that sound like a good bargain to you?"

"You can't mean . . . force a man like that to obey us?"

"Why not, Flossie? He owes me plenty."

Randee lay awake for hours after the girl was asleep. Was this what Marsh considered the insurmountable obstacle between them? Was he afraid his stormy past would follow him here one day and destroy those around him? Was that why he pretended to be the Durango Kid, hoping to go unrecognized as Storm Hayden? Was this why he couldn't and wouldn't commit to her? Did he fear she would become entangled by his lethal past? But what, she wondered sadly, did that dark past include? Was he guilty of murder and robbery? How so, when he even paid for the dynamite he stole in Brownwood? No, Marsh Logan could not be a vicious criminal, a wanted outlaw! Surely he had been framed or compelled to act as he had! Maybe those deeds had been terrible mistakes during his misguided youth. Maybe those deeds were the reasons why he hadn't been able to go home after his father's explanation. Yet, why hadn't he revealed such things to her? If Marsh "Storm Hayden" Logan was such good friends with Miss Sloan Peters and she knew of his dark past, then why had he lied to Pete about them? Where, she asked herself jealously, was Marsh spending the night, alone, or with that ravishing woman?

She sighed wearily as her troubled mind was plagued by endless questions about the man she loved. Was it a hopeless situation between them? What if they went far away for a fresh start, where no one could find Storm Hayden? What if they found a way to outrun the law? He couldn't have been too infamous, as she had never heard this name before tonight. Was he tired of looking over his shoulder for the long reach of the Kansas law? Kansas! If he was still wanted there, then how could he return to help her defeat Payton Slade?

I want to trust you, Marsh, but how can I, with all this evidence against you? Have you lied to me? Used me, like Payton has done with my mother? Please God, don't let this story be true, she prayed.

Marsh's evening went differently from Randee's. He talked with several men in the saloon and played three hands of poker. He learned of the Epson raid near Jacksboro and hoped it wasn't in retaliation for Jim's attack on their friends' camp. When George Light arrived for a night of pleasure, Pete introduced the two men, at Marsh's request. He figured Light wouldn't guess the truth about him.

President Grant's agent said, "I heard you're the lawyer who's handling the land sales for the Mid-Texas Land Company. I have a nice spread near Jacksboro that I might consider selling if the price is right. My parents owned it, but they're dead now, victims of one of those raids by the Epson bunch. Who's buying, and what are they offering?"

The silver-haired man replied, "The company owners want their names kept secret for a while longer. Give me the details and I'll see if I can get an offer for you."

Marsh complied, then remarked, "I don't like selling out to ghosts, Mr. Light. It's my home, so I wouldn't want to see it destroyed again. What do they want with so much land?"

George Light sipped his drink and eyed the man before him. "I'm just their lawyer, so I can't answer that question. I do know they're planning something big and important for this state."

To draw the man out, Marsh revealed, "Williard Mason over at the paper is the one who steered me your way. He said you were an honest man and would make me a fair deal. I tried to see him when I got into town tonight, but he's not around."

George informed him, "I believe he said he was going to Austin on business. He's been trying to do a story on the company I represent, but that group isn't ready to reveal their news yet."

Marsh chuckled and said, "Knowing Mr. Mason, I'm sure he's anxious to be first with the story."

George responded coolly, "If you ask me, he's a damn nosy fellow; I guess all newspaper men are. But if he isn't careful, somebody might chop off his big nose one day. People don't like strangers getting into their private affairs and exposing them."

"I know what you mean," Marsh replied, wondering if he'd been too careless with this cunning man. "I have some business in San Antonio this week, but I'll be back around the twenty-fourth. I'll stop by your office and see if we can make a deal on my land."

"That's fine with me, Mr. Logan. If you'll excuse me, I have other plans for the evening," the lawyer hinted as he eyed one of the pretty saloon girls. Since he was the representative for the Mid-Texas Land Company, there was nothing unusual in a man approaching him about a land sale, so he forget about the Jacksboro rancher . . . .

Marsh lay in bed reflecting on his time with Randee during that violent storm. She had said, " . . . man she loved . . . I'm not ready to give Fate the chance to do that to me." Had she been telling him something? Or had she made a slip? She had also said, "Whatever it is between us . . . we have to allow it to take its course." Wasn't that true? Didn't he owe them the chance to discover what this bond was and how strong it was? This mission couldn't last forever, unless one or both of them were slain. What about afterwards? Could he ride out of her life and never look back? Or look back only on occasion?

At dawn on Thursday, the Epson Gang raided near Wadesville, and news reached Fort Worth and Marsh by noon.

Marsh knocked on Flossie's door and waited for either female to respond. When it opened, Randee said almost emotionlessly, "Good morning, Marsh. Is it time to leave?"

Marsh eyed her closely, noticing that she appeared tired and reserved. "If you're ready to ride, we'll head for Wadesville."

"Wadesville?" she echoed, clearly intrigued.

He glanced into the room and sighted no one else, but he said cautiously, "I'll explain on the trail." As Randee gathered her belongings, Marsh asked politely, "Need any help?"

"No thanks, I can manage. Are the horses saddled and ready?"

"Waiting out back," he replied, becoming curious about her odd behavior and mood. "Where's Flossie?" he asked.

Randee answered, "She's washing her hair and getting ready for work tonight. I've already thanked her and told her good-bye."

Randee followed him toward the back door. Miss Sloan Peters met them there and bid them farewell and good luck. The blonde watched as Pete gave Marsh a hug and a kiss and told him to "please return soon." Marsh thanked the redhead for her help, then Randee did the same. They mounted, waved to the saloon owner, and rode away.

A mile or so outside town, Marsh reined in and signaled for Randee to do the same. She followed him off the well-traversed road to a place behind a rolling hill where they couldn't be sighted by travelers. He did not dismount, but smiled before opening their conversation.

Marsh felt a cold stab in his gut when Randee merely watched him without warming. He instinctively knew that something was wrong between them. Now that they were alone, he mused worriedly, why was she still acting like a frosty morn? Maybe it had been a mistake to take her into a place where women sold themselves to men for money, where sex was given without love and bonds. To pull her from her shell, he plunged right into his explanation, "I met George Light last night and tried to get us a break in this matter." After revealing their talk in the saloon, Marsh asked, "What do you think?"

"About what?" she inquired.

"About what I just told you," Marsh responded. "Is something wrong, Randee? You seem a little strange today. If you're wondering if I spent the night with one of those saloon girls, I didn't."

Randee realized she had to stop thinking about what she had learned last night, as it was affecting her behavior toward him. She had to wait until Marsh broached that dark secret and confessed all to her. It wouldn't be the same if she forced him to expose his past. She decided to use a jealousy ruse to cover her

335

slip. "I had a very interesting evening with Miss Flossie. She told me lots of things about you men. It seems that you and Pete are very good friends and you visit her often."

A grin captured Marsh's mouth and got bigger and bigger as his blue eyes sparkled with amusement and relief. "Is that jealousy I detect in that beautiful body, Miss Hollis?" he teased. "I certainly hope so."

Randee stuck her tongue out at him and scoffed, "Why not? You are a hot-blooded man, Mr. Logan. I'm sure you have plenty of other women waiting for you in every town. I just never expected to meet any of them. If you'll recall, you did warn me once that jealous people do crazy things. Forget I said anything stupid and acted like a donkey's rear end. I guess I'm just a little tired and fussy because we girls talked nearly all night."

Marsh chuckled and caught her hand in his. "You don't have to fret over me playing around while we're together. Besides, I wouldn't have enough energy to keep more than one female satisfied at a time."

Randee apologized, "I'm sorry, Marsh. I don't mean to sound selfish or possessive, but I don't want to share you while we're together. What you do afterwards is your private business. Is that agreeable?"

"Absolutely, woman. Relax, partner, you don't have anything to worry about where I'm concerned. I'm perfectly content with you."

"Just so you understand my feelings and meaning, I'm not trying to make demands on you, Marsh, but you should play fair with me. Any time you want out of our relationship, just tell me, and it's over. No strings, no tears, no arguments, and no regrets. All right?"

"Sometimes I'm afraid you're too good to be true," he murmured.

"The same goes for you, partner," she retorted with a

laugh. "Let's drop this vexing topic and get back to business. Was your talk with George Light one of those bold moves you mentioned?"

"Yep, I want to see if his boss takes my bait. Somebody has to sign those sale papers, and I want to see whose name appears on them."

Randee reasoned in alarm, "What if you can't see the papers without signing them? Surely you wouldn't sell your place just to get a smidgen of information. What about using the Carson Ranch as bait? Since I have no legal claim to it, my sale wouldn't be binding. Anyway, my sale would be less suspicious than yours, considering the company lawyer associates you with Willard Mason."

Marsh disclosed, "That's one of the reasons why we're heading for Wadesville. Too, there was another raid near there at dawn this morning. I want to do some snooping around while you distract Sheriff Wade." At her look of surprise, he clarified, "This is going to be a bold move, partner, but we need to make it and get on with this mission. This is what you'll tell him," Marsh began, then related his daring scheme. "He's going to be mad as hell, so you can pull it off?"

Randee considered his ruse and nodded. "It sounds like a cunning plan to me. But you're right about Brody not taking my actions well at all. He'll do everything he can to stop me from leaving again. At least this will give me the chance to reject his proposal and stop him from waiting around for my return."

"No, you can't do that," Marsh protested instantly. "You have to let him believe you're coming back to him after we finish this task. If you don't keep him on the hook, he'll give us all kinds of trouble. The only way he'll let you leave town peaceably with me is by leading him on for a while longer. You can't let him even suspect the truth about us. Maybe you should accept

337

his proposal."

"What!" she nearly shouted at him. "You can't be serious. That's cruel, Marsh. I can't treat anyone that badly, especially a friend. It's wrong and mean to use Brody like that."

Marsh released her hand and stated firmly, "We have no choice, Randee. Once we commit to this perilous scheme, our path is set. I can't allow a spurned sweetheart to mess it up, or to endanger us by trailing you and begging you to reconsider his proposal. Dammit, woman, this mission is more important than one man. We have to use Brody Wade to obtain a victory over that murderous bunch. If you don't agree with this plan, then go back to town and wait for me there."

Randee asked softly, "How important is your victory, Marsh? More important than using anyone to obtain it? Tell me, just how far would you go to defeat that gang?"

Marsh looked at her and realized he had spoken too harshly and coldly. He comprehended that deceiving Brody wasn't her only concern; she was afraid he would use her, too, if the mission called for it. "Listen to me, Randee; I don't want an innocent person used any more than you do, but it's better than hundreds more getting killed or being driven out of their homes because we can't find another way to operate. We've been on this case for weeks, and I've been on it for over a year. It's time to make daring moves to force that gang into the open. If that means hurting Brody's feelings for a while, then we must."

Distressed by this entrapping situation, she asserted, "Obviously there's a lot you don't know about people, or you'd be more considerate of others' feelings. There's something else you don't know, Marsh. Flossie told me about a customer of hers that she hates and fears. She perfectly described the leader of the Epson

338

Gang: big and mean, redheaded, frigid black eyes, and a lame right leg. She says he visits her every so often. Why can't we hang around Pete's place and capture him? Or follow him back to his hide-out and dynamite the whole gang? His name is Carl Bush. Of course that might not be his real name; sometimes men do change their names for one reason or another."

"We could wait around for weeks or months before Bush decides to visit Flossie again, if he ever does. That gang's been laying low for a while, but they're on the move again. I doubt their leader would take time out right now to spend the night with a saloon girl. If you'll recall, that gang takes plenty of women when they're raiding, so Bush doesn't need to ride into Fort Worth to sleep with Flossie. She doesn't know who or what he is, does she?" After Randee shook her head, he continued, "That tells you it's nothing more than sex for him. Did you drop any clues to her?" Again, Randee shook her head. "We need to visit Wadesville, partner, and I've been avoiding it because of the danger to you. Since the gang struck there this morning, their pattern says they'll head some place else to raid next. That means it's safe for you to visit right now, and Brody gives us the perfect return cover. As you pointed out, woman, the Carson Ranch is the only one that's been spared from total destruction. There's a clue there, Randee, and we have to find it. Don't you see, the only way we can get in and out of Wadesville is by you revealing yourself to Brody and duping him? If you can't do that, I'll understand and let you out of this assignment. But I can't permit you to thwart my plan by showing up and not carrying it through. What's your decision, partner?"

Randee weighed all the information and risks, and she couldn't argue against Marsh's clever but devious plan. Besides, he wasn't insisting she do as he said;

there was no force or coercion involved. She also wondered why Carl Bush had spared the Carson house and on whose order. Before she relented and agreed to her lover's ploy, she related, "I told Flossie to stop worrying about that evil bastard because you would hunt him down and kill him for her. She doesn't want Pete to know about his cruelties to her, because Pete would blame herself for not protecting one of her girls, and Bush threatened her if she exposed him. I gave Flossie my word we would save her from that beast and we'd keep her secret. I know you and Pete are good friends, but this time, my word includes yours. Agreed?"

"Agreed," Marsh responded, then waited for her answer to his previous question. He didn't want to leave her behind, where trouble could find her while he wasn't around to help protect her, but he wanted to get this matter settled so they could get on with their lives. They had committed to this task, and hopefully Light wouldn't associate them with the rancher he'd met last night. They had no choice but to pursue this until the end, and the faster they succeeded, the better and safer for all involved, especially for him and Randee. He knew he was asking her to do a difficult and dangerous thing, but Randee was more than capable of handling herself and this assignment. If he didn't trust her implicitly and have full confidence in her, he would never allow her to set foot in Wadesville or to continue this mission at his side.

"Even if I agree to go along with your clever plan, aren't you afraid I'll panic or go soft and mess it up?" she asked.

Marsh looked her straight in the eye and replied, "If you give me your word of honor, that's good enough for me, Randee. I know your skills by now, so I have every confidence in you and in them. In fact, I think I believe in you more than you believe in yourself." He smiled

340

and tugged on her hair. "I realize you don't like this part of the plan, but it's necessary, woman, or I wouldn't ask you to do it. Do you think for one minute that I want you being mushy with Brody Wade? My teeth want to gnash just thinking about what you'll have to say and do to fool him. Dammit, woman, about the last thing I want is Brody Wade wooing you! If there was any other way to get this thing moving toward victory, don't you think I'd use it instead?"

Randee smiled at that admission. "I don't like it, but I'll do it."

"Good girl," he said tenderly, then caressed her cheek. "As soon as we finish our task in Wadesville, we'll ride back to Fort Worth to check in with Willard. I'll give him Carl Bush's name and see what he can discover about the man. If we're lucky, either you or me will get a bite on our land offers."

"Is that all for now, partner?" she asked.

Marsh smiled wryly and shook his ebony head. He had not forgotten about the name he had signed impulsively on the reward release paper for Brody Wade, so he knew he had to reveal and explain that fact. Mercy, how he hated to deceive her again, but it was necessary at this point in time and in this case. But, as soon as this mission was over, he was going to trust her with the truth about himself. His parents had died thinking he had turned out badly, and he could never forgive himself for that heartbreaking mistake, so he wasn't about to let this special woman go on thinking the worst of him for a minute longer than need be! He would make his false explanation simple and direct, and hope for the best.

He began slowly, hesitantly, worriedly, "There's . . . something I have to tell you, partner . . . before we reach Wadesville, because Sheriff Wade will delight in doing so and . . . causing problems between us. I'm

341

. . . I'm not the Durango Kid." When she looked surprised and baffled, he hurried on, "I only used that familiar identity to win your trust in me and my skills. Since we were strangers about to head into the wilds together, I thought you would be more at ease with me if you thought you knew something about me — especially since the Kid is reputed to be such a good fellow. We do favor each other greatly, and I am mistaken for him quite a lot. That's why I used him to win you over. My real name is Marsh Logan, but I've used 'Storm Hayden' during my travels."

"Storm Hayden," she echoed, allowing time for her wits to sharpen. She was eager, yet afraid, of his coming words.

He sighed loudly and deeply. "I know, I lied to you, but I thought it was the best thing for both of us. I don't want you learning this news from anybody except me, so please hear me out before you get mad and call it quits with our partnership. I did lots of drifting after I left home, and I got into big trouble in Nebraska. I was accused of killing and robbing a man there, but I didn't do it. I was using the name Storm Hayden because I didn't want to stain my family's name. Of course, at the time, I thought I had changed it because I didn't want to be Marshall Logan's son anymore. I got into plenty of suspicious mischief, so it seemed natural for them to put the blame for that crime on my shoulders. I was a loner, wild and rebellious, smartmouthed and arrogant. I tried to clear myself, but I couldn't. I escaped just before they were going to lynch me without a trial. After I came back to Texas, I made friends with Willard Mason and told him all about my problem. He keeps up with the news from everywhere, so he was trying to get information to clear me, or let me know when it was safe to go back and do it myself."

Randee knew he wasn't finished, so she held silent

342

and alert.

"That's one of the reasons why I couldn't go home; it might have endangered my parents. After I saw my family that last time, I was heading for Nebraska to set the record straight. Before I could return home and tell them the truth, they were killed by that gang, killed believing I was a notorious gunslinger. That's what I blame myself for more than not being there to protect them. You don't have to worry about lawmen chasing me; that case is closed now. The trouble is, some people know me as Storm Hayden and I still have enemies I made there. Some folks can't remember or accept when a man's exonerated. They only recall he was accused, and they act as if he's gotten away with a clever crime and they never fully trust him.

"When I was in Wadesville, Brody called my bluff on being the Durango Kid. Without thinking, I signed that release paper for the reward money as Storm Hayden because I didn't want Brody Wade knowing who I really was. If he discovered the truth, he would put the facts together and know we've duped him. When a man's mad, his tongue gets loose and he tries to spite you. When you see Brody, I'm sure he's going to tell you who he thinks I am." He inhaled deeply and noisily. "I didn't want to tell you about my misbegotten youth, but I don't want it to come as a shock and cause you to doubt me."

She inquired astutely, "You said the case is closed now, so why are you still apprehensive? Still on the run? Still living as Storm Hayden or the Durango Kid?"

Marsh responded quickly with part of the truth about himself. "The law closed the case, but the people involved still believe I'm guilty. Once in a while, they send someone to harass me, hoping I'll be killed legally in a showdown. Willard has two detectives searching

343

for the real killer, so I'll be off the hook when they succeed. Until then, I have to keep watching over my shoulder. So you see, partner, we both have people to outrun. There's one other thing: my reward posters were called in, but some may still be laying around somewhere to mislead people about me. I can't relax my guard until every angle of this Storm Hayden mess is straightened out. It would be easier to do if some of the rotten things they said about me weren't true, but it's too late to change the past. I did 'em, so I have to pay the price."

"Surely defeating the Epson Gang will go in your favor, Marsh. Maybe one day you'll be able to get your past behind you. I hope so."

"So do I, Randee, but it'll take time and patience, which a man like me usually doesn't have much of. But don't worry, 'cause I'm not giving up," he said, trying to sound light and merry.

As they traveled along, Randee pondered what Marsh had confessed. She wanted to believe him, but something in his expression and voice prevented total trust. She sensed he was withholding additional facts, or skillfully coloring those revealed to suit his purpose — whatever that was. Perhaps she was allowing her love for him to blind her, but blind her to what? Even if he wasn't guilty of what that poster claimed, was he guilty of other "rotten things"? Had he only confessed this secret because he knew she would learn about it soon from Brody, or because he knew or suspected she had learned about it last night? Marsh Logan was still a mystery to her, one she had to unravel . . . .

They camped over halfway to Wadesville, but talked little that night, as both seemed caught up in their own thoughts. Randee was waiting to see if Marsh exposed anything more, and Marsh was waiting to see how the blonde reacted to his shocking revelation. She could tell that Marsh wasn't ready to give more answers or to reconsider a commitment to her, and Marsh was glad she wasn't pressing him on either score. They watched each other furtively, and slept separately.

They were up early Friday morning to complete their intimidating journey. Just before reaching town at three o'clock, Marsh halted them and asked for a certain garment from her saddlebag. When she passed it to him, he rubbed it in the dirt, shook out the excess dust, handed it to her, and told her to dress in it.

"What's going on?" she asked, staring at him strangely.

"If you've been on the trail for weeks since your Indian capture and my rescue, then you can't look so neat and pretty when we ride into Wadesville. We'll hide your belongings here, then retrieve them on our way back to Fort Worth. You ready to take on this assignment?"

"Ready," she responded unflinchingly.

Marsh smiled encouragingly and said, "Let's ride, partner."

Chapter Sixteen

As she dismounted before the Wadesville jail, Randee Hollis felt as if her body was stretched tauter than a sheafing cord. It was normal to feel anxious, guilty, and uncertain — but annoyed and repulsed? Reviewing the matter of Brody Wade, she knew why.

The closer she had ridden to this office alone, the more she had been assailed by enlightenment, apprehension, and anger. Yes, anger — anger at herself and at Brody Wade. She had changed her mind about the persistent lawman. Perhaps it had been time and distance that had opened her eyes to the truth. It now sounded ridiculous to think she had ever been tempted to marry him, but she understood why she had made such a mistake. She had been under a terrible strain before and after running away from home, and following the tragic deaths of her kin. At first, Brody had seemed a wonderful part of a new life, a clean and happy one. She had been flattered and touched by his attentions and hot pursuit. At times, she had been scared, alone, and vulnerable. She had needed someone to lean on, and the handsome sheriff had seemed to fill her needs. She had assumed she liked him, could even love and marry him, but she had fooled herself.

To be honest—Brody Wade was too nice, too sweet, too much in love with her, too cloying, and too manipulative. If she gave herself to him, he would suffocate her, absorb her, want too much from her. He had made her feel vulnerable and helpless, tried to trick her into yielding to him. Brody Wade was more cunning and demanding that she had realized. Thanks to Marsh, Brody had lost his appeal: physical and emotional. Suddenly she didn't want him around her at all.

Randee knew she needed to pull off this duplicity, and prayed she could succeed. Yet, she was wary, tense, even a little afraid. She hadn't told Marsh about such ridiculous feelings because she could not explain them even to herself. Maybe she was simply unsettled about having to be falsely romantic with another man since she had already given her heart and body to Marsh Logan. Maybe she was merely worried that, after she led him on, Brody Wade would intrude on her love affair and dangerous mission. Maybe she was afraid she would do everything wrong today. Or, maybe she was only panicked at the thought of Brody knowing and telling her things about "Storm Hayden," which she didn't want to hear. . . .

Randee was glad she was seeing Brody alone, yet she also wished Marsh was at her side. She wondered what, if anything, her ebony-haired lover would discover at the Carson Ranch today while she was facing this incredibly difficult task. She hated being separated from her partner, and she looked forward to rejoining him before dawn.

Randee stealthily approached the door to the sheriff's office. She heard a voice which she recognized, and halted. Heavens, how she dreaded facing this man today, or any day! It wasn't conscience or morals that troubled her about seeing and fooling Brody, it was something else. *I don't want him touching me or wooing me or anythinging me!* It was strange, even dismaying, to comprehend and accept the fact that she actually did not like Sheriff Brody Wade, much as she had tried to do so and had convinced herself she did. She realized it was the Carson's and townsfolk's respect and affection that had influenced — no, misguided and controlled — her feelings, along with her distraught state. Now that she thought about it honestly, the rugged lawman made her wary! Maybe Brody was one of the things she had been trying to flee with this mission!

Randee peeked around the door jamb into the sheriff's office. She eyed Brody Wade's broad shoulders as he leaned against the cell, talking with a prisoner. She flattened her back against the outside wall and tried to steady her erratic respiration. She had fooled Brody once before; surely she could do so again.

Marsh Logan flooded her thoughts. Since he wasn't the Durango Kid, what little she had "known" about him wasn't true. Who was Marsh Logan, alias Storm Hayden? If each bit of information was measured by teaspoon, she wouldn't have enough to fill a coffee cup! He must have had plenty of experience and practice to become as skilled, as swift, as accurate, as deadly, as fearless as the real Durango Kid. Undeniably, Marsh Logan was better than most gunslingers. He did not hesitate about taking on one, three, five, or more opponents!

Just as she thought Marsh was opening up to her and she was learning more about him, he retreated or added more mystery, or destroyed her old thoughts and impressions. Yet, she loved him. Perhaps the strain on her nerves was caused by not having him close since their passionate Sunday together, and the discovery of his deceit. For now, she had to forget about her stormy love and concentrate on duping another man. Randee swallowed hard and composed herself before she stepped

348

into the jail and announced, "Brody, I'm back safely."

The brown-haired man whirled—dropping the cell keys—and stared at the nervous blonde in her dusty dress. Sheer astonishment filled his eyes and face. Then, a wide grin captured his mouth. "Dee!" he practically shouted in excitement. Forgetting about the man behind him, whom he had just released, he rushed forward and embraced her. "Heavens above, you had me scared stiff. I've been checking every day to see if the Army had rescued you. I've been crazy with fear and worry." Glancing past her and out the door, he noticed no military escort, and was puzzled. "Lord, woman, how did you get away from those savages?" As he spewed forth questions, his chocolate eyes were scrutinizing her for injuries and changes. "Tell me everything; don't leave out a single day or word," he persisted hastily.

As she witnessed his love and concern, Randee's courage and confidence threatened to vanish. Misgivings chewed on her, but she cast aside such disturbing and intrusive feelings. She mentally and emotionally committed herself to carrying out Marsh's plan. She captured his face between her hands and urged, "Relax, Brody, I'm fine now. Why don't you finish with your . . . charge and we can talk privately?" she wisely suggested, nodding toward the man who was awaiting his freedom, an action which would allow her time to get over this initial moment of difficulty.

Brody smiled cheerfully before turning to the pale man and saying sternly, "Get out of here, Buster, and don't let me hear of you causing trouble again. Next time, I won't be so lenient with you."

The freed man nodded sheepishly and hurried out the door, which Brody closed and locked behind him. The sheriff returned to Randee and pulled her into his arms. As he spread eager kisses over her face and hair, he murmured passionately, "Dee, Dee, you've come back like you promised. I knew you would." He leaned his head backward to look down into her lovely face as he inquired worriedly, "Where have you been? What happened to you out there?"

To avoid meeting his keen gaze as she deceived him, she rested her head against his hard chest and encircled his waist with her arms. She had no choice. "It's been a long and hard journey, Brody, but I have you to thank for my rescue, not the Army."

"What do you mean?" he asked confusedly, tightening his possessive embrace on her. His body trembled noticeably at her bold contact and amorous behavior. Fooled, he made no move to release her.

Randee felt her stimulating effect on him and she wanted to run from him and this distasteful chore. She couldn't; she mustn't. Careful not to mention any of Marsh's names, she declared, "You hired that gunman to come looking for me, even offered him your entire savings. That was a very kind and unselfish thing to do, Brody. I can't tell you what it means to me. The Indians who abducted me kept moving around a lot and concealing our trail, but they never harmed me. All I had to do was work for them — cooking and washing and such. That gunslinger you hired tracked me down and stole me from their camp one night. He demanded five thousand dollars to bring me home. He said that was how much it had cost him to come after me, rather than accepting a job for some rancher in southern Texas. Of course I agreed to reward him with some of the money I have in the bank from the Carsons."

Randee knew Brody was about to interrupt, but she rushed onward with her false tale, "He's to return Sunday for his payment, so I'll need to get to the bank to make a withdrawal before it closes today for the weekend. I'm so happy you hired him and he located me. At

350

first I was terrified with those Indians; but later, I realized they only wanted slaves, not whites to torture. I was biding my time until I could find a way to escape. Then, your fearless gunman showed up one night. He's a smart and daring man, Brody. He eluded those Indians as if it was the easiest thing to do in life."

Brody did jump in here. "I'm surprised he came after you, Dee. He refused my offer when he was in town, even though I begged and reasoned and bargained and threatened. I took the liberty of telling him you would sweeten my offer. I hope you don't mind."

"Certainly not," she responded softly, cuddling up to him as a distraction. "He said the search for me sounded more exciting and lucrative than his job offer in Austin, or some place down that way."

The lawman said hesitantly, "I hope you understand why I couldn't come searching for you. I don't have any authority in Indian Territory and I don't know my way around there. I could have made things worse for both of us. I figured the Army knew what was best and was trained to handle situations like that. I've missed you terribly."

Randee claimed boldly, "I'm glad you didn't rush off to save me. They would have killed you, Brody. White men they hate, but white women they tolerate. You did the right thing, and I'm glad he decided to accept your offer after leaving town. He can be a most unpredictable and exasperating man. And real bossy too. But I finally got used to him. Or rather, I learned how to get along with him."

As the sheriff leaned away to separate their bodies so he could kiss her, the silver necklace which Marsh had given her became tangled on one of his shirt buttons. As he freed it, he asked, "Where did you get this? It's new, isn't it?" Knowing Spanish, he mentally translated the message, and jealousy flooded him as he wondered if

Storm Hayden had given her the necklace.

To conceal her startled expression, Randee glanced down at the cherished item. Quickly coming up with what she considered a plausible story, she replied in a casual tone, "While we were in Fort Worth, a saloon girl named Flossie gave it to me. I slept in her room at Sloan's Pleasure Palace one night because the hotels were full. Flossie liked me because I helped her fend off a mean customer with flaming red hair, so she gave me this necklace. It says 'Friends Forever.' I think one of her many admirers probably gave it to her. She must not have liked him very much, or she wouldn't have parted with it." As she lightly fingered the silver circle before dropping it inside her denim dress, Randee added, "It's lovely and it seemed to mean a great deal to her for me to accept it, so I did." She felt Brody force himself to relax, and she tried to do the same.

Brody believed her because her voice and look were so convincing, so innocent, so radiant — or he read what he wanted to see. His lips covered hers and he was thrilled when she responded eagerly to his action. He kissed her hungrily as his hands roved her back and played in her silky hair, which was bound with the blue ribbon he had given to her on May eighteenth. His mouth nuzzled her neck and ear, and she laughed softly and nestled into his arms.

"I love you, Dee. Will you become my wife now?" he asked.

Randee met his gaze, and prayed hers didn't reveal her trickery. She didn't know how she had endured his touch, but she had. It was time to enlighten Brody about her future plans, and persuade him to accept them. "I can't just yet, Brody. I've agreed to partner up with that gunslinger to help hunt down clues on the Epson Gang. We — "

Brody was stunned. He interrupted angrily. "You

can't leave with him! He's only after you and your money! It's too dangerous!"

Randee smiled and teased, "Don't be jealous of a man like that, Brody, and don't be so angry and harsh with me. He isn't the kind of man I could love or marry; you are. Don't you understand? I can't remain here endangering you and this town. Until that gang's locked up or slain, none of us are safe. I have to do this for all of us, especially for you and me. I was captured because of that gang, because I was cowardly running away from them. And because of them, I can't come home or marry you. They're controlling and ruining my life, Brody. I have to help thwart them so I can settle down with you."

Brody hoped he was hearing and understanding her correctly; yet, he was concerned over her imminent intentions. "What are you saying?" he questioned anxiously. He eyed her closely, intently.

She laughingly responded, "I'm saying I'll marry you just as soon as it's safe to do so. That's why I came back to visit rather than sending you a letter or a telegram. I wanted you to hear this answer from my own lips: I accept your proposal, but our wedding has to wait a while longer." She saw his smile fade gradually and knew she had to do some fast and clever talking. "After what I've been through recently, I'm not afraid of them. Besides, according to rumors and newspaper stories, lots of them have been killed in the last few weeks. They're getting careless and weaker, and leaving clues behind. Once those clues are collected and passed along to the law, they can be halted. Then, we'll be safe and we can marry and settle down here."

"What kind of clues have you discovered?" he asked eagerly. "I'll help you track them down so we can finish this matter quickly."

Randee shook her blond head and told him, "You

353

can't go along, Brody; they might recognize you as a lawman. That would put us all in peril. We have to be very cautious and sneaky. Don't worry about me," she coaxed as she teased her fingertips over his cheek. "I'm a good shot and a skilled rider, and so is my partner. As for those clues, I promised I wouldn't reveal them to anyone except the State Police in Austin. That's where we're heading when he comes after me Sunday. Hopefully before this month's out, we'll have that gang leader and his bunch behind bars or buried so they can't harm anyone else. All I can say is that some people have seen him and a few of his men, and given us descriptions. With what she told me, the State Police will be able to make up some posters real soon and circulate them."

Brody trailed his fingers over her shapely lips and smiled. "Posters should help all lawmen lend a hand with their captures. I'll make sure the State Police send me plenty of them to post around here. But why do you have to tag along with this notorious gunman? He can't be trusted, Dee. And this isn't a job for a woman."

Randee clicked her tongue disapprovingly. "Now, Brody, don't go telling me that men are better at riding, shooting, and tracking than women are. My father taught me how to do all of those things and do them better than most men, and that isn't idle boasting. I promise I won't take any unnecessary risks, but I have to do this. Don't you realize how involved I am by surviving one of their raids? I won't be safe until they're defeated. And until I'm safe, we can't begin our life together," she disclosed cleverly. "I'm tired of running and hiding from danger. I was right in the beginning with my plan, but I let you and that gunman dissuade me from trying it. Now that he's seen I can take care of myself on the trail and he's willing to let me hire him, I have to proceed with my original idea. I honestly think they're up to something clever like a land grab. If we can prove it, their real leader and motive will be exposed. That lame boss isn't the gang's leader. Someone very cunning and powerful and wealthy is."

"Where did you come up with such ideas?" he inquired curiously.

Attempting to prove how smart and brave she was so he would back off, she revealed, "It's obvious to me because they only raid in a certain area. I don't see why the law hasn't grasped that reality and investigated it. I suppose you heard about those careless raiders who were gunned down by soldiers from Fort Richardson. It seems those beasts and their leader like to visit saloons when they're not ravishing innocent women during raids. She'll be the death of him," she asserted coldly, unaware of the revealing slips in her own words. . . .

"I still don't want you chasing after that gang. What happens if you do locate them? You couldn't kill anybody. Turn your evidence over to the authorities and let them handle it from here on. That bunch isn't stupid, Dee. They've been raiding for over a year and haven't been caught. What makes you think you two can defeat them?"

"They're not stupid, Brody, but they aren't smart either. Whoever their real leader is, he's the one making the plans and giving the orders. Once he's unmasked, those raiders will get out of Texas as fast as their horses will carry them. Men like those are cowards inside. Another thing, with small groups of them being ambushed here and there, if we're lucky, they'll believe their boss is finished with them and is having them wiped out a few at a time. Just think of the damage to that gang if they start distrusting their real boss."

"But how can you tell who's involved? What if you two slay innocent drifters or do something illegal?" Brody reasoned desperately.

"That's where instincts come in, Brody. Criminals are

given away by their behavior. We simply watch for strangers in town."

Brody shook his head and refuted, "Nothing's that simple, Dee."

She gazed into Brody's worried expression and asked, "Have I gotten any mail or visitors while I've been away?"

"Yes, but we aren't through discussing this matter."

"Mail or visitors?" she asked, ignoring his last words.

"Mail, two letters. Hear me out, Dee, about—"

"Where are they?" she pressed, cutting him off sweetly.

Brody frowned at her persistence. "A letter came from Kansas for the Carsons, so I guess it's yours now. The other letter is from a land company in Fort Worth. I guess it's about you selling the ranch. I put out the word you were seeking a buyer. I'll get them."

Brody reluctantly released her to locate the letters in his desk. He handed them to her and said, "You can read them later. Right now—"

"Brody Wade, you're impossible," she softly scolded, then kissed his mouth lightly and tantalizingly. "These could be important. Let me go over them quickly. I promise you can say anything and everything you want, but I'm not changing my mind. You're wasting your breath and our short time together by arguing with me. If you love me and want me back swiftly, you'll cooperate with me."

"Cooperate!" he scoffed. "Cooperate by letting you take off on a reckless scheme with a black-hearted rogue like that!"

She corrected, "He isn't so bad. He's good with a gun and he isn't scared of anything. Don't you see, he keeps me from getting into trouble out there? I can assure you that all he wants from me is money. If that weren't true, he would have tried something with me by now. I'm only using him to get my life back to normal so we can marry. Is that so terrible? What can I say to convince you he can't come between us while we're working together?"

"I love you, Dee, and I can't bear the thought of losing you again. Stay here and forget this nonsense. Or let me go along and help."

Randee shook her tawny head and narrowed her green eyes to appear serious and steadfast. "I can't do either one, Brody. I have a deal with him, and I gave my word. I have responsibilities to myself, to you, to this town, to my murdered kin. Haven't you heard a word I've said? I love you and I'll be back to marry you soon, but only when it's safe and justice has been done. Isn't that enough for you? If it's not, then I'm sorry, because I'm going to do what I have to do. You can't stop me or interfere, or I'll leave and never come back."

Brody exhaled loudly and scowled. "You beautiful vixen, you'll be the death of me with your courage and stubbornness. I can see it's useless to quarrel, but I'm not through reasoning with you. Read your letters while I fetch us some coffee. I need to settle down and gather my wits."

Randee ripped open both envelopes and read the letters, slowly and carefully. She stuffed the one from her mother to the Carsons into her pocket, but she pensively tapped the one from the Mid-Texas Land Company against her lips.

Brody handed her a cup of steaming coffee and asked, "Well?"

Randee fused her gaze to his and questioned, "Have you ever heard of this company before? Mid-Texas Land Company of Fort Worth," she supplied when he looked puzzled.

"I don't think so," Brody told her, then sipped his coffee. "Why?"

"On our way back here, we made several stops along the trail at old raid sites. Lots of them had been purchased by this same company. Don't you think that's odd? Perhaps suspicious?" she hinted.

Brody's dark brow lifted and he thought a minute before shrugging. "Odd for a land company to buy land? I don't see your point."

Randee slapped the letter against her palm several times as she informed him, "If there's a sinister motive behind these raids, what if this company's involved? It's happened before, lots of places. Why would this area be so valuable to someone?" she asked, walking to a map on his wall and circling the target area with her fingertip. "Why would a company want this territory so badly? What's there to crave?"

The sheriff's brown eyes studied the area before he speculated aloud, "Nothing unusual or exceptionally valuable. Several huge cattle drives pass through this area on their way to market. You also have stage routes and freight lines taking these roads. Someone could fence off the land routes and charge a toll to cross them, but that's a little far-fetched. Even purchasing the land cheaply to be sold later for a hefty profit is improbable. I don't deny it's superior graze land, but to go to such bloody and risky lengths to obtain it . . . No, Dee, I doubt there's a sinister scheme involved. Just mean, greedy, lazy villains who want what others have. Who owns the company?"

"We don't know. Its lawyer won't say. Have you heard of George Light?" she inquired, her tone and gaze skeptical of the man.

Brody chuckled. "Of course, I have. Few people haven't. He's widely known and highly respected in Texas and the South. He's handled lots of business for the governor and other important men. I got to meet him once when I was in Fort Worth delivering a prisoner to the jail there. Seemed very nice and pleasant, very powerful. From what I've heard, when he used to be a trial lawyer, he never lost a case."

Randee scoffed, "Such an upstanding citizen. I wonder why he's connected to this land company. If I sold them my ranch, the owner would have to sign the sale papers. Perhaps his name would give us a clue. I'll write to Mr. Light and say I'm accepting the company's generous offer."

"Generous?" Brody echoed, baffled by her tone and expression.

"Most of the offers have been small, practically steals. This one is more than fair. Another odd thing, Brody, the Carson ranch house is the only home that's been spared by those bastards. I wonder why . . . . Do you think this boss wants the house for some reason?"

"It is beautiful, but so were lots of those that were destroyed. Maybe they were in a hurry that day, or one of them didn't carry out his duty. I wouldn't want to live there, not where people, especially family, were brutally murdered. I think you're wise to sell it. But I think your imagination is playing games with you about this land grab plot. Who could have enough power, wealth, and men to carry out such an enormous scheme? Or be that cold-blooded?"

She looked him in the eye and vowed, "I don't know, but I aim to find out before this task is done."

"I can't let you go, Dee. I can't let you get yourself killed. Don't you understand what kind of men you're dealing with? War made a lot of them this way."

"The war's been over for six years, Brody."

"Plenty of men haven't gotten over it and some never will. Many lost everything they had and they haven't been able to start fresh. During the war, men did and saw horrible things. I've seen men have gut-ripping nightmares about what happened to them and others, about things they were forced to do to survive. Once you've killed, it gets easier every time you do it again. War makes men hard and bitter. Losses make them greedy and death doesn't affect them anymore. The gang you're after is like that: cold, cruel, and heartless. I can't even think about what they could do to you. I love you, Dee. Stay here and forget this nonsense."

Randee eased her arms up his chest and laced her fingers behind his neck. Pressing her sensuous body close to him and using her most seductive look, she murmured, "If you want me, Brody, you have to let me do this. Please don't try to stop me or interfere. When this is settled, I'll come home and marry you."

"You're right, I'm wasting my breath and time trying to change your mind. If that gunslinger gets you . . ." He halted and his eyes brightened. "There's something I have to tell you about him, Dee. He isn't who you think he is."

To thwart his impending argument, she disclosed, "I know he isn't the Durango Kid. His name is Storm Hayden. I don't care who he is, because he's as good as the Kid, and better than most gunmen. If you're worried because of those reward posters that claim he's an outlaw, a murderer and a thief, there's no need to fret. Those charges have been dropped in Nebraska. He wasn't guilty. As soon as all of those posters are out of circulation and the real killer's apprehended, no one will be chasing him. And he won't have to use the Kid's identity to prevent trouble. That's why he tricked us when he came to town."

Brody looked surprised, and disappointed. "He told you about that trouble he had in Nebraska? And you believed him?"

"You must have too, or you wouldn't have hired him to come after me," she teased, making a clever point which he couldn't argue.

He stated gruffly, "I had no choice. I was desperate to save you. Still, I don't trust him and I don't like you traveling with him."

"Calm down, Brody. He's been a perfect gentleman. We have a deal which he doesn't want to damage, so he'll be careful. I can assure you, I'm safer with Storm than I would be staying here."

"Where is Storm Hayden now?" Brody inquired.

She answered casually, "Visiting a friend south of here. He's to return Sunday for his money and his partner. You can talk to him and see for yourself that I'll be just fine."

"I'll do just that, even if it annoys both of you. Will you tell him we're in love and planning to marry, so he won't go after you?"

"He's already guessed our feelings and plans. That is why you sent him after me and it is why I'm here now. He understands."

"If I swear I won't tell a soul about what you're doing, will you promise to visit me and write me as often as you can? Please don't make me worry about your survival."

"I'll contact you whenever possible, but don't get nervous and come after me. You could endanger all of us. I'll answer these letters tomorrow, and you can mail them for me on the Tuesday stage."

Brody started to tell her that a new mail route had been established since her departure — with a pickup in the morning — but he didn't. His mind was on a crucial task to be handled that afternoon.

"Tell me about the raid yesterday morning," she coaxed.

Brody reluctantly complied, then said, "Those aren't the words which should be filling these lovely ears. Wedding vows are."

"Did that Marshal Foley Timms visit here before or

after the raid?" she questioned, ignoring his last statement.

"Marshal Timms?" he echoed, looking baffled. "Why?"

"I was just wondering. It seems he's usually around at such times. I'm trying to decide if that's odd."

"You mean 'odd' as in suspicious?" he queried.

"Yes. Was he around either time?" she pressed.

"Not that I know about," Brody responded.

"If he does show up today or anytime soon, let me know."

"You're getting yourself in deeper and deeper with these crazy suspicions. Foley Timms isn't a man to cross. He used to be a Texas Ranger, and they can be tough and mean when need be. If you're asking questions or making insinuations about him, I'd be careful. He was hired by the governor himself. He has quite a large reputation for bringing in the worst vermin alive. It's my guess he's after that gang too. Surely you've heard that Rangers fear no man or mob. You met him before you left town. Did he seem like a villain that night?"

She jested merrily, "If you'll recall, my mind was elsewhere, so I didn't notice much about him. If he's so famous, why haven't more people heard about him and his daring exploits?"

"I thought everyone knew his legend. You sure they don't?"

Randee shrugged. "They didn't seem to when questioned. At least I know he's a real lawman now, so I can strike him off my list of suspects. He just seemed like the perfect scout for that gang."

Brody laughed aloud. "Ex-Texas Ranger and U.S. Marshal Foley Timms, a gang member?" he jested, then chuckled again.

"It does sound impossible, doesn't it?" She pretended to concur. "It's getting late. Right now, I need to get to the bank before it closes. Storm will be angry if I don't have his money. You want to walk me over and guard me?" she invited cheerfully.

"I'll take the time, but we'll have to hurry. I was about to leave on duty when you arrived. I'm to pick up a rustler at the Klemens place. I should be back by dawn. How about you come with me? We can talk and have more time together," he coaxed.

"I'm too tired, Brody, but I'll spend all day with you tomorrow. Before dusk, I need to get some clothes and a hotel room. I'll write those letters and rest while you're away. You understand, don't you?"

"I'm sure you're exhausted, Dee. You rest and get your chores done while I'm gone. Tomorrow I plan to convince you to remain here and marry me," he warned with a playful smile.

"I'm certain you'll try," she laughingly retorted.

At seven o'clock, Randee was sitting in her hotel room, relieved by Brody's absence. She had purchased some jeans, shirts, and vests at the mercantile store. She had the five thousand dollars packed in the canvas bag she had bought, which also contained her new trail garments. Her purchases and bank withdrawal had been actions to throw Brody off guard. She had eaten a tasty meal downstairs, then retired to her room to write her letters and to wait for Marsh's return late that night.

Randee knew that she and Marsh would be heading back to Fort Worth during the night to visit the land company, but she couldn't tell Brody and she knew her letter to them would mislead him. She had sworn him to secrecy about her actions and questions, and believed her deluded fiancé would honor his word to avoid losing her. One thing she was positive about, Brody Wade wanted her fiercely.

In her Mid-Texas Land Company letter, she asked, "What are your plans for my ranch if I agree to sell it? Since it is my home and I will be living in Wadesville as the wife of Sheriff Brody Wade, I could not bear to see it ruined . . . . I must ask you to increase your offer because the house is still intact. My ranch is valuable and beautiful and I hate to part with it. I will do so only because of the grief and tragedy which I endured there. I want to sell as quickly as possible, but I will not give the place away . . . . Unless this date is unacceptable, I will be in Fort Worth on June thirtieth to discuss the matter with you . . . . I am interested in purchasing a smaller ranch near Wadesville if you have one available, perhaps partly in exchange for the Carson place. Please hold this news in strictest confidence as it is to be a surprise wedding gift for my husband-to-be, Sheriff Wade." Randee sealed the letter. If anyone read it, it should be cleverly misleading.

To her mother, she wrote a letter from "Sarah Elizabeth Carson." She didn't want her mother to continue to worry about her, and this was the only way she could get word to Dee Slade without alerting Payton to her whereabouts. "Everything is fine here and everyone is busy with the cattle and crops . . . . I do hope and pray your health is fine. Please send word about the baby's birth and how you're both doing . . . . I received a letter from Randee last week from New York." She created a lovely and colorful story to fool Payton and to lessen Dee's worries. She wrote that "Randee has a job at a publishing company. Isn't that fun and exciting? She's being courted by a lawyer and sounds very happy. Don't worry about her, Dee, because Randee is mature and brave and she's safe . . . . Randee hinted that she might be coming home for Christmas, probably with her new husband . . . . Randee told me about running away, but children are like that sometimes. Ranching isn't much of a life for a single girl of nineteen who loves adventure . . . . She wanted to give you two lovers more privacy. I'll let you know if I hear from her again. She didn't include an address, so I don't know where to contact her . . . . "

Randee sealed the second letter and laid it atop the first one. She wrote Brody a note, telling him Storm Hayden had returned early and wanted to leave immediately for Austin. She apologized for departing before his return, but it was necessary. She claimed she loved him and would contact him soon. She ended the note with "Maybe it's best this way, Brody. I can't let you stop me. Please understand and be patient. I'll return soon and marry you. Remember your promises not to follow me and to keep my confidence. I love you, Randee."

When she had purchased the writing paper earlier, the clerk had told her about the new mail route and schedule. She went downstairs and handed the three envelopes to him. She paid him to mail the two letters the next day, and to give the sealed note to Sheriff Wade upon his return to town in the morning.

In her room again, she gathered her belongings and went to the water closet down the hall to bathe.

Hours away, Brody Wade was meeting with several of his men. If he wanted his dream to come true, he had to stop Storm Hayden's intrusion. Soon, he would be rich and powerful beyond belief. Once his primary goal was attained, he would sell off the excess land.

He had ordered the Carson home spared because he knew Randee would be hiding somewhere inside. Even if she had been sighted, none of his gang would have harmed the woman he loved, loved as much as his dream. He knew Randee wouldn't be suspicious of his departure today, because he had invited her along, knowing she would not accept. He had gathered numerous clues, disturbing clues, from Randee's words, words which had told him where his problem areas were located, words which had revealed just how smart his beloved vixen was. He had to correct his errors and oversights immediately. He had to order that big-mouthed prostitute slain. He needed to warn Carl Bush and Foley Timms to be more careful.

Now that he had a poster on Storm Hayden, he could hire a bounty hunter to hunt down that notorious outlaw without suspicion falling on his head. He would tell his gang to be on the lookout for Randee and the galling gunman, with orders to slay Storm and orders to keep Randee safe from all harm. After which, he would find a way to "rescue" her and entrap her. He wanted no more clues, mistakes, or tracks left behind. To cover himself, he needed to order raids in other areas to throw Hayden and his love off the right trail, as well as any other foolhardy champions of justice like them. Now that he had Randee under his spell and would soon have his ultimate victory, he had nothing to worry about, nothing except staying on schedule. More time, that was what he needed, just a little more time and Randee Hollis beneath him on a marital bed.

Brody smiled wickedly as he realized he had nothing to fear. No one would ever guess that a small-town sheriff had enough wealth, power, cunning, and intelligence to pull off such a daring scheme.

He nodded to the men who approached the campfire. "Good to see you, Carl. Foley," he acknowledged and smiled. "Jack, I have a new job for you," he told the steely hearted bounty hunter.

Jackson Fuller grinned, but his eyes remained cold and clear. As his fingertips lovingly grazed his gun butts, he said, "About time, boss. My fingers are itching for action. What you got for me?"

"I need you to kill a man named Storm Hayden. As for you, Carl, you need to visit Pete's place in Fort Worth and neatly slice a pretty whore's throat. Let's have a drink and get our business done. I have a woman waiting in Wadesville to become my wife."

Hours passed as Randee dozed and waited. She was packed and dressed, ready to leave the moment Marsh arrived. When he did, he shook her lightly and aroused her.

"How did it go?" he asked as she stretched and yawned.

"Like we expected, he fell right into your clever trap." She told him about the two letters and her answers, and he smiled approval. However, she didn't tell him about her questions and revelations because, after mentally reviewing her visit with Brody, she knew he would be angry. Since he had plenty of secrets from her, there was nothing wrong with her having a few from him! Brody wanted her badly, so he would keep his mouth shut. How else could she get answers if she didn't poke around? Besides, she was a little puzzled and annoyed about Marsh's continual dishonesty: He had claimed Foley Timms probably wasn't a real lawman, when the man was a legend in Texas! If he would delude her on one point, perhaps he had done so with others. Why, she didn't know. Marsh did seem genuinely amused by Brody's reaction to her claims about Storm Hayden. Yet, he didn't ask about what happened between them personally, and she wondered why.

"What did you learn today?" she asked.

"Nothing new. I searched the Carson Ranch, but it eludes me why they spared it. I also checked out that other raid site. No clues there either. As we agreed, I didn't ask any suspicious questions. 'Course that was easy, because I didn't see anyone at either place."

"At least we have one victory; the land company did contact me about selling out. That gives us the perfect excuse to visit them and do some snooping. And, I did learn that my mother is doing fine and Payton isn't out searching for me."

"We have another victory, woman: If Brody hears about our travels, he won't get suspicious and come running after you. You did convince him of your undying love, didn't you?"

"That was my order, boss man, and I carried it out successfully."

"I know it must have been difficult, Randee, and I'm grateful."

She looked at him oddly. He appeared totally serious. "Actually, it wasn't as hard as I imagined it would be, nor the first time I'd duped him on your request. Under the right circumstances, a person can be quite an efficient liar. You'd better watch out, Logan, or I might get too good at this acting and fool you one day."

He caressed her cheek as he asked roguishly, "Why would you ever want to do that?"

"For the life of me, Durango—I mean, Storm—I mean, Marsh—I can't figure out why I shouldn't be totally honest with a man like you who never keeps secrets from his trustworthy partner."

"Why don't you forget I'm anyone except Marsh Logan?" he suggested, pulling her into his arms and kissing her.

When their lips parted, she replied, "That would be easy if I knew the real Marsh Logan. Frankly, I'm not sure he exists anymore. You're a lot of different men rolled into one body, and I doubt Marsh can ever be totally and successfully removed from the others."

Marsh fell back wearily on the bed. "I guess you're right."

Randee watched him for a moment, then laughed softly. "I wasn't insulting you or scolding you, Logan. There's nothing wrong with being a complex male, nor with being a private person. I was only saying I don't know much about you. Nothing about Durango is true about you, and I know little about Storm Hayden, even less about Marsh Logan. I suppose it makes me a little nervous to be so deeply involved with a stranger, even if he is a handsome and irresistible rogue. Perhaps you'll enlighten me after this mission is over."

Marsh sat up and yanked her against his hard chest. "I'll make you a promise, woman: When this task is over, I'll tell you everything and anything you want to know about me. Just trust me and be patient."

She laughed against his lips as she murmured, "Both will be difficult, partner, but I wouldn't refuse a promise like that one."

Marsh stood, and pulled Randee to her feet. He cuddled her in his arms and revealed huskily, "Let me get you out of here before the sun rises and Brody comes a callin' again. If Brody looked me in the eye, I doubt I could fool him about having no special feelings for you."

"I doubt that, partner, because Brody sees what he wants to see. If not, he wouldn't have fallen for my terrible ruse today. I cringed every time he touched me. So far, this has been the hardest part of our job," she confessed, snuggling closer to his entreating body.

"Does that mean he's lost his hold over you?" he asked hoarsely.

"Brody Wade means nothing special to me, Marsh. I thought you knew that by now. As you said once before, I only have enough time and energy for one lover, and I'm pleased with the one I have."

"Good, 'cause I'm more than pleased with the one I

have."

He lifted her chin and fused their lips, his tongue skillfully darting into her mouth and intoxicating her with his flavor. As his mouth roved her face and his hands stroked her back, he murmured, "We'd better get out of here before we start something we don't have time to finish. Brody has his watchdog sleeping downstairs to guard you."

Randee revealed in an emotion-filled voice, "Brody's out of town, Marsh. He left this afternoon after our talk. He had to pick up a prisoner and he won't be back until morning."

Marsh glanced toward the window and assessed the time. He muttered, "I don't like hurrying when I'm in bed with you, woman. We should have been on the trail an hour ago."

She traced his strong jawline and caressed his cheek. "I suppose you're right. It's just been so long since Sunday night."

His loins burned and ached. He chuckled and teased, "It was early Monday, but that's still too long to go without having you."

Marsh undressed them and placed her on the bed. As his mouth and hands sought her lips and body, he murmured, "Yep, much too long."

Their bodies flamed with desire, and passions raced wildly and freely as the bed squeaked sensuously beneath them . . . .

Brody stood and stretched his fatigued body. Everything was set. It was time to get back into town. He was anxious to see Randee in a few hours, and to try once more to persuade her to give up her foolish scheme, which he doubted he could do. Fortunately for him, it wouldn't last much longer, not after Jackson Fuller killed Storm Hayden and allowed himself to be talked into bringing Randee back to Wadesville "to prove she wasn't that outlaw's partner." Without Hayden to help her, Randee would relent and marry him.

Come Sunday morning, Jackson would be ready to trail them and get rid of his nuisance. Then, to throw off the law, raids would take place east of Fort Worth, outside of that "target" area which Randee had revealed. Frankly, he was amazed, even pleased, with his love's intelligence and courage. Randee Hollis definitely was the right woman for him. Soon, he would own enough land in vital areas to carry out his dream. Afterwards, as for what his clever wife might think or suspect, he would deal with that later . . . .

Chapter Seventeen

At three in the morning, a temporarily sated Randee and Marsh dressed and straightened the telltale bed. They sneaked from the hotel and left town without being sighted by Deputy Matthew Johnson or anyone else. Along the trail, they halted briefly to retrieve Randee's hidden possessions and to bury most of the five thousand dollars.

He cautioned, "Remember this spot, Randee, in case something happens to me. I don't ever want you being vulnerable to anyone again. If we don't succeed, I want you to get out of this area pronto. Go where you'll be safe from this gang and your stepfather. Promise?"

The moon was heading for its full stage in a few days, so she could see Marsh's face clear enough to read the concern and affection displayed there. Recalling his promise to expose all there was to know about him when this task ended, she smiled and hugged him. "I promise," she vowed before kissing him feverishly.

Marsh chuckled as they parted, and he warned. "Don't heat me up again, woman. We have to get our tails moving fast."

"Don't blame me," she playfully scolded. "I can't help

it if you affect me this way. You shouldn't be so over-powering." Her voice and gaze waxed serious as she added, "I really like you and enjoy you, partner, and I almost hate for this task to end."

"We still have that nasty job ahead in Kansas, re-member?"

"Afterwards, maybe I can persuade you to take me on another adventure. This kind of life gets in your blood, doesn't it?"

"I'm glad to see you're getting to understand me better," he responded. "Now you know why I love this existence so much. The freedom, the excitement, the challenges, the fun, even the danger . . ."

Randee sighed dramatically and admitted, "I'm afraid I do, my handsome drifter. When our jobs are done and I have to settle down somewhere, I'm going to miss you and such stimulating times."

He reminded unexpectedly, boldly, meaningfully, "Don't forget you offered to tag along on occasion. I've gotten used to having you around, and I find it most pleasurable and helpful."

"You flatter me, partner, but I love it."

As Marsh remounted, he retorted, "That wasn't flat-tery, my impulsive vixen; that was the truth. Fact is, I've been trying my darncdcst to keep you from getting under my tough hide, but you surely do make it diffi-cult, and people don't have much use for a soft-hearted gunslinger. Rumor claims they get themselves killed too easily because they're distracted. So if you want me to stay alive, stop tempting me."

"Why, Marsh Logan, how could you possibly accuse me of doing such a wicked and selfish thing?" she teased.

He jested in return, "Because I know it's true. You've been working on my defeat ever since we met. I wouldn't be at all surprised to learn you intentionally bumped into me that first day. You're a naughty girl, Randee Hollis, and a dangerous one."

Randee laughed and confessed humorously, "I surely hope so."

"Move it out, woman, before we get caught by your sweetheart."

When Sheriff Brody Wade reached the hotel shortly after seven thirty, he was more than angered to find Randee gone without a trace. He read her note to him, and couldn't help but smile triumphantly. He took possession of the two letters, telling the clerk he would mail them for his fiancée. He hurried to his office, unlocked the door, and went inside. Taking a seat at his desk and lighting a lantern, he brazenly opened the letters and read both.

The letter to the land company sent his heart to racing madly and joyfully. If she would put such revealing words into a letter, then they had to be true. Any doubts he had had about her feelings toward him vanished. Even his stony heart warmed at reading she wanted to use the money to buy a ranch for them. Since it was supposed to be a surprise, he would have to remember not to mention it to her.

It was the other letter which astonished him. Bewildered, the insidious lawman read it a second time, slowly and thoroughly. Why did Randee want this Dee Hollis Slade to think everything was fine here in Texas, and that she was living and working in New York? Why did she write the letter as Lee Carson's wife, and why hadn't she revealed their deaths? The letter indicated that Dee Hollis Slade was Randee's *mother*. Randee had never mentioned trouble at home or running away from Kansas! If the Carsons had known the truth, why had they concealed Randee's presence? It was clear that

Randee didn't want someone back there to know where to locate her. The question was, why?

A letter full of lies and deceptions . . . How strange and distressing. If there was trouble back in Kansas, why hadn't she confided in him? This mystery had to be solved, and solved quickly!

Brody pulled out a desk drawer and withdrew a copy of the advertisement which Randee had placed in several newspapers to lure a partner here. He put it into a large envelope along with a clipping of the local news story about the raid, revealing the deaths of Lee and Sarah Elizabeth Carson. He included a note about Randee's current and dangerous preoccupation with capturing the Epson Gang, aided by a notorious outlaw named Storm Hayden who was still wanted in Nebraska. He added that the Mid-Texas Land Company was eager to buy the ranch for a very large sum.

He looked over his packet and grinned. That should lure somebody down here to explain matters to him! If, after Storm Hayden's death, Randee attempted to hire another partner, perhaps fear of something in Kansas would compel her into his protective arms! There was also the matter of the Carson Ranch. If Randee wasn't the Carsons' heir, he needed the real owner to appear soon and sell it to his company. If trouble found its way here and threatened Randee, perhaps he could impress and ensnare her by getting rid of the problem for her . . . .

Brody sealed the expanded envelope and addressed it to Dee Hollis Slade in Kansas. By sending it out with the mail runner today, it should reach the Wichita train by Wednesday, then the woman to whom it was addressed by Thursday or Friday. Within another week, somebody should arrive to clear up this mystery. Soon, he wanted Randee in his clutches and in his bed.

He wrote another letter to a friend in Nebraska,

asking him to check out the Storm Hayden puzzle, and telling him where the alleged outlaw could be located. If by some miracle Storm eluded Jackson Fuller, the Nebraska authorities might be interested in him!

Lastly, he sent a letter to San Antonio to the real Durango Kid, informing the famed gunslinger of an imposter who was soiling his reputation and using it to his advantage. That should infuriate the Kid and put him hot on Hayden's trail.

Between all those threats, Hayden, you don't stand a chance of living past this month. I warned you not to cross barrels with me.

Brody took Randee's letter to his land company in Fort Worth and resealed it with melted wax. Randee's false letter to her mother had been enclosed in the packet, which would expose her cunning lies. He smiled wickedly. "Sorry, my love, but it has to be my way."

Wanting and needing to put as much distance as possible between them and Wadesville, Randee and Marsh rode all day, with only a few short rest stops. They camped late, placing them two-thirds of the way back to Fort Worth.

They ate quickly, then cuddled on overlapping bedrolls. They were too tired to talk and it was too perilous to make love, so they only kissed and embraced for a short while. Soon, they were asleep.

Randee could not believe what Pete was telling them: Flossie was dead, perhaps murdered in her sleep. She had been found that morning, sprawled on her mussed bed, not breathing. There was no sign of a struggle and no indications of physical injury. The stunned blonde listened as Marsh questioned Pete about a lame man with red hair, but Pete claimed she hadn't see anyone

376

like that and had no reason to lie.

Worried about Randee's safety in the saloon, Marsh took her to the hotel and registered her there. He told her to get some rest while he did some checking around, to which she protested.

She paced the floor with a tormented look on her lovely face. "I knew Flossie was terrified and in danger. It's partly my fault she's dead, Marsh. I knew how dangerous that beast was, and I shouldn't have left her at his mercy, or total lack of it."

Marsh captured her in his arms and held her tightly. "You aren't responsible for her death, even if it was murder, and even if Carl Bush did it," he refuted firmly. "She lived a hazardous life. She knew it."

Randee argued sadly, "She begged me for help and I promised it to her. Maybe she got scared and told him she had made that slip to me. Maybe he knows all about us."

"She wasn't too bright, Randee, but she wasn't that dumb. Let me do some nosing around. Then we can decide how to handle this. I have to meet with Willard, but I don't want anyone seeing you visit him. Don't forget, you have a meeting tomorrow with George Light. It wouldn't do for him or one of his hirelings to get suspicious of you."

"You're right, I can't endanger us by tagging along today. I'll stay put and rest, not that I need it," she jested to calm her tension.

"Keep this door bolted and don't let anyone inside," he warned.

"When will I see you again?" she inquired nervously.

"You've had little rest or sleep in two days, so get plenty of both. I'll see you early in the morning, about seven thirty. We'll go over my talk with Willard before you see that lawyer."

"Marsh, you will be extra careful today, won't you?"

Marsh drew her against his hard body and embraced her. Then, he lifted her chin and fused their mouths in a heady kiss. His mouth drifted down the silky column of her throat and his hands wandered through her tawny hair. A hungry groan escaped his throat and his mouth fused greedily with hers again. Suddenly he drew away and said in a hoarse voice, "I'd better get out of here just in case we're being watched. Someone might wonder what I'm doing in here so long."

"Why don't you come back later tonight?" she asked shamelessly.

"The way these rooms are located, there's no way to sneak in. I can't risk being seen at your door during such odd hours."

"I don't care what anyone thinks about me," she asserted.

As he caressed her flushed cheek, he corrected, "Yes, you do, Miss Hollis, and so do I. Besides, aren't you forgetting you're Sheriff Brody Wade's fiancée?" he teased, cuffing her chin.

Randee knew she couldn't say, *I only belong to Marsh Logan and I don't care who knows it.* "Suffer in silence, suffer alone . . ." she said aloud.

"At least you have the pleasure of knowing I'll be doing the same."

Randee frowned at his jest. "Some comfort, Logan."

Marsh chuckled. "Yep, I certainly do enjoy having you as my partner, you witty and greedy vixen. I'll see you in the morning."

Placing her arm across her forehead, she sighed deeply before murmuring, "Alas, if I don't expire from hunger first."

Marsh's hands and lips roved her sensitive flesh as he countered huskily, "If you do, my love, I'll revive you with a tasty feast."

She warned seductively, "Get out of here, Logan,

before I act like a wanton tart and ravish you."

"Yes, ma'am," he responded, grinning broadly at her.

Randee bolted the door after his departure. She was hot, tired, restless, and hungry. She needed a good meal, a cool bath, fresh clothes, and lots of slumber. Instantly she dismissed Marsh's precautionary orders and went about taking care of each need in order.

Later, curled in her bed in a clean nightgown, Randee boldly sipped the sherry she had purchased downstairs. Gradually her body and mind relaxed and she entered dreamland.

Marsh sat on Randee's bed going over what he had learned from Willard Mason the night before. The newspaperman had explained his futile search for the Mid-Texas Land Company's owner or owners. Willard had explained how he had gone from town to town to trace an intricate trail of companies—one company owned by another company owned by another company and so forth, each with a different name on record, leading nowhere of interest or value.

"So even if we both signed over our deeds, we wouldn't have the real boss's name on our records. Damn!" she declared in vexation. "Is that legal, Marsh, to use fictitious names as owners?"

"As long as the real leader can prove he owns all or part of those companies, he's in the clear, and we can't unmask him."

"Damn, damn, damn," she swore angrily. "What now?"

"We did get one break, Randee. Carl Bush is reputed to be one of Quantrill's ex-raiders, so we can bet some of those other bastards are too. There's still a reward poster out on him. If we can capture him, he's dead. So you see, you did move us forward with that sneaky piece of information."

"One step forward and six backward, some accomplishment."

"Don't get discouraged, woman. I need those keen wits working at their best. Another thing, Foley Timms is an ex-Ranger and currently a U.S. Marshal. That surprised me, because I'd never heard of him or run across him during my travels. Seems he's one of the governor's best secret agents, a tough and determined lawman."

"You mean . . . Timms is for real?" she asked, astonished, disappointed, confused. That explained why Brody Wade had found her accusation amusing and why Brody had known the suspicious man. She was beginning to think that Brody . . .

Marsh cut off the remainder of her budding doubt with his reply, "All we have to do is discover if Timms has become a gang member, or if he's pretending to be one to defeat them, or only coincidentally being in the right place at the right time. Frankly, I find him suspicious."

"So do I," Randee concurred. "His pattern is too accurate."

"I might as well give you some more bad news," Marsh began reluctantly. "That man I had Willard check on from Kansas, he was working for your stepfather until eight months ago, and so was one of those three raiders whom I killed in Granbury."

Randee paled noticeably. "Is there a connection between Payton Slade and this Epson Gang?" she asked worriedly.

"I don't think so. It seems your stepfather employed several of Quantrill's men at one time, but he's let them all go. I guess to avoid suspicion. I suppose they drifted here and joined up with the Epson Gang."

"You don't think it's odd they were working with

Payton in Kansas, now with this gang that's terrorizing this area?"

"I honestly believe it's only a coincidence. Men like those seem to locate and join up with others like them. They have no other place to go. The war ruined them, so they keep on raiding and killing. After what Quantrill's men did during the war, this is nothing new for them. It's my belief that the real leader intentionally searched out these men, knowing they had no consciences left, but plenty of greed and bitterness. He's actually exploiting them, but they don't know it."

"My heavens, Marsh, this is crazy," she remarked sadly.

"I know, love, but so was the war," he replied, unaware of the pet name he had picked up recently and was using with her.

Randee noticed it, but wisely didn't point it out. "I might as well see George Light, even if I doubt we'll learn anything new."

Randee was surprised by her conversation with the company lawyer. The man was highly educated, pleasant, and nice-looking. She hated to admit she was very impressed by George Light.

She was becomingly attired in a soft-blue summer dress and matching hat which she had brought along from her trunks in Wadesville for this meeting. "As I said, Mr. Light, I just wrote you a letter Saturday in Wadesville, but I decided to come here and talk with you personally. I cannot bear the thought of the ranch being ruined for any reason, so I have to make certain your reasons for buying it are honorable. How did you hear about my desire to sell?"

The man appeared totally relaxed and honest as he replied, "You have nothing to worry about, Miss Hollis.

My client desires to purchase large spreads, then divide them into smaller ones which the average man can afford. He wants to see this area of Texas prosper. It's my responsibility to locate properties which have fallen on hard times. Sad to say, most of the sales have resulted from raids by this vicious gang which is terrorizing our state. I check all newspapers for news of raids and approach the heirs about sales. As you know, most of them wish to sell quickly and leave the area. I give them as much money as possible to help them begin fresh elsewhere. Hopefully after this trouble is settled, some of them might return and repurchase their old spreads, or parts of them. Currently our plan is to hold on to the lands until the law has dealt with these murders and the areas are safe once more. Afterwards, we'll divide the larger spreads and sell them to several buyers. With the profits, we plan to build churches, schools, and businesses. This way, numerous people will benefit from a dreadful situation. We're interested in development, expansion, and improvements. Progress, Miss Hollis, that's our primary goal."

"The ranch house is still intact, Mr. Light, and it's beautiful — one of the few places spared by those horrid beasts. Naturally that means I'll have to ask a higher price than you mentioned in your letter."

The man thought for a moment, then responded, "I'll have to consult the company owner about raising my offer, Miss Hollis. I only have permission to spend a certain amount on each spread. I'll need a couple of weeks to contact him and get an answer for you. Will it be possible for you to return here . . . say after July fourth?"

Randee sighed artfully and said, "I had really hoped to get this matter settled as quickly as possible. Are you sure you can't make an exception this time?"

George shook his head. "I'm afraid not, Miss Hollis.

My authority is limited. To be honest with you, my offer was most generous and I'm not certain I can get a better one for you."

Randee did not want to appear overly eager, so she remarked, "Yes, but it was probably based on the erroneous fact that only the land existed, as it is uncommon for a raid site to escape total destruction. Surely the house makes my spread worth more?"

"Ah, but I did know the house was unharmed; that's why my offer was so reasonable. Surely you read the newspaper account of the raid? It mentioned the curious oversight by that awful gang."

That shocked Randee, and it showed in her expression. She admitted, "No, I didn't know about the story."

George smiled kindly. "You were very fortunate, Miss Hollis, but what's to stop that gang from destroying the house before we can sell it to another buyer? You are aware that those outlaws often strike the same place again? If I get my client to raise his price and the house is burned later, he's out a great deal of money which cannot be replaced with a sale."

"But, Mr. Light," she cleverly argued, "the raiders only strike a second time if people and cattle are present to make it worth their while. Since my ranch is deserted, what would it profit them?"

George grinned broadly. "You could be right. I'll approach my client about your request, then give you his answer on July fifth."

Randee grasped the polite dismissal in his tone and by the way he rose from his chair. "I can see you're a busy man, Mr. Light, but I have one other request." She watched the man take his seat again and look expectantly at her. "This must be held in strictest confidence. I'm looking for a nice, but smaller, ranch near Wadesville. You see, I'm to marry Sheriff Brody Wade soon and we want to get into ranching. As soon as election time comes around, he's stepping down as sheriff. I want to surprise him with a ranch as a wedding gift. I would like for you to be on the lookout for a superior ranch in that area, but one I can afford with the sale of my land, and one which leaves enough money to buy cattle and build a home. Is that possible?"

"Sheriff Wade is a lucky man to have won not only a beautiful woman but also a very generous one. I will do my best to fill your needs. With luck, I'll have both answers for you when we meet again. It was a pleasure to meet such a charming and intelligent woman."

Randee stood and shook the hand which was extended across the polished desk. "I look forward to doing business with you, sir. I shall return at ten o'clock on July fifth. Hopefully your news will be good."

George Light leaned back in his chair after Randee's departure. He absently scratched his taut groin as he envisioned the blonde beauty. He decided that his boss was indeed a very lucky man to have ensnared such a special creature, if indeed he had. George wasn't so sure about that, as this female was very bright and clever. Thank goodness, he had been warned by one of Brody's men to expect a visit from her soon, but not this soon. He had stalled her as ordered, but for how long?

Jackson Fuller came in the back door, a lopsided grin on his face. "So, that's the boss's little treasure. Can't blame 'im for wanting that writhing beneath him in a bed every night."

"Remember your orders, Fuller; she isn't to be harmed, only her partner in this silly chase. You have the poster on him?"

"Yep, in my saddlebag. His death will look real legal, and maybe it is. I got rid of that whore at the Pleasure Palace. Simple as breathing," he hinted and laughed coldly. "I guess she found it hard to catch her wind with a pillow over her painted face. Carl couldn't risk being seen in town, so he let me get rid of her for 'im. Must say, I wouldn't have minded a piece of her before she went out so easily. I been tailing those two ever since they hit town Sunday afternoon. Hayden visited that newspaperman and stayed a long time, but I couldn't get close enough to hear anything. The girl kept to her room all night, alone. 'Course that don't mean ain't nothing between 'em."

George Light swallowed his sour disgust with this repulsive killer-for-hire. If he had known so many people would be slain during this job, he wouldn't have taken it. He had been led to believe people would be scared out, but not this horrible way. Now, he was as deeply involved as Brody Wade and that malicious gang. If they were exposed and hanged, he would be too. He would be glad when this scheme was over, the sooner the better. What did it matter if he was going to be a wealthy and powerful man, when he had so much blood on his hands? "Anything else?" he asked when Fuller didn't move. He wanted this satanic bastard out of his office and life. The bounty hunter had no conscience; he enjoyed the pain and death of others. Yet, George Light hated to see Randee Hollis in Brody Wade's control . . . .

Jackson Fuller commented dryly, "I had to ride all night and day to beat 'em here. I'm tireder than a doggie who's been stampeded for hours. Can't rest yet 'cause those two won't stay put long. It's my guess they'll leave within the hour, and I'll be on their butts. By dusk, Hayden will be dead; that's a sure bet, Light."

George scowled at the mention of his one weakness, the vice which had gotten him involved in this bloody mess. "Then, I suggest you get back to work, or they'll sneak away before you know it."

The bounty hunter boasted calmly, "Nobody escapes me, Light. I've captured or killed every man I've gone

385

after. I'm the best; that's why Wade hired me. I was trained by the Apaches, so I have skills most trackers only dream about possessing. Hayden don't know it, but he's a walking dead man. Too bad the boss wants that girl with him."

"Make certain you don't forget that point, Fuller, or you'll be the walking dead man when Brody sends that gang after you."

Fuller threw back his head and laughed sardonically. "Don't tell me she teased your craw too. Don't worry, Light, I ain't met the woman who could make Jack Fuller forget himself."

George Light had not seen or met Storm Hayden, so he did not realize or suspect that Brody's nemesis was the same man whom he had met earlier as Jacksboro rancher Marsh Logan . . . .

Randee and Marsh camped early that night, a half day's ride from Fort Worth. They had talked little after discussing her nonproductive meeting with George Light and leaving town immediately thereafter.

She glanced at Marsh as they dismounted and unpacked their supplies. He had been unusually quiet this afternoon and she wondered what was on his mind. To break the heavy silence, she asked, "Do you think George Light knows what he's doing for this unknown boss? With all those false companies involved, maybe he doesn't even know whom he's actually working for." When he remained silent and distracted, she asked, "Is that possible, Marsh?"

"Possible, yes, but probable, no," he replied.

"Where to now?" she questioned, having failed to draw him out.

"I don't know," he confessed almost sullenly. "All we can do is ride around trying to get rid of more raiders while Willard continues his paper trail and his investigation of Carl Bush and Foley Timms."

"What's wrong?" she asked tenderly. "You're too quiet tonight."

"I don't like that business with Flossie. My gut instinct tells me someone is on to us. If I'm right . . ." He fell silent again. "I think I'll take a swim to get rid of some of this restlessness."

She watched him pull a bottle from his saddlebag and take several deep swallows of whiskey, an uncommon action for this strong male. As if forgetting her presence, he did not politely offer her a sip, although she would have refused that potent drink. Something had him worried, and that alarmed her. Yet, she tried to appear calm and confident and cheerful. With a wisdom beyond her years and experience, Randee was careful not to behave like a selfish or nagging woman by demanding he explain his moodiness.

Her father had told her long ago during one of their special talks, "When you're trying to rope your sweetheart, Randee, remember that men aren't like women when it comes to feelings. You women show yours and talk about them; men think they have to control theirs and be quiet about them, because that's how we're raised. Us boys are trained to hide our tender feelings and use self-control. We're not supposed to show fear, pain, doubts, or flaws. That makes people think you're less of a man, makes *you* think you're less of a man. That may sound silly, daughter, but we can't help ourselves. No matter what happens, we aren't supposed to burden you womenfolk with any problems, no complaining or tears or whining about cruel fate. We're supposed to be strong enough to handle anything. When trouble arises, we need to withdraw into our silent worlds to work through our feelings, to solve nasty situations, to deal with our failures. When your man does this, don't harass him with questions and tears and pouting. Be kind, and patient, and understanding until he opens up to you. He'll love you all the more for being so smart and unselfish. Don't be provoked to intrude on his silent retreat. When women behave like that, I'm sorry to say, we're bad about striking out in self-defense, because your reaction makes us feel weaker and more intimidated. A man constantly needs to prove his strength and worth."

As the blonde observed Marsh Logan and considered her father's words, she decided they were wise, but so hard to obey. Yet, she would try. With a radiant smile, she told him, "I'll start our supper while you get rid of that nervous energy, Logan. We'll talk later, if you're in the mood. If not, don't worry about it."

Marsh glanced at her and half grinned. "Only a smart woman knows when a man needs to be left alone. And you, Miss Hollis, are brilliant. Thanks. I'll be back shortly."

Randee watched his retreat, worried about him. He had to keep his wits sharp to avoid trouble, and they were anything but clear and active tonight. There was nothing she could do except wait for him to explain, if he cared to do so. She built a fire and began their meal.

Suddenly she was seized from behind, a strong arm imprisoning her throat and cutting off her breath. She felt a gun barrel pressed painfully between her shoulder blades and heard a frigid voice in her ear warn, "Be still and quiet, or you're dead, Miss Hollis."

The man did not release her. Instead, his grip tightened and she feared she was going to be strangled. Then, it loosened slightly. "If you don't do what I say, this bullet has your name on it. Call your friend back to camp. Storm Hayden and me have a little problem."

Randee grasped the name her assailant had used in speaking of Marsh, and the frightening use of her own name. She didn't know what to do. If she called Marsh and didn't warn him, her love could be slain, probably would be slain. If she did shout *danger*, the man would shoot her and still go after Marsh. "Wha-t d-do y-ou wa-nt?" she asked, struggling to get each word past her captive throat.

"Your friend out there owes me something, his life. It's yours or his or both; your choice, Hollis," he replied, his voice icy.

Horror seized her. "Why?" she questioned frantically.

"Money."

"I do-n't un-derst-and. What mon-ey?"

"He's a wanted man, one with a big reward on his head."

"Do you ha-have to ch-oke me?" she asked, twisting to loosen his grip so she could get more air in her lungs.

"When I let up, you best call him over, or your pretty ass is mine, bitch, if you catch my drift. Cross me, and I'll get rid of you real slow and painful after I finish him off. Obey, and you go free. You have my word, woman; 'cause you don't interest me, just Hayden."

"I should believe that?" she challenged after drawing a deep and ragged breath. No time to think, she had to listen closely.

"You got a choice?" he asked sarcastically.

"What if I pay you more than his reward to let us go free?"

"You ain't got twenty thousand dollars on you, and I don't trust nobody. Shut up and call him," he demanded contradictorily, jabbing the gun barrel sharply into her back.

Suddenly Randee realized that Marsh might suspect trouble when she used his false name, so she yelled, "Storm! Storm Hayden, come quick! I've burned my-self badly! Get over here! Pronto!"

Marsh appeared almost instantly — behind them, and

with a gun in each hand. But the alert bounty hunter had not boasted falsely to George Light about his skills; anticipating and hearing Marsh's stealthy approach, he had whirled and placed Randee between them.

"Drop 'em, Hayden, or she's dead." He shoved his gun roughly against her spine and wiggled it, causing her to jerk backward and to scream in pain. Her captor laughed malevolently. "You might get me, but I'll get her before you do. Lose the guns," he ordered coldly.

For a time, Marsh held his ground—a few feet away—with only a blanket wrapped around his dripping body. Wet hair fell over his forehead, and his unshaven face looked hard. His blue eyes narrowed and his jawline grew taut, and he knew he had made an incredible error. The warning had been in her words and he had grasped it, but he had underestimated the prowess of this killer—a stupid and possibly fatal mistake. He cursed his blunder and hastily assessed the situation. He dared not shoot with Randee as the man's shield, particularly with such a dangerous and alert bastard who was quick and agile. This opponent was highly trained, highly skilled, highly perilous. Here was a man hard to trick, one who couldn't be bargained with or fought fairly. Marsh was too far away to risk attack, leaving him no way to defend his woman. Yet, he adopted a nonchalant stance and grinned. "Seems you caught me with my jeans down, partner. What's the deal?"

"No deal, Hayden. If you want this woman to live, stay right where you are. No sudden moves or heroics. Your poster says you're worth more alive than dead, so I'd like to take you in kicking. The guns, toss them toward me, real slow and careful, barrels first."

Randee's life depended on his unselfish decision. For now, Marsh knew he had no choice but to surrender, and that enraged him. He pointed his weapons downward and uncocked their hammers. Flicking his wrists, he let his revolvers slide through his hands so he could grip their barrels with his fingers and toss them on the ground. He watched the now useless weapons hit the hard earth, out of reach. The number one rule for being a survivor was never to give up your gun for any reason; this time, he had to break it because he knew the man would shoot Randee without a second thought.

"That's better," the man said smugly. "Kiss the ground with your belly," came his second order, an even more embarrassing one. When Marsh obeyed, the man added, "Spread-eagle, Hayden!"

Marsh cursed his oversight of not concealing a knife behind his back. In that one moment of the man's distraction from apparent victory, he could have . . . He ordered himself to clear his mind of debilitating intrusions. Swallowing his pride and mastering his fury, he stretched out, knowing how vulnerable and helpless the position made him. Before he could decide a course of action, the man threw Randee aside and struck him forcefully on the back of the head, rendering him unconscious. The last thing he heard was Randee's scream . . . .

"Move one inch, woman, and you're a goner." Pulling a rope from his pocket, Jackson Fuller bent forward and begin to bind Marsh.

Randee rubbed her sore throat and coughed. She shifted to her knees as she pleaded, "If you let him go, I'll give you the money. I have that much in a bank in Wadesville, also a valuable ranch. You can hide him somewhere until we fetch it. No tricks; I swear."

As the bounty hunter turned to scowl at her, shaking his head, she fired the pistol which she had drawn from her boot. The bullet struck him in the heart. She fired again. A shocked look briefly crossed his face as he grabbed at his chest before he collapsed, dead.

Randee stared at his unmoving body as her respiration came in short, shallow gasps. Her hands went cold and started to shake. For a time, she couldn't move or think. She had killed him, but he had given her no choice. Doubtlessly he would have slain both of them, or at least killed her beloved. Finally she crawled over to Marsh on watery legs. She checked his injury, blood staining her trembling fingers. Impelled into motion, she rushed to their saddlebags and withdrew a clean cloth. Grabbing a canteen, she returned to her love's side. She washed the wound and bound it tightly. Retrieving a bedroll, she spread it beside Marsh and eased his limp frame onto it. She waited for him to rouse, avoiding a single glance at the body nearby.

Nearly a half hour later, Marsh moaned and stirred. As his keen wits cleared swiftly, he tried to bolt upward to challenge their attacker. Randee placed her hands on his shoulders and pressed him to the bedroll again, saying soothingly, "He's dead, Marsh, relax. You have a nasty cut and I don't want it to start bleeding again."

Marsh twisted his head and glanced at the body nearby, then looked at the pale woman sitting beside him. "What happened?"

Randee related her story in a quavering voice. "You wondered if I'd panic and if I could shoot a man. I guess I proved myself tonight."

Marsh was concerned by the hollow sound of her voice and the anguish in her green eyes. "You saved my life, Randee, but thanks doesn't mean much at a time like this."

"You were willing to do the same for me; that's why you gave up your weapons. I tried to reason with him, tried to buy him off. He was going to kill us. I had to do it, didn't I, Marsh?"

"Yes, love, you made the right choice," he said comfortingly, then drew her down into his arms.

Time passed as neither spoke nor moved, only drew solace from each other's embrace. Both had faced demanding moments-of-truth tonight, and both needed privacy to deal with them.

Marsh released her and sat up, saying. "I'll get his body out of camp and check out the area. I've been real careless tonight, and I nearly got us killed. You stay alert and concealed until I return."

Randee started to refute his guilt, but decided not to do so. Her words would only intensify his bad feelings, not remove them. As her father had revealed, Marsh needed time and silence to deal with this crushing failure. Admitting his weakness aloud had been difficult enough without her trying to appease him. His ego was bruised, his pride singed. He was unaccustomed to defeat and to being rescued by another person, especially a mere woman. She let him leave without a word, and obeyed his orders while he was gone.

Tuesday and Wednesday they traveled, but sighted nothing suspicious. They rode, rested, ate, and camped in near silence. Randee kept telling herself to leave Marsh alone while he worked through his emotions, but it was difficult, frustrating, tormenting. Each hour, he seemed to become more guarded, more troubled, more driven . . . more elusive. She hated this distance and coolness between them. She had tried to be cheerful, supportive, considerate; she had done everything she could to let Marsh know she was there for him when he decided to relent. Nothing seemed to work in her favor.

Did Marsh blame her for his vulnerability, his stunning defeat? Didn't he realize he wasn't the only man with superior skills and prowess? Didn't he realize that no mortal man was unconquerable, matchless, infallible? He was riled by his careless slip, by the one-sided battle. He knew he could have been slain; she could have been slain. Was that the first time this unique male had faced real death, real defeat?

Yet, if the only things between them were sex and stimulating adventures, they did not have enough for a good and permanent relationship. If they couldn't talk, couldn't console each other, couldn't share the bad as well as the good — couldn't reveal their innermost feelings to each other — their relationship was nothing more than a physical one. If that was true, they had no future together. How long should she be "kind, patient, and understanding"? How much time and energy, how much of herself, should she give to this . . . arrangement before she made certain it would grow, deepen, and last?

Marsh was so accustomed to keeping everything to himself and to being alone that he did not realize he was shutting Randee out completely, and seemingly coldly. He had so much on his troubled mind. He was certain that Brody Wade was behind that bounty hunter's attack, and Marsh felt to blame for rashly exposing his Storm Hayden identity to that jealous bastard. But, was Brody's order given for only Storm's death? How could the sheriff be sure that his *fiancée* wouldn't be injured or killed, possibly by accident, by his stone-hearted hireling? Was Brody's only motive to get rid of him and to force Randee to go home to marry him? His answers depended upon how much Brody loved and wanted Randee, on whether or not the lawman had believed her story . . . . Then, that business with George Light had him plenty worried and baffled. Why had the lawyer hesitated, postponed a deal with Randee? And what was so damn special about the Carson Ranch!

He mentally eyed his lengthy list of enemies and problems: Carl Bush, the Epson Gang, Foley Timms, George Light, bounty hunters, misguided lawmen, and possibly Brody Wade and Payton Slade. There were too many perils involved, too many dangerous people to allow Randee to continue working and traveling with him . . . .

Chapter Eighteen

In Kansas on Thursday morning, Payton Slade curiously eyed the fat packet which had arrived earlier with his wife's name on it. The Wadesville, Texas return address caught his attention. He knew that was where Dee's older brother lived on a sprawling ranch, which was reputed to be one of the finest in the Lone Star State.

As he was heading toward the house, Payton abruptly halted and stared at the bulging envelope. What, his wicked mind asked, if it contained news of Randee? A surge of delight and eagerness was promptly replaced by dread. What if that cunning bitch had shown up at her uncle's place in Texas and betrayed him to her kin, and they were warning Dee, or threatening to take legal action against him? He shuddered and scowled. He could handle his groveling wife, but Lee Carson or the authorities . . . Payton experienced a moment of shock and terror at the thought of being unmasked and punished, of losing all he had obtained. That petrified sensation enraged and hardened him, as did the memory of his stepdaughter's humiliating trickery. He vividly recalled the wintry night she had guilefully enticed, seductively enchanted, and rashly duped him.

A mixture of powerful emotions raced wildly through his mind and body, but the most dominant one was erotic revenge because it encompassed so many feelings and desires: lust, vengeance, triumph, and pleasure. Never, he smugly decided, would Randee Hollis expose her dirty little secret and risk humiliation, or risk being held all or partly to blame for the sinful episodes. Nor would she risk shaming and hurting her mother, or forcing her mother to bear witness against her. Never would Randee challenge him without evidence, and there was none; he had made certain of it. If there was one thing that girl knew, it was how dangerous he could be, which was the obvious reason why she had not exposed him before escaping.

Payton grinned satanically as he begrudgingly admitted he was impressed by Randee's courage and daring. His ravishing and tempting stepdaughter was a rare treasure to own and use. The girl was smart; she knew when to be afraid and when to be brave. She had spirit, fire, vitality; and he wanted to be the master of all her traits.

Intoxicating excitement charged through him and sent his mind to spinning madly. What if there was still a chance of locating that reckless vixen and bringing her back home as his slave? Naturally, the insidious man mused, after she was properly disciplined and cowed! When he finished with her punishment and subjugation, she would never again trick him or disobey him or leave him . . . or refuse him anything.

Payton hurried to the barn for privacy. His hands trembled with anticipation as he ripped open the missive, spilling most of its contents on the ground. He scooped them up and leaned against a stall to read them. He was astonished by the incredible enclosures. He nervously paced back and forth as he went over each paper, time and time again.

He laughed heartily as he murmured, "By God, girl, yore quite a woman, a real spitfire. You fooled yore step-pa once, but n'er again."

Immediately Payton Slade mentally planned his journey to Texas to recover his beautiful stepdaughter and to look over his new property. After he checked out the Carson spread, he would decide which ranch to sell and where to live. He needed to take along a few of his men to deal with this "notorious outlaw" who was playing games with his golden treasure. He wouldn't tell his wife anything about this business, until it was settled. Besides, she was still in bed from her miscarriage last week and didn't deserve to be treated kindly after daring to lose his first child. If he could get Randee back under his control, he wouldn't need to get his current wife "to breeding" again soon! Actually, he concluded evilly, he wouldn't need Dee Hollis Slade at all . . . .

Salacious dreams filled his distorted mind. He could be in Wadesville within a week, seeking control of both his valuable properties. If he could get hold of Randee and the Carson Ranch, they could begin a new life where nobody had to learn he had been her stepfather before his wife's — her mother's — tragic demise . . . . In Texas, he would be far away from where he had committed so many as-yet-undiscovered crimes. He would be safe and happy, prosperous and powerful, rich and sated . . . .

It was late that same afternoon when Marsh finished his letter to President Grant. If anything happened to him, or to Willard Mason — one of the few men who knew his real identity — he needed to share the information he had gathered on the Epson Gang with someone he trusted above all others: his boss, the President. A small town was located not too far from where they were resting; he could mail this crucial missive there and also obtain current information on the gang's actions, as he needed to learn where they were raiding this week. The next thing he needed to do was take Randee back to Fort Worth and place her in Willard Mason's care, to be sent back East swiftly to join the newspaperman's family, where she would be safe until this case was solved.

Marsh glanced over at the reclining woman who had stolen his heart and softened it. The sun was beginning to set, causing a seductive golden glow on Randee's tawny hair and skin. The suffusion of honey-colored light which generously flowed over her was seductive, alluring, enhancing. He recalled her anger at his calling her a golden treasure, but that described her perfectly. Her green eyes were closed, unmoving. Her lips and skin were soft, inviting. Her flaxen hair fell gently to the bedroll upon which she was possibly asleep, presenting him with a favorable look at her silky throat. He wanted to spread kisses down it, across her face, over every inch of her from head to toe.

Marsh's body and spirit ached for a union with hers. They hadn't slept together — made love — in nearly a week. There had been no time or place or proper mood for it. He admitted the truth to himself: He didn't want sex from Randee Hollis; sex could be taken anywhere and at any speed from any obliging female. He wanted to love her slowly and sweetly, swiftly and ravenously — but all with special meaning, with total giving and sharing and taking. Mercy, how he missed being close to her, physically and emotionally.

From the beginning, they had respected and accepted each other in all ways. They had valued each other's strengths, and accepted each other's weaknesses. She had always been there, was here, for him whenever he reached out for her.

Yet, his love and desire for her could get her killed. He had to break off their relationship while he still possessed the strength, means, and time to do so. He realized he had been distant — moody and unresponsive — lately, and that should work in his favor . . . .

Randee lay still and quiet as she wondered what Marsh was doing and thinking and feeling. To whom was he writing? About what? Why wasn't he being a partner anymore — sharing information, thoughts, ideas, suspicions, his skills, himself? She perceived that something was happening inside that handsome head. Marsh had not made love to her since Wadesville. He had not touched her or been open since she killed that bounty hunter and saved his life. She sensed that he was getting ready to drop her, to desert her, to end their love affair and partnership. The sad blonde knew she would protest loudly and fiercely, but she doubted it would do any good this time . . . .

Randee sat up as Marsh announced, "Let's head to a small town nearby so I can mail this letter. When we get there, I want you to hide and wait for me. I'll need to visit the saloon for information, and you're not allowed inside. I shouldn't be gone more than an hour, two at the most. Then, we'll head to that private place to camp so we can talk. There's something we have to settle tonight."

Dread — and relief — filled Randee at his last statement. He was being secretive about the letter, acting warily, and she thought it best not to press him until later that night. It was definitely time for them to have a talk, an honest and enlightening one. She nodded understanding and agreement, then stood to pack and leave.

Aware she had hardly spoken to him or looked at him today, he started to ask her what was wrong, then realized how contradictory that was. Obviously she was responding in like manner to his mood and behavior. He wanted to apologize, to comfort her, to explain, but he couldn't. He had to stand firm and appear selfishly insensitive if he was going to persuade her to leave his side tomorrow.

Marsh slipped into the *Texas Sentinel* office and scanned the papers for the last week, discovering something curious about the gang's raids. Secondly, the ebony-clad man sneaked into the stage depot and placed his letter to President Grant—under a code name—in the appropriate pouch. According to the schedule posted, the mail would be picked up tomorrow and should be . . . Marsh's eyes widened and he stared at the poster on the wall before him:

STORM HAYDEN
WANTED DEAD OR ALIVE
FOR CRIMES IN NEBRASKA
TWENTY THOUSAND DOLLARS REWARD

Marsh felt his respiration speed up, as did his heart rate. This wasn't one of the old, false posters from a past mission. This one was newly printed, different, and his sketch was revealingly accurate. The reward was a lie. Somebody wanted him dead, swiftly, badly.

It was night, but plenty of light was available because the moon had been full yesterday. Marsh left the office and headed down the street, where his horse was waiting obediently. He never had to secure the stallion's reins to a hitching post, which was a big advantage when he was forced to leave town or escape camp quickly. The animal was highly intelligent, exceedingly well-trained, and totally loyal.

Marsh went to full alert as he noticed other posters tacked up here and there, proclaiming perilous lies. Some enemy had been real busy during the past few days! He wondered if these false posters were everywhere by now. If they didn't get him killed, they positively would compel him to straighten out this devious matter before continuing his mission. Maybe, he decided with a frown, that was the motive behind them — to slow him down or to halt him permanently from chasing the Epson Gang. The question was, who was responsible for them?

A shout to Marsh's left seized his attention: "There he is! It's him all right! Come on, boys, let's earn us twenty thousand dollars!"

Marsh reacted instantly, taking cover behind a building and firing warning shots in the air. He whistled for Midnight, who came galloping to his rescue. Marsh knew he could not kill innocent but misguided people, even if his life was at stake. Yet, if he was chased and captured, he probably would be slain before he could convince the money-crazed mob of his innocence. The best thing was to make a run for it, then clear up this matter later, from Fort Worth. He leapt upon the stallion's back and raced from town. Marsh wished he could have fled in the other direction, away from where his beautiful partner was hiding. He heard gunshots, shouts, and hoofbeats behind him. The pursuit was on, but he had to lead them away from his love.

Randee heard the thundering hooves coming in her direction, then suddenly veer off to the left. She mounted the chestnut's back and topped the rolling hill before her. In the bright moonlight, she saw Marsh galloping across the open grassland with a group of seven men chasing him, firing at him! She observed the way her love headed back to the right, toward the trees, and realized he had skirted the area where she was concealed. She tried not to panic, because Marsh had a good head start on them; yet, he was not defending himself . . . .

Randee quickly and intelligently assessed their pace and direction, the perils involved in helping Marsh, and the chances of her success. She patted the chestnut's neck and murmured, "Let's help him, Rojo."

The blonde rode swiftly and skillfully to intercept the rider and pursuers. It was apparent Marsh was not returning their gunfire, so he must have a good reason, one in which she mustn't interfere. She couldn't do anything to cause his capture or to force him to defend her. She needed to slow the men down, give Marsh time to lose them.

Randee topped another hill and checked out the situation again. They were galloping down the road which eventually curled back toward her, not far away. Marsh and Midnight had a good lead on them now. She left her mount hidden and hurriedly made her way to the dirt road. After securing one end of her rope to a tree, she stretched it across the road on the ground. Then, she concealed herself behind a large tree to keep Marsh from sighting her and halting. In the dark, and with the noise, he should miss her intervention, which was probably for the best.

After Marsh galloped past, with trembling fingers, she hastily raised the rope and secured the other end tightly to the second tree. She heard shouts and pounding hooves, and her heart throbbed fearfully. She ran toward the bushes and fell on the grass behind them, making certain she was out of sight, motionless and silent.

Yelps of surprise and pain filled her ears as the riders were yanked from their horses by the taut rope barrier and sent thuddingly to the hard ground. The men had been grouped closely, which disallowed reaction time to avoid being unhorsed and having the wind knocked from their lungs. She heard frightened animals whicker and paw the ground in tension, and heard a couple run off down the road as their owners tried to regain enough breath to shout to them to halt. Within minutes, curses reached her alert ears, and strange words . . . .

One man remounted quickly and went after the two runaway horses. The others dusted themselves off and checked for injuries. The cowboys were angered at being tricked and at losing their valuable captive. Until their friend returned with the two lost mounts, they cursed and fumed and planned what to do. The unanimous decision was to search for the cunning outlaw. Assuming the man they were chasing was alone, had duped them, and had continued his escape long ago, they mounted and galloped down the road again, taking Randee's rope.

Randee waited until the sounds faded into near silence, then returned to where Rojo was secured. She mounted the mare and galloped to a hilltop to scan the area. Sighting a thick cloud of dust, she knew which direction the irate band of men was taking. Her keen gaze searched the area for any sign of Marsh, but found none.

The logical thing was to return to where he had left her and to wait for his return. But the men from town were riding in that direction, making it dangerous for her and Marsh to head that way. She pondered how they could link up again. Assuming she would guess why he didn't return to her side, what would he expect her to do? Where would he look for her? If he looked for her . . .

Randee knew she was west of Fort Worth by at least a day's ride. Wadesville was southeast of her present position; Fort Richardson was northwestward. "Which one, Marsh?" she murmured thoughtfully.

Recalling what he had said about "that private place to camp," she tried to remember the mumbled directions he had mentioned before leaving her outside that little town. Her mind elsewhere, Randee had paid little attention to words which she had not realized she would need. She closed her eyes and concentrated, trying to envision the scene earlier and trying to hear Marsh's words.

Taking a chance she could locate the campsite, Randee headed eastward, away from the town and away from the last direction in which she had seen her partner heading swiftly. And his pursuers.

Shadows surrounded her and moved eerily in the breeze. She remained on full alert. She had to travel slowly and gingerly, as peril could be lurking behind any tree or hill. Randee rode for over two hours before reaching the location which she felt certain was the correct one. Before her, in the thick cover of trees and tangled underbrush, stood a small shack. Cautiously she approached it, and was relieved to find it empty. She looked around and heard nothing threatening.

After Rojo was unsaddled, the chestnut mare grazed on lush grass and drank water from a narrow stream nearby. Randee did not enter the shack, as she did not want to be entrapped there if danger arrived in any form. She made camp behind the unpainted wooden structure, which could last another five years in this climate. She did not make a fire and she did not eat. After spreading out her bedroll, the anxious blonde sat on it and waited.

Randee heard the sounds and movements of nocturnal birds, creatures, and insects. She was not afraid of nature, but she was afraid for her love. What if he hadn't gotten away tonight? What if others had found him? What if he didn't think to look for her here?

The moon had gone beyond its overhead position, telling her it was long past midnight. Still, she sat on the bedroll, staring into the darkness which surrounded her. She was too apprehensive to be sleepy or hungry. If Marsh didn't appear by morning, what should she do?

After ambushing Marsh's pursuers with the rope, she

had been hiding close enough to the road to hear most of their words. What was all that talk about "wanted" posters and a huge reward for Storm Hayden? Marsh had told her that Nebraska outlaw episode was settled. And why were they saying to be careful not to harm the "female hostage" who was being forced to travel with him? Since she had heard the words "Sheriff Brody Wade's fiancee," didn't that explain the perilous matter to her troubled mind? The men had talked of whether or not Storm Hayden was riding with the Epson Gang, which was now raiding *east* of Fort Worth, out of the target area. Randee went over many facts, speculations, and doubts. Too many things made sense to her . . . .

Marsh's voice sliced coldly and abruptly into her rambling thoughts, "You shouldn't have come here, Randee, but I figured you would. It's too damn dangerous to hang around me; our partnership is over. I can't call off this quest, but you can't continue it with me. Get away from me and this bloody mess before you're injured or killed."

"No," she responded calmly, firmly. "We stick together."

Marsh dropped to his knees before her and shook her shoulders. "Listen to me, you stubborn woman. You aren't safe with me no matter which identity I use! I thought those fake 'wanted' posters had been destroyed long ago, but they're being reprinted and circulated again."

"By Brody Wade," Randee disclosed confidently.

"How do you know that?" he queried, settling his seat on the soles of his boots. He watched her as she lifted her head to answer him.

"I don't know where Brody got a copy of that poster or how he got it circulated so fast, but I'm sure he's behind it. What does it say?"

"Lies," Marsh replied angrily. "It isn't the same one

which was printed years ago. It has my current description on it and a hefty reward of twenty thousand dollars. Just like that bounty hunter said, so maybe he was only working for himself. There's no telling how many of those posters are around, or how many men will try to collect on my head. Get back to Fort Worth and Willard, where you'll be safe."

"Everyone knows we've been traveling together, so I'm probably considered your sidekick, or whatever it's called. If you send me away or desert me, I'll wind up in jail, or be tortured for information about you. Surely you realize how tempting that much money is? Some people will do anything to earn it, including killing me. I don't know why Brody would endanger me, if he truly loves and wants me. Unless," she began hesitantly, "it's true what your pursuers said about me supposedly being your hostage and I'm not to be harmed."

"Where did you hear that? When? How?" he demanded. "Did you sneak into town tonight before you came here?"

Randee exhaled loudly and frowned before she admitted, "This probably means you won't speak to me again for three more days, but I'll tell you anyway, so we can grasp what's happening." She revealed what she had seen and done that night, then remarked peevishly, "If you don't like my second intrusion, it's too bad. I had to try to help you; that's what partners are for. Shut up and let me finish," she demanded when he started to speak. Then she related the remainder of what she'd overheard.

Randee clarified her thoughts and feelings. "I think these raids east of Fort Worth are cunning tricks to fool us and the law. I don't think this unknown boss wants control of the entire area around Fort Worth. I think he only wants the area you've got marked on that map in your saddlebag." Her troubled gaze met his alert one as she asserted, "I think Brody Wade is a member of the Epson Gang, at least some kind of spy for them. I think he's responsible for that trouble with the bounty hunter, for those fake posters, for Flossie's death, and for these new raids outside the target area. And it's all because I revealed too much to him while I was in Wadesville. So you're right. I don't deserve to be your partner, or even your friend. Because of me, Flossie is dead, innocent ranchers are dead, and you could have been killed. I should have confessed my stupidity earlier, but I was angry with you for all your deceitful actions and secrets. And I . . ." She faltered and lowered her gaze to gather the strength to continue.

"I really thought Brody loved me and would keep my confidence. I should have known what a bastard he is; that's why I can't stand him and wouldn't marry him if he were the only man available. He's probably warned Timms, Bush, Light, his boss, and the gang by now. Because of these loose lips and a missing brain, by now, they all know what we've been doing, what we know, and what we plan to do." After making certain she made a complete disclosure to Marsh about her visit with Brody, she asserted, "So you see, Mr. Logan, I'm to blame for you getting your masculine pride stomped the other night and for you getting chased tonight. It's my guess you were planning to end our partnership this morning, so do it. But don't expect me to run to Willard Mason for protection. I'm going to do exactly what I set out to do: defeat that gang, by starting with the traitorous Brody Wade."

Before Marsh could respond, Randee told him exactly what she had been thinking and feeling Wednesday night about him and about their relationship. "Whether you ever accept it or not, Marsh Logan, you aren't perfect and you can't survive alone! And if the only things I'm good for are sating your desires and

408

having fun, then we have no real friendship." She raced onward almost breathlessly, "I've tried to follow my father's advice, but you make it so damn hard. Isn't there a time limit on how long a woman has to be the lone giver? You don't have to share everything with me, but can't you share at least a little bit of yourself, besides when things are good between us?"

When Marsh lowered his chin and exhaled loudly, Randee — misunderstanding his reaction — shoved him forcefully, causing him to fall to the bedroll on his back. "Damn you, you headstrong rogue! Don't get huffy with me because I'm speaking the truth and you don't want to hear it! It's time for an understanding, Mr. Logan! I was willing to return home after our two jobs and begin work on my ranch, learn how to run it alone and how to defend myself and my property. I was perfectly willing to let you drift in and out of my life whenever the mood struck you — which I hoped was often, because I enjoy you and being with you. I was willing to accept any part of you, big or little, frequently or only occasionally. No demands or promises, just a reasonable understanding, a tiny compromise. But no, you don't think that's fair to me because you believe only you would be getting what you want and need. Well, Mr. Logan, that isn't true at all. My needs would be fulfilled, probably better than yours. Contrary to what you have convinced yourself to believe, I wouldn't be sacrificing a family, respect, or anything else. If you get out of life whatever makes you happy, why do you need more?"

She quickly answered her own question. "You don't. Even without commitments, I'm happy with you, happier than I would be enslaved to some husband I don't love and to some boring existence as his shadow. I give you what you need, Marsh, so why are you miserable? So damn stubborn? So friggin' blind to the truth and your good fortune? I'm not your slave or prisoner, and you aren't taking advantage of me. If I decided not to wait around for you to change or die, then I wouldn't have to. I'm a free woman, so I can do as I please. That's my choice, Marsh. Surely you know me by now. I'm not a weak or foolish woman, a silly girl, a clinging vine, a beggar or a trickster. I've reasoned this out, and I've taken plenty of time to avoid a mistake. It's only a compromise. For how long, I don't know. It's so simple, Marsh. You want me and I want you. If we can be together only for short periods, isn't that better than sharing nothing at all? Or refusing to ever see each other again because we know we can't have anything permanent? Life's too short to be miserable. Real happiness is hard to find in most lives, so we have to grab it whenever and wherever it's available. Why is our situation so impossible for this keen mind to understand and accept?"

Randee moved to his side, as he had not shifted since she had pushed him down, and he seemed to be paying close attention to her words and expressions. "Can't you understand my feelings and believe me, Marsh? I don't want to marry a man just to have a husband and children, to fulfill my duty to society as a woman. And I can't fall in love with someone else until I no longer want you, and I'll keep wanting you until I've had my fill. How can I, if you stay away because you feel guilty or intimidated by this bond between us? You should feel guilty only if I mean nothing to you or you're misleading me. Neither is true. You can't help the way you feel; I accept that, Marsh. I won't try to change you, but I will try to have you as much as I can."

"Is it my turn to get a few words into this conversation?" he asked, rolling to his side and propping his jaw on his hand. He watched Randee present her profile to him, then rest her chin on her raised knees. "There isn't much for me to say, because you've summed up my same suspicions. I was having doubts about Brody Wade, and now I'm convinced he's involved with that gang. Obviously they're paying him a lot of money to do their dirty work, money he wants to use to buy a ranch for his new wife: one, Miss Randee Hollis."

Her head jerked around, causing her flaxen hair to tumble wildly about her shoulders. "I'm not responsible for his greed and evil. If you'll recall, the raids were going on long before I escaped to Texas."

Marsh sat up and took a cross-legged sitting position. His tone and look were serious as he replied, "I know, woman, and I wasn't accusing you of provoking him into becoming a criminal. What we need to learn is when Brody joined them and what he does for them. At first light, we should head for Wadesville, not Fort Worth. We'll abduct him and take him somewhere private and force him to confess. Don't you see, partner, your slips were perfect strategy. They made him race off to see his boss and friends to reveal what you told him. That's probably where he went that night, not to pick up a prisoner. Now that he's unknowingly exposed his hand, we can use him to entrap the others. Another thing, woman, I understand why you mistrusted me, but I can't help being secretive about some things. There's a lot you don't know about me. I'm sorry, but I can't be open and honest with you any time soon; it's impossible for several good reasons. So, you see, I have good cause to feel guilty about our relationship. I do mislead you by withholding things, even outright lie to you sometimes."

Randee's mind seized on his words "several good reasons." She was surprised by his casual admission of his devious behavior. Yet, she sensed that he did—or believed he did—have a valid motive for dealing unfairly, dishonestly with her. If she didn't give up on him . . . Randee met his steady gaze and said, "Keep your

411

secrets, Marsh. I only want to know one thing for now: Is our personal relationship real? I mean, do you honestly care about me and accept this bond between us?"

Marsh wondered what was the best, not particularly the truest, thing to say. "I don't want to fool you or allow you to fool yourself, Randee. Deep inside, you'll always be hoping and believing I'll appear one night at your ranch and decide to stay forever. I'm a gamble, woman, and the stakes are high. Can you really put your life in limbo because of a dream about conquering me one day?"

Randee smiled and challenged, "Is it only a dream, Marsh? Can you look at me and swear you aren't tempted to settle down with me? Or swear there's no way or time you'll ever leave drifting behind?"

Without his awareness, Marsh's expression and mood seemingly implied what Randee wanted to hear. He could not tell her the truth about his love and need for her, because he was worried about her refusal to leave him if the time came when it was crucial. He had to find a way to keep them alive until he could finish this mission and could finish changing, and could yield to her. "It can't be, Randee, at least no time soon. And if one of us is slain, it can never be."

Randee knew Marsh had lost his family and was possibly afraid of losing someone else he loved. He was so wary, so intimidated by strong emotions. For a loner, that wasn't hard to understand. She teased, "I'll wait around for a while, Marsh, because you're worth it."

"It isn't fair to—" he began to protest, but was cut off.

"Stop telling me what's fair to me! Let me decide what I want and need." She laughed merrily before jesting, "By the time we complete our two jobs, maybe your magical grip over me will vanish. Then you won't have to worry about using me or getting rid of me."

"I don't know how you manage it, woman, but you've

412

done it again. Every time I'm about to put your safety and survival above my selfish desires, you find a reason why I can't leave you behind. With all our enemies on to us, the only place you can stay is with me." Marsh pulled her into his arms and ventured bravely, "We'll have an understanding, Miss Hollis; from now on, I won't think about or say how unfair our relationship is to you. I'm going to accept your word that you're getting enough from me to make it worth your while. I'm not going to make you any promises or denials, but I will admit you're very special to me, and I'd like to keep you alive and with me."

Randee hugged him and asked, "Was that so hard to admit?"

Marsh's arms encircled her body and held her closely and snugly. "You're darn right it was. Don't forget, this is all new to me, Randee, having a woman with me all the time. Even if you aren't verbally pressing me, I feel like you're doing it in other ways, and that makes me terribly nervous. You're a cunning vixen. You're getting me hooked on you so I'll be miserable when we're apart. Why didn't I see it before?" he teased. "You're the one being unfair to me."

"I would be unfair and dishonest only if I played guileful games with you, Mr. Logan, which I don't. I never offer you anything which isn't yours to take, as much as you desire and for as long as you desire." She hinted seductively, "Even if I were trying to hook you, I am feeding you lots of pretty worms to sate your hunger."

"Sate my hunger? It's more like whet my appetite."

"I guess that means I'm not very appealing or satisfying."

Marsh leaned back and looked down at her in bewilderment. "What does that mean?"

"Either you don't get hungry very often, or I'm not

413

very good at whetting your appetite, or very skilled at sating it."

"You must be joshing me, woman. You have my tummy growling and my mouth drooling in hunger all the time. I could make love to you six times a day and still want you all the other hours."

At that staggering and stimulating disclosure, Randee's stunned gaze locked with Marsh's amused one. She witnessed the flames of desire which were burning brightly in his eyes. She felt the heat of fiery passion rising in his body, and she snuggled closer. She wanted him so much that it startled her, mildly panicked her, almost took her breath and reason away.

Marsh hinted meaningfully, "I checked out this area carefully before I rode in. Nobody's around for miles, and no one should be stirring for hours. Would you like to take unfair advantage of me?"

Randee laughed happily as she replied in a seductive tone, "Nothing would please me more, Mr. Logan, than to ravish you here and now." She unbuttoned his shirt and parted it, then pressed her lips to the golden flesh and ebony hair on his compelling chest. As her mouth trailed sensuously over his torso, her trembling fingers eased the shirt from his body and cast it aside.

Randee removed her own vest and shirt, and nestled her naked flesh against his as her lips wandered up his neck and sought his mouth. She urged him backward to the bedroll and lay half atop his virile frame. As she kissed him feverishly, her breasts brushed provocatively over his hard chest.

Marsh's quivering fingers fumbled with the buttons on her skirt, loosened them, and shoved the sturdy material downward to expose her soft — but firm — buttocks to his grasp. He gently kneaded the silky flesh before shifting her body so his mouth could capture the smoldering peaks of her brests, which were hot against his flesh. He groaned as his hunger reached a ravenous level and he feasted wildly on the delicious buds.

Randee felt her head spinning blissfully as Marsh labored lovingly on her body, swiftly increasing their desires. It felt wonderful to be in his arms and possession again. Hope, joy, and rapture filled her. She refused to think about the perils which they were facing; all she wanted to know and feel was this special moment, this unique love.

Soon, their bodies were free of all garments and their spirits were free of all inhibitions. Their secluded haven was quiet and romantic; it was seductive and dreamy. The moon shone down on their naked bodies, and the scent of wildflowers teased their nostrils. A cooling breeze wafted over them, but their heat increased despite it.

Marsh's teeth nibbled at her earlobe before his lips roamed to her mouth and greedily fastened to it. His manhood slipped skillfully into her receptive body, and her response welcomed him to her paradise and encouraged him to visit a long time. For what seemed like hours, he tantalized and stimulated them with his movements and talents. The pleasure and hesitation were almost painfully ecstatic, forcing him to use every ounce of his self-control. Suddenly Randee was clinging tightly to him and writhing wildly beneath him, and sending forth sounds which could only mean she was ready to fall over the precipice of passion. Marsh cut the leash on his body and raced after her, swiftly catching her pace and location, and completing this blissful ride together.

Marsh did not cease kissing her and caressing her for a long time after the rapturous moment subsided into a peaceful afterglow of contentment. He held her tenderly in his embrace and closed his eyes, fully absorbing the uniqueness and strength of this moment and bond.

He admitted to himself that Randee was right about him wanting and needing to settle down with her, was right about him being unable to stay away from her, even for a short time. Yes, he was hooked by her. .

"Good-night, Marsh," she murmured sleepily, nestling closer.

"Good-night, love," he whispered against her silky hair. Marsh was content, yet worried. In his arms was the answer to his needs, but beyond them was a threat which could rip her from them. What a dilemma! She wasn't safe with him or without him. Mercy, how he wished this moment could last forever, how he wished there was no such thing as the Epson Gang or his troubled past. How he wished he could ride home in the morning and introduce his love to his parents. He had already lost his family to that vicious gang, and if he wasn't careful, he could lose his first and only love to their brutal evil.

Marsh glanced at the precious bundle beside him. A bittersweet smile claimed his lips. *What a sly vixen you are, Randee Hollis. You kept chasing me until you convinced me I wanted to capture you. I do love you and want you, but I can't let you die because of me. Somehow, I have to find a place where you'll be safe until I can come back for you. Whatever I have to say or do to keep you alive, I'll do it. . . .*

Chapter Nineteen

In Wadesville on Friday, Sheriff Brody Wade received a big surprise. A lawyer from Austin arrived to see Randee, explaining to Brody how he had just learned about the Carsons' deaths and how he needed to show Miss Hollis the will which made her the heir to the ranch. Shocked, Brody cleverly revealed that he was Randee's fiancé and that she was away visiting relatives to get over her grief before their marriage. Deceived by the sheriff's claims, the lawyer disclosed how Lee Carson had changed his will two months ago, cutting off Dee Carson Hollis Slade and naming his niece Randee Marie Hollis as sole inheritor of his estate.

The lawyer confided, "I think there was an awful reason why Mr. Carson did not want his sister to inherit his property. He was most adamant about getting his will changed quickly and leaving all he possessed to his niece. Perhaps it had to do with Miss Hollis' stepfather, this Payton Slade. I remember clearly that Mr. Carson's look was most cold when his sister's second husband was mentioned."

Brody stared at the man's retreating back and wondered if he had made a mistake in alerting Randee's family to her location. And if he had made a mistake in sending out those fake posters. If someone wanted the money badly enough, they might injure his love trying to claim it. He knew Storm had been sighted late yesterday in a small town near Fort Worth, but Randee hadn't been with him. He read the telegram again, glad Foley Timms was sneaking down their trail . . . .

Upon rising late that morning after their long night, Marsh wrote another letter to President Grant, using their code names for secrecy. He had to update the President about Brody Wade's involvement and about the clues he and Randee had gathered last night. He told his blond partner that the letter was to a trusted friend — which was the truth — just in case something happened to either or both of them.

He and Randee discussed the matter of how to get the letter mailed, as it seemed dangerous for him to be seen in this area before he could reach Willard Mason with his second letter and have the man straighten out this new mess. "Willard knows I'm not guilty and he has proof of it. He'll find some way to clear the record and get those new posters recalled. Until such time, we have to be extra careful, woman."

"He needs to do it quickly, Marsh, to keep us out of peril. If we can't move around freely, we can't defeat that gang. Of course, that's probably the reason for them trying to get at you. This tells us that we're getting too close to them and they're getting nervous. I'm sorry I was the one who gave them a weapon to use against you."

"Don't think that way, my clever partner. We couldn't have planned better strategy to draw them into the open."

"I'm glad you aren't angry with me. After all, I did do it for the wrong reason, and they were careless slips. It won't happen again."

"This time, I'll hide outside of town and you'll ride in to mail these two letters. I know a beautiful stranger will snatch some attention from the locals, but try not to be more enticing than necessary," he teased.

"I'll be on my best behavior, Mr. Logan," she promised.

"Let's get out of this area first. I know a small town a day's ride from here, where it might be safer to handle this task. We can't risk meeting up with those eager cowboys again. We'd really be in big trouble if we started shooting down innocent citizens who've been cleverly misled, even to save our hides."

By three o'clock Saturday afternoon, Randee had mailed the two letters at the stage depot, to be picked up Monday morning. She remained alert, and decided no one was taking particular notice of her. But to be on the safe side, she pretended to shop leisurely for a while in the mercantile store. Later, she went to a restaurant and purchased a nice meal for an early supper with her waiting partner.

Marsh had told her they would ride until dark to put distance between them and this second small town. By Monday evening, they should make it to Wadesville to work on Brody Wade. She realized it was a good thing that Marsh had not come into town; this one, as with the other place, had posters of Storm Hayden mounted in the stage depot and in other locations! That told her how widespread the false posters were. Clearly, her love was in jeopardy.

Randee rejoined Marsh and reported her activities. He smiled at her success and confidence. They talked a few minutes, then headed for the overland trail to Wadesville, as being seen on a public road would be dangerous. It did not matter, as trouble struck quickly.

After topping a hill and heading down the other side, Marsh suddenly motioned for Randee to halt. They reined their mounts, and he looked around. Tension showed in his gaze and expression, and in the way his body was taut. Randee asked, "What's wrong?"

"I heard a horse whinny. My gut instinct says something's up."

She watched him twist in his saddle and scan their surroundings. He was wary and alert, and had good reason to be. Riders came at them from all directions, shutting off any escape route. Fear seized her.

Marsh quickly assessed the situation and knew flight was impossible. He couldn't shoot the men, who obviously made up a legal posse. All he could do was curse his second blunder and wait for the riders to approach them. He hastily warned, "No gunfire, Randee."

"What are we going to do?" she asked frantically, noting the size of the group encircling them, and the silver stars on several vests.

"Nothing we can do except surrender," he replied sullenly.

"After you explain—"

Marsh interrupted her, "Let me do the talking. Keep quiet."

Randee froze as she recognized one of the lawmen. "That's Foley Timms on the big roan," she murmured fearfully.

"Recognize any of the others?" he asked instantly.

Randee's gaze looked over the posse and she shook her head. "I must have been seen and trailed," she whispered. "I'm sorry, Marsh."

"It wasn't your fault, woman. This was a neatly planned trap, and I stupidly rode right into it. Seems Wade and Timms outguessed me."

"They can't harm you, because those posters aren't for real."

"Look at those faces. Do you think they would believe me?"

Randee eyed the numerous riders and the guns in

their hands. It looked bad for them, especially for her love. "You have to try," she said.

Foley Timms halted his mount nearby and grinned triumphantly at Marsh. He announced to his men, "We got him, boys. You'll each get your share of the reward when it arrives. He's tricky, so keep your eyes and ears open. Wouldn't surprise me none if he's been riding with that Epson Gang." To Marsh, he said, "We heard you were in this area, so we've been waiting for you to ride this way, figured you would. Your wicked days are over, Hayden. We're gonna hang you at noon Monday. Too late to do it today and Sunday ain't proper."

Marsh knew he was wasting his breath, but he tried to bluff the posse. He responded pointedly, "I bet you have, Marshal Timms. There's only one problem; those reward posters are false. You boys can't earn any reward on me 'cause there isn't one. I've been trailing that gang for months, and somebody wants me stopped. This little trick won't work, 'cause I'm not Storm Hayden; I'm Marsh Logan from Jacksboro. I'm after that gang because they raided my place and killed my family. If you don't believe me, check with Willard Mason in Fort Worth. He can prove I'm innocent of this ridiculous charge."

Timms scoffed, "You can't fool us, Hayden. We got you dead to rights. Every place you've been seen, bodies have been left behind. I've been investigating you for weeks. You can do all the denying you want, but we don't believe you. Do we, boys?"

The greedy men promptly concurred because they didn't want to lose their slice of this big reward pie. "Let's get him back to jail."

"You heard 'em, Hayden," Timms said, laughing coldly.

"What about the girl?" one of the men queried.

Foley's eyes roamed the apprehensive blonde, and he

grinned at some private joke. "We can't leave her out here alone, too dangerous. We'll take her into town with us and I'll question her there. If the report's correct, she's not involved with Hayden's crimes."

"That telegram you showed us said she's Sheriff Wade's woman, said she's Hayden's prisoner. That true, girl?" another man asked.

Before Randee could answer, Marsh replied, "The stage she was on was attacked by Indians and I rescued her. I'm taking her back home because she's paying me to do so. She's in no danger."

"She is wearing a gun," another man remarked.

"He probably has her fooled. You know how trusting women are."

"Yeah, you said he was a sly varmint, Marshal."

Randee and Marsh had no choice but to be led back into town. At the jail, the names of the posse were recorded and a promise of payment was given. Marsh was locked inside a cell, and Foley Timms told Randee to take a seat at the local sheriff's desk.

After everyone cleared the office, Timms leaned against the wall and glued his gaze on Randee. "You best git out of this town on the next stage, girl, or you're in big trouble. I'm only releasing you because I know you're Brody Wade's sweetheart, and he's spoken up on your behalf. If you stay here, you'll have to witness Hayden's hanging at noon Monday, and that ain't a pretty sight. Once people learn you were traveling with him, your reputation will be blacker than old ink. These townfolk are mighty nervous about that gang, and might get nervous about you. It would be kind of hard for one marshal to protect you against a bloodthirsty mob."

Randee glared at the cocky man and said, "You know he isn't guilty! If you harm him, you're the one who'll be in big trouble. Contact Mr. Willard Mason at the Fort Worth newspaper. He'll tell you the truth. He's known

Marsh Logan for years."

"Well, now, I can't rightly do that, Miss Hollis. You see, Mr. Mason was reported killed a few days past. If he's the only one who can clear Hayden's name, I'm afraid Hayden's in a terrible bind."

At that stunning disclosure, Randee's lovely face paled and she trembled. "Willard's dead?"

"Afraid so," Timms replied nonchalantly. "Anything else I can do for you?" he offered almost sarcastically.

"Let me speak with Marsh privately," she demanded, rising.

"I can't do that, Miss Hollis; he's a dangerous prisoner. Why don't you go get yourself settled at the hotel, and get ready to catch that Monday morning stage heading southward?" he suggested.

Randee angrily retorted, "I want to speak to the local sheriff. He'll listen to me."

"He's gone home. I'm in charge here. Didn't you know, U.S. Marshals have more authority than local lawmen? What I say, goes."

"Damn you! You know this is a frame!" she shouted at him.

"Where's your proof, Miss Hollis?" he taunted.

"This isn't over, Marshal Timms. You'll regret this day."

The man straightened and scowled. "Are you threatening the law, Miss Hollis? Do you realize I can imprison you for such insults?"

Randee knew she couldn't help Marsh if she allowed this vile beast to capture her, so she frowned at him and fell silent. She glanced at the alert Marsh and sighed in distress. She whirled and left the office, heading for the telegraph station. She knew Foley Timms was watching her from the window, but she didn't care. If he had lied about Willard Mason's death, she had to alert the man to their peril. It probably wouldn't do any good, but she would telegraph Brody Wade for help. If he wanted to impress her, perhaps he would halt this crazy episode, even if she had to marry him to get Marsh free!

It was almost closing time when she reached the telegraph station. To her horror, she was told that the lines were down and no messages could be sent out before Monday's repairs! She asked how far she was from Fort Worth and from Wadesville: Both were too distant to allow her to get there, obtain help, and return before . . .

No! her mind screamed, she could not let Marsh hang. But if she tried to break "Storm Hayden" out of jail, she would be viewed and chased as a criminal. She was partly responsible for her love being captured and threatened, so she had to think of something.

Saturday night was busy and noisy in the small town. Randee had registered at the hotel and was pacing her room pensively. She figured that Marsh would be guarded closely until noon Monday, so how could she rescue him? Their horses and gear were in the livery stable down the street, but how to get Marsh out of jail was the problem.

Inside the jail, Foley Timms and two of his men were harassing Marsh. With a satanic gleam in his eye, Foley taunted, "I have you at my mercy, Logan, and these hands are itching to get at you. Ever experienced real pain? I bet a tough gunslinger like you would die before bending or breaking, wouldn't you?" Timms looked Marsh over sullenly and scratched his greasy head. "Maybe I'm giving you too much credit for strength and prowess. It don't make no never mind, because I'm gonna see how much you got. You would be real disappointed in me if I didn't prove you right about me, wouldn't you?"

Marsh held silent, but caught the name Timms had used. That told him the insidious lawman believed him and was ignoring the truth, which revealed how dangerous and evil the man was. Never—even when captured by the bounty hunger—had Marsh felt more vulnerable or helpless than he did at this minute, locked inside a sturdy jail. Or so the secret agent prematurely thought . . .

"You've guessed the truth, haven't you?" Timms taunted merrily. "Won't do you any good. You'll hang Monday, just like I said. How much does the girl know? Speak up, the truth, or she's dead too."

"You're making a big mistake, Timms. I'm a U.S. Marshal, who's working undercover on this mission. I've already reported my findings to my superior. I know about you and Brody Wade's connections to the Epson Gang, and my report's been filed. If you're involved in my hanging, they'll have all the evidence they need to hang you in return. The law won't believe my death was an accident, a mistake made because of those fake posters—not with you handling it."

"You're lying," Timms declared, but looked anxious at that news.

"You willing to bet your life and neck on it?" Marsh challenged.

"I've already sent word to Brody that I have you and the girl. He'll arrive just in time to see you swing and to carry his woman home to comfort her in his big bed." When he saw Marsh's uncontrollable reaction to those statements, he laughed devilishly. "I think I'll go fetch that girl and lock her up as your accomplice. If you're really a lawman, then you know what her fate will be inside a jail or a prison. By the time your little report is read and acted upon, your little whore will be used up by those prison guards. Tell me what you know, who you notified, and keep your mouth shut to her—and she'll be safe."

For two hours, Marsh was beaten brutally and questioned, but he held silent. His pride was injured as badly as his body was. There was no way he could save his love, no way to protect her. It looked as if he was going to die this time, die without Randee knowing the truth.

Mercy, this defeat tasted bitter in his throat, especially when combined with the metallic taste of his blood. If only his hands and feet weren't bound securely and he wasn't getting weaker by the minute from this savage assault. No escape. No help. No future.

Randee went down the hall to the water closet and pretended to be bathing. She eluded her guard by sneaking out the window. She located the local preacher's home and explained her perilous dilemma.

"Please, sir, you have to help us. At least find a way to get this message to Willard Mason in Fort Worth. They told me the lines are down, so I can't telegraph for help."

"I can't ride to the next town this late at night, Miss Hollis. I have church services in the morning; it's Sunday."

"God will forgive you for missing services one time in order to save an innocent man's life!" she stormed at him angrily. "Please, you have to help us. They're going to hang him at noon Monday."

The religious man considered her plea and relented slightly. "I'll send my older son with your message. Will that do?"

Randee smiled and nodded. "Tell him to hurry, and not to fail. I'll reward both of you as soon as possible. Thank you, sir." Randee gave him the letter to Willard, which explained the dire situation and asked him to bring help and proof of Marsh's innocence quickly.

Randee sneaked back inside the hotel washroom and

426

unlocked the door. She returned to her room and prepared things for her daring plan. She could not depend on help arriving in time to save Marsh's life; she could only hope that Willard's imminent explanation would call off the search for them after she aided her love's escape.

She needed to see Marsh to try to let him know of her plans. She went to the jail and knocked persistently. When Foley's man answered, she demanded to see Marsh Logan. The man refused.

Randee's gaze went past his thin frame and saw Marsh's battered body secured by ropes to the bars. Her eyes widened in disbelief. "What have you done to him? This is an outrage! This is criminal!"

"He tried to escape while being questioned," the man lied.

"That's ridiculous! I swear you'll all be punished. Don't you know how much trouble you're in? He's a lawman who's working secretly for the governor," she alleged desperately to frighten the guard. "When the State Police arrive and they see what you've done to their best man, you'll be the one hanged! If you keep him alive until they get here Monday, I'll speak in your favor at your trial. Let me talk to Marsh, see if he's injured badly. He might need a doctor."

"Marshal Timms said nobody was to get inside."

"Marshal Timms is a liar and a villain! He's responsible for those false posters because he wants to get Marsh Logan off that gang's trail. If you ask me, Timms is part of that vicious gang. If you allow him to harm Marsh, you'll be just as guilty of murder. The governor will have all of you hunted down and killed."

"What's the trouble here?" Foley Timms asked from behind her.

Randee turned and glared at the offensive man. "You're a disgrace to that silver star, Marshal Timms.

How could you beat an unharmed, imprisoned man? I insist on speaking with Marsh Logan."

Timms shrugged and said, "Fine."

Randee could not conceal her astonishment. She was led inside to Marsh's cell and the door was unlocked. She feared a trap, but had to continue her action. "Marsh?" she called to him, shaking his sagging shoulder. His eyes opened slightly and looked at her. "I'll get a doctor."

Marsh summoned his flagging strength and said, "Don't bother, woman. Just get out of my sight. You're the reason I'm here. If you hadn't distracted me with your pretty face and body, I would be free."

"What?" she murmured confusedly, anguish gnawing at her.

Marsh had to say anything to get Randee out of there, or she would be in worse peril than he was. He had to save her because he loved her. He wanted her gone. He didn't want her seeing him and remembering him like this — a beaten animal, one caged and whipped.

"You heard the man, Miss Hollis; go home. He's already confessed, so there ain't nothing you can do to stop his hanging."

"I've sent for help, Marsh; don't give up hope. We have until Monday noon. After all you've done to help capture that gang, even if you're guilty of being Storm Hayden, they'll pardon you."

"Get out, woman; it's too late. Those posters are for real."

Randee didn't care if the men heard her words as she refuted, "You're just saying that to make me leave. I won't go!"

Each word came forth with agony and difficulty as he scoffed deceitfully, cruelly, "Don't you understand, woman? I was only using you. I'm no better than Payton Slade. I wouldn't ever marry a woman I could have so easily. I was only enjoying you on the trail and aggravat-

428

ing Brody Wade. I wanted that reward you were offering so I could leave Texas. I told you I was no good, a carefree rogue, a drifter; but that's the only truth I spoke to you."

"That isn't true! Why are you saying such things?" she asked painfully. "Let me help you. When the telegraph lines are repaired, I'll alert the State Police. Help will arrive in time to save you."

He tried to say coldly and unfeelingly, "Are you deaf, woman? I'm guilty, so they won't release me. You don't know me. You're just as blind and gullible as your mother, and I duped you as easily as Payton Slade duped her. Get her out of here, Marshal."

"You heard him, Miss Hollis. Consider yourself lucky we caught him before he used you up and while Sheriff Wade still wants you. He's the one who put out that false tale about you being Hayden's captive so you wouldn't be harmed or arrested. As a favor to Brody, I'm letting you go, but you deserve to hang with him if you ask me."

Randee stared at Marsh, who was eyeing her so bitterly and coldly. Tears dampened her lashes and she could not seem to move. "Are you sure this is the way you want it, Marsh?" she asked sadly.

"Don't beg, woman, you're too strong and proud for groveling. I rode my path like I wanted to; now, it's time to pay the price. If I don't try to escape again and get myself beaten for it, I'll be able to walk to the gallows like a man."

"Is that how you want to be remembered, for dying like a man?"

"What else is there in the end? Go home, Randee, and beg your sweetheart to forgive you for letting me make a fool of you."

"You certainly accomplished that, Mr. Logan. You won't mind if I don't hang around to watch you go out with pride."

"You should. Spurned women should enjoy their revenge."

"I'm only vengeful when it comes to the Epson Gang. Too bad you won't be around to witness their defeat. Good-bye, Marsh."

Marsh glanced at her, praying his gaze and voice wouldn't expose his torment and love. If she believed him and left town, she would be safe. He knew she wouldn't return to Brody Wade, and he hoped she would recover the hidden money and go somewhere to begin a new life. Mercy, how he hated for that life not to include him.

Randee looked at Marshal Foley Timms and said, "It appears you were right, Marshal Timms, but I'm not going to apologize. No matter who or what he is, what you've done to him is terrible. Whatever happened to civilized law and order?"

The defiled lawman sneered. "It exists only when and where men allow it, Miss Hollis. I'll escort you back to the hotel."

Randee replied, "No thank you. I can find my own way back. I'm used to taking care of myself. What time is the stage Monday?"

"Ten o'clock," the other man answered.

Randee hurriedly left the sheriff's office and returned to her rented room. She flung herself across the bed and cried. Not because she believed Marsh — she did not — but because of how cruelly he had been treated and because he had groveled to save her life.

"What now, my love?" she murmured, feeling utterly helpless.

At the jail, in a desperate attempt to obtain information, Marsh was beaten again by Foley Timms and his two men. . . .

* * *

Randee arranged her bed to make it appear as if she were sleeping there, in the event someone peeked into her room during the night. After scanning the area below, she climbed out her window and dropped to the ground in the alley. She halted and listened for danger, detecting none. She made her way to the livery stable and broke into a side window. The nervous blonde saddled both horses and sneaked them out the back way. Gingerly she walked them to the rear of the store next to the jail and dropped their reins to keep them from leaving.

She cautiously made her way to the barred window of Marsh's cell and, using a discarded wooden box, peered inside the jail. There was one man on duty inside the office, asleep with his head on the desk. Marsh wasn't moving, and she dared not try to signal him. Was it her imagination, she wondered, or did he look worse?

Randee looked around the corner of the building and saw another guard on the porch, one who was leaning against the wall and appeared to be dozing. Her narrowed green eyes roamed the dark street and she prayed no other guards were hidden from sight. It would be like Foley Timms to expect her behavior and to be ready to thwart her.

Still, she had to take this chance as security might be tighter tomorrow night. She drew her pistol and edged her way along the wall. Reaching the man, she rendered him unconscious with a blow to the head. Positioning him so he would not fall over, she propped his hat to cover his eyes. She searched his pockets and found no key. She would have no choice now but to awaken the guard at the desk and try to bluff her way into the jail. It was unnecessary, as the door was not bolted.

She inhaled deeply and wondered if she should halt this madness. She could not. She eased open the door and slipped inside, watching the dozing guard carefully. She sneaked closer and closer until she reached him, then rendered him unconscious in the same manner. Grabbing the cell keys, she unlocked the door and rushed to Marsh's side.

He had been beaten again. She tried to arouse him, but his injured body resisted. She fetched a water bucket and splashed water on his face, slightly reviving him. "We have to get out of here, partner," she whispered close to his ear.

Marsh's swollen eyes blinked in confusion and he tried to speak through lips which were puffy and bruised. He ached all over and he feared he had broken ribs. Dried blood and still-flowing red liquid seemingly covered his handsome face. "It's to-o late, Ran-dee. Get a-way . . . from here."

"Not without you, partner. Gather your strength and help me get you to our horses. I'm not letting you hang, Monday or ever."

Throbbing pain viciously attacked him when he tried to obey, and his mind spun dizzily when he lifted his head. He knew he could not make it and she was endangering herself. "Get out, wo-man; I don't wan-t you . . . near me."

"That's too bad, partner, because I'm saving your ass whether you help me or not." Randee threw a blanket to the floor and rolled Marsh off the bunk as gently as possible. When he groaned in agony, she ordered, "Shut up, Logan; you've been in worse pain and perils before." Grasping the edges of the material, she shrugged and heaved as she dragged him along the floor until she reached the back door, breathing erratically at her arduous exertions. "Damn, but you're heavy. Lend assistance any time the mood strikes you," she teased.

Randee unbolted the back door and looked outside. All appeared safe. She left Marsh where he was, out cold again, and went to fetch a drunk who had fallen in the alley. She managed to get the dazed man on his feet, and

432

helped him wobble into the cell. She placed him on the bunk and covered him, hoping he would be mistaken for Marsh long enough for them to get far away from this dangerous town.

Returning to her love's prone body, she finally managed to arouse Marsh enough to get him to his horse. She was overjoyed when Midnight obeyed her command to get down closer to the ground. She labored until she had Marsh bound securely to his saddle. Quickly, she returned to fetch his weapons. She closed the jail door and mounted Rojo, hanging Marsh's gunbelt over her pommel.

Taking Marsh's reins, she walked the two horses down the alley to the edge of town. She hesitated for a few minutes and listened intently, then walked them away from the shelter of the last building. Marsh was unconscious, but he couldn't fall off his horse, and hopefully he couldn't feel much pain, as the impending ride would be swift and tormenting in his battered condition. There was no time to tend his injuries, so she headed for a secret place which she recalled, a place which would require over a day's ride without many stops. . . .

An hour later, Foley Timms unlocked Randee's door and sneaked a glance inside. Noting the shapely bundle in her bed, he grinned and left. He had them both fooled. He wasn't planning to hang Marsh Logan Monday; that would be too dangerous and suspicious. He was planning to let Miss Randee Hollis free him tomorrow night, after she saw him again and couldn't help herself. He wasn't deceived by their words and conduct; those two had something between them, something Brody wasn't going to like at all. Once the ravishing blonde helped Marsh escape, he would take a posse to hunt them down and have Marsh slain during his attempted escape. Who could blame him under the circumstances? No one, Foley decided smugly.

At the jail, the guard outside had awakened. He had looked inside to see the other man sleeping peacefully and the prisoner still lying on his bunk. He assumed, that while dozing, he had struck his head against the wall and knocked himself out cold. When Foley Timms walked over to check on things before retiring for the night, the man unknowingly pointed inside to the drunk and said, "All's fine, Marshal. Not a peep from anyone." He closed the door.

It was nearly three in the morning. The devious marshal was exhausted from his gambling, whoring, drinking, and from the beating of his captive. Foley Timms stretched and yawned. "I don't expect trouble tonight, but keep alert. She'll make her move tomorrow just like I said. We'll set our plan into motion in the morning. Good night."

Randee pushed them all night and all day Sunday, halting briefly several times for the horses to rest and graze, and to handle a few vital tasks. At each stop, she forced water down Marsh's throat and checked him closely. She had bandaged his injuries as best she could at the first available opportunity, paying special attention to his cracked ribs, which she had bound snugly with cloth and rope. She knew he needed to be lying flat, but it was impossible to stop. She couldn't even risk going to another town or fetching a doctor, because the same thing could happen. Or worse, they could send for Marshal Foley Timms. Surely by now their escape was known and a posse was swiftly pursuing them. They had to keep going, even if the unconscious Marsh wasn't aware of their actions and progress.

Randee had taken every precaution she could think of,

from dusting their trail with underbrush, to traveling in water to conceal their tracks, to doubling back, to making a false trail one time. But she couldn't afford any more delays. She had to get Marsh to a secluded line-shack on the Carson Ranch where she could take better care of him. Thank goodness, she knew a lot about injuries and doctoring, but travel was the worst thing for a man with such injuries. The house, and the attic, were both too dangerous to use because Brody would probably check them and have them watched. With luck, no one knew about the deserted shack in the thick tree line miles from the house. . . .

Chapter Twenty

Daylight was almost gone by the time they reached the line-shack. Quickly, Randee checked the sturdy structure and surrounding area, relieved to see that it appeared as safe and secluded as she remembered. She coaxed Midnight to lie down so she could cut the ropes which held Marsh to the animal and saddle. She let him remain there a while, knowing he must be in agonizing pain from their swift journey — if he had enough awareness to even feel pain. The few times that he had roused, it had not been fully, and she could imagine the haze of torment which must be dulling his mind.

She prepared a rope corral near a stream and led the horses there to graze and rest. She talked soothingly to them, thanking them for their assistance and hoping they could understand they had saved two lives with their demanding pace and loyalties. As gently as possible, she dragged the unconscious man inside and labored until she had him on a cot. She removed his boots and clothes and checked his injuries. His body was bruised and bleeding in several places. She tended him gently.

Not once did Marsh stir, and she was worried. She paid close attention to his head injury and blackish-blue rib area. What if she had pushed him too hard and done worse damage to her love? No, she scolded herself, it was worse to hang for crimes he hadn't committed.

Randee knew they needed food. Marsh especially would need hot soup to revitalize his ailing body and to get past his tumescent lips. Hopefully Brody would assume she couldn't make it this far and this fast with a badly injured man so he wouldn't check the Carson Ranch today. She mounted Rojo bareback and headed for the house. If she was lucky, there would be vegetables still growing wild in the garden, and the telegraph lines would still be down, preventing a message to Brody.

The young woman approached the area cautiously. Everything was still and quiet. No doubt Brody would arrive tomorrow and place a guard on the house. Hurriedly she went inside and gathered supplies, then raced to the garden to pick vegetables. She carried as much as she could manage to where Rojo was waiting patiently. After covering their tracks, she headed back to where she had left Marsh.

Randee locked the door and approached Marsh. He hadn't moved. Again, she tended his wounds — this time with the medicine which she had taken from the house — but he did not stir. She prepared a fire, concluding it was safe to allow escaping smoke at night, and cooked a large pot of soup. She mashed the vegetables into a soft mush and added liquid, then tried to force some down Marsh's throat. She succeeded in getting only a little inside him, but that was better than none at all. Time and sleep were what he needed most.

The sun would be rising soon, so Randee doused the fire. The covered soup would stay warm a long time, and she would try to feed him again in a few hours. Randee hadn't slept since Saturday morning, and it was nearly dawn Monday. She was exhausted; her body ached and pleaded for mercy. She examined Marsh once more, and believed he was breathing easier this time. She tossed a thin cover over his naked frame. After unrolling her sleeping bag, she collapsed on it and closed her eyes. If trouble came, there was little she could do, and nothing if she was too dazed by fatigue to think or react.

"Help us and protect us," she prayed, then yielded to slumber.

Shortly after noon, Randee was yanked from dreamland by Marsh's moans and thrashings upon the wooden cot. She was at his side instantly. "It's all right, Marsh. We're safe now. Lie still and quiet."

His tumid blue eyes moved and opened very slowly. He tried to clear his wits, but the pain from head to foot attacked him maliciously. He groaned and winced and breathed erratically.

She caught his hand before he could rub his sore eyes and held it. "Don't move or try to talk, partner, or you'll do worse damage than I did with that bone-jarring ride. We're miles from that town, Marsh, so you're safe," she told him soothingly. "I was afraid to look for a doctor, but I've tended you as best I could. Can you eat some soup? It'll make you stronger."

"Where . . . are . . . we?" he asked, struggling with each word. "How —" He was too weak to finish, but she understood.

Randee explained the jailbreak and their location. "Is there anything I can do to lessen the pain? Did I miss an injury?"

Marsh looked at her pale face, so full of love and concern, and he tried to smile. He grimaced instead because his jaw and mouth hurt; even his teeth protested. "I said . . . some . . . terrible —"

Randee touched his swollen mouth lightly and hushed him. "I know you didn't mean them. You were only trying to save my hide."

"Don't make me laugh," he entreated almost pitifully. "I'm one big ache."

438

"Sorry, partner. It's just that I'm so damn glad you're alive and awake. You had me worried. You've been out since Saturday night."

He glanced at the window. Randee had shielded it, so he couldn't determine what kind of light was filtering inside. More so, he had a hard time focusing his puffy eyes. "What day is it?"

"Monday," she replied, just before he went back to sleep.

Randee stroked his ebony hair and kissed his forehead. "Don't worry, my love, I won't let anyone harm you. I love you, Marsh Logan, and I can't lose you now, not ever. Please get well."

Marsh roused again about nine that night. Randee was at his side quickly to force him to lie still. When he asked about the date, she told him it was still Monday, the day he was to have been hanged.

He struggled to clear his wits, but it was difficult. He gazed at the woman kneeling beside the cot and was amazed by her actions. "You making a practice of saving my life, woman?" he asked.

"You would have done the same for me, partner. If not for you, Marsh Logan, neither of us would be alive tonight. You've taught me so much and done so much for me. You inspired this courage and determination which saved you back there. I couldn't have done this without your training. I was able to rescue you and avoid recapture only because of what we've done together. If you weren't so damn special, I wouldn't have broken you out of jail and become an outlaw."

"Don't give me the credit, woman," he argued softly.

"I have to, Mr. Logan. You taught me stealth, persistence, patience, and prowess. You've shown me what it is to put someone else's life before your own. You allowed us to be friends and partners, even if I am only a woman. I depend on you, I trust you, I learn from you." When she saw his look of skepticism, she coaxed, "There's no reason to be embarrassed about your capture and condition; it happens to the best of us. I know it must be hard to feel vulnerable and helpless. But if you were right and perfect all the time, Marsh, you wouldn't be human. Can you get some soup down?"

Marsh was touched by her words and mood. He felt the same way. He tried to smile as he nodded. He knew he must look a mess, and he felt awful. He hated being unable to take care of her, and hated always endangering her. Never had he met a woman, or man, so compassionate and so unselfish. This time, she had risked all to save his life, and he would repay her generously. He watched her prepare his meal and return to his bed. She gently placed her sleeping roll beneath his head to raise it. Then, she fed him the nourishing soup as if he were a sick child. Even if he had been able to help himself, he would have allowed her to do this task which made her happy. It was strange: Half the time, he was angry and humiliated at being helpless; the other half, he didn't seem to mind at all. His pride was as bruised as his body was, but she made it easier to endure his weakness.

"Where did this come from?" he inquired between spoonfuls.

She told him what she had done upon their arrival and saw him about to protest her perilous conduct. "Don't scold me, Mr. Logan. We have to eat, and I was careful. I used all those skills you taught me. You finish this soup and get more rest. That's an order, partner."

Marsh was too weak and fuzzy-headed to disobey. He thanked her after he finished, and soon fell asleep. Randee did the same.

* * *

By Tuesday at midday, Willard Mason had sent word to every sheriff's office within three days' travel of Fort Worth, telling them the posters were fakes and to destroy them. He had the governor's office issue a statement saying Marsh Logan was a special agent for the Texas authorities and was not an outlaw, which Willard published in his newspaper and sent to all others in the area to do the same.

Willard knew he was destroying most of Marsh's cover, but it was the only way he could end this perilous situation involving Storm Hayden, and keep his friends alive. He cleared up the episode about the jailbreak, explaining it had been necessary to prevent an illegal and erroneous hanging. Since there was no evidence against Foley Timms yet, all the man received was a reprimand and a personal warning from his superior. Willard reported in the newspaper how the gang was responsible for the false posters because Marsh Logan was hot on their trail and about to unmask them. He wrote of how Marsh had been framed and nearly killed. He warned everyone to destroy those fake posters and to leave the special agent alone to complete his mission, which would benefit all Texans. Afterwards, all Willard Mason could do was hope Randee and Marsh got the news and realized it was safe to come out of hiding, if they were alive and well.

In the shack, Marsh was awake again. He felt a little stronger, but his body ached all over and his mind wouldn't seem to unfog completely for any length of time. Randee hovered over him, forcing soup and water into him and tending his injuries. Most were healing, but his cracked ribs gave him terrible pain when he breathed and moved. He knew he had no choice but to remain abed until he was stronger. What use was he to anybody, especially to them, in this sorry state?

His head cleared for a while today and he stayed awake longer each time he roused, but it was difficult. He realized he must be terribly weak because he couldn't stay awake for more than twenty minutes. He figured it would be a week or two before he could ride. He wondered what was happening away from this secluded cabin. And he wondered what he should say to this woman he loved.

Randee returned from her bath at the stream and smiled at Marsh. "Would you like me to wash you off a little?" she offered. "I'm sure it would refresh you greatly. However, my bearded lover, a shave is unwise with those facial injuries. We don't want any wayward whiskers getting into these healing cuts."

"If you help me, I can make it to the stream."

"You would pass out before you reached the door and injure yourself again. That would be bad for me. Let me tell you, partner, you're heavy when you're out cold."

"It's my bullheadedness that weighs so much."

"I see we're feeling better today, joking a little bit. Good. That still doesn't mean you can get up and dance around. After that jarring ride I gave you, it's a wonder you survived. Stay in bed a few more days. Your body's trying to heal and it needs your cooperation."

"Yes, ma'am," he replied, yawning as his eyelids grew heavy.

Randee did not tell Marsh she was lacing his soup with laudanum which she had taken from the ranch house. Now that he was getting stronger, she felt she needed it to keep him abed to heal properly. He was so stubborn — yes, bullheaded — and would be up too soon to get back to their task. She knew he was worried about their safety, and about what she had done to rescue him. Until the matter was cleared up, they were both fugitives.

* * *

Hours later, Randee pan-bathed him and helped him eat more soup, rabbit this time, which she had snared. She assisted him with sitting up for a while, until the drug sent him back into dreamland.

Wednesday, Randee allowed Marsh to get up twice and walk to the door and back a few times to get his circulation moving. She almost felt guilty when he commented on how weak and shaky he was. She vanquished it by telling herself she was only doing what was best for her love, letting him heal and keeping him out of danger. If she let him get back on the trail now, he would be placing his life in jeopardy.

Thursday morning, she let him walk outside for a while and get fresh air and a little more exercise. That night, she helped him to the stream to wash off, which enlivened him until he devoured the last of the soup with its medication.

As Randee watched him sleep, her eyes lovingly traced every line on his handsome face. The bruises had changed colors, indicating they were getting better. The swelling around his eyes and mouth had lessened. The small breaks on his face were closing up nicely and shouldn't scar. She teased her fingers over his chest, enjoying the silky feel of the moist black hair which curled around them. Her heart fluttered wildly and her body warmed with desire. She loved this man and wanted to spend her life with him. Would she be given the chance?

Friday morning, Randee did not tell Marsh he was devouring the last of the biscuits and gravy and coffee. She watched him enjoy the meal as she planned her trip to the ranch for more supplies. She should have gone last night while she had the cover of darkness, but hadn't thought of it! When he asked why she wasn't joining him, she smiled and said she had eaten before he awakened — which wasn't true, and she hoped he didn't notice her growling belly as she sipped coffee. She waited for him to succumb to the laudanum before she left the cabin.

Surely no one was searching for them in this area, so Marsh would be safe for a few hours. She had to fetch supplies, and she could not let him stop her. She left the chestnut mare hidden in the woods near the house and covered the rest of the distance on foot.

She quickly gathered what she needed and was about to leave when she heard horses approaching. She looked out the window and nearly fainted; it was Brody Wade, her stepfather, and several men! She hid the bundle and concealed herself behind a sofa near a side wall, as there was no way she could sneak out of the house and risk capture.

Brody and Payton Slade entered the house, talking. Randee listened closely to their revealing words, shocked by her discoveries.

Brody was saying, "As I told you, Mr. Slade, the lawyer from Austin told me Randee inherited everything. Lee Carson changed his will two months ago, from your wife to his niece."

Payton responded, "Randee and me are very close, Sheriff, so that ain't a problem. I just want to look around. Any news on her?"

"That business about arrests and jailbreaks has been cleared up. Seems it was a stupid mistake over fake posters. The governor sent out word he was innocent, claimed the man is an agent working for him. It was in all the newspapers this week. Those false posters have been called back, and Hayden — I mean Marsh Logan — has been exonerated."

"No charges against my stepdaughter for bustin' him

444

outta jail?"

"None. She had no choice. Marsh Logan is a free man. As soon as he hears the news, he'll turn up some place. So will Randee."

"What's goin' on between those two?" Payton inquired, his tone and expression lewdly suggestive.

Brody caught signs which he didn't like. "I wouldn't know."

"I thought you said you two was to marry soon. Ain't you a mite curious about what they been doin' out there alone? Randee's a beautiful woman, a mighty temptin' one."

"I explained how Randee hired him to help her track down the killers of Lee and Sarah Elizabeth Carson. I don't have anything to worry about where's he's concerned. She loves me."

"You best worry where I'm concerned," her stepfather disclosed. "Randee's ma lost our baby a while back an' ain't doin' too well. Me an Randee will probably marry an' settle here if Dee don't make it. I'll give you a warnin', Sheriff, me an' Randee love each other, so don't interfere in our private business. 'Course, we didn't know it till after I was strapped with her ma. If her ma don't live, Randee will want me over you or that drifter."

"What are you talking about?" Brody asked coldly, suspiciously.

"That's why Randee left home, 'cause she was pinin' for me. When I find her, she'll be mine. I plan to sell my place in Kansas an' move here, even if I have to give up her ma. You the one who sent that packet of information to Dee?"

"What packet?" Brody asked deceitfully, riled by his mistake.

"I got this package with newspaper clippin's about the raid an' an offer to buy the ranch. 'Course I won't sell it for any price. Strange thing, there was a letter from

Sarah Elizabeth enclosed. I wonder how a dead woman wrote a letter about Randee being in New York." He chuckled. "That girl is a real surprise. She was just trying to lure me here an' let me know where she is. Real clever, ain't she?"

"Yep, she's very clever," Brody concurred. "What did your wife say about you coming here to chase after her daughter?"

Payton grinned at the other man. "Dee ain't too smart; she don't know nothing about me an' Randee. Naturally I didn't tell her about the packet, an' she don't know where I am or what I'm doin'. I want to look around a bit, see how much damage was done to the house. When I get finished here, I'll plan a way to locate Randee an' get her back. She's probably scared an' ready to come home to me."

After they talked a while and Payton went upstairs, Brody motioned to his man near the open door. He whispered, "I want this crazy bastard ambushed and killed today. If he thinks I'll let him walk in and take everything, he's dead wrong. Now I know what drove Randee from Kansas; the man's loco and mean," he murmured.

Two days before, Brody had received a shocking and baffling reply to his query to the Nebraska authorities. The response said that Storm Hayden was not and never had been wanted there. Apparently the man was Marsh Logan, a U.S. Marshal, as he and Willard Mason had claimed. Thank goodness, Timms hadn't killed an agent and brought suspicion down on them! But if Logan had filed a report with his superior, as he had claimed to Timms, it would have caused trouble for them by now. Obviously Logan had been bluffing. Brody wondered how much Randee knew about Logan and his assignment. . . .

* * *

Randee remained hidden until the group left, then gathered her bundle and hurried back to the cabin. Willard Mason was still alive, and he had cleared up that Storm Hayden mess. They were free! Safe! Brody was going to have Payton killed before tonight, so her wicked stepfather would be out of hers and her mother's lives forever! No doubt Payton had lied about her mother's condition, and was probably planning to kill Dee the moment he returned home to sell out in Kansas. With his death, her mother would be safe until Randee could reach her. She was glad the lecherous bastard was going to pay for his sins, and she did not feel guilty about not warning him about his lethal peril.

Another thing, Brody had read her mail and sent a warning home, unaware of what he was doing until today. How very thoughtful of the insane Payton to inform the very man who would destroy him. At least Brody was about to do one good thing: rid the world of a demon like Payton Slade. Recalling what she had put in the letter to the land company and what she had told George Light, maybe she still had Brody fooled, even if he knew she had helped Marsh Logan escape.

Marsh Logan, an agent for the governor . . . Was that true? Or had Willard Mason convinced the man to help them with a ruse? It would play right into their hands, as she could use it to further dupe Brody to get evidence against him. How could her fiancé fault her for working with a government agent? Of course, she would claim she had known all along, but had been sworn to secrecy. That would also explain why she had aided Marsh's escape. It was perfect. . . .

Randee observed her sleeping love and wondered how much to tell him. More so, when to tell him. Once he heard this information, he would be up and out of here, injured or not!

*　*　*

For five days, Randee held her silence while she helped Marsh regain his strength and heal. She ceased giving him the laudanum and worked hard to restore his health to normal. She was ready to get this mission going again, to get it over with and see where they stood.

It was shortly after dusk on Wednesday, the twelfth day after he was arrested and beaten. They had eaten early and were strolling around outside. She could tell he felt stronger and his ribs were better. She smiled and asked, "Are we still in pain, partner?"

Marsh looked at her and grinned, then rubbed his sore jaw and side. "Only when I laugh or move or walk or eat," he teased.

"Then you shouldn't do any of those things yet," she replied.

"Does that mean no more secret drugs, partner?"

Randee blushed and inhaled sharply. "How did you know?"

"I didn't until my head cleared; then I figured it out. That's one way to keep a drifter where you want him, but very sneaky, woman."

"Knowing you, Marsh Logan, it was necessary, or risk losing you to a relapse. I didn't save you to let you get yourself killed before you were back at your highest peak of prowess. Ready to tangle with them again?" she inquired, hating to leave this peaceful place.

Marsh stroked his freshly shaven face and gazed into her eyes. "Not tonight, woman. Tonight, I only want to tangle with a reckless vixen," he murmured, pulling her into his embrace.

She cautioned seductively, "Careful or you'll reinjure yourself. You aren't up to physical exertion this soon."

Brushing his lips over hers, he whispered huskily, "Oh, but I am up to this, Doc Hollis. In fact, it's the only

448

medicine I need to get me completely well again. You wouldn't deny your loving patient what he needs, would you?"

Randee grinned receptively, eager to surrender to him after their lengthy abstinence. Every night she had dreamed of this moment, causing her passion to smolder more fiercely each hour. At his touch and smile, it burst into fiery need and her body glowed from within. It was so serene here, so romantic, their natures so close to the wildness that surrounded them. She surrendered uninhibitedly to his caresses and kisses, feeling weak herself for a change.

Marsh knew she had unleashed her bridled desire and was as ready to ride love's wild stallion as he was. His mind spun wildly, but this time it wasn't because of medication; this woman was utterly intoxicating. His bold kisses and caresses were provocative, stimulating, pleasurable. Presently, the only ache he was conscious of was the one in his heart and loins, which would soon be sated. Marsh trailed his lips over the satiny skin of her face and throat, causing her to moan sensuously. Mercy, she was irresistible and tantalizing.

She willingly yielded to his deft hands as they undressed her, then unclothed himself. Marsh's touch was gentle, yet strong and confident as he skillfully explored her trembling body, and Randee responded with all her being. No shame or hesitation threatened to halt their actions. She cuddled against his hard body and enticed him to continue their heady journey in this sensual haven where stars twinkled overhead and night creatures sang to them and playful breezes tried vainly to cool their torrid flesh.

Marsh's lips traveled her shoulders before he lifted each feminine hand to spread kisses over them, hands which had tended him so gently and lovingly. The partial moon did little to lighten the tree-encircled area where they were standing on passion-wobbly legs. He watched the shadows dance over her face and body, and his fingers followed their delightful game. His troubles receded quickly and his thoughts were of Randee alone.

Without unsealing their mouths, Marsh guided them to the lush grass, where they embraced and kissed each other feverishly. As if one entwined spirit, they worked together on increasing each other's desire and on sating the other's needs. Marsh's tongue teased over her chin and down her throat, as if the carefree drifter he was reputed to be. But he knew his destination, and provocatively journeyed to her breasts. His mouth roved the taut peaks which revealed the intensity of her desire. As his lips traversed her torso, his hands moved lower and lower with titillating leisure. His fingers encountered another peak that seemed to beg for attention, which he eagerly supplied.

Randee caressed the sleek muscles of his shoulders and arms and back. Her fingers playfully traced the hard ridges of his spine, all the way to his firm buttocks, which she seductively massaged. It enlivened her to stimulate and pleasure him. Her hands quivered with delight. His body was beautiful, so firm and yet so smooth. She knew he enjoyed making love to her, thrilled to her uncontrollable responses.

"I need you, Marsh, now," she whispered hoarsely. She had made love enough times to assess her distance and pace. She could wait no longer to feel him within her, have him joined to her.

Marsh's throbbing manhood entered her, and she arched to meet his gentle probe. He felt it quiver and threaten to explode as powerfully as the dynamite in his saddlebags. She was so all-consuming that she was his only reality, his only mission tonight. It staggered his senses to taste and feel and hear her surrender.

Locked together, they labored sensuously for the prize

450

which awaited them at the end of this blissful race. They clung together, riding rapturously across love's prairie, which was ablaze with a wildfire. They explored, searched, journeyed, and wandered until they located ecstasy, their destination, and raced into that wondrous paradise . . . .

At last, they relaxed side by side upon the crushed grass. They remained silent, embracing and allowing the beauty of this episode to wash over them serenely. The air was cooler now, as were their bodies. The melodies of crickets, frogs, and night birds still filled their ears. The moon was overhead, giving them more light in their blissful enclosure. The sky was clear of clouds, but scattered with millions of blinking stars. Contentment encased them.

"How did I ever get along before I met you, woman?" he asked tenderly. "You've softened a part of me that I thought was hard forever. It's past time I explain a few things about me."

When Randee remained still and silent, Marsh glanced down at her. He smiled happily. She was cuddled against his side, sound asleep. He realized she must be exhausted after her long vigil over him and utterly relaxed after their passionate bout. He kissed her forehead and murmured, "I don't know how it happened, Randee, but I love you."

Without arousing her, he lifted her in his arms and carried her into the cozy shack. He placed her on the bunk, and he took the sleeping roll on the floor. She curled onto her side, toward him, and sighed dreamily. Another smile curved Marsh's healing mouth upwards. He felt wonderful tonight, strong, alive, invigorated, happy.

The jet-haired man lay on his back, thinking. Tomorrow, he had to expose himself to the woman slumbering nearby. Not only did she deserve the truth, but he couldn't conceal it any longer. In order to protect her from criminal charges and possible injury, he had to reveal his identity to the local authorities — naturally excluding Brody Wade and Marshal Foley Timms. He had to find a way to get her out of this mission so she would be safe until he could complete it quickly. If only he could find some hard evidence against that gang and their accomplices, he could settle the matter within a week or two.

Marsh ran his fingers over his sore wounds and damned his attackers. He vowed that Foley Timms and his boys would pay for their assault and for forcing his love to imperil herself trying to help him. Recalling her actions, his heart seemed to burst with pride and love, and gratitude. He tried not to feel bitter over his recent weakness and defeat. It was hard, because he had allowed them to get captured; he had allowed himself to get beaten and humiliated. But he had weakened only enough to protect Randee. He hadn't betrayed his job and identity: the reasons for the harsh beatings. He envisioned Timms's fury at his silence and strength, but he hadn't let the man break him. The only way Timms could have gotten the information he so desperately and savagely wanted was to have used, threatened, his love. Since the man had feared to do so, did that mean Brody Wade had more influence and authority with the gang than the guileful marshal did?

Marsh glanced over at Randee, and felt his heart drum madly. Soon, she would be walking at his side daily and sleeping beside him every night, if she would marry him. And he would have to be a blind fool not to realize she was as much in love with him as he was with her. He looked around the cabin and reflected on their days here. Maybe this enforced solitude hadn't been so demanding after all . . . .

* * *

Thursday morning, Randee stretched and yawned contentedly as memories of the night before played joyfully through her steadily clearing mind. She felt wonderful: rested, enlivened, lighthearted. Abruptly she realized she was lying on the wooden cot. She sat up quickly and looked around, but Marsh wasn't inside the cabin. The door was open, and she heard birds chirping gaily. Noticing the sleeping roll on the floor, she knew he had taken that position last night after giving her the only bed. She remembered falling asleep in his arms outside, which meant he had carried her here. She smiled and warmed.

Tossing the light cover aside and rising, Randee saw that she was still naked. What she needed was a quick bath before dressing and beginning breakfast. Sighting Marsh's shirt tossed over a rickety chair, she pulled it on and grabbed a blanket with which to dry herself. She headed to the stream, then halted and wondered if she should alert him to her approach. "Marsh? Where are you? Do I need to wait a while?"

He did not respond, and she panicked. She feared he had overexerted himself last night and perhaps damaged his ribs again. She ran toward the stream. He was not there, nor was Midnight. She called his name several times. Nothing. She raced to the edge of the tree line and scanned the horizon for him. Nothing. Surely he wouldn't leave her here while he went off to . . .

Randee chided herself for her wild imagination. Of course he wouldn't, she reasoned, because he did not know there were no charges against them. As far as he was concerned, they were fugitives. And he wouldn't leave her here to face danger alone, not without telling her. Where had he gone? What was he doing?

Hurriedly she bathed, returned to the cabin, and dressed. He was going to return; he had left his belongings here! To distract herself, she made a fire on the hearth and started their morning meal.

Soon, Marsh entered the cabin and warned, "You have to put out that fire, woman. I saw a curl of smoke from a mile away."

Startled by his silent arrival, Randee squealed and whirled in alarm. "Don't do that! You scared the wits out of me," she scolded him. "Where have you been? I was worried about you. How's your side? You shouldn't have lifted me last night in your condition."

Marsh chuckled heartily. "A real chatterbox this morning, are we?" he teased mirthfully. "One question at a time. Let's see," he murmured, trying to remember them. "I went riding to test my strength and to give Midnight some exercise. He's been lazing around as long as I have. As to my health, Doc Hollis, I feel great today. How about you? Besides being annoyed with me for sneaking off and sneaking up."

Randee shook her head as she noticed the roguish sparkle in his eyes. "Marsh Logan, you're a beast. Why didn't you leave me a note?"

Marsh's smile faded and his blue eyes chilled. "I couldn't, no supplies. That snake Timms stole half the stuff in my saddlebags. He took our notes and maps, and the dynamite." Marsh was glad his Presidential papers and badge were sewn inside the area under his cantle, the raised section on the back of his saddle. When he needed them, all he had to do was slit the stitches and withdraw them.

Randee was dismayed by that news. If she had known about the theft that night, she could have searched for their belongings. "I'm sorry about our evidence, Marsh. I didn't even look inside your saddlebags when I retrieved the horses and saddles, and I haven't thought about them since we've been here. By now, Timms has probably destroyed them. I did remember to take your guns from the sheriff's office," she remarked, even though she noticed he was wearing them.

"Thanks," he remarked, his fingers grazing the gun butts absently.

"What now?" she asked. "Do we start from scratch again?"

"First, put out that fire, or we might attract company. Then—"

She injected, "It isn't necessary. The law isn't looking for us anymore." Randee related what she had overheard at the ranch last Friday between Brody and Payton. As she made her disclosures, she observed Marsh's astonishment, and vexation. "Hopefully Payton Slade is dead by now, so my mother's safe for a while. Willard's alive, Marsh, and the ranch is really mine. We're safe and free."

Marsh irrationally accused, "Why did you deceive me, Randee? I trusted you and depended on you. The only reason I've remained here so long was because I was so weak and I thought we were in peril. I've stayed here to get back my strength so I could go after them and prove our innocence. While you were drugging me and holding me captive here, those bastards have been hiding their trail better than before."

Stunned, Randee shouted at him, "That isn't fair, Marsh Logan, and you know it! There was nothing you could do until you healed properly, even if we were free to leave at any time. If you had known, you would have taken off too soon and harmed yourself."

Without being aware of it, Marsh responded in the same tone which she had used, "You shouldn't have kept this from me! This mission is vital; I have work to do. If I had known we weren't in danger I would have been chasing their butts yesterday. You knew I was able to ride and work days ago, if not for that sneaky medicine. There's no telling what Wade, Timms, and Light have been up to while I've been trapped here. Maybe I could

455

have defeated them by now."

"Without proof? In your condition, they might have snared you again and killed you this time! Damn you, Marsh Logan. You—of all people—know how evil and cruel they are. Now they're desperate. They know all about us and will be guarding their backs every day."

"That should have been my decision, woman; I'm in charge."

"You weren't in any condition to be in charge, *partner*."

Marsh paced angrily, but the anger was at himself and those villains, not at Randee, whom he seemed to be taking it out on at this time. He was flustered by this new setback and wasn't thinking clearly or calmly, which was unlike him. "Damnation," he swore. "Now they know who and what I am. Getting them will be harder. Willard should have waited for permission to unmask me."

Randee's brow wrinkled in confusion. "You mean it's true about you being a secret agent for the governor? You're a lawman?"

Marsh turned and met her troubled gaze. This was not how he had meant to explain matters to her this morning. "Not for the governor, Randee, for the President. I'm a United States Special Agent, chosen and appointed and authorized by President Grant. I'm accountable only to him, and few people know what I am. Most of my missions are secrets, so I've used lots of covers, like Storm Hayden. The original posters were made up so I could earn my way into a gang of rustlers in Nebraska. I didn't commit any crimes and I was never an outlaw. I handle cases other law enforcement agencies can't or won't touch. I work in any state, but mostly Texas and her surrounding neighbors. Since there was no real Storm Hayden, I wasn't worried about that old identity causing us trouble, until new fake posters started showing up."

Randee felt weak and nauseous. She sat down at the

small table. "What's your real name?" she asked without looking at him.

"Marshall Logan, Jr. That was my parents' ranch we visited, and the Epson Gang did murder them. Until I capture or kill every one of those bastards, I've refused to take on any other assignment."

An old and distressing line of thought came to mind: How important was his victory? Would he use anyone, anything, to obtain it? How far would he go to complete his current "assignment"? Now she understood his references to their "mission" — no, to *his* mission.

Randee informed him, "I knew about the poster and Storm Hayden before you lied to me about them. Flossie saw one in Pete's desk and told me about it the night I slept with her in the saloon. She tried to convince me you were lying to me, but I figured you had a good reason. I didn't confront you because I wanted you to trust me and . . . enough to confide in me. First, you're the Durango Kid, then suddenly you aren't; next, you're Storm Hayden, then suddenly you're not. I don't know who or what you are anymore. Are you sure you're really Marsh Logan?" she asked sarcastically.

"I didn't mean for you to learn the truth this way, Randee. I was going to tell you everything this morning. I had to keep silent; I was sworn to it by the President. I don't even have permission to be revealing this stuff today, but it can't be helped."

"You're right, Mr. Special Agent, because Willard destroyed your cover in an effort to save our lives. Is he also a Special Agent?"

"He works with me on most cases. He's a good man. I want you to remain here while I finish this job, then —"

"Because you no longer need a partner, even one who knows their faces! You were only using me for information. The only important thing to you is your job, and your damned revenge!"

"That isn't true, Randee. You're very special to me."

"And you have the gall to accuse me of deceiving you! You've lied to me from the start. You're only confessing now because the news is out about your secret identity. You're a bastard, Marsh Logan."

"I know I am, woman, but it couldn't be helped at the time. I'm heading for Fort Worth to speak with the law there. I have enough facts and suspicions to get some help with this matter. I'm going to find Foley Timms and force the truth out of him, then go after Brody Wade for the same reason. Once I have hard evidence, this case can be closed. Stay here where you'll be safe. Please," he urged.

Randee looked at him, her gaze frosty. "No, I'm going to Wadesville and work on Brody myself. Payton is dead by now, the ranch is mine, we aren't fugitives, and you're not an outlaw—so I'm in no danger. Brody can't blame me for working with a lawman, and he won't suspect how involved we were because he believes I love him and want to marry him. I didn't start this task to stop before it was finished. I've put almost as much into it as you have. I'll watch him closely and get the evidence the law needs to punish my family's killers."

Marsh was worried about her warring emotions. "The only way you can get close enough to spy on Brody Wade is to marry him."

Marsh did not realize that his statement sounded suggestively hopeful, not blatantly discouraging as he had meant it to be. Randee's heart lurched painfully to think that her traitorous love would allow her to wed such a villain to defeat that vicious gang. "You can't stop me."

"Listen to me, Randee," he began, but she shook her head.

"Never again, Mr. Logan. As soon as I have my coffee and biscuits, I'm leaving. And don't you follow me or try to halt me."

Randee fetched a cup of coffee, added honey for nourishment and her impending ruse, and sipped it, even though the heat pained her lips. "Go ahead, do your job, Special Agent Marsh Logan."

Marsh decided aloud, "I'm going to saddle Midnight and load up while you settle down. Then I'm returning. We aren't through discussing this matter, Miss Hollis."

Randee turned and glared at his retreating back. *Oh, yes, we are, you treacherous snake!* she mentally shouted at him. Randee poured another cup of coffee and generously laced it with laudanum. She added a little honey to conceal the taste of the drug. After dumping out the rest of the coffee so he couldn't fetch himself a different cup, she began packing her possessions to be ready to leave quickly.

Marsh came back as promised. When Randee placed her coffee cup on the table, Marsh lifted it and drank from it. Tasting the sweetness, he thought nothing of it, as he had seen her add honey earlier. He needed to settle himself down. He had to explain why she must remain here: He loved her and wanted her safe. He feared she might not believe his claim since he had deceived her so many times in the past. Would she doubt him? Think it was a sly, but cruel ruse?

While Marsh was thinking, planning, fretting, the drug was working swiftly and potently. He was so distracted that it was too late by the time he realized what she had done. He stared at the blurring cup, then tried to turn and speak to her. His tongue wouldn't work. His mind wouldn't work. His body wouldn't work. He passed out cold.

Randee caught him before letting him crash to the hard floor. Tears ran down her cheeks as she gazed into his sleeping face. "Why, Marsh? I love you, and I thought you were beginning to . . ."

She could not think about his deceit at this time. She

had work to do. She had to get away from him. Even as she cursed him, she shoved him onto a bedroll and made him comfortable by removing his boots and guns. She read the paper and eyed the badge which he had brought inside to show her, his Presidential authority. There was no denying his real identity and status. She removed the silver necklace and placed it with his belongings. Taking one last look at him, she closed the door and headed for the stream. After kindly unburdening Midnight, she saddled Rojo, mounted, and rode away.

Chapter Twenty-one

Randee reached town before three that afternoon. After leaving her horse at the livery stable, she registered at the hotel. Reclaiming her trunks from the storage room, she donned one of her prettiest dresses and bonnets for her impending visit with Brody.

At his office, she was told by Deputy Matthew Johnson that Sheriff Wade was not in town and wouldn't return until late tomorrow afternoon or Saturday morning. She asked Matthew to give Brody the message that she was back home and was staying at the hotel, adding that she wanted to see him the minute he arrived.

Matthew asked her if she knew the charges against her had been dropped, and she replied with feigned cheerfulness, "Yes, that's why I returned today. I'll explain everything to my fiancé when I see him. After that scare, I decided my task was too dangerous for a woman. I'm letting that Special Agent finish his mission alone." She smiled innocently and fluttered her lashes dreamily. "I've missed Brody and I'm ready to settle down and get our ranch to working again. Any news on that gang, Matthew? I don't want them returning to raid us again, just as Brody and I are rebuilding the place."

"They were raiding the other side of Fort Worth. But for the past week, they've mostly worked northwest and southwest of here. If the newspaper was right about that agent having evidence on them, maybe it won't be long before they're caught. I hope so. Lots of good people have been killed or run off. I sure am glad they don't raid towns."

Randee noticed the man's fear of that malicious gang, and she concluded that Matthew Johnson wasn't working for Brody in that evil area. That was good, in case she needed his help in an emergency. They talked a while longer, then she smiled and left the sheriff's office.

In her hotel room, Randee paced and planned. She wondered if Marsh Logan would come here after he awakened soon, and she hoped not. She wanted him to carry out his decision to head for Fort Worth. Whatever he had done to her personally, she still wished him luck and speed with this perilous assignment. She had believed she was getting to him, and maybe she had. But Marsh was so used to being on his own, so used to secrecy and self-reliance, so used to controlling and hiding his emotions, so used to keeping his heart stony to avoid more anguish. If only he weren't so caught up in his blinding desire for revenge and justice, he would recognize the strong bond between them! When the strain of his current task ended, perhaps he would. She loved him, so she wouldn't give up hope.

Suddenly a daring idea came to mind, and Randee prepared herself to carry it out . . . .

Marsh moaned and opened his eyes. As his mind cleared, he briefly fumed at what Randee had done. He sat up and rubbed his head. His mouth was cottony dry and tasted foul. He grabbed a cold biscuit from the table and devoured it to clean away the bitterness on his tongue. He didn't have to search the area to know Randee was gone, or try to speculate on her destination and scheme.

He got to his feet and opened the door, checking the sky for the time of day: between four and five o'clock. She had loaded him up good, as he had been out for hours. He looked down at his bare feet. Turning, he saw his boots and guns near the bunk, and noticed he had been lying on a bedroll. His papers and badge had been placed by his holsters, as had the silver necklace which he had given to her.

Marsh scowled and exhaled loudly in annoyance. If she had given him more time, none of this would have been necessary! On second thought, he couldn't blame her for feeling and acting as she had; all he could blame were himself and his damned secrecy!

A mischievous smile claimed his mouth as he noted the clues which told him she still cared about him, even if she denied it to herself and to him. Soon, he would make her listen to his explanation. If things were as good between them as he believed, she would forgive him and relent. Surely by now he knew Randee Hollis well enough to be certain she loved him and would marry him.

If he pursued her to Wadesville, that would interfere with her plans there. She needed to carry out this part of their mission, for herself and everyone else. His intrusion could prevent her success and might endanger her. Reflecting on what she had in mind, he realized it was a clever idea and might work. He had to give her the chance to succeed. He would visit Willard Mason and the authorities in Fort Worth, to file his report and to obtain more help on this case. Then, he would go to Wadesville to make sure she was all right. As smart and brave and cunning as his love was, she would be safe on her own for a few days.

Marsh gathered his belongings and stuffed the necklace into his pocket, vowing it would be around her neck again soon, along with a wedding band on her finger. When his love had time to calm herself and think clearly, she should realize that she had won his heart and know that he would return for her soon. If he rode fast and hard, he could reach Fort Worth late Saturday night. With luck, he could be on his way back to Randee sometime Sunday . . . .

Randee walked to Brody's small house near the north end of town. She hoped the door key was still hidden where she had seen him retrieve it one day when he had stopped there on their way to a picnic. She lifted the rock by the back steps and smiled victoriously. She let herself inside and began to examine the house, being careful to put everything back into its proper place.

She searched behind, beneath, and inside furniture and rugs. Nothing. She looked in the fireplaces and inside supplies. Nothing. She checked the floors and walls and closets for a hidden compartment. Nothing. She went through his clothes. Nothing.

Feeling discouraged by her futile investigation, she sat in a chair and tried to imagine where a man — a criminal — would conceal something of such importance as clues to his wicked actions. There had to be evidence somewhere, as no man could contain everything inside his head, certainly not legal deeds or numerous instructions!

Cautious in the daylight, Randee sneaked to a small shed which was attached to the back of the house and searched it. After rolling two empty barrels aside, she took a shovel and dug beneath them to check out her intuition. She was shocked to find that the hard objects which she had struck were gold bars! She worked harder and faster. She unearthed payroll sacks which had been stolen from various banks, companies, and the Army! There was a fortune here! Was that Brody's role, to be the banker for that gang and land company? Hastily, she recovered the treasure, smoothed the dirt, and replaced the barrels.

Randee went inside again and took another look around. She needed more proof than she had discovered; she needed something in writing, something with names and dates and places. She needed undeniable black words, not golden speculations. She found no new or suspicious stitches on the furniture or mattress and, when she squeezed them, she heard nothing crackle to indicate that something was hidden inside one of them. Her eyes settled on a framed map of Texas on the far wall. *Pictures!* her mind shouted to her. She had not checked behind pictures. She jumped up and hurried to the wall, taking down the map.

Excitement flooded her when she noticed the slit on the back of it. Gingerly she withdrew papers and another map, which she unfolded. She studied the map and realized what she was holding: the motive for the raids. But that wasn't all. She read the papers concealed there, and was horrified to comprehend that Sheriff Brody Wade was not a gang member; he was their boss! She shuddered at that revelation.

Oddly, her first thought was about her mother. She understood how Payton Slade had duped Dee Hollis. Just as she had been irresistibly drawn to the devious Marsh Logan and had been deluded by Brody Wade, her mother had made similar mistakes with her stepfather. Randee realized how clever and guileful and convincing some men could be. If she could be so easily and completely fooled, so could Dee Hollis. Randee's heart softened toward her mother's error in judgment. Yet, she could not vanquish the resentment she still felt about how Dee had kowtowed to Payton and how her mother had changed so drastically. Perhaps losing Randall Hollis had weakened her mother. If Marsh were slain, how would she behave? No, she decided, it would not destroy

465

her. It would tear her apart, but she was a survivor.

Randee refocused her attention and concentration on the map and papers. Brody owned the Mid-Texas Land Company, and the other, diversified companies which Willard Mason had uncovered during his investigation. The map revealed the existing railroad lines in the West and the lands already purchased or designated for future railroads. She noted how Brody had inked in his own wishful lines to connect the Southern Pacific Railways from Louisiana to El Paso, and from Fort Worth to the Atchison Topeka & Santa Fe Railroad in Kansas: All speculative routes traversed the targeted area which she and Marsh had marked on their map, an area which had been terrorized by the Epson Gang for over a year, an area almost entirely in Brody's control now.

It was a brilliant, but insidious plot: Obtain the land, sell rights-of-way to the railroad companies, and make a fortune. Then, with the land he owned on either side of the future rail lines, he would earn even more money with depots, stockyards and such. And with that much money and land came enormous power and prestige. The sheriff's motives and desires were only too clear to the trembling blonde.

She also grasped why the Carson Ranch house had been spared. Its location, beauty, and size made it the perfect home for such an important man. Too, Brody must have suspected she would be hiding there and he hadn't wanted her slain. Otherwise, he would have ordered his men to make certain everyone there was murdered, or he would have gotten rid of her by now. No, she refuted, because he needed her alive to sell the ranch to his land company! Having discovered she actually owned the beautiful ranch, she was relieved she hadn't closed a deal with George Light that day in Fort Worth.

Panic began to build within her as she wondered if Brody did really love her after all. Maybe the ranch was

466

the only thing he craved from her. If so, she was in real danger. Yet, despite the fact he had fooled her so deeply, she believed he truly loved her and wanted her as his wife. The fact that Foley Timms or other gang members hadn't tracked her and Marsh down and forced her to relinquish the ranch made her doubt Brody would slay her. A soon-to-be-rich and powerful man needed a wife, and obviously he had chosen her.

Randee started to take the evidence and leave town immediately to locate Marsh or Willard Mason. That was reckless. Brody could return at any time, even if Matthew had said he wasn't expected home until tomorrow or Saturday. If he discovered these papers missing, he would telegraph his men and have them set a trap for her. Then, she would be dead for sure! Alone, she couldn't battle a band of black-hearted villains. If only Marsh were here with her . . .

He wasn't, so she had to decide what to do. Randee went to Brody's desk and withdrew two pieces of paper. Skillfully she copied the map and made notes of the information on the papers. Afterwards, she replaced the originals and rehung the picture. The apprehensive female checked everything to make certain her presence wouldn't be noticed. Cautiously she locked the door and put the key back under the rock.

In her hotel room, Randee hid the evidence inside a pocket of her trail coat. It was seven o'clock, and she was safe. She mustn't do anything to call suspicion to herself. She went downstairs and ate leisurely. Following a short stroll, she returned to her room to plot her next move. Even though Marsh had betrayed her for one reason or another, this mission was vital. She had to find a way to get this information to him or the authorities. She reached for her necklace to toy with it nervously, but it had been left behind. If Marsh had been coming here after her, he would have arrived by now. She was slightly annoyed and disappointed that he hadn't. Obviously he had continued with his assignment and was on his way to Fort Worth, probably furious with her and planning some way to repay her. She wished she was important enough for him to pursue her as his first priority. . . .

The next morning, Randee took a stroll after breakfast so as to be seen before she sneaked out of town. She had decided against waiting for Brody and trying to dupe him. If she did, she might not be allowed another chance to escape with her crucial evidence. With luck, Brody wouldn't return until tomorrow, too late to halt her imminent actions.

She saw a black-clad figure enter a mercantile store down the street. She hurried that way and entered the store. Grabbing the man's arm, she tugged on it and began, "Marsh, I didn't expect—"

He turned and looked down at her. Embarrassed, she blushed and stammered, "You—you aren't M-Marsh Logan."

Sending her a smile which could charm the bloomers off the chastest of females, he replied in a tingly voice, "Sorry, miss, but I wish I were. Name's Durango. What's yours, if I might ask?" he inquired politely, disarmingly.

Randee saw the resemblance immediately. He was just as devastatingly handsome and virile as Marsh Logan! When she realized how she was staring at him, more color suffused her lovely face. "Randee Hollis," she replied, flustered.

"This Marsh Logan, he's the one who's been using my name, isn't he?" Durango questioned in a mellow tone, and smiled again.

"Yes, but I can explain everything," she responded quickly, not wanting them to tangle in a gunfight. "It was—" she faltered as those ice-blue eyes fused with her wide green ones.

"Why don't we talk about it over coffee in a more private place?" he suggested, eyeing her with interest and appreciation.

In the hotel restaurant, Randee revealed the complicated situation to the famous gunslinger, who seemed amused by it, but most impressed with her. When she finished, she asked, "Are you sure you two aren't related? You favor each other enough to be brothers, almost twins."

"I don't know my real name or who my parents were. I was abandoned at a mission in San Antonio when I was a baby. I was raised by a local family until I left there at seventeen. You might say I got tired of being a slave to a family who made sure I knew what I was."

Randee heard the bitterness in his tone and saw it in his eyes. Her heart warmed to this man who was so like her love. "I'm sorry, Durango; that must have been a terrible life. But you've done well for yourself. From what I hear and read, you've a beloved legend, a good man, well-liked and widely respected."

He grinned and said, "I learned early in life that you don't kill another person without good reason and provocation. I don't look for fights, but I don't run from them. Nothing's worse than being a coward."

Randee looked him in the eye. "How do you feel about female partners, a woman boss?" she asked unexpectedly.

"Don't rightly know, never had either one. What you got in mind?" He leaned forward and propped his elbows on the table, intrigued.

"I need to get to Fort Worth, pronto. Would you be willing to hire on as my guard? Say for . . . two hundred dollars a day?"

Durango observed her closely and intently. "Those are steep wages, Randee," he said, calling her by her first name this time.

"It's a dangerous job, Durango. I've made lots of enemies lately."

"How could anyone want to harm a beautiful woman like you?"

"I have this way of annoying people when I'm after something important," she teased, laughing softly. "Your life would be in constant peril if you sided with me."

"That's nothing new for me," he remarked and chuckled.

She informed him, "I have to drop off something in Fort Worth, then I'm going to check out a clue . . . on the Epson Gang. Interested?"

Durango's surprise wasn't concealed. "Dangerous isn't the right word, if that's what you've got in mind. Why me?"

"Three reasons: You're here now, I need help and protection, and you're the best man for the job. You won't have to work alone; I'm an excellent shot and rider, and I'll be glad to prove both to you."

"I read the papers, Randee, so I'm already aware of your skills. That jailbreak was a fine piece of work. Took real courage and cunning. Where's this Marsh Logan? Why did you two split up?"

"He got tired of working with a woman and thought he could move faster and better without me." She related her personal motives for wanting to defeat the Epson Gang. She told him about Flossie's murder, which saddened and riled him. "You see, I'm not only involved, but I'm also in danger until they're stopped. Besides, I think I know where they camp between raids. All we need to do is check out the location, then we'll report it to the authorities. You needn't worry; I don't plan for us to tangle with them. I'm brave, but not stupid."

"You amaze me, woman," he murmured, looking and sounding like Marsh. He extended his hand across the table and said, "You've got yourself a new partner. When do we leave?"

"Immediately," she announced, rising gracefully.

"I'm afraid that isn't possible, Randee. My horse is being reshod at the livery stable. The blacksmith is busy today. Said it would be late this afternoon before he could get around to my job. What about leaving at first light in the morning?"

Durango noticed her worry and hesitation. He asked, "Any special reason why you need to get out of town today?"

"Could be," she responded absently and prayed Brody wouldn't return until they had departed. After a moment, she met his astute gaze and said resignedly, "It can't be helped. First light, partner."

"You need a guard tonight?" he asked, his tone lacking any wanton suggestiveness.

"Not unless the local sheriff returns before we can leave. We're supposedly betrothed, but I would never marry him. I let him believe it because I needed to spy on him. He's . . . a gang member," she half confided. Later, she would reveal more to him.

"I see," he murmured thoughtfully. Durango realized something he doubted the beautiful blonde did: She was trusting him and treating him as if she had known him forever, as if he were his look-alike . . .

Randee left town the next morning at dawn with the Durango Kid. He had suggested they not be seen together again before their departure, so she had spent the evening alone in her room.

At their first rest stop, Durango told her, "You can relax, Randee; I'm not going to make a play for you this soon. Not that I ain't tempted; I am. You're a beautiful woman. But you're a real lady, and I don't want to give

471

you a bad impression of me. This isn't the time to be thinking of romance if I'm going to keep my concentration on protecting us. Later . . ." he hinted with a charming grin.

Randee returned his smile and calmed her tension. She felt she could trust him to keep his word and distance, for now. The trouble was, he was too much like Marsh in appearance and personality!

Romance — what an unusual word to come from a gunslinger's mouth and head. As with Marsh, this man could be as gentle as he was tough. Frankly, she had a hard time keeping her eyes and thoughts off of him. But she knew why; she had comprehended the attraction last night in her room. Durango couldn't be the twin son of Marshall and Judith Logan, but could Marsh be their adopted son? Could he be this man's brother? If not, why were they so much alike?

As Randee prepared their meal that night in camp, she noticed one of the differences between the two men. Marsh always helped with chores, but Durango tended the horses while she cooked supper.

Later, while resting on their bedrolls, Randee told Durango as much as she knew about Marsh Logan, except for his being a Presidential special agent. On that matter, she let him believe the recent account in the newspaper about his working for the governor.

Durango wanted to ask if there was something between her and Marsh, but he didn't want to point out their similarities as the reason why she kept looking at him with those enchanting green eyes which exposed love and desire. He had taken an instant liking to her and he wanted her fiercely. Before their partnership ended, he must convince her why he was better for her than his mirror image . . . .

In Fort Worth, Marsh was talking with Willard Mason, having awakened the man upon his late arrival. Willard promptly informed him it was Randee's urgent message — brought to him by a preacher's son because the telegraph lines had been cut — which had alerted him to their peril. Marsh realized how frantic and desperate she must have been. He revealed his love and intentions to his friend, who was delighted.

"We'll meet with the U.S. Marshal and State Police in the morning. After I report all I know and suspect, they can go after Timms while I get my hands on Brody Wade. I don't want Randee near him any longer than necessary. I'll head there after our meeting."

In Wadesville, Brody was pacing the floor, drinking whiskey while he pondered this new situation with Randee. It didn't make sense that she would leave town suddenly with the Durango Kid. Matthew had seen them meeting in the restaurant Friday, then ride off at dawn this morning. He didn't think she was heading for Fort Worth to make up for the July fifth meeting with George Light, which she had missed because of the capture and jailbreak. He knew she and Logan were on to Timms and Bush, and were suspicious of Light. But they had no proof against any of his men, and certainly not even a tiny doubt or clue about his involvement! He had destroyed the evidence which Timms had stolen from Marsh Logan, but the persistent man would try to gather more. He had to leave Monday to meet with his men to give them their final orders, as there were only two more ranches to be conquered, plus Randee's. He had to warn all of his men to be extra careful these days. He needed to finish his task quickly; he was too close to success to turn

473

back or halt. Logan had nothing valid against him, and the man would die before he could obtain it . . . .

Marsh left town Sunday at one o'clock and headed overland for Wadesville, passing within miles of Randee and the Durango Kid.

Randee and Durango reached town too late to visit Willard Mason that night. They planned to see him the following morning before heading northward to check out the curious dot on Brody's map. They registered at the hotel, freshened up, then met downstairs to eat.

She enjoyed her evening with Durango. He told her stories about his adventures and how his colorful legend had started and grown. She was surprised and pleased when he confided that he was weary of his exciting and dangerous lifestyle, and wanted to start fresh somewhere.

"What would you like to do, Durango?" she asked.

"Ranch. I've had jobs here and there on ranches, and I always hated to leave. But trouble had this way of dogging me and making the bosses nervous. If I had my own ranch, I could remain in one place."

"What about becoming a ranch foreman until you can buy your own spread? After this task is over, I'm heading back to Wadesville. I have a large spread there which needs lots of work and a good foreman." Randee told him about the Carson Ranch and her plans for it. "Once this gang is halted, I can rebuild. I was reared on a ranch in Kansas. My father had no sons, but I was as good as one. I know as much about ranching as most men, and that isn't boasting."

Durango's blue eyes sparkled as he remarked seriously, "I have no doubts you are. In all honesty, you strike

474

me as a woman who can do about anything. I watched you on the trail, and I know you work as good with your hands dirty as you do in a lovely dress like that one. I can't explain it, but you seem like a lot of different women, yet only one woman — a very special one. This isn't flattery and it has nothing to do with my eventual pursuit of you."

Randee's face glowed with pleasure and she thanked him for his sincere compliments. It was wonderful to be appreciated for more than her looks and sex. She liked this man and found him most interesting. She hinted, "You didn't answer my question. Would you like to continue working for me, at the ranch? Or do you need time to think it over?"

"Your offer is as tempting as you are, boss lady. One question, would it be permissible for your foreman to romance you?"

"That's one question I'll need time to think over," she jested.

"We'll both think hard, then talk it over when I return you home."

Miss Sloan "Pete" Peters, owner of the Pleasure Palace, was speaking to Willard Mason on the street. She was telling him about seeing Randee Hollis with the Durango Kid last night in a lovely restaurant, being "very cozy." She revealed how they had sat talking and sipping wine for hours in a secluded corner, baffling her.

Before Willard could respond, he saw Randee and Durango headed toward them. He quickly told Pete he would see her later.

Randee smiled and spoke to the redhead as they passed on the sidewalk, curious about the woman's coolness to her. When they reached Willard, Randee said, "We need to talk privately, Mr. Mason."

Inside the man's office at the newspaper, Randee related what she had done and discovered in Wadesville, stunning both men. She handed the map and her notes to Willard and said, "You know what to do with these. Durango and I have an errand to handle, then I'll check with you again Wednesday before heading home. To stay this time."

"Marsh is on his way to Wadesville now to work on Brody Wade. Why don't you remain here while I telegraph him to return quickly?" Willard didn't think it was his place to reveal Marsh's personal reason for heading there in front of another person, especially a man.

"We have something to do first. I'll be back Wednesday." She wanted to check out that suspicious dot before telling Mason about it. Too, if she stayed, it would appear she was only waiting for Marsh.

Willard tried to reason with her, but Randee held fast to her decision. If Marsh wanted her, let him come after her! His conquest of her had been too easy for a man accustomed to difficult challenges. Let him worry and chase for a change!

Willard watched them ride out of town, northward, before hurrying to the telegraph station to have a message waiting for Marsh the minute he reached Wadesville sometime that night.

Randee and Durango made it to within twenty miles of the dot before they halted to camp. Both knew it was unwise to approach such a perilous location with exhausted horses and bodies. They ate the cold food they had brought from town and settled down to sleep.

Durango wondered why Randee hadn't wanted to wait for Marsh Logan's return and assistance, but he was glad she hadn't. Perhaps something bad had happened between them, and she wanted to avoid the other man. *Other man* — that was what Marsh Logan was now, his competition for this unique and ravishing creature. He wished he had met Logan before so he would know how to battle his opponent. All he knew was what Randee had told him, which was plenty. Obviously this Logan was a special man, or he wouldn't have captured Randee Hollis' eye and heart. But the man must have problems, or Randee wouldn't be here, with him, at this moment. If he played it smart and careful, he could be all the good things Marsh Logan was and avoid all the bad. To imagine a future with this woman warmed his heart and his loins.

Randee sensed Durango's eyes and hunger. It was flattering to know that two handsome and masterful men wanted her. Durango was so unique, just like Marsh. But Durango was straightforward, so open and honest, so direct. If only she knew where she stood with Marsh . . .

Marsh reached Wadesville at dusk. He had ridden hard and fast, fatiguing both himself and Midnight. He left the loyal steed to be tended to at the livery stable, and walked to the hotel. He was shocked to learn Randee had left town Saturday morning, with the Durango Kid! The clerk had watched them mount and leave at dawn, but knew nothing more. He learned that Brody had returned, then left again this morning, but the deputy couldn't tell him where the sheriff had gone, because the man didn't know.

As Marsh stood outside the hotel trying to decide what to do next, the telegraph operator approached him with a paper. Marsh read it, his eyes widening, then narrowing:

"R and DK here today. Has all we need. All. Left town. Returning Wednesday. Get back quick. W.M."

Marsh knew he couldn't push his horse and himself again this soon. He checked into the hotel for a few hours sleep while Midnight rested. He wondered where Randee and the Kid were going, and why she had left Wadesville with a stranger. He reminded himself that he and his love had been strangers when she had taken off with him, believing him to be the man with whom she was now traveling. He knew the Kid's good reputation, but still he was worried. Randee was a tempting woman; he should know!

What, he pondered, was the proof Randee had obtained in such a short time? Willard had stressed it was "all" they needed to wind up this case. If he left early in the morning, he could reach Fort Worth sometime Wednesday, the same day Randee and the Kid were to return.

Marsh tossed for two hours, barely managing to doze off and on. He couldn't stop thinking about Randee being with Durango, and Brody's sudden departure after theirs. He wished she had remained in Fort Worth until he could get back.

He sat up in bed and rubbed his tired eyes. "What are you up to, woman? Hell, I can't hang around here! I can catch a nap or two on the trail. At least I'll be heading your way. Just wait until I get my hands on you again," he vowed anxiously. If he left now, even with enough stops along the way for Midnight, he could reach town early Wednesday morning, probably before dawn.

Shortly after noon, Randee and Durango sneaked up to the camp of the notorious Epson Gang. Three cabins were located in a densely wooded area which bordered a lovely clearing beside a peaceful river. Two large corrals—undoubtedly for confining stolen stock—were positioned nearby, and stacks of goods seemingly littered the huge area. *Tianges* — shelters made of four posts set into a square and covered either by brush or colorful material — were sighted in the sunny clearing and were being used to ward off the blazing sun. The mere size of the camp was intimidating and enlightening. Only a few men were present, but it was obvious Randee and Durango had found the right place.

"You two looking for something?" a familiar voice asked from behind them. "Move real slow and easy and lift those hands high."

Randee, as well as Durango, noticed the number of shadows that darkened the grassy bank before them, and they made no threatening moves. Slowly they turned, raising their hands as ordered.

"Well, well," Foley Timms said mirthfully. "If it isn't Miss Hollis, and with the real Durango Kid this time. You're one clever woman, but you won't get out of this new predicament so easily."

As she heard the thundering of numerous hooves, Foley's eyes raked her lewdly as he remarked, "Looks like the whole gang's back, just in time to greet our beautiful visitor and her legendary escort."

Chapter Twenty-two

While the gang members were dismounting and tending their horses, Randee and Durango were disarmed and taken to one of the three cabins, to be held captive there. She bluffed bravely, "You're in big trouble if you harm us, *Marshal* Foley Timms. I'm looking for Brody. Durango wants to join up with him, and I have important things to report. If he isn't here, then tell me where to find him quickly. He has problems which he doesn't know about, and he's in danger."

The man's head fell backward as he laughed wildly. "You ain't fooling me twice, girl," he informed her coldly.

Randee desperately scoffed, "I wouldn't have fooled you before if that Marsh Logan hadn't blackmailed me! He was going to tell Brody we were lovers. I had to help him escape. He planned it all when you were closing in on us that day near town. Then, after we were in hiding for days, I learned he's a Special Agent and we aren't fugitives. When he showed me a newspaper story about our jailbreak and laughed about how he'd tricked all of us, I knocked him out and escaped. I rode to Wadesville to tell Brody all about him, but Brody was gone. Durango showed up, so I hired him to help me find Brody so I can warn him before Logan catches him."

The man looked her over skeptically and asked with a wolfish snarl, "Do you expect me to buy that wagonload of horseshit?"

Randee glared at him and shouted angrily, "How dare you speak to me like this! When I hired Marsh Logan, I didn't know who he was. He told me and Brody he was the Durango Kid, and we believed him. Look at the Kid. Seeing how much they favor each other, anyone could have made that mistake." Randee knew she should show anger and hostility about the ranch raid, so she did. "Your men killed my aunt and uncle during that raid and burned my property! That's why I hired a gunslinger to hunt you down and punish you. At that time, I didn't know Brody was your boss and he was only after the land. It's mine now, so everything's worked out for him. And that suits me just fine because my kin were trying to send me home. Brody knows why I couldn't return to Kansas; that's probably why he ordered the raid on the Carsons. He's told me everything. Are you forgetting we're to be married soon?"

"I ain't forgetting nothing, girl. Nothing," he stressed icily.

Randee continued, while Durango watched and listened, "Logan probably made those posters himself and had them circulated so he could fool Brody and get close to him. He figured the gang would believe he was an outlaw, just like them, and try to hire him away from me. He was going to pretend he had taken my job for the money, but really wanted to locate you so he could join up. It was a clever plan, but Logan didn't realize how Brody and I felt about each other. I admit I don't like what Brody's doing to get control of this area, but I suppose he thinks it's best and I have to trust him."

"You don't know nothing, girl, but I know what a sly vixen you are. I can't wait for Brody to turn me loose on you."

Randee asserted hotly, "You're a stupid fool, Timms! If you aren't more careful, you'll ruin everything and

Brody will have you slain. I know all about Brody's plans for several railroad lines across Texas. If you don't believe me, I can give you their exact routes, and I can list the companies he owns as covers for the Mid-Texas Land Company. I know everything because he trusts me. Brody was letting me stay with Logan to mislead him, but you interfered with that enlightening capture. If I had let you hang a marshal, we'd all be defeated by now! Brody's going to be furious when he hears about this."

Foley grabbed her arm, twisting it as he demanded, "How did you find this camp, and how do you know Brody's plans?"

Durango lunged at the man to help Randee, but was clubbed on the head by another outlaw. Randee jerked free and knelt beside her unconscious friend. She looked up at Foley and vowed, "You'll regret this, you bastard! If there's one thing Brody admires, it's courage and loyalty. When I tell him what you've done to us—"

"He'll be here in the morning, so you can tell him then. He's in Fort Worth on business, but he's heading this way."

"He's probably discussing something with George Light. When he arrives, you'll be sorry you ever insulted and harmed us!"

"It's my guess, tomorrow, you'll be the sorry one," Timms hinted, then left them locked in the cabin, with a guard posted outside. In his riled state, he forgot about his two earlier questions.

Carl Bush joined Foley and asked, "What's going on, Timms?"

A devilishly grinning Foley explained the excitement. He cautioned, "Make sure your men keep away from her until Brody decides her fate. I'd be willing to bet the boss ain't gonna want her anymore."

Carl licked his lips. "If he don't, I'll take care of her for him."

Foley looked at the flaming-haired gang leader with jet-black eyes and grasped the man's sadistic meaning. He chuckled.

Randee removed her bandanna and bound the bleeding wound on Durango's head. She peeped through the loose-weave curtains and observed the talk between Carl Bush and Foley Timms. From the way both men kept glancing at her cabin and grinning lewdly, she could imagine the topic of their conversation: her. Dread filled Randee as she recalled what these violent outlaws had done to defenseless women. Her gaze slipped around the cluttered camp. There were so many of them and their evil was so enormous. How could she get out of this terrifying situation? How could she endure it if escape was prevented?

When Durango roused, she said, "I'm sorry I got you into this trouble, Durango. When Brody arrives tomorrow, he'll know I'm lying. He'll probably kill us." She showed him the small gun hidden in her boot, but remarked sadly, "It only shoots two times. There are so many of them outside. I don't know how we could escape tonight."

Durango pulled her into his arms to comfort her. "Don't worry; we'll think of something. That was some clever talking you did earlier."

She retorted gratefully, "That was some brave action you took on my behalf. How's the head?"

"Hurts like h — crazy," he replied, touching the aching spot.

"You'll have a big knot by morning. This was my dumbest idea," she berated herself. "I should have thought about guards being posted."

Durango felt he was the one who shouldn't have made such a simple and reckless error. He had been thinking about taking a quick look so they could hurry back to town where he could pursue her. He had always lived by his wits, skills, and on sheer luck. He could not believe his life would end like this, not now. "I don't believe my luck's run out, Randee, but if it has, it's a shame. I've never met a woman like you before, and my only regret is in not having more time with you."

Durango's lips closed over hers and he kissed her thoroughly and tenderly. The action was gentle, yet enticing and very pleasant. Randee needed his comforting arms about her. She needed this show of affection, this encouragement in the face of probable death in a few hours. She needed him to stand in for Marsh in her final moments on earth. She returned his kiss and embrace, wishing it were Marsh, yet relieved it wasn't her true love here with her, facing death.

The door opened and Foley Timms peeked inside, grinning and taunting, "Now ain't that a pretty sight. Brody's gonna love this news."

Randee knew they had been seen, so there was no need to jerk free as if they were doing something wicked. She remained in Durango's embrace, which tightened protectively. Her bluff hadn't worked with Timms, and wouldn't work tomorrow with Brody. She despised the thought that this horrid beast was going to get away with his crimes, but only for a while longer. She was glad she had visited Fort Worth before coming here. At least the authorities had the evidence they needed to defeat this gang.

Randee thought about returning Timms's taunts by telling him what he would be facing soon, but it was rash to alert him to his imminent peril. She glared at him and held silent. For a time, she was tempted to draw the concealed weapon and use Timms as a hostage, but the odds were against them. No doubt those villains outside would let her shoot Timms rather than allow her and

Durango to escape!

Timms said, "I was only checking to make sure you two were behaving yourselves. I'm damn glad you weren't. Carl is real anxious to punish you for the boss. You know what I mean, don't you, girl?" he hinted wickedly and cruelly, then left chuckling.

Randee explained the villain's threatening words to her friend. Durango was infuriated and alarmed over her peril, but there was nothing he could do to save her. Or, he mused, was there . . . ?

She and Durango sat snuggled together as different thoughts raced through their minds. How she hated for her life to end this way! Why hadn't she told Willard about her suspicion of the camp? Why hadn't she stored her pride and waited in town for Marsh? But if she had, would they all three be facing death together at this moment?

Around midnight, Durango suggested a desperate plan for escape. Randee agreed. He went to the door and called the guard. When the man responded, Durango told him Randee was very sick. The man peered inside and saw her on a bunk, moaning and clutching her stomach.

"I'll git the boss over here," he said, just before Durango yanked him inside, clobbered him, and scized his weapon.

Holding a gun in each hand, he motioned Randee forward. "This is it," he whispered, then kissed her soundly.

Before they could round the corner of the cabin, shots were fired at them, and Randee was hit in the shoulder. Three men surrounded them and forced Durango to give up the guns. He carried Randee into the cabin, and Foley Timms appeared within minutes.

"I told you two not to try anything," he scolded them.

"Bring me some bandages," Durango ordered coldly.

Timms glanced at the blonde's bleeding shoulder and frowned. Brody wasn't going to like this, not without his permission. He told one of Bush's men to bring water, clean cloths, and medicine. After which, he left them alone for Durango to tend her.

He had to see Carl Bush and warn the gang leader to get better control over his band. They couldn't harm Randee until Brody said it was all right. But afterwards . . .

"The bullet passed through clean, Randee, but you're bleeding heavily." He pressed a wad of cloth against the wound to stanch the flow, and watched the beauty grimace in pain. But she did not cry aloud.

"Damn them," the black-clad man cursed softly. He had seen plenty of bullet wounds, and he knew this could be a serious one if he didn't halt the bleeding. "You have to lie still and I have to keep pressure on it. I know it hurts like hell, but . . ."

Randee read emotions in his expression and tone which touched her deeply. "I know," she said weakly. "Listen to me, Durango; please try to escape again. Brody won't kill me if I'm here alone. He wants me too badly. He'll threaten me and force me to marry him, but he won't harm me. You, he'll kill. Please, get away if you can."

"No way am I leaving you here with those bastards!" he protested.

"Whatever their plans for me, you can't stop them. Go, please. Now that I'm hurt badly, they won't be expecting another attempt."

"I haven't known you long, Randee Hollis, but you're damn special to me. I'll fight them to the end," he vowed honestly, worriedly.

Tears blurred her vision because she knew he was a

man of his word, an honorable man, a death-marked man. She argued, "You're very special to me too, so escape while you have the chance. I don't want you to die, Durango. That would hurt me more than this wound."

Durango pulled her into his arms and held her gently while she cried, partly from physical pain and partly from emotional anguish. She knew she would never see Marsh again. She knew she was responsible for this man's impending death. She knew she would never see her mother again to explain everything to her. Fate had defeated her.

Marsh arrived in Fort Worth late that night and spoke with Willard Mason. He viewed the evidence with a fatigued mind and body. "When she gets back tomorrow, I'll jail her if need be, to keep her put while I finish this case! I love her, Willard, and I don't want her hurt."

Later, Marsh dropped wearily on the bed in Willard's spare room. He was exhausted. He had traveled for days with little food or rest, and hardly any sleep. He collapsed and was out soon.

Before dawn Wednesday, Marsh awakened suddenly, the curious black dot on Brody's map tormenting his slumber and arousing him. He sat up quickly, instantly alert. He realized what it meant and where Randee had gone. He awakened Willard and revealed his suspicion.

"Get a posse together as rapidly as you can! I'm heading out now. Have them follow immediately. She's in trouble; I know it."

"You can't challenge that gang alone, Marsh; it's too big. Gather the posse and ride with them," Willard advised frantically.

"I can't wait. I'll get some dynamite and ammunition, then take off. Work fast, Willard. I have a gut feeling she's in danger." Marsh added, "And have George Light arrested so he can't warn them."

Marsh rode as if the demons from hell were pursuing him, and he reached the area by four o'clock. He figured guards would be posted. He looked for them and, one-by-one, noted the locations of the lookouts. Spying on the large camp, he knew his love was trapped in there. He studied the area through his field glasses, deciding she must be in the cabin where two additional guards were posted outside.

From the number of horses, the entire gang had to be present. It was July twelfth, a hot and clear and dazzlingly bright day. Many of the raiders were lazing around outside beneath shade trees and *tianges*, playing cards or chatting or cleaning weapons. All were guzzling whiskey. He counted seventeen men, which didn't include those inside. Marsh had to assume — from the number of horses in the corral — that just as many raiders might be inside those other two cabins, doing the same things or napping or eating. The odds and risks were staggering.

Another reality forcefully hit home. This was one time he could not challenge or face danger alone; it was too dangerous for his love. All he could do was wait for the posse to arrive and assist him. No, he instantly concluded, he should go meet them and make a battle plan.

The wait seemed endless and nerve-racking. Fear such as he had never experienced before chewed at him. The hot sun blazed down, and the shade of the tree did not cool or calm him. He prayed.

When the posse finally arrived, Marsh talked with the men, forty of them. He explained the situation and suggested a plan. He warned them to be careful of Randee's presence, and the Durango Kid's.

* * *

488

Shortly before dusk, Marsh sneaked around disabling the lookouts. The men in the posse took their positions. The attack on the sluggish camp came without warning. Hearing it, Durango barred the door with a chair so none of the men could enter and use them as covers. Loud explosions and multiple gunfire were heard. Yells and whinnies filled their ears. Stacks of goods were dynamited to get rid of protective covers for the bandits and to rapidly end this struggle, which was endangering Marsh's love. The thunderous noise terrified the outlaws' horses and they tried to break free of the corral. Gunfire sounded in all directions, and messages were shouted back and forth on both sides.

Randee lifted her head and asked, "What's going on, Durango?"

"It's my guess we have help out there, plenty of it. Lie still and quiet or you'll open that wound again," he cautioned, wishing he had saved Randee's concealed weapon for this crucial moment. If he hadn't acted rashly, she wouldn't be injured.

Randee somehow knew who was out there, but she was too numb to be happy. She felt weak and dizzy from her loss of blood, and her shoulder burned and throbbed. From past experiences with wounds, she concluded it would take weeks for this one to heal. She wished she were out there helping to destroy this vicious gang. She smiled faintly at her friend and said, "Seems your good luck has rubbed off on me, Durango. I think we're about to be rescued."

The battle continued for a short time. The gang members who weren't killed, finally surrendered—all except Foley Timms, who escaped. Carl Bush had been slain early during the attack on his camp.

When Marsh beat on the door and was let inside, he went to where Randee lay, and dread filled him. He eyed her closely and asked, "What happened to you, woman?

489

You all right?"

Randee realized she and Durango had been saved from horrible deaths, saved by the slayings of brutal beasts beyond her cabin door. A mixture of emotions raced through her. This sudden change of fates was a shock to her dazed mind and injured body, and she needed time to adjust to this dark lethal-defeat-turned-glorious victory. "Fine," she replied, smiling happily at Durango over Marsh's shoulder. "I've had a good doctor. Durango, this is Marsh Logan, the man you're looking for. Don't get nervous, Marsh; he knows why you borrowed his name."

The two men eyed each other, noticing how it seemed as if each was looking into a mirror. Randee also noted the undeniable resemblance, which was most revealing to her but not to the men.

"Brody hasn't arrived yet, has he?" she asked, breaking the spell around the two matching males.

"He's not outside," Marsh replied as he checked her injury.

"He was in Fort Worth. He might have witnessed the action and gotten scared. He's probably on his way to Wadesville to recover that gold and money I found, so he can escape justice. It's hidden in the shed behind his house. Let's go after him before he gets away."

"Not you, woman. You stay put. I'll go after him."

"You aren't leaving me behind, Marsh Logan. I found this evidence and this victory is mine," she argued, not thinking clearly.

He refuted tenderly, "Victory is the most important thing, woman, not who obtains it. You've done more than your share; you got the proof we need to end this madness." Marsh looked at the Durango Kid and asked, "Could you leave us alone for a few minutes? I have something private to tell Randee."

Durango glanced at the pale blonde, who nodded and

490

said, "It's all right, Durango. He owes me a good scolding for something I did."

After the gunslinger left reluctantly and closed the door, Marsh dropped to his left knee beside the bunk. He gently caressed her cheek as he told her, "You've had me scared out of my mind, woman. I ought to spank you good. If you weren't injured, I'd do just that. I have to go after Brody before he gets away. He's responsible for the deaths of my parents, your kin, and plenty of others. If he gets away, he could try this bloody game some other place. We can't allow that, Randee. I have to bring him in or kill him. I can't give him time to escape, so I have to leave immediately. Don't you realize, he won't be expecting anyone to come after him so quickly? You're hurt badly, love, so you can't go with me this time."

When she didn't respond, he said, "The posse is going to camp here tonight, then head for town at first light. You rest and leave with them. They'll protect you for me." Marsh smiled roguishly as he stroked her hair. "If you hadn't drugged me the other day, you would have stayed at the cabin after I told you why I wanted you safe. Because I love you, Randee Hollis, and I need you. When I get back to Fort Worth, we have some serious talking to do. You might say, you made me an offer too tempting to resist."

Randee thought he meant her offer to let him drift in and out of her life when he so desired. She didn't want that anymore; she wanted something permanent. She wanted to settle down, build a real life with this man. She wanted a home, a family, a husband who was around every day and night. She was amazed by his confession of love, but couldn't help but wonder if it was timed to make her stay put. Her hesitation brought a worried look to his face.

Marsh asserted, "I know you love me, woman, so don't deny it. This partnership isn't over, even if the Kid wants to take my place."

Randee could not suppress an amused grin. "Is that jealousy I detect, Mr. Logan?" she teased.

"Damn right it is," he admitted freely. "You're mine."

Randee's hand lifted to playfully cuff his stubbled jaw-line: This wasn't the time or place to question him about his feelings and intentions toward her. "I'm not a piece of property, Special Agent Logan."

Marsh relaxed and chuckled. He kissed her passionately before replying, "Nope, you're my equal partner, and I like it that way."

Randee didn't want to get her hopes up if she was misreading his signals. Lightly touching her wounded shoulder, she remarked, "I have no choice but to stay here with Durango. He'll take care of me. Go after Brody, and we'll talk later. I'm too muddle-headed and weak right now. After all I've been through lately, my mind refuses to function any more today. Remember when we were on the trail and you needed time and privacy to do some thinking and accepting? Well, I need those same things right now. I was expecting to die this morning, so I prepared myself. Now that I'm going to live, I need to get back to normal. I was kind, patient, and understanding when you needed silence and distance; now, you have to do the same for me."

At first, he was surprised that she — a woman — hadn't flung herself into his arms and wept in relief and joy. Then, he reminded himself that Randee wasn't a coward or a weakling, so she wouldn't go to pieces. She wasn't the hysterical or weepy kind. Another thing, she probably didn't know how she was supposed to behave under these circumstances and with him. "You sure you're all right?" he asked again.

Marsh was right about her thoughts and feelings. One good thing, she decided, she now grasped Marsh's past feelings of weakness and defeat. She despised and resisted them as much as he had. She hated to admit she had been careless, vulnerable, and terrified. This dreadful, nearly fatal experience hadn't been all bad; she had learned from it. "I'll be perfect in two weeks; I promise. Now, get going."

Marsh called Durango back inside and said, "You make sure she stays put for a while. Take her to Fort Worth to the doctor, and keep her there until I get back. I'm making you responsible for her."

Durango eyed the other man closely, intently. He felt the heady mood in the cabin, and guessed their feelings for each other. He had suspected it all along, but still he was disappointed. "I'll take good care of Randee. You needn't worry."

Marsh glanced at the man suspiciously. He didn't like the tone of Durango's voice or the look in his eye. It was worse when Randee said, "Go do your duty, Special Agent Logan. Durango will be with me."

Marsh knew he had to move fast to keep Brody, the gang's boss, from getting away. But he hated to leave. The other man was too much like him, and he didn't want Randee to get them confused! Yet, he had to trust his instincts, which told him she loved him but feared to reach out until she knew he was serious. As soon as he had Brody in custody, he would make certain it was very clear to her!

The following morning, when the posse headed for Fort Worth, Randee and Durango rode toward Wadesville, very slowly and cautiously. She wanted to go home, home to the ranch. That was where she and Marsh needed to talk privately. That was where she wanted to heal, to rest, to enjoy this peace which she had helped bring about yesterday.

* * *

Brody Wade reached his home town at mid-afternoon on Thursday. He had witnessed the commotion in Fort Worth yesterday morning, and knew his dream was ending. He was frantic; he was terrified. His evil mind snapped. He had to fetch part of his treasure and make his escape while the posse was raiding his gang's camp. There was no law here to warn about his arrival, because he was the local law. Soon, Marsh Logan would come after him, but he would be gone.

Retrieving the gold and money which were concealed at his house, he loaded them into a wagon and covered them. Rapidly, he gathered supplies and packed them. He had treasures hidden in other spots, gold and money and jewels, stolen during the war and during robberies since it ended. One beautiful dream was lost, but perhaps another one wasn't: Randee Hollis. He wrote a letter telling her he loved her and wanted her to wait for his return one day. He drew a map which indicated the places where he had the rest of his valuables hidden. Surely that show of love and trust would delight her and keep her faithful to him.

He took the letter to Matthew Johnson and told him to make sure Randee received it when she returned. Long before dusk, Brody Wade mounted the wagon and drove it away.

Marsh reached Wadesville Friday before noon. He discovered Brody had been there and left, yesterday. As soon as Midnight was fed and rested, he began his tracking. The wagon wheels were easy to follow as the heavy gold created deep and clear depressions. Marsh realized that Brody was in too much of a hurry to conceal his trail, if the crazy sheriff even thought about such a precaution.

For hours Marsh persistently and patiently dogged

him, as Brody had a big head start on him. The agent knew that Brody might be too wildly excited to get fatigued, but his horses would demand rest. Marsh finally saw the sheriff and wagon in the distance. He raced after them. Brody heard him coming and opened fire.

Marsh tried to get the insane man to surrender, but Brody refused. The sheriff jumped off his wagon and ran straight at Marsh, firing rapidly and cursing his nemesis. Marsh had no choice but to defend himself, as there was no cover nearby. He tried wounding Brody to halt him, but the man found enormous strength from his hatred and madness and kept coming at him. Clearly, it was one or the other's life in jeopardy. They exchanged shots, and Brody Wade was slain. Marsh loaded the body into the wagon, covered it, and headed back to town, knowing it would be a slow journey.

Randee and Durango reached Wadesville Saturday afternoon. The sheriff's office was locked and they couldn't find anyone who knew about Brody and Marsh. Since neither was in town, that meant Marsh had to be chasing the villainous boss. Durango insisted she see the local doctor to make sure her shoulder was healing all right, so she agreed. The physician checked her wound and bandaged it, placing her arm in a cloth sling and telling her how to tend it properly.

"How about if I buy us a wonderful meal?" she suggested as they left the doctor's office.

Durango clasped the hand of her good arm. He smiled and said, "That sounds like a great idea. I'm starved."

"So am I," she concurred, laughing softly.

Matthew Johnson saw them and delivered Brody's letter to her. She opened it and read it, shocked by its contents. She passed it to Durango to read, and his brow lifted in astonishment.

"You'll be a mighty rich woman, Randee," he remarked.

"That gold is stolen and has to be returned to its owners."

"How do you know who it belongs to?" he questioned.

"I'll turn it over to the authorities and let them decide. I'll insist they return everyone's ranch that was stolen by Brody. They'll be able to track down the gang's victims. I couldn't keep the gold. Which reminds me, Durango, I owe you for eight days' work, so far. I'll pay you when the bank opens Monday. What about the other job offer?"

Durango took her hand in his again and met her soft gaze. "Why don't we wait until you have your talk with Marsh Logan before we decide if you still need me as foreman?" he suggested meaningfully.

Her gaze and answer were direct. "While we were partners, Marsh told me many times that he wasn't the kind of man to settle down. He doesn't want to ranch or make commitments."

"What if he's changed his mind?" Durango ventured.

Randee knew it wouldn't be wise to hire this man if she and Marsh . . . But if Marsh didn't commit to her, she would need help at the ranch, help from a man she liked and trusted. She knew her lengthy silence told Durango he was her second choice, but she couldn't prevent it. "I'll be honest with you, Durango. I do—"

"Randee! Randee!" Marsh was shouting from the wagon, which was pulling up before the jail. He had witnessed them standing there, too closely. He wanted to jump down and yank Durango away from her, but that was silly.

Marsh joined them and asked, "What are you doing here?"

She hurriedly and furtively looked him over for injuries, and was relieved to find none. A sunny smile brightened her green eyes and lovely face as she replied, "I wanted to come home. It's safe now."

"How's the shoulder?" he inquired anxiously.

Glancing at it, she related, "I've already seen the doctor. This wound isn't as bad as we thought. Did you . . . did you get him?"

Both were conscious of Durango's eyes and presence. Marsh motioned to the wagon and said, "He's dead. He wouldn't let me take him alive. I'll need to fetch the undertaker, and the banker to lock up that gold. Why don't I meet you in the hotel restaurant after I tend to these chores?" he suggested, hoping Durango would leave them alone.

"Durango and I were headed there now. We're both starving for a good meal. Join us when you finish," she invited politely.

Marsh pulled out the chair next to Randee, annoyed that Durango wasn't sitting across the table from her. They had been laughing and talking when he arrived. "All finished," he announced.

Randee removed the letter from her pocket, passed it to Marsh, and asked him to handle it for her. She recalled what Brody had once said to her about her being his one weakness, the only thing which could hurt or harm him, that she would be the death of him because of her courage and persistence. In a way, all of that was true. Yet, she hated it that Brody Wade had been the gang's leader, because so many people had loved, trusted, and respected him. She could not understand how he could be responsible for ordering the deaths and destruction of his old and current friends. How could anyone want riches and power at such a price? Surely he had been insane, perhaps driven mad during the war for the reasons he had revealed to her.

Randee didn't want to discuss Brody or the depressing

case, so she didn't question Marsh about either one. She wanted to feel alive and happy again. "Let's order," she suggested in the ensuing silence.

Marsh disclosed to her, "I have one more task, to apprehend Foley Timms. Brody blamed him for his failure, so before he died, he told me where to find Timms. I'll be heading after him in the morning. He should be holed up in another hide-out near Jacksboro. I'll return in a few days. Will you be all right until then?"

Randee laughed merrily as she retorted, "You know how well I can take care of myself. Besides, Durango is coming to work for me as my foreman. He'll keep me out of trouble, won't you?"

Durango grinned and replied, "Be more than happy to fill both jobs, Randee. I've gotten used to working for you, woman, and I'm crazy about it."

Marsh frowned, and both people noticed. He asserted boldly, "I thought you were planning to hire me for those two jobs, partner. Something change your mind?" he asked almost sullenly, his tone and gaze replacing the "something" with *someone*.

"You?" she teased. "If I recall correctly, Mr. Logan, you told me several times that you're a permanent drifter and you don't like ranching or farming. I plan to do plenty of both. So does Durango. He's more than ready and willing to change his lifestyle. I'm glad, because we've become very good friends and I'd like to see him survive and enjoy life. The same goes for you, ex-partner." She was telling the truth. She wanted both men to give up their perilous existences. She loved Marsh passionately, and Durango was like a brother to her.

Their meals arrived, so the strained conversation ceased while they ate. So far, she had been open and honest with both men. She had been genial and direct. Randee made it a point not to flirt deceitfully or unconsciously with Durango to worry or annoy Marsh. She didn't want her love getting angry, defensive, and withdrawn. She wanted him to speak his mind, all of it. Yet, she found it impossible not to be friendly with the gunslinger who had shared her near lethal fate. She liked and admired Durango, and it was obvious to both men.

When Marsh was done, he stood and said, "If it's possible, Randee, I'd like to speak with you alone in about an hour. Finish your meal and get some rest first. I'll come to your room later."

She noticed how tense and quiet Marsh was, and that concerned her. What kind of revelation did he have in mind? Whatever he had to say to her, she must hear it tonight. "That's fine, Marsh."

Randee observed his retreating back, as did the Durango Kid. She lowered her lashes and sighed heavily. What to expect?

"You love him, don't you?" the man inquired knowingly.

Randee met Durango's gaze and nodded. "It isn't enough for me anymore. When this all started, I thought it would be. He likes his freedom and doesn't want —" She fell silent as Marsh returned.

Marsh bravely revealed, "I can't wait until later to tell you I love you and want to marry you. Please wait for me until I can finish my assignment. On second thought, I'll send word to the law at Jacksboro and have them capture Foley Timms. Vengeance isn't more important to me than you are, woman; nothing is." He grinned roguishly and said, "Sorry about the lack of privacy, but this has to be said here and now. She's mine, Durango, and I'll fight any man or problem to keep her. I just have to remind her she feels the same."

Durango grinned broadly and his blue eyes twinkled. He remarked mischievously, "Thank goodness, you came back and confessed. I was afraid I was going to have to take you behind the barn and beat some sense into you. I've known all along she's in love with you, but you can't blame a man for craving such a treasure — especially if his competition is fool enough to give it up. I think it's about time you two found a less crowded place to talk. I'll see you in the morning."

Marsh looked at the gunslinger in surprise, then smiled in understanding. "Thanks, Durango. Come along, Miss Hollis," Marsh said, helping her rise and leading her away.

At the door to her room, Marsh halted and said, "I shouldn't come inside. Since we'll be living in this town after our marriage, we don't want people gossiping about us. You get to bed and get well, so we can marry soon, tomorrow if possible." When she started to protest his departure, his fingers silenced her lips and he whispered, "I'll take you to the ranch in the morning, then we can really talk privately. Does that meet with your approval, partner?"

Randee smiled happily. "You're right, as usual, partner. I am feeling very weak and tired and sore. Be here bright and early, won't you? We have so much to do, so many plans to make."

Marsh withdrew the silver necklace from his pocket and fastened it around her neck. "It actually says: *You are in my heart forever.*"

"I know. I sneaked back to the store and asked for a translation," she confessed. "Why else would I have been so patient with you while you were getting over your fear of love and commitment? I love you, Marsh Logan, with all my heart. Yes, I'll marry you."

"Get inside and lock the door before I forget about protecting our reputations," he warned playfully. "I'll join Durango downstairs and lend him a shoulder to cry on. You're a terrible loss, woman, but a wonderful find. I can't wait to see my ring on this hand."

As he was kissing each of her fingertips, she ventured

softly, "Marsh, do you think there's any possibility you and Durango are close kin? When I look at him, it's like seeing you. It's uncanny. I don't think this heavy resemblance is coincidental. What do you think?"

"Frankly, neither do I. We'll talk about it later, after I do some snooping around about us. You get to bed, woman. I love you."

"I love you," she responded, kissing him before he left. She closed the door and leaned against it. Her heart fluttered madly in joy, but her knees wobbled in warning. She craved him fiercely, but she wasn't in the best condition to prove it or enjoy it. Trembling with a combination of weakness and desire, she walked to the bed and lay down. Soon, Marsh Logan would be hers forever.

Randee Hollis stretched out on the bed and closed her green eyes. She allowed her dreamy mind to retrace her heady adventures with the daring rogue she loved and would marry soon. At last, Marsh Logan had only one identity; he was only one man, her man.

Chapter Twenty-three

Six weeks had passed since Randee Marie Hollis and Marshall Logan, Jr. had married on Sunday, July sixteenth. Afterwards, they had recovered the five thousand dollars which they had buried outside of town on June seventeenth. The money, gold, payrolls, and jewels that Brody and his gang had stolen were being returned to their rightful owners, as were the ranches which had been wrongfully taken. Foley Timms had been captured and hanged. Lawyer George Light was in prison. In exchange for mercy, after revealing everything he knew about Brody Wade's evil scheme, George was helping the authorities straighten out the mess which Brody had made during his reign of terror.

Marsh and Randee didn't know it yet, but they were expecting a child, the first of three in their long and happy life together. The H/L Ranch—for "Hollis bar Logan," their new brand—was being rebuilt, and soon would be prosperous and beautiful again.

Marsh Logan had retired from his job as Special

Agent for the President. He had told Randee how he had become good friends with Sloan "Pete" Peters and what Flossie had misunderstood long ago when the saloon girl had overheard them talking and laughing about that false Nebraska incident. The adventurous and daring Miss Sloan Peters had been one of the best agents for the American government during the Civil War. The multitalented Yankee lass had met Marsh during one of her missions while he was working with the Galvanized Yankees. After Marsh became a Special Agent, they had worked together several times on other cases, especially when a couple was needed.

During that horrible war, in one of Sloan's covert and perilous cases, she had worked against Quantrill's Raiders by using a strategy similar to the one which Randee and Marsh had used against the Epson Gang. She had been exposed and captured one day while passing information to her contact. As punishment, Sloan had been beaten and ravished by two of the raiders and left for dead. Sloan's illegitimate daughter had been the result of that brutal incident. Three years later while working in a small town, one of those raiders had come upon her and the child. He had demanded to know if the little girl was his, behaving as if there was a way Sloan could know which man was the father, and acting as if he had fatherly rights where the child was concerned! Fearing her daughter would be in danger and might discover her dark heritage if she were allowed to remain with her mother, Sloan had sent the girl back East to her parents, to be schooled and reared there until she could make enough money to join them. To swiftly earn more, Sloan had gone to work in the Pleasure Palace. She eventually became the owner's mistress, then his partner, and lastly, the sole owner.

But having a lucrative business which provided the money for her child's and parents' support, and knowing a woman could not find such a profitable job back East, Sloan had been unable to join them yet.

Without her knowledge, Fate had intruded on her dream. During a drunken bout, Sloan's ravisher had revealed those wicked tales to a new friend named Carl Bush, who had found a way to use the information.

Neither Randee, nor Marsh Logan—who had known about Sloan's misfortune and child—had seen any reason to tell Sloan of Carl's vicious treatment and blackmail of Flossie. There was no need to hurt the lovely redhead, who recently had sold the Pleasure Palace and moved back East to live with her parents and to rear her daughter. A wealthy gambler had come to town, recognized the good prospects for the place in this rapidly growing area, and had made Sloan an enormous offer for it. Making sure she left no trail behind for either of her ravishers to follow, Miss Sloan Peters had joined her family to begin a new life.

Before long, the Texas & Pacific Railroad would plan and build routes along the very lines which Sheriff Brody Wade had marked on his dream map. Fort Worth would become a giant in the cattle-shipping business. The progress and expansion which George Light had mentioned also would come to pass within a few years.

Astonishingly, a letter had been found in an old mail sack from a robbery long ago—a letter to Marsh from his parents.

The President—knowing of the trouble and heartache for Marsh and his parents due to the secrecy and dark allegations which were vital to Marsh's job—had written to the Logans to reveal their son's position with him, and he had sworn them to secrecy to protect Marsh and themselves. But the missing letter was one which had been sent—to prevent it from falling into the wrong hands—to Marsh, in care of the President, in response to the truth which the President had revealed to them. Recently located in the discarded mail sack, it had been sent on to the President, who had forwarded it to Marsh four weeks ago.

The letter—dated only a week before his parents' deaths—expressed their love and pride in their son and their remorse over their lack of faith in him. It revealed how Marshall had confessed his adulterous guilt to Judith, and she had forgiven him. Marshall had taken the blame for driving Marsh from home and for the trouble between them, and for what he had believed falsely about his son. The now-deceased man had gone on to explain:

> "I guess I was trying to prove I was a real man after my many failures that year. We'd never been able to have a child, so I was perhaps trying to see if that failure was also mine. Although you were adopted, Marsh, we couldn't love you more if you were our own flesh and blood. We don't know who your real parents are. We got you at a mission in San Antonio when you were a year old . . . ."

Afterwards, Marsh had talked the matter over with the Durango Kid, who was almost a year younger than Marsh. The two had concluded they were brothers, and had decided it didn't matter who or what their parents were. Marsh had signed over the Logan property near Jacksboro to Durango so his younger brother could also begin a new life on his own ranch. Randee and Marsh had insisted on Durango splitting the many rewards for the defeat of the Epson Gang so he would have money to buy stock and to build a home and barns. Fortunately, everything was working out for all of them.

Dee Hollis Slade had sold her property in Kansas and moved to Wadesville, using the money to buy the town hotel and Brody's home. With a place to live and a way to earn a living, Dee could be on her own. She could meet new people, and give the newlyweds privacy. Dee was swiftly becoming the woman she had been before the evil Payton Slade had entered her life after her love's stunning death.

Randee had met with her mother after the woman's arrival so they could talk about the past and about Payton's fate. Dee had confided shamefully, "I used Payton to get over the pain of Randall's loss. I know it was wrong to feel betrayed and angered by his death; I even blamed him for dying and leaving me. I needed someone to fill my time and mind so I couldn't think about your father. I was so alone, Randee, so terrified and miserable. There was so much work and responsibility for you and the ranch. I feared what would happen to us. I had no one to hold, no one to comfort me, advise me, help me, defend me. I was so selfish that all I thought about was me, me, me!"

"It was a difficult time for you, Mother," Randee noted softly.

"Not as bad as it was for you. I pulled away from you. I used you to punish Randall for deserting me. You are so like him, Randee, and I couldn't bear that resemblance sometimes. That was wrong and cruel, Randee, but I couldn't help myself. Every hour of the day and night, I knew Randall was gone forever. I wanted him and missed him so much that I ached all over. I don't know what got into me. It was like . . . like I went crazy for a while, as if I had to move fast, as if I would suffer and die if I slowed down or stopped to think. Something evil and powerful was pushing me onward, was controlling me."

"You've had a long trip, and you have lots of unpacking and settling in to do. You don't have to talk about this today, Mother."

Dee stroked her daughter's blond hair and refuted gently, "Yes, I do. Now that I understand what possessed me, I have to explain it all to you. I have to earn your forgiveness and love."

"You know I love you," Randee said honestly.

"Please, hear me out while I have the courage and words. Payton entered my life and took over when I was too vulnerable and too weak to resist. All I had to do was obey his orders and he would handle everything for me. I didn't have to think or worry or be afraid. Nothing concerned me except love and pleasure, or what I thought was a second chance at them. I got in deeper and deeper with him and lost myself. It was as if I were walking and living in foggy woods where I could see only mist, not myself or you, or what he was doing to us. I wanted to feel young, feel carefree and whole again. I wanted to smile and laugh, to be kissed and caressed. I wanted the terrible agony and emptiness to go away. In my crazed mind, I wanted to show your

507

father I could replace him. For a long time, I honestly believed Payton was filling my dreams and needs."

Dee halted to catch her breath, but Randee held silent for her to continue in a few minutes. "I know you hated and mistrusted Payton. In my crazy state, all I feared was you driving him away and leaving me alone again with that awful anguish I'd endured at your father's death. I was tormented by terror. I was irrational, blind, stupid. Payton was so clever and enslaving that I lost myself to him."

"What made you come to your senses?" Randee asked kindly.

A pained expression filled Dee's eyes and her voice choked. "After the baby was lost, I saw him as he was. He was mean and cold and cruel. He dominated me and humiliated me. It was clear he only wanted Randall's ranch and a respectable image, and it was clear he was only using me. Hints and signs had always been there, but I had ignored and denied them because I couldn't face the ugly truth about myself. I was so weak, so confused, so foolish. Randall wasn't to blame for dying; he didn't betray or desert me. He wasn't careless and he didn't want to leave us through death. How could I have pushed you away and punished you so cruelly when you needed me the most? We needed each other, Randee. I'm sorry I was too dazed and selfish to realize what was happening to me. Can you ever forgive me?"

Randee embraced her mother and smiled through happy tears. "Of course I forgive you and love you. I'm glad you told me everything, Mother, and I truly understand. Don't continue to blame yourself for a mistake. Father loved you dearly and you loved him. I can see how his sudden death grieved you and changed you.

Maybe you can let go of that pain and loss now and begin anew here."

Dee returned her daughter's smile and agreed, "Yes, I think the dark past has finally freed me. I'm going to have a new life here, a happy one like Randall would want for me. I'm going to forget Payton Slade ever existed, and I hope you'll do the same."

Randee felt it would accomplish nothing by revealing Payton's evil toward her, so she held silent about it. Dee had suffered enough, too much. She let her mother believe the man had come to Texas to seek possession of the Carson Ranch, an act which had gotten him savagely beaten and killed in an ambush by "bandits." She also didn't think it wise or kind to tell her mother about the arrests — thanks to Marsh's Kansas contacts — of Payton's hirelings, or of their involvement in Randall Hollis' murder. If Dee learned she had been sleeping with the man who had slain her love and who had tried to ravish her daughter, the woman's new existence might be endangered.

* * *

Marsh and Randee cuddled together in their bed, talking and planning. She remarked cheerfully, "I think everything is going to work out wonderfully for Mother and Durango. They both have new lives, good ones. Too bad she's too old for your brother," Randee teased.

"You trying to find Durango a replacement for you?" he jested.

"Nope, just trying to find Mother a man almost as great as you."

"If you're looking for a proper match for Dee, I might know just the man. My old friend Jim Brinson has finished his duty at Fort Richardson and is heading

509

this way to become our new sheriff. He's the right age and has good breeding. He's nice-looking, kind, gentle, and strong; you know, all those traits you women love in a real man." He chuckled and nibbled at her ear. "After you meet Jim, you can decide if we should have them both to supper on the same night."

Randee recalled the Army officer from the attack on the raiders near Jacksboro. Yes, she remembered, he was very nice-looking, a man with a sunny smile and a muscular build. After learning Jim Brinson was arriving soon to take Brody's place as the sheriff of Wadesville, Marsh had told her all about his old friend. Yes, she concluded, Jim was the perfect selection for Dee Hollis Slade . . . .

Marsh kissed the nearly healed wound on her shoulder, hating to imagine what his life would be like without Randee. Her arms encircled his neck, and their kisses intensified their cravings.

He nuzzled her ear and murmured, "It amazes me, woman, but the more I have you, the more I want you. Mercy, but I love you and I'm glad I found you."

Randee hugged him tightly as she teased, "Settling down isn't so bad after all, is it, my roguish drifter?"

Marsh ticked her and replied huskily, "With you, nothing is bad, Randee Logan. And certainly not this."

Her fingers wandered over his hard body, admiring its texture of soft skin over hard muscles. He made her feel so loved, so special.

Randee hoped her mother and his younger brother would one day find a love like theirs: strong, rich, wonderful, and enlivening. She wondered, If Marsh had been the youngest child and the men's roles had been switched by Fate years ago, would she be married to the Durango Kid? Somehow she knew she would have loved and chosen and wed this man here with her tonight, no matter which role in life he had been given, be it Marsh Logan or the Durango Kid.

Their kisses and caresses waxed bolder. They stimulated each other to higher yearnings. Their passion blazed fiercely and brightly in the dark room, and the heat of it inflamed them. As if his lips were a branding iron, he marked his possession of her from head to foot.

Greedily, Randee responded to her handsome and virile lover, her cherished husband. He was so consuming. She writhed beneath him and urged him to take her fully and rapturously, which he did.

Together they savored the bond which would never be broken between them. Together they claimed passions wild and free . . . .

Dear Reader:

If you would like a Janelle Taylor Newsletter and Bookmark, please send a legal-size SELF-ADDRESSED STAMPED ENVELOPE to:

> Janelle Taylor Enterprises
> P.O. Box 11646
> Martinez, GA 30907-8646